Taste for Trouble

The Blake Brothers Trilogy

Book One

Susan Sey

For Claudia and Greta, always.

For Bryan, who reads with me.

For the staff at the North Oaks Bruegger's, because they provide me with a bottomless mug of coffee and a friendly place to write that smells delicious.

And for the guys at the table next to mine who provide me with stuff to write about. I try not to eavesdrop but...

CHAPTER ONE

Jilted brides were nothing new to Belinda West. A girl didn't churn out two wedding cakes a weekend for ten plus years without witnessing every disaster that could possibly befall a wedding party. Nothing about a groom making a last-minute break for Cozumel—with or without the bride's sister—surprised Bel anymore.

But it always surprised the bride. *That* was the part Bel didn't understand. Because when your groom wasn't totally on board with the whole marriage thing, there were signs. There were always signs. And if Bel, the total stranger manning the cake table, could see them, surely any bride paying even the tiniest bit of attention could see them too.

Which meant either these women weren't paying attention to the details (something for which Bel had little sympathy) or they were willfully ignoring them (something Bel didn't even comprehend.)

Then she got jilted. On live TV.

It wasn't like she'd been sleepwalking through the day with a wedding planner at the helm, either. No, indeed. She'd tackled her wedding personally, and with the same soft-spoken, detail-oriented implacability she'd used to transform herself from a semi-solvent wedding cake baker into the *Kate Every Day* baking maven. The series of segments she'd shot on baking your own wedding cake had been among the highest rated all season. Kate herself had taken Bel out to lunch when the numbers came in.

And had rewarded her by putting Bel's wedding at the heart of the season premiere. The *live* season premiere.

Kate's trust lit on her like a butterfly—so delicate and tentative as to be sensed rather than actually felt—and Bel devoted herself to living up to it like the heir apparent she aspired to be.

Her wedding, she was determined, would be perfect. She planned. She predicted. She envisioned. She managed. She checked details, then doubled checked. Triple checked. No decision was beneath her notice. And on paper, in rehearsal, in theory, everything *was* perfect.

But in reality? Somewhere between hand-picking the cottage-white, rustic-finish, wooden-not-metal folding chairs and personally glue-gunning three hundred and forty three red-foil-wrapped, dark-chocolate hearts to the hand-lettered place cards, something had gone terribly wrong.

Which meant, as Kate had frostily pointed out later, that somehow, inexplicably, Bel had missed something. Something important. A harbinger of doom had passed right through her hands unidentified. The proverbial wolf in sheep's clothing.

No, Bel thought darkly. That wasn't entirely true. She'd seen the signs. She just hadn't understood them.

Annie had been right. She should have paid attention to the swans.

CHAPTER TWO

Earlier, at Kate Davis' Hunt House

Bel was sitting in front of some sadist posing as a hairdresser when her assistant Annie appeared in the mirror behind Bel's shoulder.

"There's a problem with the swans," Annie announced. "You need to come with me."

"Don't move," the hairdresser/sadist said. Bel didn't move. The woman rewarded her by stabbing one last hairpin directly into Bel's scalp. Bel breathed through the pain and thought of perfect wedding pictures.

"There," the woman said, giving the yard of tulle she'd just attached to Bel's head a satisfied little fluff. "That ought to hold it."

"I should hope so," Bel murmured, but smiled at her reflection. Then she spun the chair to face Annie and her smile spread into something delighted and genuine.

"Well, look at you. If that dress isn't perfection," Bel said with satisfaction. She wasn't ordinarily a gloater but Annie had put up a vicious stink about wearing lilac satin. And maybe it *had* been a risk, mixing Annie's edgy, tattooed, art-school vibe—not to mention her Lucille Ball red hair—with a delicate Easter egg of a dress. But nobody could argue with the results.

Annie rolled her eyes, which Bel ignored.

"Didn't I tell you it would be perfect?" Bel said. "You look like Marilyn Monroe." She tipped her head and squinted. "Well, if Marilyn Monroe was a red-head and recovering from a rockabilly phase. Where have you been hiding those curves, anyway?"

Annie crossed her arms over that surprising chest. "Can we please not talk about this dress? It's a testament to our

3

friendship that I'm wearing it at all. But if anybody should happen to see me in it on TV, friendship be damned. I'd have to exercise my connections. My Uncle Luigi is a made man, you know."

Bel cocked a brow. "You'd have me whacked over a dress?"

"I'd think about it. Now come on."

"What? Where?"

"The swans."

"What about them?"

But Annie was already out the back door and trudging down the gentle, grassy slope overlooking the pond. Bel tucked the yard of tulle cascading from her head under one arm and followed her out the door.

The heat hit her like a sweaty embrace, hot and thick with summer's last kick. Her oxford button-down clung damply to the instant film of sweat on her back. Thank God she hadn't been through makeup yet, she thought. Or been sewn into her dress. Still, with the flowers to approve yet and the cake to assemble...

She glanced at her watch, a beautiful gold and silver Hermes bangle. She didn't usually indulge her taste for glitter even now that she could afford the occasional splurge, but timeliness was the closest thing she had to religion. She checked her watch hundreds of times a day. Why not look at something pretty?

What she saw there now had her mentally nudging a few bullet points around her to-do list and picking up the pace. "I know you think the swans are a bit much," she said to Annie's back, "but trust me. What seems over the top in person works just fine on the small screen. Swans are a time-honored symbol of fidelity, and having a pair on the pond during the ceremony makes a beautiful statement."

"They're making a statement all right." Annie stopped in the shade of the white canopy under which the ceremony would take place in—Bel checked her watch again—one hour and fourteen minutes. "But from what I'm seeing, that statement is less *look at our beautiful love* and more *holy hell, we're taking sniper fire.*"

"What?"

"See for yourself." She shot a purple fingernail toward the pond.

Bel frowned at Annie, then out at the glassy blue pond upon which glided two gorgeous swans. Except they weren't gliding. They were jerking around in irregular zigzags, heads low, eyes slitted and suspicious. Every now and then one of them blatted out an affronted honk.

Her stomach dropped. "What on earth? They were fine! Two hours ago they were *fine*. What happened?"

"Hell if I know." Annie's lips were a grim line. "When I brought the tent people out here to set up the arbor they were fine, like you said. Then I stopped back a few minutes ago to see if the techs had the lighting levels down for the ceremony and there they were. All...disturbed."

"Okay." Bel pulled in a deep breath of warm, wet air that did nothing to clear away the buzz of anxiety trying to fill her head and erase her thoughts. "Just give me a minute here. I have to think."

"Bel, listen." Annie's voice softened, and she put a hand on Bel's arm. "I know you were heart-set on this but I just don't think it's going to work."

"No, it will," Bel said. "I can fix this." And she would. She'd sunk countless hours of painstaking preparation into this afternoon. Rearranging a single minute of it on the say-so of a couple of deranged birds went against everything she believed. Everything she was. Bel had a *plan*. And the swans, by God, would get on board. Then everything would be fine. Better than fine. *Perfect*. Everything would be perfect. She'd make sure of it. "They'll have to be tranquilized."

"*What*?"

A hot breeze snatched at her veil which yanked unmercifully at her scalp but she breathed through the pain. Her veil was beautiful. It was perfect. It was exactly what she'd envisioned. So it hurt like the fires of hell. So what? Perfection cost, yes, but Bel didn't mind paying. The swans might do well to remember that.

She tucked the end of the veil carefully under her arm

and said, "Annie, please. I still need to approve the flowers, assemble the cake, and get through makeup. Then I have to okay camera placement for the ceremony itself and get sewn into my dress. I don't have time to counsel a pair of traumatized water fowl out of whatever neuroses they've hatched in the past two hours. They'll need to be tranquilized. Can you get the breeder on the phone?"

Annie stared at her from under a short chop of bangs. "You want to drug *fidelity* and *everlasting love* into a photogenic stupor? That's just wrong, Bel. It's *all* wrong. Can't you see that?"

"Don't be melodramatic." Bel dug her iPhone from the front pocket of her shirt and began scrolling madly for the swan guy's number. "They're just swans, for heaven's sake. The world's not going to come to an end if we—"

"This isn't about the damn swans!" Annie shouted. "Will you listen to me?"

A shock of surprise lifted her stomach, and her fingers froze mid-scroll. Because Annie had just shouted at her. *Annie.* As Bel's personal assistant and best friend, Annie told her no all the time. Of course she did. Every time Bel tried to double-book herself, overshoot the budget or work through another weekend, Annie was right there with the not-so-fast. It was her *job* to tell Bel no. But that was the thing. That was why Bel adored and appreciated her. Annie was *good* at no. Calm, efficient, practical. Annie's no was utterly drama-free.

And Annie had just shouted at her.

"Of course." Bel put her phone away. "I'm listening."

Annie's eyes slid toward the water, then back to Bel's. "You can't do this," she finally said, twin spots of color burning in her pale cheeks.

"Do what?"

"Marry Ford. I'm serious, Bel. This is a sign. You can't go through with this."

Bel's eyebrows came together. "Because my swans have some kind of stress disorder?"

"Because you don't love him. And he doesn't love you."

Love. The word dropped a cold stone of distaste into

Bel's stomach. The very last thing in the world she wanted was to be in love.

"Ford and I have something better than love," Bel said, her voice carefully calm and assured. The breeze snatched her veil out of her grip again, lifted the tail and dropped it on top of Annie's firecracker-colored head. Annie swatted it away.

"Better than love," she said, her mouth a skeptical knot. "Like what?"

"Like compatibility," Bel said. She unwound Annie from her veil and pinned it under her arm again. "Similar temperaments, goals and lifestyles. A great deal of mutual respect and affection. We have a *partnership*, Annie. A good, lasting one. Marriage simply takes it to the next level."

"I hate how you do that. Make it sound so rational and justified." Annie gave her head a hard shake. "No. Compatibility, my ass. It's cold-blooded and it's wrong and you know it. People need to be *loved*, Bel. High esteem and great affection just don't cut it. You're cheating yourself, and worse, you're cheating Ford."

"Cheating? Please." Bel gave a weary chuckle. They'd covered this ground ad nauseum. But how were you supposed to explain reasonable prudence to the fearless? "Love is nothing more than an excuse to be fickle, impulsive and selfish. People shouldn't build a lunch date around it, let alone a marriage. I don't feel deprived, and I doubt very much if Ford does either."

"Only because you've convinced him that this is as good as it gets. And it's not." She spat the words like they were poisonous. "I don't know who hurt you so badly, Bel, who broke your heart or whatever. And if you don't want to get over it, fine. Your choice. But this is bigger than you. Now Ford's in it, too, and he's a sweet guy. He deserves better."

Bel stared at her assistant through the early September sun that poured down in rich, buttery waves. It bathed the afternoon in exactly the sort of light Bel had known it would. The pictures would be perfect. So would the cake and the flowers and her hair and the dress and the three hundred and forty three guests arriving in an hour. They, along with the entire *Kate Every Day* at-home audience, would see that perfection. Would bear witness while Bel finally achieved the life she'd been planning since that day twelve years ago when she'd stumbled onto an episode of *Kate Every Day* while waiting for her mother to come home.

Her mother hadn't come home—not for three days that time—but that was all right. By the time she did, Bel had found a new home. An imaginary one, sure, but at least it was available every day from three to four, eastern. *Kate Every Day* had taught Bel everything she knew about the good life and how to build it.

And after today's ceremony, Bel's life would be very good indeed. She'd have job security, a solid relationship, and a stable, predictable life. She'd have a future that stretched out toward the horizon in a beautiful, straight line. Everything was going to be perfect. And she wasn't about to let some rogue waterfowl—or her best friend's disapproval—get between her and that future.

"Annie—" she started.

"Oh, God, the *be reasonable* voice." Annie slumped inside all that purple satin, defeated. "Okay, fine. Here's me being reasonable. Ready?"

Bel's lips twitched in spite of herself. "Ready."

"You're my friend, Bel. I care about you and I want you to be happy." She fixed Bel with shrewd, troubled eyes. "But I don't see how that's going to happen when you don't love your husband."

Affection flooded her and Bel let go of her veil. "Oh, Annie." She snatched the shorter woman into her arms and hugged her hard. The veil streamed out in the breeze and pulled viciously at her scalp but she didn't care. "I love *you.* Is that good enough?"

"No." Annie pulled back and glared. "Because you love Ford just the same way."

"Of course I do. He's my other best friend."

"Yeah, well, most people want to feel something a little warmer than friendship for the guy they're going to sleep with for the rest of their lives."

She grinned cheerfully. "Not me." She checked her watch and stopping grinning. "Oh, yikes. Annie, listen. Thank you for yelling at me. I know you love me and want what's best for me, but you're going to have to trust me on this. Ford and me? We're good. We really are. And we really, *really* don't have time to discuss it anymore. The swans—"

"—are a sign," Annie said through her teeth.

"No, they're not. They're just—"

She stopped when a golf ball sailed over the box hedge that separated their lawn from the neighboring estate. It whistled in from the east and detonated in the pond like a hand grenade. The swans wheeled madly and sent up a chorus of betrayed honks.

Bel and Annie stared speechlessly.

"Oh my lord," Bel said finally. "Was that a golf ball?"

"Looked like." Annie squinted into the pond. "Well. This explains a few things."

CHAPTER THREE

"It came from the Annex," Bel said. Not a question.

Annie frowned over the hedge. "Yep."

"James Blake and his insane brothers are *at home*?"

Annie scratched her nose as they watched another golf ball scream over the bushes and explode into the water. "Must be."

"At home and *using my wedding for a driving range*?" Bel tried to modulate her tone but dismay vibrated inside her, with fear sneaking in underneath on slippery little feet. She'd planned this out very carefully. The nouveau riche red-neck neighbors *should not be home*.

"Miss West?" The florist appeared at Bel's elbow, his bald head sweaty in the afternoon sun. Too sweaty. A dash of foreboding swirled into the nerves already churning in her gut.

"One second," Bel said to him. She turned back to Annie. "I thought you said the Statesmen were playing in LA this weekend."

Annie frowned down at the swans, who were heaving themselves out of the pond with offended dignity. "They are." She lifted open hands. "At least that's what it said on the internet when I checked their schedule. I don't really follow professional soccer so maybe I misunderstood, but it said *Statesmen vs. the Galaxy*, LA, one p.m. Which, adjusted for the time change is—" She glanced at Bel's watch. "—about now."

"So what is their star forward doing *teeing off on my swans*?"

Annie didn't have an answer for that one.

"What's this? We have a tee time?"

Bel turned and found Ford striding down the manicured green carpet of the lawn toward them. Hunt House rose up behind him, as solid and square as Ford himself, and the sight of the two most dependable things in her life steadied her.

The florist tried again. "Miss West," he said, his plump hands clenched together, his face round and unhappy.

"I'm sorry, just one more minute." She held out her hands to Ford who took them in his big warm ones.

"Hello, Bel," he said. "Are we going golfing?"

She kissed his cheek. "Yeah, I don't think so."

He laughed and patted her veil. "Can't blame a guy for trying." He winked at Annie, then just stared.

"Good lord, Annie. Is that you?"

Color rushed into Annie's cheeks. She closed her eyes and gave her bare shoulders a furtive pat as if verifying that she was, indeed, displaying several times more skin than usually met with daylight in a calendar year. "A great deal of me, yes," she said, her smile weak.

"That dress," Ford said seriously. "It's...a revelation."

The blush deepened. "Bel's idea."

"Of course. She's always putting unusual ingredients together and making them into something delicious." He put an arm around Bel's shoulders and gave her a fond squeeze, his brown eyes crinkled with laughter. "She's famous for it, isn't she?"

A wave of gratitude swept over her. She wasn't in love with Ford, no, but she absolutely loved him. How could she not? Kindness ran through his character like an underground stream, as deep as it was predictable. If Bel's life was a ship, Ford was her safe harbor. And she planned to drop anchor permanently in less than an hour now.

"Even my magic has its limits," she said on a sigh. "Because I can't think of a single ingredient in my kitchen that would make this situation taste better."

Ford's brows lifted. "What situation?"

"Evidently the Blake brothers are playing—"

She broke off as another golf ball sailed over the bushes and landed in the pond. The swans honked their displeasure from the safety of the shore, then turned speculative eyes on the catering tent. Fresh alarm clutched at Bel's chest and she swallowed an ugly word or two.

"—hooky."

"I see." Ford squinted. "Actually, that looks like golf."

"It is." Bel smiled grimly. "Only they're supposed to be playing soccer today. In California."

"Ah."

"Miss West?" The florist tried a third time. "Please, if I could just—"

"Sorry, one second more." She turned to Annie. "Will you *please* see about the swans? Keep them out of the catering tent if nothing else?"

Annie jerked one shoulder. "Yeah, okay." She trudged down the hill, her pale shoulders squared.

"And me?" Ford said, his eyes trailing Annie to the edge of the pond. "How about I go next door for a little man-to-man?"

Bel gripped his hands gratefully. "Would you? It would be such a favor."

"Not at all," Ford said, his hands warm and solid inside hers. "It'll be nice to feel useful for a change."

She blinked, uneasiness tightening her smile. "I've made you feel useless?"

"Honey, no." He gave her a wry smile. "That wasn't a slap. You've been a dream bride, honestly. I've barely lifted a finger. Men the world over only wish they were me." He put a kiss on the end of her nose and Bel thought fleetingly of Annie. *People usually want to feel something more than friendship for the guy they're going to sleep with for the rest of their lives.* "But dealing with unruly neighbors? That's a man's job. Leave it to me."

She laughed. "Right. Okay. Go man it up, then."

"Roger that." He turned and she watched him march back up the lawn, his shoulders square and broad in his perfectly fitted tux.

"*Miss West.*" The florist looked ready to cry.

"Sorry," she said, and mustered up a polite smile. "It's a little crazy around here."

He didn't smile back. In fact, he looked ready to stroke out. She half wished he would. Then he could keep his bad

12

news to himself. *A small, mean thought*, she scolded herself. *Unworthy*. She dredged up a little more sincerity for her smile. "You have some flowers to show me?"

"That's just it." He clasped his hands together in front of his apron. "I don't."

A mild buzz started in Bel's ears. She flicked a glance at Annie who was flinging breath mints from her purse into the pond. The swans appeared to be debating the merits of going after them. "I'm sorry?"

"There was an accident on the beltway," he said. "Our delivery van."

"Oh." The buzzing intensified. The swans reached a decision and waddled into the pond. Bel struggled to focus. "Is everybody okay?"

"Yes, thank God. But your flowers. Oh, Miss Bel, your beautiful flowers." He shook his head. "All over the expressway, all those cars..." He spread helpless hands from which Bel surmised a terminal diagnosis. Her flowers were DOA.

"Do we have *any* of the flowers?" she asked.

"Just the bride's bouquet and the groom's boutonniere. I hand carry those to every job."

"All right. Okay."

She broke off as another golf ball sailed over the box hedge and detonated in the pond. The swans squawked their displeasure—*screw the breath mints*—and paddled for shore.

It's all coming apart, Bel thought. *Spinning, spinning, the center starting to give*. The old darkness crept in with sneaky fingers, tried to crawl up her throat, burn her eyes, turn her hands leaden and useless.

She shook herself. No. She was fine. She was organized. She could handle this. She'd built room into her schedule for a few mishaps, hadn't she? She hauled in a nice deep breath and held it until her lungs gave in and absorbed some oxygen.

Think, Bel. Just think.

"Okay," she said. "Okay. You see that white picket fence to the left of the main house? Go through the gate in the center. About fifty yards straight back you'll run right

13

into Kate's rose garden. You have half an hour."

The florist's eyes widened. "You want me to..." He made a snipping motion in the air between them, as if the word was too horrible to say out loud. "In Kate Davis' personal rose garden?"

"Yes. I'll answer for it. Make me a miracle." She checked her watch. "Forty nine minutes."

He swallowed. "Right. One miracle, coming up."

"That's the spirit. I'll be in the catering tent assembling the cake if you need anything."

She started for the kitchen at a dead run.

Fifteen minutes later, Bel had four tiers of ivory-fondant-coated, pink-polka-dotted, bow-topped perfection on the cake table before her. She was just piping her new monogram on the top tier and expounding for the camera on the finer points of lettering with royal icing when Kate strode into the catering tent. Bel glanced at her boss' face and froze mid-letter.

Surviving as the heir apparent to Kate's hand-crafted domestic fiefdom was less a matter of talent than of being able to instantly and accurately gauge her boss's mood. And the fixed, on-camera smile on Kate's face sent Bel's Mood-o-Meter clear into the red zone.

She straightened. "If this is about the rose garden, I gave the florist permission to—"

Kate's smile went a bit grim around the edges. "The flowers are fine. It's the groom we seem to be missing."

"Ford?" Bel's mind went blank.

"Unless you have a back up groom waiting in the wings?" Kate lifted a well-shaped brow.

"Of course not."

"Then yes, Ford. The photographer is asking after him. He seems to be missing."

Bel's heart stuttered, then just stopped. "He's not back yet?"

"Back from where?"

"He went next door," she said. "The neighbors were using the pond as a driving range again, and he was going to—"

"You sent your groom on an errand? An hour before your wedding?" Her tone implied, with all due politeness, that this constituted a massive error in judgment.

Bel handed Kate her pastry bag. "I'll go get him."

"Of course you will." Kate handed the bag to one of the myriad assistants who orbited her at all times, invisible until their presence was required. "Take a golf cart. And hurry back. You still have makeup and wardrobe, and the ceremony starts in—" She consulted a discreet gold twinkle at her wrist "—thirty two minutes. Cameras are rolling, Belinda."

Bel ran.

CHAPTER FOUR

James Blake twisted the cap off a fresh bottle of beer, dropped an elbow over the back of his lawn chair and watched his new buddy Ford take a crack at yet another range ball. James' older brother Will sat in the lawn chair at James' right elbow, his younger brother Drew sat in the lawn chair to his left. They all watched as Ford addressed the ball, then sent it curving deep into the woods south of the neighbor's pond.

"Hooked it." Will sighed with deep disgust and lifted the beer bottle dangling from his fingertips.

"Amen." Drew helped himself to the cooler.

James squinted after the ball, then back at Ford. The guy would have a right pretty stroke if he'd just relax. Not that he didn't *look* relaxed. With that easy smile on his magazine-pretty face and that thousand dollar tux—not rented—he wore like skin, the guy practically dripped smug assurance. Like he was about to marry the prettiest girl in the country club. Richest, too. Probably was.

But James had a sense about these things. Ford was an unhappy man. Not that it took a psychic to figure that one. Half an hour before his scheduled *I do* and the guy was on his third beer and his second bucket of balls with a bunch of strangers. Plus that was one vicious hook for a dude who looked like he'd been born with a golf club in one hand and a silver spoon in the other.

"Now boys," James said. "That's a lot of club right there." And it was. A soccer-mad Titleist sales rep had gifted James with a prototype driver, and he and his brothers had spent a very enjoyable afternoon putting balls all over creation with it. "Give the man a minute to get a handle on it."

He stretched his legs out in front of him, pulled his ball

cap low enough to take a nap under and nodded Ford toward the bucket of balls. "Relax, son. And remember, a golf club's like a woman. Just keep your hands soft, pay attention, and for God's sake don't rush her. You'll find the sweet spot soon enough."

Ford took a pull off his beer and gave them a wry smile. "You're assuming they all have one. A sweet spot."

"Well, I guess that depends." He grinned. "Are we talking about golf clubs or women?"

Ford shrugged. "Either."

James winced inwardly. So it was like that. The prettiest girl in the country club lacked a sweet spot. Or his new buddy Ford hadn't located it yet. Bummer. That would explain a lot about the stiff shoulders and self-mocking smile.

James glanced at Will, who shook his head and gave him a look that said *so not your business, bro*. James plucked the beer bottle from Ford's hand and nudged him toward the driver again. He waited for the guy to address the ball then tossed the beer off the patio.

Ford burned a ball into the lawn. Will and Drew made twin noises of pained disgust. James gave them a mild look. Drew shrugged and Will rolled his eyes but they shut up.

Ford shook his head. "Okay, I'm done. No point embarrassing myself further." He set the club aside and looked around for his beer.

Drew glanced at James, raised a brow toward the cooler in silent question. James shook his head. Bad enough that, given the sweet spot issue, the poor guy was already in for a lifetime scored to *Ford's Flaws: The Greatest Hits*. Best not put 'Drunk at our Wedding' on the playlist.

"There's no shame in a learning curve," James told him. "Nothing more admirable than honest hard work. But, listen. Ford. There's working hard and then there's forcing it."

"Forcing it?"

"Sure. I mean, you can't force something into place if it doesn't want to—Ow! Damn, Will, watch your elbows!" He rubbed his biceps and glared at his older brother, who mumbled a wholly unconvincing *sorry*.

17

"As I was saying," James continued with a hard look for Will. "You can't force anything into a place it doesn't want to be. And it's been my personal experience that if it feels too much like work, either the timing's off or the fit isn't right. Not saying there aren't tough times, of course. But it shouldn't be uphill all the way. Life's too short and too hard to make work for yourself. Some things ought to *flow*, you know? Roll. They ought to just..." He spread his hands. "Sing."

"Oh, for God's sake," Will muttered, sinking back into his lawn chair with a beer.

"Sing." Ford repeated the word slowly, rolling it around in his mouth as if it were some new and delicious food he'd never tasted before. A food he'd never even imagined existed, or if it did, that he'd never received permission to try. He frowned over it, puzzling it into place as all the other pieces scattered to make way.

Then his gaze shifted over James' left shoulder, locked there. All that moneyed polish fell away and a radiant joy spread over his face.

"Annie," he breathed. "Annie."

Uh-oh. James glanced back, saw a woman standing there looking like she'd stepped out of one of those black and white detective flicks. Only this girl was in full color—candy-apple curls springing around her pale face, purple silky dress, a few swirly tatts playing peek-a-boo with her neckline. Her eyes were cats-eye green and full of yearning, but her pretty rose-bud mouth was clamped down hard. Fighting it.

"You're late," Annie said to Ford.

"I know. I should've said something months ago."

Annie closed her eyes. "For your *wedding*, Ford. You're late for your wedding."

"Screw the wedding." Ford strode past the lawn chairs, swept the girl into his arms and planted his mouth on hers with an energy that suggested he knew exactly where to find her sweet spot. Had possibly already found it a time or two, if James read things correctly. Annie hesitated—still fighting it—but then her arms rose up and wound around his neck.

18

Drew leaned in. "Thought he said the bride's name was Bethany," he whispered, as if they were at the theater.

"He said Belinda, dumb ass." Will didn't bother to keep his voice down. The happy couple didn't seem to mind. "And that's not her."

"Ohhhhhh." Drew nodded sagely and settled in for an entertaining scene. Will delivered a shot to James' shoulder. "I *told* you not to get involved."

James winced. "What did I do?" He rubbed his arm. "I just said—"

"All your bullshit about flow and singing and what not." Will snorted and tipped the last of his beer down his throat. "God."

Ford came up for air at the precise moment a golf cart zipped around the house. It had barely skidded to a stop before a woman leapt off, a whole lot of veil streaming from her head. A paunchy guy with a muscular camera in his hands wobbled out of the other side of the cart. James watched, amused, as the guy sucked in a couple of deep breaths then made a furtive sign of the cross in apparent gratitude for having survived the ride. He shouldered the camera and followed the woman.

Tall and slim, the bride-to-be marched toward them on yard-long legs. A glossy river of hair the color of good maple syrup swung between her shoulder blades. Strong cheekbones in a striking, rectangular face. Dark, snapping eyes. That thoroughbred gait. James lifted his brows. Appealing, he supposed, in a polished, corporate sort of way, but not the prettiest girl in the country club. And probably not the most patient regarding balky sweet spots. Her own or anybody else's. He almost turned back to root for the curly red-head.

Then he noticed her mouth. That plump, bee-stung mouth that had surely been created with a man's pleasure in mind. A mouth that, given the rest of her face—hell, given her entire vibe of crackling, practical energy—was a searing shock. Blatant, flag-waving evidence of a sweet spot just waiting to be discovered. He stared, arrested.

Drew leaned in again. "Belinda?"

Will cracked a fresh beer. "Who else?"

"Not what I expected," James murmured as she reached the cool shade of the eaves, propped the flat of her hand to her forehead and squinted into the shadows toward the happy couple.

"I love you, Annie," Ford said, staring down into the dazed face of the woman he'd just kissed senseless. "Marry me."

Belinda froze. "Oh," she said. "Oh my goodness."

Annie jerked away, horror filling her big green eyes. "*Bel*. Oh my God, Bel. I'm so sorry. I didn't, we didn't—" She broke off to cast stricken eyes up at Ford. "I mean, we never would have—"

Ford put an arm around Annie's shoulders and cut in gently. "I'm sorry, Bel," he said, and James had to give him credit. The guy did look genuinely sorry. "I wish to God I'd said something sooner. But I didn't know myself until just now."

Bel pressed the heel of her hand to her chest, seemed to put all her concentration on forcing some air into her lungs. The camera man shifted around her for a tighter shot of Ford and Annie.

"I tried, Bel," Ford went on. "Please believe me, I tried. You're everything I wanted in a partner—smart, ambitious, independent, successful. But we just never..." He looked down at Annie, his eyes soft. "We never had *this*."

Annie closed her eyes and made an agonized noise. Ford gave a helpless shrug. Belinda stared at them, pale and wordless. "I'm sorry, Bel," Ford said again. "I know the timing is awfully inconvenient for you. I wish there were something I could do, some way I could make this less..." He glanced at the camera's avid eye. "Awkward."

"Awkward," Bel said slowly. "Yes, it is that."

The curly red-head seemed to shrink inside that flower-petal dress of hers. "I never wanted this, Bel," she whispered. "Please believe me. I fought it so hard. We both did. Neither of us would hurt you for the world. We love you, Bel. But you can't fight your heart. It'll only make you crazy in the end. And my heart—" She broke off, turned an adoring face up to Ford's, squeezed his hand. "—*our* hearts belong together."

Bel stared at them, that strong, angular face so bloodless that James rolled up to the edge of his chair. He wasn't about to let her crack her head on his pavers in the event she passed out. She looked like the suing sort.

"We discussed this," she said to Ford with a cool self-possession that had James reconsidering the existence of that sweet spot. "The possibility that one or both of us might at some point be attracted to somebody outside our marriage. But we concluded that our partnership was worth more in the end than gratifying a short-term attraction. So please forgive me for speaking so bluntly, but in the interests of clarity and closure, I need to know. Are you making this decision with your heart, Ford? Or with your libido?"

"With my heart," Ford said without hesitation. "I'm in love."

"Are you?" She didn't sound surprised. Just tired.

"I know this is hard for you to understand," Ford said. "Hell, it's hard for *me* to understand. Because until Annie, I was exactly like you. I had no idea what it was to feel this way. I know you think—we thought—that love was nothing but a myth. Now I understand that my life is nothing without love. You and I, we were great friends and kindred spirits. We got along. Enjoyed each other. It was comfortable and predictable and easy. But this?" He snugged the girl into his side and she melted into him. "Annie and I? We just *sing*, Bel. We flow."

"And that," Will said, saluting James with his beer bottle, "is why you should have shut up twenty minutes ago."

The woman—Bel—flicked her gaze toward James and his brothers. She took them in, their lawn chairs facing the action like seats in a theater, then zeroed in on James.

"You did this?" she asked.

James rose slowly, palms out. "Easy now. I didn't do anything."

Will smiled at her. "Except tell your boy Ford that life ought to flow and sing." He wiggled his empty bottle at her.

"Care for a beer?"

James gave Will a killing look, then turned his attention back to the woman staring icicles into his chest. "Bel, right? Your name is Bel?"

"Yes." She advanced on him, and he noticed the hint of a pair of delicious dimples carved deep into the softness of her cheeks. "Pleased to meet you."

Impressive, he thought. The way she turned a simple pleasantry into something so chilly and sharp. "Now, Bel, be reasonable." James gave her his best aw-shucks-ma'am face.

"I have been reasonable," she said in that same deadly polite voice. "I have been imminently reasonable. But this—" She waved a hand in the air, a tight little circle that James understood encapsulated the whole distasteful scene she'd just endured. "This is not reasonable. This is ridiculous and immature and impulsive. And apparently your suggestion."

James glanced at his brothers as Bel advanced on him, cold purpose vibrating in the air around her. But it was the touch of panic shimmering underneath the purpose James found most compelling. And he'd thought Ford was unhappy. This woman was so unhappy she didn't even know she *was* unhappy.

No wonder Ford couldn't find her sweet spot.

"It wasn't a suggestion exactly," he told her. "It was more like—"

"Unsolicited advice," Will supplied when James paused to grope for a word.

"A philosophy," James said with a dark look for his brother. "Sharing my personal philosophy about life."

"What I don't understand," Bel said as if nobody had spoken, "is what you're even doing here." She closed the gap between them to poke a finger into his chest. He could feel the sharp bite of her nail through his t-shirt. "I read the papers, Mr. Blake. I know that the DC Statesmen paid an ungodly amount of money for your services. For your golden boot and your physical presence on the field or the pitch or whatever you call it in soccer. You have an away game today. In a series of away games. You're supposed to be playing *soccer* in *California*, not playing *golf* off your *patio*. Not talking my *groom* into following his *bliss*. Certainly not *sabotaging my career*. *What are you doing here?*"

James weighed his options. No answer seemed really palatable.

"He got his ass suspended," Drew informed her with the unholy cheer of an adored youngest child. "Fighting."

"It wasn't really fighting," James told Bel, then gave Drew a black stare.

"No, that's true," Drew admitted. "You totally cold cocked the guy. Kind of unsporting, now that you mention it."

"There was an incident," James said to Bel. "A particularly heated match and—" He trailed off. This wasn't going well.

"I don't care." She brushed one elegant hand through the air between them, shooing away all his pathetic excuses. "I don't care why you're here. I don't care about matches, heated or otherwise. I don't even care what you said to Ford. But I have three hundred and forty three people sitting in folding chairs on Kate Davis' lawn at this very moment. I have duck canapés circulating and fifty bottles of a very nice '96 Moët chilling for the champagne toast. I have a four-tiered cake with pink polka dots and my new monogram sitting on a cake table beside a Waterford knife. I have *ice sculptures*." She said this last bit as if it were the clincher. Had to get married if there were ice sculptures on the line.

"So I don't care about your fights or your philosophy. All I want you to do is *fix this*."

She stabbed a finger toward Ford and Annie. Or at least toward where they'd been. Because Ford and Annie were gone.

"Oh no," Bel said.

Drew made a noise of deep satisfaction. He did love a good scene, especially one with a happy ending. Will snorted his disgust and James turned sheepish eyes on Bel.

"You, uh, want that beer now?"

CHAPTER FIVE

Four hours later, Bel stood outside the door of Kate's Hunt House office and wished she'd taken James Blake up on the beer. The end of her career—hell, the end of a life-long dream—was bound to sting. A little alcoholic anesthesia might've been nice.

But no. She'd never taken refuge in alcohol before. She wouldn't do it now. She'd fallen, but not that far.

She hiked up her chin and tapped softly on the doorframe.

Kate, perched on a French provincial lady's chair behind the Queen Anne table that served as her desk, waved her in without looking up.

"I've dealt with the last of it," Bel said, looking at the ruler-straight part in Kate's ash blonde hair.

"Have you?"

"Yes. The caterer was gone over an hour ago. The tent's broken down, the tables and chairs loaded. The leftovers were boxed and sent to St. Joan's shelter. Gifts were returned to the appropriate givers. Your lawn is back to normal."

Kate glanced out the enormous window behind her. "Aside from my denuded rose garden, yes."

Bel winced. "Kate, I'm so sorry. If I'd had any idea this might happen—"

"That's just it, isn't it? You *should* have had an idea, Belinda." Kate finally looked up, and Bel's heart sank at the grave finality in the older woman's face. The Mood-o-Meter had never failed her before and it wasn't failing her now. This wasn't a dressing down. This wasn't *don't disappoint me again*. This was The End. Waterloo. Utter disaster, prettied up in an Ann Taylor sweater set.

"I'm sorry, Kate," Bel said quietly.

Taste for Trouble

"As am I." Kate set aside her pen and rose, tall and statuesque against the arching window. "But weddings do fall through, Belinda. Grooms elope with assistants. Flowers suffer grievous accidents on the beltway. These things happen, so please don't misunderstand this. I'm not punishing you for bad luck."

Oh God. Bel's stomach cramped and she clamped down on the urge to check her watch. What, did she want to mull it over later? How many minutes it took Kate to deliver her career a killing blow? Compare it to the number of years she'd spent building it?

"What I object to isn't your luck, or lack thereof," Kate continued, a rueful half-smile on her patrician face. "It's your lack of attention to the details."

"The details?" Bel echoed, astonished.

"Yes, dear. The details. Oh, you have a fine sense of fashion, of taste. And I'll be honest, I've never seen or tasted a cake to equal one of yours. But the simple fact is, your two closest companions engaged in an inappropriate love affair over the past year right under your nose. They battled against it, but eventually, at the worst possible moment for all of us, lost that battle. And you didn't see it coming."

Kate clasped her hands in front of her neat linen skirt. "You're a fine baker, dear. Gifted, even. But an error in judgment this egregious, a lack of awareness this persistent? I'm afraid you simply don't have the vision I require in a partner, let alone a successor."

Bel absorbed the shock, the bitter sting of failure. It bowed her shoulders, sent shameful tears rushing to her eyes. She dropped her gaze and waited miserably for Kate to finish her off.

"You're fired, dear," Kate said, and even now Bel had to admire the woman's style. She delivered the blow firmly enough to discourage unseemly argument yet with just enough compassion and regret to take the edge off. Kate Davis wasn't the queen of etiquette for nothing.

It steadied her somehow, this small demonstration of the values Kate represented on TV every day. The values Bel herself had absorbed like plants absorbed sunlight, and would have practiced with pride had she been found worthy. Tact, graciousness, and calm conviction.

Bel bit back her tears and steadied herself. Maybe she was a failure but she wasn't a coward. She forced her spine straight, lifted her head and, with clear eyes, met Kate's gaze.

And found it filled with...relief? Kate was *relieved* to be rid of her? After three years of grooming Bel as her potential successor, after countless other mistakes she could have easily parlayed into legitimate grounds for dismissal? Why on earth would Kate wait for a screw up of epic proportions to give her the boot? And why would she be happy about it?

"I'll give you two weeks to vacate the Dower House," Kate said gently.

Bel closed her eyes as a rush of panicked sorrow drowned out everything else. Of all today's losses—and they'd been staggering—it was losing the Dower House that finally drove her to her knees. She'd loved that tiny cottage behind the rose garden, the third spoke of what had once been the single enormous estate surrounding the pond. Kate's Hunt House. James Blake's Annex. Bel's Dower House. Her home.

No, she thought. *Kate's* Dower House. *Kate's* show. *Kate's* vision. Not mine. None of it mine.

"I'll..." Her voice broke, and she cleared her throat. "I'll start packing."

"I regret this, dear," Kate said as she seated herself at the desk once more, tucking her skirt properly under her thighs.

You do not, Bel thought. But, distasteful chore dispatched, Kate had already returned her attention to the endless work of being *Kate Every Day*. Bel walked silently out of the office.

Two weeks later, her entire life squashed into the back of her catering van, Bel drove away from the Dower House. She didn't look in the rearview mirror. She couldn't bear to see it behind her. But it didn't matter if she didn't look. She knew it by heart.

A story and a half of pink Virginia brick personally stomped, shaped and fired by Hunt House's own masons over two hundred years ago, the Dower House was a sturdy little white-shuttered island in a sea of hollyhocks, ivies, and climbing tea roses. A weeping cherry tree shaded the porch and every year sent the smell of spring wafting through Bel's tiny, beloved kitchen, through the heart of her house. The heart of her.

Looking in the rearview mirror, watching it grow smaller until it disappeared would be like having that heart torn out by tiny, torturous degrees. So she didn't look.

She focused instead on the pretty twist of macadam road unspooling across the lush green countryside of northern Virginia. She drove as if it required every ounce of her concentration, blanking out the sorrow and focusing instead on the loose ends she couldn't stop tugging.

Because something wasn't right. She knew it in her gut. There was more behind Kate's decision to let her go than a spectacularly failed wedding. But despite two solid weeks of turning the problem around and around in her head, despite gnawing at it from every possible angle, she couldn't figure out what had happened.

There was hope, however. One person who knew more about the myriad plans, plots and machinations in Kate's head than Bel did. Her own personal Wizard and Bel was, however reluctantly, on the yellow brick road. Which led, in this case, to the heart of DC. To the man who'd plucked her and her cakes from obscurity and plopped them on TV next to Kate Davis.

She was going to Bob Beck. To her and Kate's mutual agent. And possibly to yet another firing. But maybe she'd get some answers before he let her go, too.

Bel hesitated, her hand poised to knock on the frame of Bob's open office door. With his Italian loafers propped on a polished barge of a desk and a cell phone glued to his ear, her agent looked more or less the same as he had for the past five years. But something made her pause.

He'd always been a square, craggy kind of handsome,

27

but the silver at his temples had taken over some serious real estate since she'd seen him last. His shoulders were still total-eclipse broad and the crease in his shirt sleeve could slice butter, but Bel had the oddest impression that he was somehow wilted inside all that starch. Like lettuce left out of the crisper.

Then he looked up and that faint weariness evaporated. He waved her in, then pointed to his phone, rolled his eyes and made a *yak, yak, yak* motion with his hand. "Uh huh. Yeah. I'll take care of it."

Bob ended the call and tossed the phone onto his desk. "So, Bel. You haven't been answering my calls."

"You'd have only wanted to talk about the hideous death spiral of my career." She plunked a pretty pie box into the center of his desk. "I was depressed enough without that conversation, thanks."

Bob lifted the corner of the lid with his pen, a solid gold Mont Blanc that had to weigh two pounds. He sniffed at the pie. "Cherry?"

"Sour cherry with an almond crust."

"Nice."

She smiled. "This pie takes *nice* out back and steals its lunch money."

"I believe you." He picked up the pie box and deposited it on the credenza behind his desk. "So, you're ready to talk about the hideous death spiral of your career now?"

"Sort of." Bel sank into the watered silk chair across from him. "I want to know what's going on with Kate."

Bob's brows inched up over granite colored eyes and he leaned back until his leather chair creaked. "Your groom ran off with your assistant on live TV, Bel. Your wedding—not to mention the *Kate Every Day* season premiere, usually a testament to good taste and high-brow entertainment—went down in melodramatic flames. And you want to talk about Kate?"

Bel bore up under the weighty truth of that one. "Yes," she said. "I can't do anything about my wedding. I clearly misjudged Ford. Annie, too. And in a highly public manner. That was my mistake. A bad one." She fought to keep the sick humiliation in her stomach from seeping into her voice. "One that reflected as badly on Kate as it did on me. She's perfectly within her rights to fire me over it. I won't argue. Not with that." She leaned forward. "But I do have a problem with the fact that she was relieved about it."

Bob frowned. "She told you that?"

"Of course not. But I'm not blind, Bob. You and I both know that Kate can be...subtle. What she says isn't nearly as important as what she means, and I've gotten pretty good at reading her. Maybe not as good as you are, but darn good. And I'm telling you, firing me was a big, fat relief to her. I could see it in her eyes. The woman wanted me gone and my rather spectacular failure made her day."

"That doesn't make sense, Bel. She sank three years into you. She made retirement plans around you. You were the golden child. Why on earth would she be happy about losing that kind of investment?"

"You tell me."

"How am I supposed to know?"

"Because you know everything." She gave him a smile, big and bright. "You're the Great and Powerful Bob."

"And as such, I'm not in the habit of overlooking problems that cost me money." His gaze went hard. "I invested in you, too, Bel. I saw something in you that Kate saw as well or she would never have taken you on in the first place. So don't sit there and tell me this isn't your fault. That you're the victim of some vast conspiracy or something."

Bel's shoulders had crept up to her ears as if to protect her from the ugly truth, and she forced them back down. "I didn't say it wasn't my fault. I just pointed out that maybe there's more than *my fault* going on here." Bob's brows headed farther north and Bel shoved her fists into her elbows. "Listen, maybe we haven't been together as long as you and Kate, but you're my agent, too. You know me. I do the work, Bob. I do it well and I do it right. And when there's blame to be laid, I don't run whining to my agent. I take my fair share."

He sighed. "I know you do, Bel. That's why I haven't signed or sent the Dear Jane letter on my desk with your

29

name on it."

She'd known that letter was a possibility. Of course she had. That was why she'd ducked his phone calls for the last two weeks, wasn't it? But her lungs went scorched and useless all the same. "You were going to void my contract?"

His shrewd gaze shifted to hers. "I didn't say that."

"So you believe me?"

"I didn't say that either."

Bel took a firmer grip on her courage. "What did you say, then? If you don't mind my asking."

Bob smiled his sharky smile. How had she ever imagined he was wilted? "I have a proposition for you, Belinda. One that might bring Kate around, save your career and iron out a little problem of mine, all at the same time."

She considered him narrowly. "I already gave you a pie."

"Resurrecting your career is worth considerably more than a pie, Bel. Even one of yours."

"I think you're undervaluing my baking, but okay." She leaned forward. "What do you need?"

"A nanny."

She frowned. "For what? Your imaginary children?"

"No, for a multimillionaire with maturity issues."

Bel considered this. "What kind of maturity issues?"

"All of them." He steepled his hands and watched her over his fingertips. "Just listen, okay? I have this client. Magnificent athlete. Like poetry in human form. On the field, he's a goddamn shrine to timing and instinct. But his personal life is a disaster. He drinks, he fights, and if he's ever had a date he didn't pick up in a strip club I've never met her."

"He sounds charming."

"Oh, it gets better. He also has a pair of moronic brothers, one of whom acts as his manager, the other as his webmaster. Now if even one of these boys had the judgment God gave a billy goat we might be all right. Unfortunately..."

Bel's stomach tightened with alarm. This set-up was starting to sound ominously familiar. "Unfortunately?"

Bob shook his head. "These boys make billy goats look

like academics. Throw in unlimited funds and—" Bob filled in the blank with a weary chuff of laughter. "Bottom line? My boy's one thin hair from being blackballed from every team in the league. Kid needs a babysitter." He fixed Bel with sharp eyes. "He's *earned* one and he's going to get one."

"What makes you think a grown man would agree to that kind of supervision?" she asked calmly even as suspicion sank sharp claws into her. Because, come on, what were the chances? Badly behaved athletes and their hangers-on were a dime a dozen. Surely Bob's billy goats weren't the same idiots who'd ruined her wedding and thereby her career. They couldn't be. Could they?

"Because the people paying him all that money to wear their shoes, drink their soda and hawk their jeans are even richer than he is. And people don't get that kind of money leaving anything to chance."

"Okay." She grabbed her logic with both hands and forced herself to focus. To listen. A hell of a lot could be riding on these next few minutes and she didn't want to miss anything because she was needlessly—probably—panicking. "Which means...?"

"Which means that the contract he's working under contains what you might call a modified morals clause."

"A morals clause?" She blinked. "As in *you'd better not be a gay Communist or you'll never work in this town again*?"

"Not quite. More like *get your stupid ass red-carded out of one more match and I'm issuing you a goddamn nanny*." He smiled. "I believe they call them life coaches these days."

"Ah." Bel digested this. "Fascinating. But how exactly is my playing Mary Poppins to a badly behaved athlete going to pull my career out of the toilet?"

Bob's smile went sharky again and Bel braced herself.

"How do you feel about doing it all to Kate's specifications?"

Bel stared. "For *Kate Every Day*?"

"No. But, damn, wouldn't that be a great segment?

31

Mary Poppins for Millionaires. *Entourage* meets *Nanny 911*. The disgraced domestic diva proving her mettle by whipping an over-funded frat house and its skeevy inhabitants into shape." Bob gave a wistful sigh and Bel tried not to look horrified. "But it's not going to happen so don't worry about it."

"Kate said no?" Relief sprinkled through Bel like rain on a dusty street.

"Of course she did." Bob curled his lip. "Something about decorum or dignity or some such nonsense. But she's agreed to give you another chance. Privately."

"She has?"

"She's a reasonable woman, Bel. She doesn't want to throw away what you've built together any more than you do."

Bel let that go without argument. Now wasn't the time to quibble over details. "What do I have to do?"

"Prove yourself."

"How?"

"By fixing my client under Kate's supervision."

Bel tried to think over the mad spiral of hope in her chest and the clanging alarm bells in her head. "What does that mean?"

"It means that each week for the next four weeks, Kate will assign you a new social grace to teach our boy. At the end of each week, she'll evaluate his performance and yours. Brutally. You pass and you get your job back in time for the *Kate Every Day* Christmas Special."

Bel studied him. "And if I fail?"

Bob gave his cell phone a spin on the glossy surface of his desk and watched her from under thick brows. "I sign the Dear Jane letter on my desk."

Bel swallowed but her throat stayed tight and dry. "This mystery athlete," she said finally. "Does he have a name?" Like she even needed to ask.

He stopped the spinning phone. "James Blake."

Bel closed her eyes. "Of course." A prickly wave of rage rolled over her at the memory of that slow, no-worries smile under a raggedy ball cap. Of those easy words and that thoughtless mouth. Of the way he'd offered her a *beer* as if it was an even exchange for blowing her career to kingdom come.

"Former soccer god of Manchester United, more lately of the DC Statesmen," Bob said. "Also Kate's next door neighbor and, after the wedding incident, her new arch enemy."

"Yeah, I know." Bel gave him a sour look. "I was there for that part." Then she frowned. "Now wait just a minute. Why on earth would Kate want anything to do with rehabilitating James Blake? Seems to me like she'd *want* him to get blackballed from the league. Then he could go into bankruptcy, lose the Annex and sink quietly into a life of abject poverty and substance abuse while Kate indulged in a private chuckle, after which she would bask in her skyrocketing property value."

"See, that's why you got fired." Bob aimed a finger her way. "You don't understand your boss."

Bel frowned and dragged herself away from the satisfying mental image of James Blake's downfall. "I don't?"

"Come on, Bel. Think. This guy fucked up Kate's season premiere, her protégée's wedding day and her retirement plans in one fell swoop. You think watching him suffer from afar is going to satisfy *Kate*?" He huffed out a soft laugh. "I'm sorry, have you even *met* the woman?"

Understanding detonated in her head like an atom bomb and she froze. "Revenge," she said, her voice hollow. "Kate wants to twist the knife." On James, of course, but on her, too. God, Bob was right. She *was* slow.

"Is this going to be a problem for you?" he asked, his eyes narrow and stern.

"What? Kate demanding her pound of flesh in exchange for a second chance?" she asked. "Or spending every waking minute of the next month with James Blake and his band of merry idiots?"

"Either." Bob watched her steadily. "Both."

She laughed bitterly. "Does it matter?"

"Yeah. It does."

Bel blinked, startled out of her momentary wallow. "Excuse me?"

"You say the word and it's off the table, the whole deal." His face was as hard and closed as always but his eyes, she saw with a shock, were full of troubled concern. Her mouth dropped open and he held up a flat hand. "Don't misunderstand, now. That Dear Jane letter is always a possibility. Kate came first, and business is business. But if you think you'll drop off my radar, you're wrong. You're talented, Bel. Beyond talented. You'll land just fine. You have my word on that." He leaned back in his chair and held her gaze. "The question is, is that what you want?"

Her throat cinched tight on a rush of mortifying tears and she swallowed hard. Bob believed in her. In her talent, anyway. That was enough right there to make her cry, that anybody believed in her anymore. But coming from Bob? This was the rough equivalent of a request to adopt her.

"No," she said when she was sure her voice wouldn't wobble. She refused to reward his faith by weeping all over his starchy shirt. "I don't want that. I want to whip James Blake's frat-boy ass into shape for Kate's viewing pleasure."

"Excellent." Bob's smile flashed sharp and hard but his eyes laughed. "Go pick out your bedroom, kiddo."

Bel frowned, and for one wild moment she wondered if Bob was actually adopting her. "My bedroom?"

"At the Annex." He propped an ankle on his knee, enjoying himself. "Nannies live in, Bel. Plus you're currently homeless, so what's the problem?"

"No problem," Bel said again if a bit more faintly. "Just...okay." She gave herself a mental slap and a stern warning to get it together. Eyes on the prize, she thought. Eyes on the prize.

"Fine. Now get out of here," Bob said, dialing. "I need to deal with some irate sponsors."

"Right." She gazed at him, searching for any hint of the tired, worn man she'd seen when she first walked in. Any hint of the fatherly concern she'd seen just a minute ago. Nothing. Now he was just kicking her out so he could work the phone.

34

"Don't forget about the pie," she said slowly. "You could stand a slice or two, and I don't want to come back here in two weeks to find it growing moss on your credenza."

He stuck his phone to his ear and waved her away in the same motion. "Yeah, okay."

CHAPTER SIX

Despite the early fall sun pouring into the van like melted butter, Bel's fingers were cold and stiff on the wheel as she pulled into James Blake's courtyard. For one weak moment, she allowed herself to wonder if she was making a mistake. But no. Last resorts were, by definition, never mistakes. When one had no choice, one couldn't choose badly, right?

Still, what had seemed like a workable idea in Bob's office felt a bit less reasonable outside James Blake's front door. She concentrated on her breathing as she parked next to the Italian fountain that had nearly given Kate a stroke when she'd seen it go up last fall. *Did you hear that thud, Belinda? That was my property value falling. Thank you, nouveau riche redneck neighbors.*

Bel actually didn't mind the fountain. She got out of the van and patted the ample backside of one of its naked frolickers. The world could use a few more women who didn't look at a Tic Tac and see lunch.

Speaking of which, Bel retrieved a grocery sack from the passenger seat of her van with a twitch of relief. She could handle hotel living—the strange beds, the cheap sheets, the generic showers. But having no place to put her milk, butter and eggs? That unleashed a blind panic in her, cracked the door on the swirling chaos she'd worked so hard to banish.

But she'd bet good money James wasn't using his fridge for anything but cooling beer, and her groceries needed a home. So she gathered them into her arms and marched up to the twenty-foot tall double doors. She pressed her free hand to her jumping stomach then rang the bell.

"Mamas Don't Let Your Babies Grow Up To Be Cowboys" bonged solemnly inside the house and Bel's stomach settled somewhat. Surely she could handle a guy who programmed his doorbell to sing Willie Nelson.

She waited a moment, then pressed the bell again. Patsy Cline this time. "Walking After Midnight." Huh. She pressed again. Hank Williams. "Down on the Bayou."

She was reaching for the button a fourth time, just to see how deep her knowledge of country music legends really went, when James Blake himself wrenched open the door.

He wasn't a huge man, maybe three or four inches taller than Bel's own five-eight, but his presence filled up the doorway and spilled out onto the veranda just the way she remembered. His hair was like shaggy sunshine, all mashed up on the one side as if he'd just rolled out of bed. It spiked down over shockingly dark eyebrows and a nose that had clearly seen the business end of a fist or two. His mouth was perfection, though, even poised to snarl. That deeply bowed upper lip, the full curve of the lower. Too pretty for a man but that magnificent beaky nose balanced it out, Bel decided. He wasn't exactly handsome, but she could see why his face ended up in the papers so often. Women would always love pirates.

"For the love of Pete," he barked, "*what*?"

Even pissed off, he stretched the words like taffy. Twelve years chasing a soccer ball around Europe (okay, so she'd Googled him) hadn't touched that West Texas drawl.

"Um, hi." Bel gave herself a mental kick in the butt. *Nice. Very good start*. In her defense, however, he *was* shirtless. He was perhaps a bit softer about the midsection than Bel would have expected from a professional athlete but his arms and chest were all leanly muscled gold and a lot to contend with on a nervous stomach. A tiny, unwelcome shock rippled through her and she clutched the bag of groceries tighter to her chest.

"I'm sorry," he said, frowning. "Do I know you?"

"Well, that's lowering. You destroy my career and you don't even remember me?" She gave him a chilly smile. "Belinda West. You single-handedly derailed my wedding about two weeks ago now." Her smile sharpened. "On live TV."

He squinted into the late morning light and pressed a thumb to the center of his forehead as if the very sight of her gave him a headache. "Oh. That was you?"

"That was me." She brushed past him into a soaring marble and gilt foyer, complete with a curving staircase that cried out for hoop skirts and grand entrances.

"No, I insist," he said to the empty doorway. "Do come in."

"Thanks." Bel gazed around the foyer. "I haven't been in the Annex before. Is the entire house decorated like this?"

"Like what?"

"Like the mausoleum where they buried restraint and good taste?"

He pinched the bridge of his nose. "Is this my punishment for giving your runaway groom a couple beers and a bucket of balls? You're going to ring the bejesus out of my doorbell at the crack of dawn and insult my decorator until I repent?"

"I have a few other duties as well, but I'm sure Bob explained them all."

"Bob?"

"Bob Beck. Our mutual agent?"

"Bob's your agent, too?"

She stared at him. "He didn't call you?"

"About what?"

"You don't know what I'm doing here, do you?"

"Besides being confusing and, I'm going to be honest here, just a tad inconvenient? Sorry, no."

She gripped her groceries and prayed for Bob's untimely demise. "We should start over."

He rubbed the back of his neck and pursed up that gorgeous mouth. "Do we have to?"

She shifted the bag to her hip and stuck out her hand. "Hello, Mr. Blake. I'm Belinda West. Your new nanny."

James squinted at this woman in his foyer. All long legs, deep dimples and impossibly soft-looking skin, Belinda West—Bel, if he remembered—looked like an angel. The tidy sort of angel that made a man wonder what it would take to get her to set aside that halo for a minute or two. Even at whatever o'clock on a Saturday morning.

But then she'd started throwing around words like *Bob Beck* and *good taste* and—God—*new nanny*. Any vague ideas about mussed angels and crooked halos vanished in the face of his first coherent thought of the morning.

As usual these days, it was *wait, what*?

God, he was getting old. Time was he could match Will drink for drink and still play out of his mind the next day. Now he was getting to be as big a pussy as Drew, who fell in love with every pretty waitress who smiled at him. He shook his head in brotherly disgust but stopped when his skull threatened to explode. God, *what* had he drunk last night? He forced his focus back to the situation at hand.

"Bob hired *you* to be my new assistant?" he asked.

"I believe the term he used was babysitter. Live in." Bel gave him a prim little smile that barely played peek-a-boo with those killer dimples. Between them, that butter-soft skin and the creases he'd bet good money she ironed into her jeans every morning, she was a damn pretty picture. But James knew exactly what pictures like her cost—a big, fat diamond solitaire and total obedience to a color-coded calendar.

The diamond he could afford, no problem. But the calendar? He got hives just thinking about it.

"Why?" he asked, cursing the hangover that had his normally glib tongue thick and stupid.

"Why do you need a babysitter? Bob said something about another red card and a morals clause." She fixed him with a bright, inquisitive gaze that made him feel like the proverbial worm to her early bird.

"I meant why you?" he asked. "And why would you say yes? You seem like a nice enough girl and it's bound to be a thankless task."

She gave him a hard look. "Are you planning to give me trouble, Mr. Blake?"

He gave her his best shot at a roguish grin. "Not you personally. But I do have a powerful dislike for schedules. Calendars, too. Systems, methods, rules. Authority of all kinds, really." He spread his hands. "It's been a trial all my life."

"I'm sure."

"But my brothers? Why, they're barely housebroken. Why on earth would you want to muck around with the likes of us?"

"It seemed only fair that you give me a job," she said. "Since you got me fired from my last one."

"Oh." James' head thumped like a disco. He cast around for something charming and apologetic to say but came up empty. If she was keeping score, and she looked like the sort who would, he'd also cost her a groom. Was she going to demand a replacement there as well?

"Wow," he said finally. "I'm...sorry."

"Thanks. Listen, do you mind if we continue our little chat in the kitchen?" She jiggled the paper sack in her arms. "I have perishables here."

"Oh. Right. Sure." He waved down a short hallway to the swinging door to the kitchen. "Through there." A change of venue might be a good idea, actually. Maybe just standing next to the coffee pot would put a dent in this vicious and well-deserved headache.

But he wasn't so hung over that he didn't enjoy the scent of her—all sunshine and sweet cream butter—as she swished past him. The sight of her pert backside wasn't lost on him, either. He followed her into the kitchen.

She stopped just inside the doorway, gazed around the enormous space. "This," she said, "is a fantastic kitchen."

He blinked at her. "I hate this kitchen. I can't find anything, and on the off chance I do, I can't figure out how it works." He moved around her to poke at an espresso maker the size of a Volkswagen parked on his granite countertop. "Like this. This is a coffee maker." He frowned. "Isn't it?"

Bel wrinkled her nose at it. "No. That's a piece of high-end kitchen art."

James sighed. "Figures. Drew probably fell in love with the salesgirl."

"Drew?"

"My baby brother. He's in charge of the kitchen."

40

She slanted him a glance. "He cooks?"

"No. But he's in charge of the kitchen."

She crossed to a stainless steel behemoth of a fridge and opened it. "So I see."

"Hey, the kid loves gadgets. And since practically everything in the kitchen plugs in..." He leaned left and followed her bemused gaze to the contents of his fridge: half a six-pack and a grease-stained pizza box. "Maybe he should stick to updating my Twitter feed."

"That might not be a bad idea." She closed the fridge. "What does your other brother do? Decorate?"

"Will? No." James pulled a long-legged stool from beneath a massive island counter and sank onto it to watch her unload her grocery sack. "He manages my career."

She paused, a carton of eggs in one hand. "How's that going for you?"

"He negotiates one hell of a contract," he said. "Boy plays with money like it's Monopoly."

"But overlooks small details like morals clauses that saddle you with a babysitter?"

"There's that." James propped his cheek on a fist and watched her tuck away groceries. It was nice, watching her. She was so...neat. Efficient. Practical. It was almost hypnotic, the way she moved around his kitchen. With five minutes and no apparent effort, she'd unearthed a sauce pan from a cupboard he'd have sworn didn't exist and boiled water. She'd hauled coffee beans from her grocery bag, zipped them into a heavenly smelling dust in a grinder (also from her bottomless bag) then performed some miracle involving the water, the beans and a glass contraption (also from the bag.) James was waiting for the loaves and fishes to pop out next when a blessed mug of strong black coffee landed under his nose.

"Wicked, witchy woman," James said, burying his face in the steam rising from the mug. "You think you can bribe me into good behavior with coffee?"

Bel studied him. "Yes."

"Damn skippy." He sighed in satisfaction as the first kick of caffeine hit his poor, battered system. Then she started cracking eggs into a bowl he'd never seen before.

"What are you making?"

She raised a brow over the dripping eggshells in either hand. "Eggs."

"For me?"

"Yep." She reached into the fridge for a carton of milk, splashed some into the bowl and started whisking the crap out of the eggs. A pat of butter melted in a pan on the stove, filling the room with the promise of forthcoming sustenance. James nearly wept.

"Wicked, witchy woman," he said again. "I will not fall in love with you so stop trying."

Her lips twitched. "I'll bear it in mind."

An odd contentment filled him as he watched her expertly flick eggs around the pan. He could get used to this woman right quick. Addicted, actually.

The thought slapped him back to reality. What the hell was he doing? Somewhere between the coffee and the eggs, he'd lost control. She'd focused on him and his needs, and he'd lapped it up like a dog instead of remembering that power came from giving not receiving. So what did Bel West need that had her scrambling eggs for strangers bright and early on a Saturday morning? And how was he going to get the upper hand back by deciding whether or not to give it to her?

"Okay, I can see what I'm getting out of this deal," he said as she slid a plate full of fluffy eggs under his nose. He forced himself to ignore them for the moment. "But what about you? With your résumé, I'm pretty sure you have other options. Why this? Why us?"

She leaned back against the stove, arms folded over her waist. "I want my old job back."

"And this will get it for you?"

"Yep."

"How?"

She gazed at him. "You really need to talk to your agent more often."

"Okay, setting that aside, why would you even want that job back?"

A wrinkle appeared between those no-nonsense brows of hers. "What do you mean?"

He sipped his coffee, considering the bafflement in her face. "Weddings go south all the time, Bel. Seems to me that if Kate Davis really valued you as an employee, she wouldn't be so quick to pull the trigger, you know? So I'm forced to conclude that Kate's maybe not that into you." Her plump little mouth went tight and James smiled. "Why on earth would you put yourself through what will surely be several weeks of misery just to prove yourself to somebody who doesn't want you?"

Bel stared at him. "I want my job back," she said. "It's none of your business why."

James shrugged, but tucked away that interesting, hunted expression for future consideration. "Your call," he said easily. He picked up his fork and laid into the eggs which were, unsurprisingly, incredible. He would have to watch this woman.

"So we're winning you back a bad job," he said. "How are we going to do that exactly?"

She smiled at him, slick and just a little mean. An unexpected splinter of lust shot into his gut at the sight of that pretty mouth curved with such a sharp wickedness.

"Why don't you call Bob and find out?"

He frowned at her. At himself. He was generally pretty predictable when it came to women. He loved them all but as a rule preferred the soft, curvy, agreeable types. Now was not the time to develop a weakness for bossy, sharp-edged women with magic grocery sacks and fallen-angel mouths.

"I'll do that," he said around a forkful of eggs. God, this woman was dangerous. "After breakfast."

Will Blake dragged his pounding head and uneasy stomach out of bed and down that ridiculous *Gone With The Wind* staircase. He smelled eggs—the greasy, salty, buttery kind that cured hangovers like magic—and he was getting his share. Right before he died of a raging headache. At least he'd go a happy man.

Well, full, at least. Will couldn't quite remember the last time he'd have classified himself as happy.

He shoved at the kitchen door, held it propped open with a foot while he steadied himself on the doorframe and squinted into the brutal light. James was already there but Drew wasn't. Good thing, Will thought. Drew ate like a Hoover.

James looked up, then hunched over his plate and started shoveling eggs into his mouth. "Nuh-uh," he said around the food. "Mine."

Will tsked. "That's not the Blake family way," he said, advancing on his brother. "What do we always say?"

"We don't say anything," James mumbled and washed down an ambitious mouthful of eggs with a slug from the mug at his elbow. Coffee? Will sniffed. Yes, indeed. There was coffee, too. Hallelujah.

"Family first," Will told him. "What we have, we share."

James curled a protective arm around the plate and gripped his fork like a weapon. "I will defend these eggs with my life."

Will shifted his gaze to the mug. "How about that coffee?"

James glanced at it, momentarily distracted, and Will leapt. God, his head. But he was going to have those eggs.

Bel rose from her squat next to the produce drawer of James' fridge just in time to see one of his brothers take him in a flying headlock and drag him off his stool. They disappeared behind the island counter, locked in pitched battle over...what? Bel leaned over the counter for a better look. Possession of the fork? She checked the drawer. There were at least half a dozen others right here. She shook her head and reached for the egg carton.

She was beating more eggs into a milky froth when the third Blake brother strolled into the kitchen. Where James and the first brother were both fair and wiry, this one was tall

44

and lanky with hair like ground nutmeg. He gave her a sweet smile and stepped over his brothers like he did it every morning. He probably did.

He paused only briefly to snap a phone-photo of the melee at his feet, then seated himself at the island counter.

"If there's any chance you'd part with some of whatever's in that bowl, I can almost guarantee I'm going to propose marriage," he said, eyes still on the phone, typing with his thumbs.

Bel grinned at him. "I'm not in the market for a fiancé, thanks. But you can have the eggs."

He finished whatever he was typing and set aside the phone to co-opt James' abandoned coffee. He tasted it and that sweet smile bloomed again across a long, angular face that was more charming than handsome. "I think I love you," he said. "Who are you?"

Bel slid a plate of eggs across the counter with a fresh fork and said, "Propose first, ask questions later, is that it?"

He sampled the eggs and his eyes lit up. "Forget it. I don't even need to know your name. We're heading to Vegas just as soon as I'm done eating."

The scuffling behind the island counter paused. "Damn it, Will, Drew's getting round two of the eggs."

"*Round two?*" Will popped up beyond the counter like a prairie dog, just his head, and he scanned the room until his gaze landed on Bel. "Who are you?"

Drew shook his head. "No, son, see the first question is always *can I have some of that*? And that's why I'm eating while you're rolling around on the floor with your own brother like the pervert you are." He helped himself to a leisurely sip of coffee. "I tweeted a photo, by the way."

James staggered to his feet in triumphant possession of the fork. He plopped onto a stool beside Drew and resumed eating as if nothing out of the ordinary had happened. Bel was afraid that perhaps nothing had. He gave Drew a black look and stole his coffee back.

Drew gave him that same sweet smile he'd used on Bel and said, "You were busy."

James grunted and shifted the mug to his other hand, the one farthest from his younger brother.

Will hadn't moved. He hadn't shifted his gaze from Bel and those hard pale eyes weighed like stones on her. "James?" he said. "Introduce your friend."

"That tone's not going to get you any breakfast," Drew told him. *No kidding*, Bel thought.

"That's Bel," James said, concentrating on emptying his plate with maximum efficiency. "Bob sent her. She's our new nanny. Live in."

Drew made a happy noise.

"Apparently, she and Bob have cooked something up that will get her back in front of the *Kate Every Day* cameras while rehabilitating my sadly tarnished public image."

"Ah." Will gave Bel an assessing up-and-down. "You bit on that, huh?"

James paused mid-bite and said, "You know about this?"

Will gave his brother a terse summary of the same plan Bob had outlined for Bel a few hours ago. James pushed back from his now-empty plate and listened in silence, sipping thoughtfully at his coffee.

"You have to admit," Drew said around a mouthful of eggs. "We could use some minding." He chewed contentedly. "I, for one, intend to write Bob a nice thank you note. You should, too. The minute you get home."

Will and James turned twin frowns on Drew.

"Get home?" James said.

"From what?" Will said.

Drew held out his hand for James' coffee. James sighed and handed it over. Drew took his time about the first sip then said, "From the underpants party."

Bel stared. "The *what*?"

"Some underpants company gives James bushels of money to wear their tighty whiteys," Drew told her. "They're having a big thing tonight. James is supposed to make an appearance."

James looked a question at Will who thought for a moment then nodded. "Contractual obligation," he said. Bel wondered if he had the wording of each individual contract in his head, available for consultation.

Drew grinned at him. "Bummer for you."

"Oh well. At least I won't be lonely." James smiled, slow and satisfied. "Because you know what we say here in the Blake house."

Drew and Will went still.

"Family first, gentlemen." James surveyed them solemnly. "Family first."

"What we have, we share," Will said as if reciting from memory. He shot a pointed glance at the coffee mug in Drew's hand.

"Your fight is our fight." Drew sighed and handed it over.

"Which means that if I have to wear a tux—" James laid a hand over his heart like he was preparing to pledge allegiance. Bel suspected he was.

"—so the hell do we," Will finished grimly. He tossed back the coffee like a shot of whiskey.

She stared at the three of them, bemused. When she was a kid, she'd wished for a sibling with all her heart. She realized now that she hadn't had the faintest idea what she'd been wishing for.

"This is a black tie event?" she asked.

Drew and James looked at Will who consulted his apparently photographic memory and said, "Yep."

"Do you even own tuxes?" she asked.

"What do you take us for, animals?" James sniffed. "Of course we own tuxes." He paused. "We just don't know where they are exactly."

"Which is why we have a nanny now. To take care of these things for us." Will smiled at her but it had a nasty, sharp edge.

Bel folded her arms. "I apprenticed under Kate Davis for *three years*," she said. "You think getting the three of you showered, sober and appropriately dressed by nightfall is going to sweat me? Please." She pointed the spatula at Will. "All the same, no eggs for you. I don't care for your tone."

Drew smiled at her with delight. "I'm serious about Vegas, Bel. Say the word."

Will gave him a disgusted look. "You proposed already?"

James gazed at her consideringly. "You're meaner than you look," he said, as if the discovery caused him significant personal pain.

"Thanks." She dumped the pan into the sink.

"I didn't mean it as a compliment." He frowned. "I don't think."

"Oh, no, you don't." Drew shook his head. "I saw her first. I already *proposed*."

"You propose to everybody," James said absently, his eyes intense and watchful on Bel. An odd lightness jumped in her stomach. Wow. When this man paid attention, he *paid attention*. She didn't know if she was flattered or disturbed.

Not that it mattered. James Blake was her job and as such had no business flattering *or* disturbing her. She'd do well to remember that.

"If you boys aren't showered in the next half hour, I'm not making lunch," she said.

James nodded slowly. "Meaner than you look," he said again. But he headed for the door and his brothers fell in behind.

CHAPTER SEVEN

The sun was just beginning to set as James nosed his black SUV into the lane of traffic leading up to the hotel. After a dozen years of folding himself into European cars the size of carry-on luggage, he derived a deep satisfaction from being the tallest, widest thing on the road. Even if all it got him was a nice view of the grid-lock between his seat and the red carpet. At least he could kick back and wait it out in relative comfort.

He got as far as shifting one elbow and straightening one knee before his tux launched a vicious assault on a few key areas of his anatomy. He hunched miserably back into his seat.

Bel gave him a sharp look from the passenger side. "What?"

He scowled. "I hate dressing up."

"Why?"

"I don't know. I guess spending all night in a suit that's trying like hell to strangle my crotch isn't my idea of a good time."

"That tux is custom-made," she said, frowning. "I noticed when I was pressing it. Why on earth is it strangling you?"

Drew poked his head between the two front seats. "Because he's, like, twenty pounds heavier than when he had that bad boy fitted."

James felt his neck going red. "Okay, so I've enjoyed our return to the Land of the Whopper. But come on. I run for a living. I couldn't have gained twenty pounds. Could I?"

"Land of the Whopper." Drew laughed. "I'm totally tweeting that." He pulled out his beloved iPhone while Bel peered at James' jacket with a concern that had the tips of his ears burning.

"I don't know," she said. "But now that I'm looking, those seams are under some serious stress."

"You know, your stats haven't been exactly up to par this season, either," Will said thoughtfully. "You could maybe use a little more conditioning."

"You want to start running wind sprints at dawn?" James shot him a look in the rearview mirror. "Be happy to join you."

"Hey, my tux fits just fine," Will said. And James had to admit, he did look pretty comfortable sprawled across the enormous backseat, an evil half-smile kicking up one corner of his mouth. "Besides, I'm not the one who runs for a living."

James glared at him, something mean and petty stealing into his gut. His stats were down, his damn suit didn't fit, he was stuck in traffic, and a pretty girl was speculating on how fat he'd gotten. Now Will wanted to pile on? Maybe his brother had a mean set of teeth, but James knew how to bite, too.

"Well, you don't have to run for a living, do you, Will?" he asked, a deliberate cool in his voice. "I do it for you."

The wicked, teasing light died out of Will's eyes. "That's right," he said. "You run for all of our livings. James, the grand and benevolent provider. How shall we show our gratitude today?"

James looked away from Will's eyes in rearview mirror only to meet Drew's. In the watery light of his phone's screen, Drew looked uncomfortably like their father, from the long thin face to the eyes full of gentle rebuke. *Temper, James.* Even now he could hear his father's voice. With every red card he earned, for every foul he threw. *Temper, James.* Drew gave his head a small, slow shake and James shrugged irritably. The seams of his tux creaked a protest.

"All right," Bel said into the tense silence, her assessing gaze bouncing between the three of them. "Enough. New plan."

Ten minutes later, James exited the truck, marginally more comfortable than he'd gone in. The jacket was gone, as was the bow tie, thank the good lord. His cuff links had disappeared into that tiny little confection Bel called a purse but she'd insisted on keeping the shirt tucked in.

"You want to look casual," she said. "But dressy casual. Not I'm-too-hung-over-to-iron casual."

"Right," he said. He eyed the simple black dress she wore, the way it skimmed her knee caps as she stepped out of the SUV. It barely showed any skin but managed to suggest a trim little body all the same. "You set some serious store by ironing, don't you?"

"All the best people do."

He had a witty retort all set to send her way, but then she smiled at him. Just nailed him with a full-on, dimpled charmer. He stared, verbal capacity utterly short circuited. Good lord, where had she been hiding that *smile*? It was all earthy promise and home-made goodness, like sugar cookies for your eyes, and he suddenly understood how somebody so prim, so buttoned-up, so *well-pressed*, could cook the way she did.

He stared at her until the smile petered out into something less amused and more uncertain. When he could think again he said, "You should do that more often."

"What?"

"Smile."

She frowned at him. "I smile."

"Not like you mean it. Not with—" He waved a finger toward her cheek and she drew back as if he'd threatened her with a red-hot poker. "—dimples."

"You want me to smile more often." Those severe brows of hers headed for the sky. "With dimples."

"Not for me in particular." God, he was an idiot. Way to keep the upper hand, James. "Just in general. It's..." He groped for an explanation that didn't make him sound like a kid with a crush. "...some smile," he finished lamely.

"I see." She studied him. "Thank you."

"You're welcome." He slammed the door behind her just a shade harder than strictly necessary.

"Hey," she said. "Easy on the seams."

"Right," he said. "The seams."

The truck pulled away and Bel said, "Aren't Drew and Will going to—"

"Nope." James put a hand in the small of her back and pointed her toward the red carpet. "Those boys are in it for the free drinks, not the press coverage. They'll park and meet us inside."

"Oh." She peered after the vanished SUV.

"Don't worry. They won't get into trouble in the fifteen minutes it takes us to walk from here to there."

"Are you sure? There could be alcohol in there. Unattended women."

He pretended to consider this. "Best not waste time."

She took off for the entrance at a trot. James grinned. She was so *easy* to tweak. He might enjoy the next month or so after all.

He followed her into the pack of photographers and fans lining the red carpet. This was without a doubt his favorite kind of crowd. U.S. soccer didn't bring 'em out of the woodwork yet—a fact he was ridiculously well-paid to change—but after the madness of English football fans he actually enjoyed the low-key U.S. crowds.

Tonight, for example, he was looking at a few disinterested sports writers, a couple eager gossip columnists and a whole bunch of star-struck kids wearing jerseys for teams most folks in this country had never heard of. The press pointed their cameras at him and clicked away in an obligatory fashion, but the kids surged forward, a jostling mass of idol worship in human form armed with pens, soccer balls, posters and photos.

James caught up to Bel and tucked her under his arm, partly because he was starting to enjoy derailing her when she got that task-oriented look in her eye but mostly because she was going to miss all the fun racing off like that. Giving this moment to a bunch of screaming kids was hands-down the best part of his job these days.

He sank into the crowd like it was a warm bath and started scrawling his name onto anything that got shoved his way. Bel, who'd gone stiff as a broomstick the minute he'd hauled her into his side, tried to sidle away but he caught her wrist.

"Going somewhere?" He dashed his signature across a poster.

"Your brothers require supervision," she said. "Why don't I just meet you inside?"

"And have the world think I'm one of those guys who abandons his date every time the cameras point his way?" The crowd heaved up a Manchester United jersey with his old number on it, and he signed that, too. "I don't think so."

Her dark eyes snapped. "I am not your date."

"They don't know that." He grinned and snuggled her a little closer. Her long, lean body fit into his like a dream. Might be something to dating tall girls after all, he thought. Then she turned her face up to glare at him, bringing that plump, curvy mouth of hers close enough to bite. *Definitely* something to dating tall girls. The cameras went into hyper-drive, painting the moment with a washed-out unreality that half-convinced him to do it. Just lean in and nibble a little. Satisfy the curiosity that had been nagging him all day without mercy.

She might slap his face but damn, it would be worth it to find out what that pretty mouth tasted like. Not sugar cookies, he decided. Gingersnaps. Hot and sweet and buttery, all home-cooked goodness with a surprising little kick of spice.

"Don't—" she began, alarm flaring in those huge dark eyes.

"Then stop telling me what to do." He leaned a little closer, his gaze on her lips. "I have a weakness for bossy women and you're making it awfully hard to resist."

"I am *not* bossy."

"Contradictory, too. Mmm."

She stepped back. He followed. Flashbulbs popped, the crowd cheered, and James, buoyed as always by a little support from his fans, made his move.

He was a wish away from her parted lips, close enough to feel her startled, indrawn breath against his chin when a soccer ball popped out of the crowd and bounced off his side.

He didn't wonder where it had come from or what he ought to do with it. It didn't occur to him that he wasn't on a soccer field and thus the ball was out of place. The ball was there, so he controlled it. He jerked up a knee, settled the ball into the inside of his thigh, then let it roll down his calf to the ground where he trapped it under foot. The crowd went berserk. James found himself unexpectedly entertained, too.

Because Bel had just grabbed herself a big old handful of his backside.

Bel watched James flip the ball into the air with another one of those effortless motions. He scribbled something on it and sent it flying back into the crowd that had shot it at him in the first place. And because her hand was still clapped firmly against his extremely fine behind, she discovered that he felt as smooth as he looked. All those lovely muscles working together in graceful concert against the skin of her palm, with only a thin layer of expensive cotton between them. Then his arm came around her waist and settled against the curve of her hip with a heavy assurance that had her stomach twirling up into her throat.

"So," he said, those green eyes hot and interested. "Where was I?"

"You were waving goodbye to all your friends here and getting inside."

"I was?" He eased forward and Bel shot him a clenched smile that said *try it and I'll bite you*. He froze.

"You were." Cameras flashed continuously and Bel gave up on the idea of appearing like anything other than a...God, what did they call women who chased soccer players? Soccer sluts? Football floozies?

"Sure, all right." He backed cautiously away from the warning in her eyes then beamed at the crowd which roared its adoration in return. "Let me just sign this one last—"

"*Now.*"

He shook his head in mock consternation and put his mouth very near her ear. "There's that boss-lady tone again.

What did I tell you about that?" His voice was all burnt sugar, hot and melty and tempting, and it sent a delicious shiver chasing down her nape. A thoroughly unwelcome and inappropriate shiver, she told herself.

"And what did *I* tell *you* about your seams?" she said.

He frowned at her. "My seams?"

"Yeah. The one in the seat of your pants, to be specific. The one your fancy footwork there just *blew out*." She glared at him. "And don't tell me you can't feel the draft either, because we're not talking about a cute little peek-a-boo hole."

"Blew..." Comprehension stole into his eyes and a dull flush mounted his cheekbones. "How bad?"

"Sizeable."

"I see." He cleared his throat. "And here I thought you were just warming up."

Bel's hand twitched involuntarily on the gaping rip in his pants, on the firm curve of his backside. She was warm, all right. "I have a sewing kit in my purse," she said. "Can we please just go in?"

He shot her a sidelong glance. "You're going to keep your hand on my ass the whole way?"

"That was my plan," she said, cheeks burning. "Unless you'd rather the press just took pictures of your shorts?"

"No, no. It's fine. I don't mind at all. In fact—" He snugged her into his side again and splayed a big hand over her butt crack. The vital heat of his touch soaked through her dress and sang through her entire body, pooling in all the most interesting bits. "I'll return the favor. Just so you don't look so forward."

"Forward!"

"Yeah. When the pictures hit the papers. You don't want to look like one of those desperate groupies copping a quick feel off some footballer who doesn't even know her name, do you? You'll come off much better if this is a mutual grope." He gave her bottom a fond pat. "Trust me."

She closed her eyes and tried to ignore the way her stomach jumped in response to his touch. This was her job now. Exchanging mock feel-ups with her newest colleague

55

in front of the cameras. Fate never failed to ding the good girls, did it?

"Fine," she said. "I defer to your vastly superior experience with public displays of bad taste. But if you *pat* me one more time, I'm going to pinch you. Hard."

He paused, arrested. "I'm starting to think you *want* me to make a move."

She treated him to an icy smile. "Try it and I'll make you very sorry."

"Yeah?" He lifted an eyebrow, more interested than wary. "How?"

She stared at him. She might as well be talking dirty to him for the look on his face. "Just try to remember that I'm the girl who's going to sew up your pants in a minute, okay? Mess with me and I can make this a very uncomfortable evening."

"You'd do that?"

"In a heartbeat."

He stared at her, then laughed. "I bet you would, too." He started up the red carpet at the leisurely amble he seemed to apply to all situations that didn't involve a soccer ball. "Only makes it worse, though, Bel. Just so you know."

She rolled her eyes. "I'll bear it in mind."

"I sincerely hope you will."

Will perused the top shelf scotch collection with an expert eye. Free alcohol was nothing to take lightly, after all. This was a big decision. And considering that Drew was already mooning around over one of the waitresses, he could use a stiff drink. Add to that the fact that James and the new nanny had gone directly from the red carpet to the bathrooms with their hands plastered all over each other and this night was shaping up to be a real misery.

God, he was sick of his life.

"I'll take the Glen Garioch," he said to the bartender. "Neat."

"It's her," Drew said, his gaze following some curvy little waitress around the room. "I know it is."

Will glanced at him, then back at the bartender. "Better make it a double."

The glass arrived in his hand, heavy-bottomed and cool, two inches of gorgeous amber liquid swirling inside it. The impulse to pound the drink back was there—always there—but it would be a crime to gulp down scotch of this quality. An insult to all the wizened little brewers who babied dank cellars full of oak barrels in the wilds of Scotland to ensure that their fine, life-sustaining product could end up here where Will needed it most.

He raised the glass slowly, relishing the moment. He loved that instant when the alcohol first hit his tongue, the way it spun into his system all lazy and reassuring. He especially loved the way it blurred the sharpest edges of his stupid fucking life. The one where his only professional, social or emotional obligations revolved around somebody else's talent. The one where Will, at thirty years of age, was still making his living off his younger brother and building his weekends around opportunities for free alcohol.

He rolled that first taste around his mouth, forbidding himself to swallow until he'd savored it. Then Drew poked him with a sharp elbow and said, "Seriously, will you *look*? It's totally her."

Will closed his eyes and let the scotch trickle down his throat. Then he threw the rest of it back in a single gulp. Fuck it.

"Which one?" he asked.

"The blonde," Drew said, his dark eyes glued to a pretty little thing with curves that, even in a waitress uniform almost made up for that salad spinner haircut. "God, how can you not remember her? From Maxwell's? Last night? I tried to get her number for hours. Ordered all kinds of drinks I didn't want."

Will remembered that. He'd drunk most of them. He set his glass down on the bar and forbade himself another for at least an hour.

"She told me she was leaving for Tucson in the morning." That was true confusion in Drew's voice. No anger, no petulance, just hurt wonder. "She *lied* to me."

"They'll do that."

"But *why*?" Honest bafflement now. Will shook his head in disbelief. Kid was an optimist, sure. Just wired like that, lucky him. But he'd have to be purely, willfully ignorant to think any woman was going to choose *him* when James Blake, superstar, was sitting across the table all alone. "I really liked her."

Will didn't bother to enlighten him, just made a non-committal noise and turned back to the bar. He thought about reducing the interval between drinks to half an hour. An hour was starting to look unreasonable. Good thing he'd treated himself to a couple quick shots before leaving the house. He'd had a feeling tonight was going to be a total cock-up and he'd been right. As usual. The curse of his genius IQ.

A movement in the mirror behind the bottles caught his attention and he turned to see James and Bel exiting the bathroom. Together. She gave his shirt a furtive tug, as if to make sure she'd retucked it properly, and it sent a black rage rolling into his stomach.

Their new nanny couldn't be bothered to scramble Will an egg but she had no problem fucking his brother in a bathroom stall her first night on the job. Proving once again that there was no limit to James' magical luck.

He checked his watch and gauged his level of sobriety. Even if he adopted the new half-hour-between-drinks policy he was still looking at 25 minutes until the next scotch. And while he wasn't precisely sober, he wasn't anywhere near drunk enough to endure 25 minutes of James' post-coital glow. Not with this ugly urge to break shit crawling up his throat. He needed to bleed it off, he realized dully. Break something small before he broke something big. It wouldn't satisfy the itch but it would take the edge off. He hoped.

He turned to Drew, slung an arm around his brother's neck with a heartiness he didn't feel.

"Hang on, now. That waitress lied to you?"

"Yeah." Drew didn't look at him. He was still tracking the not-into-him hottie as she wove expertly through the crowd with a tray.

"That, my brother, is an insult we can't be expected to bear."

Drew finally looked at him, those big brown eyes suddenly wary. Maybe the boy wasn't purely stupid after all. "What? No! Will, don't—"

"Oh, but it's my pleasure." He smiled and Drew actually took a step back. "Pay attention, now, son. Justice is about to be served."

CHAPTER EIGHT

Bel frowned critically at James' backside and nodded. "It'll do," she said.

"As long as I don't try to sit, stand, run, walk or move."

"Right." She smiled and it felt deliciously evil. Goodness, where was this coming from? Why was she having so much fun torturing the poor man? What had he ever done to her?

Oh, right. Now she remembered. He'd torpedoed her life-long dream with his thoughtless mouth and his stupid brothers, and hadn't had the good grace to even remember her face later. She'd made him eggs and pressed his tuxedo and he'd accused her of being bossy. Then he'd split his stupid pants and rather than let photos of his underwear turn up on the front page of tomorrow's sports section, she'd thrown herself into the breach. Smashed through several personal-space boundaries in the process, but she was a good sport and a dedicated worker. She did the job, no matter what.

And how had he repaid her? By threatening to kiss her in front of hundreds of people with cameras? By insinuating that she was begging for it? He deserved to squirm a little, and the extra two inches she'd taken out of the crotch of his pants would ensure he did.

"You're enjoying this," he said.

"Nooooo." Then she gave up resisting and sank into her pettiness with a happy sigh. "Just doing my job."

"How many times do I have to tell you the wedding thing wasn't my fault?"

"You think I'm paying you back for ruining my wedding and derailing my career?" She gave him big, innocent eyes. "How insulting."

He studied her. "There's only one other reason for you to hate me so."

"I don't hate you."

"Well, that's it right there." He beamed at her as if she were a particularly bright and amusing companion and the sudden bounce back to easy camaraderie had her head spinning. *He's like a golden retriever*, she thought. *Happy by default*. She found herself caught between a pang of envy and the urge to throw her purse across the room to see if he'd fetch.

"That's what right where?" she asked instead.

"That's why you're so mean to me."

"Because I don't hate you?"

"Exactly." He took her elbow and they strolled into the crowd. "If you hated me, you'd have just let me kiss you."

"Um, no. I wouldn't have."

He patted her arm. "Sure you would. And then you'd have had yourself a good, long laugh at my moves. Then you'd have called my brothers over so they could laugh at my moves, too." He shot her a sidelong look. "But you didn't do that, did you? There's something interesting snapping away between us and you're curious, too. You wanted me to kiss you but *shouldn't* is getting all tangled up with *wanna* and it's causing you some grief." He smiled at her, a potent combination of understanding and temptation. "And that's why you're so mean to me. You're into me and it's got you downright pissy."

She stared at him. "That's a ridiculous suggestion."

"Is it?"

"Yes," she said firmly. *Yes*, she told herself.

"Suit yourself," he said cheerfully. "But don't blame me when you finally erupt in a massive explosion of repressed lust and beg me to satisfy your sexual urges. Because I'm only a man, Bel. I'll have to say yes."

An unwilling smile tugged at her lips. "I won't blame you in the event that I erupt like a sexual volcano, okay? Now can we please go find your brothers?"

"Sure, okay. I need to talk to Will anyway."

"Why?"

"I want to find out who I'm supposed to say hello to tonight. Be nice to ask after their wives and kids by name, too."

"And Will has this information?"

"Boy's got this crazy memory. Remembers every little thing he's ever read and most of what he's heard or seen. Damn handy in a manager."

"I'll bet."

"He can do mental math, too. Huge numbers. Fun stuff at a party."

"Huh." She let James tow her through the crowd while she chewed on that interesting bit of information. "What does Drew do?"

"Drew?"

"Yeah. What's his superpower? I mean, you're an elite athlete—your current out-of-shapeness notwithstanding—Will's some sort of brainiac. What does Drew do?"

James thought for a moment then smiled. "Drew's a two-fer."

"A two-fer? How's that?"

"Well, on one hand, he can charm the circuits off any e-thing you've got. Jacked our first Wii so that Will double faulted at deuce every time he got to the finals at Wimbledon. It took weeks for Will to figure it out and deliver the beat down." He smiled fondly, the memory of his brothers pounding one another to a pulp evidently warming his heart. "Kid was all of fifteen."

"And on the other hand?" Bel asked, amused. "What's Drew's other superpower?"

"He falls in love."

Her eyebrows shot up. "With whom?"

"Everybody. He's our heart and soul. Our conscience."

"Some conscience." She sniffed. "If I remember correctly, he sat by like a beer-swilling lump while you talked my fiancé into abandoning me on live TV."

He gave her a look of mild exasperation. "Setting aside the fact that the wedding thing *wasn't my fault*, why would Drew squawk about a guy deciding to follow his heart?"

"Setting aside the fact that it *was too your fault*, a decent conscience doesn't let you shame, humiliate or otherwise harm somebody like that. Following your bliss is no excuse to damage other people."

"So you should go ahead and marry somebody you don't love to keep them from getting hurt?"

"No. But you should keep your promises."

"And if you can't?"

"Then the burden's on you to make it right."

"To whose satisfaction?"

She frowned. "What?"

"Who gets to call when it's tit for tat? When you've paid enough? What happens when you have the bad luck to owe somebody who's never going to be satisfied?"

"Everybody's satisfied eventually."

He snorted out a laugh, then swallowed it when she cut him a razor sharp look.

"There is nothing funny about living up to your obligations," she told him.

"No, ma'am," he said, suddenly sober. "There surely isn't."

They walked in silence for a few moments then arrived at the bar. James looked around, nonplussed. "Well, this is unusual."

"What?"

"This here's an open bar. And Will and Drew aren't glued to it." He peered into the milling crowd. "I reckon we'll just have to wait for it then." He turned to the bartender. "You don't happen to stock Shiner Bock, do you?"

The bartender popped the cap from a beer bottle and passed it over. James dropped a twenty in the brandy glass posing as a tip jar on the counter and glanced at Bel.

"Don't tell me. White wine spritzer?"

Bel studied him. "No, thanks. Wait for what?"

James took a pull on the bottle. "What?"

"You said we'd have to wait for it. Because Drew and Will aren't here. Wait for what?"

"Oh." James leaned an elbow on the bar. "You'll know it when you hear it."

"Hear what?"

Will's voice rose above the din of a hundred conversations. "Hey, why so unfriendly? You wiggled your ass for tips last night and now you won't even talk to us?"

Bel froze and James set aside his beer.

"That," he said. A grim resignation replaced the perpetual cheery optimism in his face and he said, "Excuse me."

Bel jerked out of her wide-eyed paralysis and scurried after him. "Hey, wait!"

She caught up with him just as he broke through the crowd that had gathered around his two brothers and a waitress.

"Will, for God's sake." Drew shoved his shoulder between the waitress and his brother, backed Will up with the force of his body and held out placating hands to the woman. "I'm so sorry," he told her. "My brother's drunk."

"Not really, but wouldn't that be nice?" Will side-stepped Drew and smiled down at the waitress. It was anything but nice.

"I don't want any trouble," the woman said, her cheeks pale, her tray flattened against her chest like a shield.

"We won't give you any." Drew shot Will a stern look and hooked him by the bicep. "We'll just be on our—"

"Screw that." Will shook off Drew's hand and leaned down toward the woman's bent head. "Listen, sweetheart. You work at a strip club, all right? You show off your goodies for tips. We probably ponied up a car payment last night alone. And now you won't even acknowledge us? What kind of customer service is that?"

Bel glanced at James. "Your favorite stripper?"

"Just a waitress, I think."

She gave him a hard look and he gave her a roguish grin in return. "At our favorite strip club, yes."

She sighed. Had she really imagined they didn't frequent strip clubs? That they didn't pay to ogle naked

64

breasts and drink themselves stupid? Good lord, what had she gotten herself into?

"Okay, that's enough." Drew shoved Will. Hard. "You're speaking to a lady, Will. Dig up some respect."

Will took a stumbling step, then caught his balance. His hands curled into fists and his lips curved into a glittering, violent smile. "Or what, baby brother?"

"What, you want me to make you?" Drew's hands—his very big hands, Bel thought wildly—clenched into fists at his sides. Oh dear God.

"Oh, please," Will sneered. "Like you're going to swing on your own brother over some *stripper*."

"Well, shit." James sighed. "That'll do it."

Panic fluttered weak wings in Bel's chest. "Do what?"

James shook his head. "Drew's real protective of women."

"He's—" Bel's tried to digest that one but her logic couldn't keep it down. "He goes to strip clubs," she said blankly. "You can't be both protective of women and patronize strip clubs."

"He's especially protective of strippers."

"That doesn't make sense."

James rolled up each cuff one more turn. "Better get in there before Drew takes that swing."

"Before Drew—" Bel couldn't breathe.

"Hmmm." James squinted. "Or Will."

"They're going to *fight*?"

"Definitely. At this point it's just a question of here or at home."

She stared, open-mouthed. He returned the stare as if awaiting instructions. She slapped his arm, hard. "At *home*, James!"

"You got it."

He jogged forward and caught Will's elbow which was—dear God—cocked back for the first punch. Then he tapped the back of Will's knee with the front of his own and suddenly Will was hopping for balance instead of swinging on his baby brother. James inserted himself neatly between his brothers and addressed the waitress.

"Pardon us, ma'am," he said. Drew scowled at Will across the breadth of James' shoulders, his jaw tight and hard. In return, Will gave him a sick parody of a grin that showed all his teeth and made Bel shudder. "My brother's an ass." James paused to give Drew a speaking look. "They both are, actually." Drew, at least, had the grace to flush and look down. Will's smile just got uglier. "We won't bother you anymore."

"Fine. Good. Excuse me." The waitress shouldered her tray and Bel finally got a look at the curves that had earned the woman a car payment's worth of tips last night. Impressive, even in the demure black skirt and white blouse of her uniform. But she also saw tendons standing out on alarmingly thin wrists as she gripped her tray. Noted the bloodless press of her lips and the doggedly down-cast eyes. The woman hustled toward escape, giving Will the kind of wide berth you'd give a growling dog.

His hand flashed out like lightning, faster than a drunk guy could be expected to move. He snagged her elbow and hauled her back.

"No, no. Come on, wait," Will said. "I'm an idiot, right? Of course. How could I forget?" He pulled a thick fold of cash from his pocket, peeled off a couple of bills, tossed them on her tray. "Women like you don't do anything for free."

"Oh my God." Drew moaned more than said it. "Shut up, Will. Now."

Will ignored him. "How much, ah, *friendliness* will that get me?"

"*Enough*," James said, and the single word cracked like a whip, freezing all the players like actors on a stage. That slow drawl, the easy slouch and the sunny grin disappeared like smoke leaving behind a man Bel hardly recognized. A man whose closed face, knotted fists, and set shoulders spoke of economical, effective violence.

A soldier, Bel realized on a slap of shock. *A warrior.* This was a man who'd made his fortune being faster, tougher, stronger than the world's most talented athletes. And she'd mistaken him for a golden retriever? Her powers of observation really were crap these days. She needed to work on that.

"That's enough, Will," he said again, his voice quiet and hard. "We're leaving. Now."

He seized Will's elbow with one of those uncompromising fists and pointed him toward the exit, but the woman slapped a hand in the center of Will's chest. James paused with grave courtesy while she stared at the money on her tray as if she'd never seen anything like it.

"Thank you," she said to James. "It's been a while since anybody defended my honor. I appreciate it. But I'd like to say something."

James nodded and released Will's elbow. He stepped back, giving Bel her first good look at the woman's face. God, she was young. Twenty-two, maybe twenty-three, tops. But that wasn't what had Bel staring. It was the girl's face. Good lord, she was *gorgeous*. No, not gorgeous, Bel corrected herself. Beautiful. The classic sort of beautiful that inspired sculptors to sculpt, painters to paint and overgrown frat boys with too much money to drop hundreds of dollars on tips. She'd kept herself so contained, head bent, eyes down, voice quiet. But now with twin spots of color raging along her milk-pale cheekbones, with her crystal blue eyes spitting fury under that golden chop of hair she was magnificent.

And she was going to shred Will.

Bel melted back into the crowd, gave the girl some space.

"Forty bucks," the woman said, still fingering the money. "Wow. Forty whole dollars." She tucked her tray under her arm and propped a hand on her hip with a calculated slink. "For this kind of money, I might bend over nice and low when I set down your drink. I might laugh at your stupid jokes and smile at your tired, lame-ass pick up lines. As if I haven't heard them all a million times already from every other asshole in the room. I might even ignore it if your hand happens to land on my ass once or twice. Because, hey, I'm not proud. I do what it takes to survive, and that means putting on the uniform—however much or little of it there may be on any given night—and doing the job. Because unlike you, I don't have a filthy rich brother to finance my life of leisure."

Will cocked a brow with a weary mix of disdain and calm curiosity. But the skin stretched taut over his cheekbones and Bel wondered if the little waitress knew how accurately she'd aimed that last arrow.

"But let me be clear on this," she went on, "because I am sick and tired of jerks like you mistaking what's for sale here. Forty bucks does *not* buy you my interest. It doesn't buy you my respect and it doesn't buy you even an ounce of my honesty."

A man with a careful comb-over, a starter paunch and an air of anxious authority appeared at the edge of the silent circle of spectators. "Audrey," he said, a warning edge in his tone. "Is there a problem here?"

"No, Jeff," Audrey said, her fierce gaze still pinned to Will. "There's been a slight misunderstanding about what's on the menu, but I'm clearing it up."

"Now Audrey, is that any way to treat our guests of honor?" Jeff sent the Blake brothers a worried smile. "I apologize, gentlemen. Our staff is well-trained to accommodate special requests. I'm sure we can provide whatever you need." He turned a pointed look on his waitress. "Why don't you take a break, Audrey? I'll see to these gentlemen."

She snapped her mouth shut, struggling visibly to reel in her temper and save her job. Bel bit her own tongue against the desire to defend the poor girl. Will was being an ass and nobody, regardless of their station in life, deserved to take crap served up from a faulty sense of entitlement. But her job was to improve James' public image and getting entangled in a high profile kerfuffle with the wait staff her first night on duty wasn't going to help matters.

She glanced at James, made a *get us out of here, pronto* face at him. But his gaze was glued to Audrey, waiting like the good soldier he was for the lady's instruction.

"But I want Audrey to help us," Will said, a sly triumph sliding through his voice. "No other waitress will do." He turned away from the manager and sent Audrey that awful smile. "Come on, honey. Be nice and there could be another twenty in it for you. As you've surely noticed, I'm pretty free with my brother's money."

Color rushed into her cheeks while something both resigned and livid leapt in her eyes. Bel caught her breath and thought *this is not going to make Jeff happy*.

"You know what? This one's on the house." Audrey elbowed her boss aside and stuffed Will's money into the breast pocket of his tux. Bel winced. There went the perfect crease she'd ironed into his hanky. "You want the truth? Okay, fine. You caught me. I lied to your brother last night. I'm not going to Tucson. Not now, not ever. It was a big, fat lie. So sue me. I didn't figure anybody would mind. Why would they? The more we lie, the more you pay. You think all those boobs are real? The hair? The tans? The interest? Right.

"But since you're suddenly hell-bent on the truth, try this on for size. I didn't give your brother my number because I didn't like him. Or you. *Or* your famous brother. You're all pathetic losers with more money than class who have to pay to see a girl shake her goodies and I don't want anything to do with you apart from dropping off your drinks and picking up my tips. Is that honest enough for you?"

Will ran his tongue over his teeth as if checking for blood. "Yeah, that ought to do it," he said. He turned his gaze to the horrified manager. "You really get what you pay for around here, don't you?"

Jeff grabbed Audrey by the arm. "I'm *so* sorry. Please excuse her behavior, gentlemen. I'll take care of this." He cut urgent eyes toward the nearest waiter, who trotted over to thrust a tray of champagne at the Blake brothers. He hauled Audrey off and Bel sighed, making a mental note to come back tomorrow to salvage the girl's job if she could.

She finally caught James' eye and he gave her the tired shrug of somebody who'd done this too often to summon up the outrage it called for. Will checked his watch, smiled and tossed back the entire glass of champagne in one swallow.

"We're leaving," James announced.

"So soon?" Will set aside his empty glass. "I was just hitting my stride."

"Yeah," he said. "I know."

CHAPTER NINE

Will rode shotgun on the way home, his face to the window. He watched the lights of DC stream by in a fluid blur and tried to ignore the silent condemnation filling up the truck like poisonous gas. It radiated off his brothers and their pretty new nanny in thick, baffled waves, pressing him deep into his seat like one of those lead blankets they put on you at the dentist. Every time he swallowed, he tasted shame and sour champagne.

"For God's sake," he said finally. "It was just a stripper."

"*She*," James snapped. "Not *it*, Will. *She*. A person. A whole human being." He steered with one hand and landed a solid punch on Will's upper arm with the other. Will's head threatened to split open and his stomach turned over dangerously. Fucking champagne. As a rule, he and alcohol got along just fine. Better than fine, in fact. But champagne was the exception that proved the rule, and Will added that last glass to his growing list of tonight's regrets. "And *she* wasn't a stripper. She was a waitress."

"At a *strip club*." Will felt dirty but he blanked his face and met James' furious eyes. "Excuse me if I don't split hairs."

"Split hairs?" James hit him again. Will relished the pain even as he prayed not to puke on the floorboards. "Split *hairs*? You acted like the girl was a two dollar hooker, Will."

"Oh spare me the outrage." Will turned back to the window and concentrated on breathing. "If it had been you doing the asking last night instead of Drew, she'd have tucked her number into your pocket personally and given you a hand job while she was in there. So do me a favor and don't try to pretend there's a big moral difference between a whore and a star fucker. It's all about currency one way or another."

Shocked silence filled the air again, along with another dose of smothering disapproval. When, oh Jesus, *when* would somebody just put him out of his misery? He didn't know how much more of himself he could take.

"Will." Drew's voice from the backseat was quiet. Careful. *Kind.* Will's stomach cramped relentlessly and oh *fuck*, were those tears stinging his eyes? "What's *wrong* with you?"

I don't know.

The answer screamed itself inside his head, the words bouncing around like those bullets that exploded after impact, sending shrapnel every fucking where. But nothing came out of his mouth. Because yeah, something *was* wrong with him. Very wrong. And honest to God, Will didn't know what it was.

But only because he didn't want to know.

See, Will's wrongness lived inside him. It *was* him—a monster with an appetite for destruction who lived in the darkest corner of his mental cellar. And when that kind of darkness starts creeping up the stairs and scratching at the door, what kind of idiot invites it in for a good look? Not Will. He, like any sane, rational soul, shoved it right back down the stairs. Alcohol worked nicely. Most of the time, anyway. And when it didn't? Well, then he had to give in and feed the thing.

Often, Will could provoke one of his brothers into kicking his ass. (Usually James, as Drew had always been more inclined to laugh than punch, the lucky bastard.) His subconscious wanted pain? Blood? Destruction? Fine. Here you go. Plus it made him feel sort of normal. Brothers fought all the time, right? Nothing weird about that.

So tonight, when his beast had seized him by the throat, Will had marched off to do some damage in the sincere hope that one of his brothers would eventually consent to bust up his face for him. Unfortunately, James and Drew were too sick of him lately to even bother taking a swing. And the rest of the world was too interested in James' money to risk punching out his asshole brother. A crazy leap of fear and pain jittered into Will's roiling stomach and he swallowed hard. He was pushing his brothers awfully close to washing their hands of him, wasn't he? It was like standing on the edge of a cliff, looking at the drop and wondering.

He dragged his thoughts away from that charming little precipice and sent them elsewhere.

To that little waitress. Hey, how about her? Audrey, wasn't it? Now *that* girl hadn't been afraid to take out James Blake's big brother. She'd put up her dukes. Dropped the truth on him like a fucking guillotine and—figuratively, at least—Will's head was still rolling across the floor.

His monster typically viewed verbal abuse as kiddie play but Audrey's tongue-lashing had been a goddamn work of art. Her scalpel-sharp dissection of his character, plus the unholy beauty of that face calmly spitting fury? It had been like watching a cathedral burn. And it had sent his monster straight back to the cellar.

He'd have to think about that.

They hit the beltway and James laid the pedal down. The truck leapt forward and Will's stomach cramped again. Christ. He must have made some sort of pained noise because James gave a humorless chuckle. "Serves you right, asshole."

Will shrugged. "Your floorboards."

"Don't you dare."

Will consulted his stomach. "We'll see."

"Fuck."

Four hours later, Bel stood at the granite island counter, spooning loose leaf tea into a paper tea bag. It was late but she couldn't sleep. She'd taken the time to put her own linens on the bed in the pretty room she'd chosen for herself in the east wing, but even the comfort of a familiar and elevated thread count couldn't push her over the edge from exhaustion into sleep.

Every time she closed her eyes, all the day's misgivings and resentments crept into her head where they started tumbling around together like a pack of cracked out monkeys. Take that along with the pointed silence emanating from the north wing where the Blake brothers had headquartered the bedlam of their lives, and suddenly Bel was dragging on her robe and padding down that ridiculous staircase—*fiddledeedee, Ashley*—to put on the kettle.

Well, to put on the pot, anyway. She hadn't had time to unload her own cookware, so she was still using the single pot and pan she'd unearthed in James Blake's gorgeous waste of a kitchen. She stared into the steady blue flame licking at the sauce pan and twitched her shoulders under that disconcerting *silence*.

The Blake brothers struck her as brawlers—hadn't they already engaged in fisticuffs over a fork, of all things? After tonight's little showdown, Bel had expected a late night full of stomping and raging and finger pointing. Violent cursing. Possibly the punching of walls.

But no. Nothing.

Okay, not nothing exactly, Bel mused, pouring boiling water over her tea bag. The scent of citrus and vanilla billowed into the kitchen and she leaned into the steam to bask in the comfort of her favorite key-lime custom blend tea. This wasn't just the absence of sound. It was like a vacuum. A black hole that sucked up everything in its gravitational pull, a menacing void that promised death and destruction, or at the very least, the permanent disappearance of anything unlucky enough to wander too near its sphere of influence.

She wondered briefly if she ought to keep an eye on the driveway. In case there was some furtive attempt at body disposal in the dead of the night.

Maybe one of those bodies would be James'. It was a comforting thought in her current state of mind. Not that she wanted the guy dead or anything, but if he happened to be the unlucky victim of fratricide this evening, some small, mean part of her might think *that'll teach you to play me on the red carpet, buddy*. Fate might always ding the good girls, but it did occasionally ding the rich, famous and lucky, too. And if ever there was a night that James Blake deserved to get a little comeuppance, it was tonight.

Because James had played her.

Her cheeks burned as she remembered the perfect innocence and sincerity with which she'd clapped a hand to his behind. She rewound the tape in her head to that exact moment, forced herself to shove away the memory of all that warm, animal sleekness under her hand and concentrate instead on his face. She played it back frame by frame until she was sure she could see the surprise in his eyes melting into calculation and then into a self-satisfied smirk.

Because accidentally-on-purpose showing off your shorts at a gala thrown by the people who paid you to wear them was a public relations gold mine. Nobody would have been embarrassed by that blown-out seam, least of all James. He probably would have gotten a bonus out of it, for God's sake. But she'd gone ahead and thrown herself—and, let's be honest, her dignity—into the breach, and grabbed herself a big old handful of James Blake's behind.

And he'd returned the favor. Her nervous system helpfully provided an instant replay of that big, hard hand cupping her own behind—

She lifted her mug for an abrupt, scalding gulp of tea, which she forced herself to swallow. That way, when heat flashed through her belly, there was a fifty-fifty chance it was from the tea rather than the memory of James' touch. There was a certain comfort in even odds.

A comfort which evaporated when James suddenly spoke from directly behind her.

"What in the name of *God* is that smell?"

Her heart crashed into triple time and she clapped one hand to her chest to keep it contained. Pain, bright and burning, flashed through her other hand as tea slopped over the rim of the mug onto her fingers. She dropped the mug in order to flap her burnt fingers in the air while mentally reviewing all the curse words she'd forbidden herself to use out loud.

The mug was no match for James' imported glazed porcelain tiles, though. It shattered, unleashing yet another wave of boiling tea in the neighborhood of Bel's bare feet.

She gathered herself for a heroic leap back, but found her feet already dangling four inches above the floor.

"Well, that was a little extreme, don't you think?" James' voice came, exasperated and amused, just below her ear. His hands were tough under her elbows, his body warm and strong against her back as he carted her bodily toward the sink. He flipped on the faucet and shoved her hand under the gush of cold water. "I don't happen to care for boiled lawn clippings myself, but that doesn't mean you can't drink them."

She spit a strand of hair out of her mouth and glared over her shoulder at him. "I didn't *intend* to drop it, you know."

He smiled at her, amusement crinkling the corners of those oddly changeable eyes of his, and she was suddenly aware that he hadn't let her go. Water flowed over their joined hands under the tap while his body nestled comfortably up against her backside. A warmth snaked into her belly that had nothing to do with the recent misapplication of hot tea to her person, so she concentrated on the painfully cold water running over her burns instead.

"Tossed it on a whim, then, did you?" He studied her gravely. "Wouldn't have pegged you for the impulsive type."

She glared at him. "I'm not. And if you'd had the manners to announce your presence instead of sneaking up behind me, I wouldn't have burned myself. Nor would I have had cause to smash the single mug you seem to own."

"Oh. Well, that's too bad about the mug." He pursed up that perfect mouth of his and considered this. Then he peeked over her shoulder and down the front of her robe. "But there are benefits to doing it my way, too."

Bel glanced down, then seized her gaping lapels together with her free hand. She was wearing a t-shirt under the robe, but it was old and baggy, and from that angle, he'd probably gotten a decent look straight down it. And since Will likely had a point about the—what had he had called them? Star fuckers?—James had probably seen down a whole lot of women's shirts. Which meant he was used to

76

ogling a female landscape quite different from the flat,
prairie-like expanse of blinding white skin she'd just treated
him to. But that was no excuse for mocking her. Benefits,
indeed.

"I beg your pardon," she said stiffly. "I realize my dress
is inappropriate. I didn't anticipate company." She stepped
to the side, putting a few badly needed feet of space between
her and the easy strength of his body.

"Now, now. No need to poker up. I was just having
some fun with you." He gave her that *shucks, ma'am* grin
she was starting to dislike heartily, flipped off the water and
passed her a dishtowel. He nodded toward her hand. "That
going to be all right?"

She patted her hand dry, gave it a quick glance and
shrugged. "Of course. I bake for a living. I get worse than
this twice a week."

He reached for the hand in question, and though her
impulse was to snatch it back and run screaming for the
safety of her bedroom, she figured that might be
overreacting. And revealing. James clearly had some sort of
investment in keeping her off balance, and if she kept
stuttering and blushing every time he touched her it would
only encourage him to keep it up.

So she gritted her teeth and let him take her hand. It
looked small and white against the tanned expanse of his big
and blocky palm. Brick layer's hands, she thought for no
reason she could imagine. But his fingers were gentle as they
brushed over each scar and nick, learning them as if by
Braille.

"You work hard," he said.

"I do," she said, and admired her tone. Brisk,
appropriate, completely unrattled. Which was great, because
her belly was flipping around inside her like a trout. God,
when was he going to let go of her hand?

"What's this one?" He brushed his thumb along a white
scar on the inside of her wrist and sent her heart trundling
into her throat.

"I, uh, cozied up to a 500 degree oven without an oven
mitt."

77

"And this?" He trailed a finger along a thin line crossing the knuckle of her index finger.

"That would be my Wusthof." One dark brow arched into the sunny spill of hair over his forehead and she said, "My first really nice chef's knife. It cost the world, or so I thought at the time. I julienned everything for weeks."

"Including yourself?"

"Sadly, yes. But I still have that knife."

He smiled at her, delighted. "You're a tool girl."

That smile, she thought, a little dazed. So easy and sunny and thought-stealing. The way he *focused* it on her. She was starting to understand how women looked at this man and decided, in spite of all the red flags, to take a flier.

"Not normally, no," she said, gripping her focus with both hands. "But this is a *Wusthof*. A ten incher. It's a beauty."

He just kept smiling at her and Bel wondered if she'd missed something, some subtext of the conversation that made it her turn to keep talking. It wouldn't surprise her. She knew she wasn't exactly a sophisticate. Getting where she was had required the kind of 24/7 focus that hadn't left any time for learning the art of light flirtation.

Not that what James did could be called light. The guy laid on the charm the way the *Kate Every Day* makeup artists troweled on the foundation. If she was going to survive this job and get her career back—get her *life* back—she was going to have to learn to either shrug it off or convince him to stop laying it on her in the first place.

Which reminded her. She ought to at least try to get her hand back.

She gave it an experimental tug but he held fast, still grinning that sunny grin at her. The urge to smile back was overpowering.

Cripes, Bel, she thought. Snap *out* of it.

"What?" she asked. "Why are you looking at me like that?"

He blinked, then shook his head. "Sorry. You were saying?" His grin went a little sheepish around the edges. "I kind of lost focus right after you said *ten incher*."

"Oh, for pity's sake." She yanked her hand back.

"What? I'm a guy."

"Maybe you haven't noticed," she said. "But that *I'm a guy* thing? Eventually, it wears pretty thin. People get tired of it, usually by the time you hit thirty or so. Then they expect you to get over being a *guy* so you can be a man instead."

"A man, huh?" His eyes lit with interest and something else Bel couldn't identify. But it made her want to step back when he stepped forward.

"Yes," she said, though it came out a little breathless. Space. She needed space. She'd never liked people crowding her, particularly not men. She edged backward only to discover the cool press of the countertop against the small of her back. "That's why I'm here," she said, a little desperately. "To help you."

"Help me what?"

She couldn't see him moving forward but every time she looked away then looked back he was closer. He was stalking her, she realized. The realization sent a hot thrill arcing into her stomach, a thrill she couldn't identify, exactly. Panic? Fear? Anger?

Anticipation?

"Transition," she said, firming her voice up with a heroic effort. "From guy to man. And from what I've seen, we have a ways to go."

"Ah, Bel. You don't give yourself enough credit." He closed the distance between them with a single bold move, propped his hands on the counter on either side of her hips and leaned in. "Since you turned up, I've been feeling more manly every minute."

She sucked in a breath but the air had gone hot and dense between them. Every molecule separating their bodies vibrated with something Bel refused to name. "See?" she said, and if there was a panicked squeak in her voice she ignored it. "That's exactly the kind of thing that was probably cute five years ago. But now?"

Not so much, she'd planned to say. *It's not so cute anymore*. But then he leaned in and nuzzled at the hair she'd tucked behind one ear.

"Now?" he asked, his voice low and pleasantly rough, like a cat's tongue.

"Now it's just—" she began but trailed off. It was hard to form a complete thought with her entire being focused on the inch of space between that gorgeous, perfect mouth of his and her earlobe. She must have wanted to say something, but for the life of her she couldn't think what it might have been. Couldn't imagine why she'd been chit-chatting while he was gearing up to do whatever this was to her nervous system anyway.

"Just what?" He buried his nose in her hair and breathed her in as if she were oxygen itself. A thrill of pure pleasure shot straight through her. "Because I have to tell you, I don't *feel* cute."

"How do you feel then?" The sound of her own voice shocked her. When had her brain given her mouth permission to speak? And who had authorized a question like that? And in that voice? All throaty and *kiss me now*?

Still, when he drew back to gaze at her with those silver-green eyes alight with lust and amusement, she stared back and waited for her answer.

"Do me a favor?" he said.

"What?"

"Shut up a minute."

"Why?"

"Because I'm about to show you."

CHAPTER TEN

"Oh." She paused while her sluggish brain connected the dots and arrived at the startling conclusion that he was about to kiss her. "Oh! No! You should definitely *not* do that. I'd prefer it if you just, you know, *told* me. Or not." She gave her watch a desperate glance. "Wow, is that the time? I really ought to get back to—" She broke off, unable to say the word *bed* with his beautiful mouth two inches from hers and intent emblazoned all over his pirate's face.

He sighed. "Bel."

"What?"

"Shush."

She frowned at him. "I'm sorry, did you just *shush* me?"

"Lord, you're making this difficult."

She stared at him. "I'm a difficult woman."

"Tell me about it."

"I just did."

He sighed again but closer this time, close enough that she felt his breath on her cheek. Her stomach jittered itself right up into her throat.

He slid one hand into the hair at the nape of her neck and she froze. Her brain said calmly *you shouldn't be letting him do that* at the same time her entire nervous system said *Yes, please.*

"Um," she said, her internal gears grinding.

"Shush," he said again.

A spike of outrage shot through her at being shushed two times in a row but it melted immediately into a confused little puddle. Because then he was kissing her.

It occurred to her, vaguely, that she might be in some sort of fugue state. It was supposed to be kind of like sleepwalking, right? Where you could walk and talk and interact, but weren't actually conscious and therefore not responsible for your actions? Fugue states weren't at all uncommon, she told herself. She'd read about them.

Besides, she couldn't think of any other possible reason why she was simply standing there, in a threadbare robe and a fifteen-year-old t-shirt, letting the man responsible for the demise of both her job and her wedding *kiss* her.

But, lord, what a kiss. If his mouth looked like perfection, she didn't even have words for what it felt like. All she knew was that he smelled like mint toothpaste and warm man, and that he took possession of her entire body with a fluid ease that had every scrap of her DNA thinking reproduction.

His body fitted itself against hers as if they'd been custom-designed to dovetail just like this. He moved with the smooth assurance of a man whose mastery of his own body was absolute, but without the air of entitlement that usually went with it. This kiss didn't demand so much as ask.

No, not really ask, she thought through the fog of his hands in her hair, the magic of his mouth on hers, the potent invitation of his body against hers. It was more coax than ask. *Come on*, that kiss seemed to say. *Where's the harm? Just a taste, see?*

He lingered over her lips, as if he had all the time in the world. As if there were nothing more important than learning the shape and taste of her. As if there might be a quiz later and he, by God, was going to ace it.

How long, Bel wondered with a start, had it been since somebody had kissed her and actually paid attention? Made *her* pay attention?

Then his mouth opened over hers. Just slightly, an invitation to a deeper dance. A hot thrill shot straight from her head into the pit of her stomach and she froze.

An invitation required a reply.

A dance took two people.

He'd asked, and now she had to answer.

She knew what she *wanted*. She wanted to open her mouth under his. She wanted to savor the hard press of his thighs against hers. She wanted that sparkly wave of heat to keep streaking straight from her belly to the ends of her hair where it turned the air around them dangerously electric. She wanted this kiss to go on and on so she could bask forever in the unprecedented luxury of being...God, it was stupid to even think it but the word that kept popping into her head was *cherished*. How else could she describe being at the perfect center of another person's mental, emotional and physical attention?

It's professional suicide, her brain said sternly.

Yep, her body answered.

It's an aberration, her brain snapped. *A momentary trick of the libido.*

Yep, her body said. *And what if it never happens again in my lifetime? Am I really going to let myself shrivel into old age without once having participated in this kind of kiss?*

Will you please grow up? her brain asked.

Will you please shut *up?* her body responded.

She hesitated, her hands awkward and uncertain in the space between deciding and doing. Then she finally released the counter she'd been gripping with desperate strength. She inched her fingers tentatively up toward that sunshiny mass of hair they'd been itching to dive into all day.

Just do it, she told herself. *For once in your life, take a chance.*

She squeezed her eyes shut and screwed up her courage and—

He pulled back and shot her a wry, lop-sided smile. She eased her hands surreptitiously to her sides.

"No, huh?" He shrugged as if she'd declined a stick of gum rather than an invitation to his bed. No, not his bed, she realized with a sinking humiliation. More likely the kitchen floor. The counter, if he was feeling ambitious. "Bummer."

Bel gaped at him. *Bummer?* Had he really just said *bummer?*

Yes, indeed, her brain said, a trifle smugly. *He is exactly the sort of man who says bummer when denied sex.*

Bel dragged the lapels of her robe together over her pounding chest and leaned back as far as the counter digging

into her spine would permit. "Do you think you could—"
She made a little shooing motion. He lifted his hands in easy
surrender and stepped back. "Thanks."

She cleared her throat and made a valiant effort to do
the same with her head. She ought to be relieved, she told
herself. Relieved, outraged and maybe even a little ashamed.
And she *was*, all those things. It had been a close call, after
all—the underdog Libido had had the reigning champion
Will Power on the ropes for a minute there. She couldn't
deny it.

But what insane, self-destructive part of her psyche had
tossed disappointment into the mix?

There it was, though. A tiny, persistent spurt of
disappointment. *Gave up pretty easily, didn't he*? it said.

She yanked out the thought like a weed from her
garden. *Of course he gave up easily*, she thought. If James
Blake were in the habit of expending any sort of effort or
patience in difficult situations, she wouldn't have a job. Or,
all right, maybe she would have a job but she'd be sleeping
with it. Him. Whatever.

Okay, she told herself. New plan.

Clearly, she had a weak spot for sunny man-children
who thought women ought to fall into their laps like ripe
peaches. It was probably in her DNA, same as her hair and
her eyes and her height. A wave of old bitterness backed up
her throat and she thought *thanks, Mom*.

But whatever, right? Just because it was part of her
didn't mean she had to embrace it. She couldn't control what
she felt, only how she acted. And lust was no different from
any other emotion when she got right down to it. *Being*
angry didn't give you a license to *act* angry, did it? No. Of
course not. Self-control. Grownups practiced it all the time,
and she was better at it than most. It had gotten her this far,
hadn't it? It would get her the rest of the way.

But at least now she knew. She had a rogue lust gene at
work somewhere deep in her DNA, the kind that, without
close supervision, derailed careers, families and entire lives.
And she ought to know. She'd seen it in action, up close and
personal, more times than she'd care to count.

It was a blow to have discovered it in herself, but at least now she could be prepared. No more sneak attacks from her own army.

She gave James a cool look. "Do you treat all your colleagues this way?" she asked.

He gave her an easy smile in return. "Only the pretty ones who turn up half-dressed in my kitchen after midnight."

Bel lifted her brows and maintained a polite silence.

"Okay, okay," he said. "They don't *have* to be in the kitchen after midnight."

She let the silence draw out and drop below freezing.

"Or half-dressed."

She narrowed her eyes.

"But hey, I draw the line at pretty. And at girls. They totally have to be women. Not that there's anything wrong with people who go, you know, the other direction. But for me, personally, I prefer girls." His smile broadened. "They smell nice."

"A ringing endorsement."

He cocked his head. "Should I apologize?"

"For what? Being a guy?" She lowered her chin and gave him what she hoped was patient look. "You've been gearing up to make your move all day, James. Do you think I'm surprised?"

"A little."

She shook her head. "Please. You have your own unique sense of timing, I'll give you that. But the move was coming, one way or the other. It's actually a bit of a relief to have it behind us."

"Is it?"

"Sure," she said, her tone nice and brisk. "Asked, answered. Check it off the list. Move along."

He stared. "Rejecting my move was on your to-do list?"

"Making the move wasn't on yours?"

He considered that one. "All right. Maybe. What else is on there? Your list?"

She grimaced. "After what I saw tonight?" She picked up the pot from the stove, frowned at the remaining water and dumped it in the sink. She might be in difficult straits,

85

but she wouldn't make tea with twice-boiled water. A girl had to have standards. She put fresh water on to boil and said, "Your family. Right at the top. Big, bold letters."

"My family?" he asked, and his sudden, intense stillness had the hair on the back of her neck standing up. "What about them?"

Bel threw him a look over her shoulder. "They're a problem, James."

"They're *my* problem," he said. "Not yours."

"Sorry, but no." She leaned back against the counter, crossing her arms over her waist. "Trust me on this one. Kate Davis' personal standard for civilized behavior does *not* include hanging around with people who a) drink to excess, b) harass waitresses into unemployment, or c) stalk their favorite strippers." She met his eyes steadily. "Your family is a problem and unfortunately for both of us, you don't have any problems that aren't mine right now."

"Okay," he said, and rubbed absently at the stubble on his jaw. Bel could hear the sandpaper rasp of it over the hiss of the gas burner at her elbow and immediately wished she couldn't. It made him too...physical. Too real.

"Fair enough," he said. "I'll give you that one. What do you propose?"

She hesitated and he said, "Come on, Bel. Don't tell me you haven't spent the entire night making a list—*Top Ten Ways to Fix James' Life*. I'll bet it's color coded and cross indexed, too. So let's have it. I know there's a sub-list titled *Family Disaster Solutions*. What's on it?"

"You're not going to like it," she said.

"I know. Say it. You won't be the first."

"I have a feeling I won't be the last either. But okay." She shrugged. "Your brothers are a problem, James. A big one. You need to cut them loose. You do, and half your problem disappears."

He considered her, then nodded slowly. "No."

"No what? No, I'm wrong? Or no, you won't?"

"No, you're right. But I won't."

She sighed. "They're grown men, James. They'll be all right."

He gave her a grim smile. "What's your family like, Bel?"

"Small."

"Brothers? Sisters? Folks?"

"Just my mom and me."

"You close?"

She gave him a grim smile right back. "No."

"Is that no, as in *we chat on the phone once a quarter*? Or no like, *I quit bailing that junkie out years ago*?"

Her smile went from grim to downright frosty. "Neither. We're just different people, and the lives we chose for ourselves don't really mesh. It took a few years for everybody to accept that but eventually it was a relief."

He gave her a skeptical look and said, "How very practical."

"Thank you."

"So now that we've established your complete ignorance of how a normal family operates, let me tell you this: my brothers and I are a package deal. You deal with me, you deal with them. Their problems are my problems."

"Even if you *are* their problem?"

"What does that mean?"

"Think it through, James. They act like overgrown teenagers because that's all they have to be. That's all you're letting them be."

"I'm not in charge of what my brothers do, Bel."

She snorted. "Please. Through you they have free housing, hot cars, unlimited funds, and access to an endless stream of women who enjoy the dubious glory of sleeping with pro athletes and their hangers on. Forgive me for being blunt, but you're the proverbial golden goose. What guy in his right mind is going to walk away from that?"

"Wow," James said, regarding her with an unexpected mix of amusement and pity. "Your childhood must've been worse than I thought."

She frowned at him, stung. "What do you mean?"

"All that crap Will was flinging tonight about who makes the money, who gets the girls, who's got the juice?

It's not about my job, or his job, or anything else." He smiled at her. "It's just what brothers do."

"What?"

"We give each other shit. It keeps us humble, see?"

"Really." Bel gazed at him in wonder, not bothering to make it sound like a question. He believed this. He truly did.

"Absolutely," he said. "Trust me on this. I don't like to brag but the fact is, I make a lot of money. A shit load. Way more than one person deserves, especially for playing a game."

"Amen," Bel said.

"And I'm not saying I don't appreciate it. Obviously I do." He grinned. "We all do. But it does complicate things."

"What kinds of things?" Bel asked. "Certainly not the rent or groceries or car payment sorts of things."

"Well, no. Granted. But it does get kind of difficult after a while to tell the difference between people who enjoy your company and people who enjoy your money." He spread his hands. "My brothers are the only people on this earth I trust to tell me the truth. They loved me before I was famous, believed in me before I'd earned it, and if I blew out my knee tomorrow, they'd still be here to help me figure out if I wanted to sell used cars or insurance, see? That's how family works."

Bel felt her eyebrows heading for her hairline and James shook his head at her. "Or should work anyway," he said.

"If you say so."

"I do. And because I know that'll stick in your craw, I'll just break the rest down real simple for you, okay?"

"Oh thank you," Bel said, laying the back of her hand against her brow. "My poor little head is just spinning. So much enlightenment all at once, you understand."

He grinned at her but it was all teeth and no eyes. He said, "You can either a) draw a big black line through anything on that To Do list of yours that involves getting rid of my brothers, or b) you can find yourself a new job." He folded his arms and leaned back against the opposite counter. "Multiple choice, just the way you like. Real easy."

Bel considered him. He stood across from her, all lazy slouch and wry half-smile. But his eyes were completely serious and she was starting to understand she needed to look there first for her clues on how to deal with this man.

"You'd do it, wouldn't you?" she asked slowly. "Torpedo your career to keep this unhealthy, inbred thing you've got going with your brothers alive?"

"Where I'm from, we call that family." He lifted a shoulder. "We're a package deal, and anybody who does business with me gets that eventually. All you have to decide is if you're willing to work with those terms."

Bel frowned at him but he just returned her gaze with equanimity, utterly unperturbed by her displeasure. She bit back a sigh. She'd never walked away from a career challenge in her life, and she wouldn't now. Particularly not with everything she'd spent the last ten years earning hanging in the balance. But that didn't mean she had to be happy with the fact that Fate had just put a big chunk of her future into the hands of a man who felt that keeping his brothers in beer and women was more important than honoring his signature on a couple dozen multi-million dollar contracts.

"I'm willing," she finally said. "But understand this: I don't work for them. And I don't work for you either. You and I? We're in this together. I'll deal with Kate, you deal with your brothers and if we catch every lucky break in the universe we might just come out of this okay."

He nodded. "Deal," he said and held out a hand.

She eyed his hand and renewed her grip on the countertop behind her. "On one condition," she said. "From now on, you'll be keeping your hands to yourself."

He smiled at her, and it sent an electric shock across her skin. "I will?"

"It's best if we keep things professional, James."

His smile widened. "Sure it is."

"And speaking of professional," she said with a small twinge of evil pleasure, "I assume you and your brothers own clothes that fall somewhere between track suits and tuxedos on the fashion continuum?"

"Sure." His smile went suspicious. "Why?"

Evil pleasure grew from a twinge into a full-on glow. "From now on, we dress for Sunday dinner."

"Aw." He hung his head. "That's just mean."

"Much as I'd have enjoyed inflicting it on you, it wasn't my idea."

"No?"

"Nope. Kate's joining us for dinner tomorrow night along with our favorite agent. They'll be delivering our first challenge on your path to rehabilitation."

"There's a challenge beyond dressing for dinner?"

Bel laughed then realized he was serious.

"How cruel are these people?" he said.

She shook her head. "You have no idea."

CHAPTER ELEVEN

"Civilization," Kate began, with a steely-eyed look that reminded James uncomfortably of his mother, "depends on our ability to quell our baser instincts in order to build something that benefits the group."

James nodded sagely and helped himself to a second piece of Bel's peach cobbler. Because, good lord, the girl could cook. Throw a scoop of vanilla ice cream on there—the good stuff, too, because Bel apparently (thank God) didn't believe in fake sugar, fake fat, fake anything—and you had yourself a big ol' bowl of heaven.

Not, he'd decided, that heaven was ever very far away when Bel was in the kitchen. He tucked into the cobbler with a happy sigh and lovely memories of the pot roast and the world's fluffiest mashed potatoes that had preceded it.

Kate nudged aside her full glass of wine and sharpened the point on that stare of hers. "It depends, James, upon being stronger than your appetites."

"Yes, ma'am." How had Kate Davis ever convinced America that she was the Martha Stewart of the South? Because if domestic bliss even existed, surely it was contained in the bowl James held in his hand. And Kate was sucking the pleasure right out of it.

"Taking control," she intoned severely, "of your *inner glutton*."

James shoved another spoonful of peachy goodness into his mouth and chewed defiantly. "Are you making a point, Ms. Davis?" he asked when he'd swallowed. And that was proof right there that he wasn't entirely devoid of manners, wasn't it?

"I am." Kate gave him a serene smile. "Thank you for putting down your spoon long enough to notice."

Across the table, Drew coughed a laugh into his hand.
James gave him a narrow glance but his eyes were all
innocence as he lifted his coffee cup. His itty-bitty coffee
cup with the useless handle that all the men, James noticed,
had finally settled on pinching rather than attempting to jam
their fingers through.

Drew appeared perfectly at ease drinking from a teeny
little breakable, however. Just as he seemed perfectly
comfortable in his slacks-and-sweater ensemble, complete
with tie. Beside him, Will looked essentially the same. Both
their ties looked suspiciously well-knotted to James.

He glanced at Bel, who was seated on his right but she
was too busy sweeping crumbs from the tablecloth into a
pile between their plates to notice.

He set down his spoon and wiped his lips with his
napkin. A cloth napkin with razor sharp creases because,
good heavens, Bel really would iron anything, wouldn't she?
He turned his attention back to the woman at the head of
James' own dining room table.

"You were saying, Ms. Davis?" he asked. "Regarding
civilization?"

"Yes," Kate said, her smooth face a sharp contrast to
the unholy anticipation he saw in her bark-brown eyes.
"Civilization. I believe it depends on an ability to master
one's own needs, and thus allowing one to give precedence
to the needs of others."

"I see." James glanced sadly at the melting mess in his
bowl. This could take a while. "And this pertains to me
how?"

Drew set his coffee aside and leaned in, chin on fist.
James frowned at him. Drew shifted to gaze at Kate like she
was the second freaking coming. Bel didn't look up from her
crumbs. Will upended a bottle of wine into his glass. In
desperation, James finally looked to his agent, Bob, who sat
at the foot of the table.

Bob only nodded toward Kate. "Pay attention, son," he
said. "You're in deep, ah—" He broke off, groping for a
word that wouldn't offend the civilization police opposite

him. "—trouble with your sponsors, and Kate here is the only ticket out I could buy you. If I were you, I'd listen up."

James sighed and turned back to the woman on his left. She gave him a smile that had James' back teeth clamping together. "You've completely lost control, dear," she said.

"I have?"

"Yes. You've become a slave to your appetites."

A dull burn crept up James' throat and headed for his cheeks. "Well, hell. I haven't gained *that* much weight."

"It's not just food, dear," Kate said with serene aplomb. "It's everything."

A twinge of recognition ricocheted around in James' chest but he covered it carefully with skepticism. "Everything? Now that's a bit extreme, don't you think?"

"All your appetites." Kate lifted a hand and ticked them off on long, elegant fingers. "Food, alcohol, entertainment, sex."

James shot a look at Will. "Am I contractually obligated to discuss my sex life with *Kate Every Day*?"

Will looked at Bob, who merely lifted one shoulder as if to say *wasn't my idea*. Will looked back at James. "Yep."

James turned back to Kate with a sigh.

"Fame and money have given you the means to live like some sort of demi-god," Kate told him. She fluttered that regal hand at his brothers across the table. "Complete with minions."

"Minions?" Drew sat back, offended.

"Minions." Will lifted his glass to James then slugged back a hefty swallow of wine.

"Indeed," Kate said. "People who do your bidding, tell you yes whenever you want to hear it, abuse those who don't agree with you, and generally facilitate this idea you've gotten stuck in your head that you deserve everything you have and should therefore use it to gratify your every whim and desire."

"Well, ouch," James said. In general, he didn't care for the idea that money was power. To him, money was just fun. He and his brothers had been poor their entire lives. Because of that, the sort of money being thrown at James now was...well, ridiculous. They all knew it, too. So why not be a little ridiculous with it every now and then? The universe was a quirky place. It would only be a matter of time before that money got snatched up and tossed some other lucky bastard's way, right? So no point in setting up foundations and trust funds and investment properties and the like. No point in getting *used* to it. The ride would be over soon enough.

But he wasn't going to tell that to this woman.

Which was a good thing, because he had no idea how to squeeze in a word when Kate Davis got rolling. And she *was* rolling.

"It's my professional opinion, Mr. Blake, that you've become over-used to being admired. You need to reconnect with the concept of service."

"Service?" James frowned at her, then at Bel who studiously failed to meet his eyes.

"Yes. And to that end, I've decided to structure your rehabilitation—and Bel's—in the following manner. You're serving out the final four weeks of a six week suspension, yes? A suspension you earned by punching a colleague?"

The way she said it, with that supercilious tilt to one blonde brow, had temper snapping up into James' chest. So he pushed back from the table, stretched his long legs out in front of him and gave her a lazy grin. "Why, yes, ma'am. I laid him out right handy. I didn't know you followed soccer."

"Four weeks," she continued as if he hadn't spoken, "in which to rediscover the pleasure of an altruistic act."

James pretended to frown. "Altru what now?"

"Altruistic," Kate said. "It means selfless."

"Right." He nodded, as if this were new and fascinating information. "Go on. Please."

"Each week for the next four weeks," she said, "I'll assign you a task which will require you to not only acknowledge the self-indulgent paradigm under which you've been operating these past several years but overcome it."

"You want I should develop a knack for that altruism thingy, then." James paused, shot her an earnest look. "I said that right? Altruism?" Kate nodded tightly. James grinned. "Awesome. I love new vocab."

"Belinda will be your guide, your mentor and your task master," Kate said, her lips curved in a tense smile that said she didn't know whether James was an idiot or making fun of her. The anger snapping in James' gut eased back a little. "She will be judged on her ability to shepherd you through the transition from your..." She paused delicately. "...current condition to that of a mature, well-adjusted member of society."

How had Bel put it? Going from guy to man? Same idea, James understood, but somehow he'd liked it better when Bel said it. Or maybe he just liked her mouth. He glanced to his right, saw her grinding those damn crumbs into a powder on the tablecloth, that pretty mouth pinched and set.

"Right." James hooked an elbow over the back of his chair and said, "Well? What's the challenge this week?" He grinned at Bel. "I'm yours, darlin'. Mold me."

Bel finally looked up and he blinked at the instant of raw, hunted panic in her eyes before she smoothed it all over and lifted her face to Kate's. "We're as ready as we'll ever be," she said.

Kate curved her lips—James couldn't rightly call it a smile, not something this cold—and tucked a wing of ash-blonde hair behind one ear.

"We'll start with the gluttony."

"Gluttony?" He blinked.

"Gluttony." She gave him that not-smile again. "You were born with a freakish talent, Mr. Blake. A surfeit of speed, strength and coordination. It's allowed you to abuse your body and still perform at a level sufficient to compete as an elite athlete. But barely."

James stifled the urge to sit up, stung. Abuse his body? He slouched deeper into his chair and rocked his feet side to side like a metronome set on lazy. "I'm not sure a couple extra cheeseburgers counts as actual abuse."

"Nourishing your body properly requires good food, and the preparation of good food is time-consuming and effortful. Becoming reacquainted with the level of time and effort good food requires will, I feel, recalibrate these rogue appetites of yours."

James squinted at her, sorting through the surfeit of words to find the meaning. "You want me to learn to cook?" he asked.

"Not just cook, but cook *well*." She smiled. "And feed others."

"Feed others?" James echoed, suspicion creeping into his voice.

She ignored him and turned to Bel. "I've booked the two of you to cater an event for twenty-five people next Saturday afternoon. An engagement party—tea, heavy hors d'oeuvres and cake. James will be your sous-chef for the week prior, then you'll instruct him in the finer points of serving."

"Serving?" James again sorted through the words and dug out the meaning. He turned incredulous eyes on Bel. "She wants me to wait tables? At a high frickin' tea?"

"Yes," Bel said, her face pale and composed while her eyes continued to burn. "Is that a problem?"

James glanced around his dining room table. He saw Bob, tough and square and unflinching, at the foot of the table. His face said *you fucked it up, you fix it*. No help there. Drew and Will sat opposite him, wearing matching smirks. Then there was Kate Davis, presiding at the head of the table, her hands folded neatly, her eyes saying *try me, buddy. I'd welcome the opportunity to kick your ass*.

James sighed. "No." He mentally resigned himself to an afternoon of having his fanny pinched by a couple dozen face-lifted socialites. "No problems here."

One week later, James stood in the shower and tried not to gag as the smell of parmesan cheese and meatballs oozed out of his pores. Between that and the clothes he'd shucked off and heaped in the corner, his bathroom smelled like an Italian deli. A really high-end deli, though. Full of culinary delights he'd have scarfed down by the fistful not so long ago. Then he'd spent the past week up to his elbows in a bowl of raw meat.

James would toss his cookies if forced to look one more meatball in the eye but happily, he wasn't required to eat the damn things. Only serve them.

He scrubbed his chapped fingers through his hair and winced at the sting of soap seeping through his many Band Aids. He no longer felt compelled to guffaw at Bel's ten-inch Wusthof, either. Damn thing was sharp.

On the bright side, he thought as he swiped a towel over his body, he might actually be down a few pounds. The last thing James wanted after the week Bel had put him through was food. He fell into bed every night, hitting the pillow with an actual poof of flour. He stayed awake just long enough to thank God for allowing him to retain all his fingers (or most of each of them) before falling into a tortured sleep during which his subconscious continued to fry, sauté and julienne until dawn.

The only upside he could envision to today's ordeal in which he'd serve the fruits of his labor to a couple dozen giggly women was that it marked the end of Bel's mission to turn him into some kind of Cordon Bleu graduate.

He tugged on a server's uniform—something like a tuxedo, only waterproof—and jogged down the stairs, eager to get this thing finished. Bel met him in the foyer, her hair smoothed into a pretty braided knot that made her look like a dancer, a white chef's jacket buttoned starched and stiff over her chest.

She plopped her fists on her hips and jerked her chin in a turn-around gesture. James rolled his eyes but complied, revolving slowly. "So?" he asked. "Do I pass?"

"We'll see," she said with a dark edge that had James sighing.

"Oh come on," he said. "My meatballs are kick ass and those little bitty egg rolls?"

"The *popiah*?"

"Yeah, those. Those are awesome. They're going to make the ladies squeal and clap like little girls. And then your cake is going to finish them off. Knockout punch. One, two."

Bel's lips twitched, but she shook her head. "I have total confidence in the food," she said. "Even your meatballs."

"I should hope so," James said. "I'm wearing permanent grease gloves because of those damn things."

"Poor baby."

"Hey, am I complaining? My cuticles have never looked better."

"I'm sure."

She grinned at him, dimples digging deep into those soft cheeks. James grinned back, a little dazzled. He stood there for a few more moments, basking in the rare radiance of her amusement, in the glow of having earned a genuine smile. Then she hiked up her sleeve and looked at her watch.

"Okay, enough stalling. We still have to get to the hall, assemble the cake and prep the rest of the wait staff. Are you ready?"

"Almost." James turned toward the stairs and shouted, "Guys! Let's go!"

"Guys?" Bel blinked as Drew and Will appeared at the top of the stairs in matching black serving uniforms. "Your brothers are coming?"

James threw her a look over his shoulder. "Of course. All for one, one for all, right? Kinda like the three musketeers. Only I guess there were four of them, weren't there? Including D'Artangne?" He grinned at her. "We'll include you, then. You want to be Athos, Porthos or Aramis?"

Bel shook her head slowly as Drew and Will landed at the bottom of the stairs wearing identical expressions of pained sacrifice. "You sure you want to do this?" she asked.

"I'm sure," James said and when Will and Drew failed to object, Bel released an insultingly deep sigh.

"All right then," she said, clearly skeptical. "Your call. Let's do this thing."

CHAPTER TWELVE

Waiting tables turned out to be a novel experience for James. He'd been a lot of things in his life—rich, poor, despised, adored—but he'd never been invisible. It was strangely unsettling.

"Excuse me," the groom-to-be said, all but recoiling from the plate James had set before him on the stainless steel kitchen counter. "Are those meatballs?"

James hadn't been to a lot of weddings in his life either but based on the five minutes he'd spent with the groom so far, Wynton Quist struck him as a real piece of work. Tall and blond with a face that landed somewhere south of Brad Pitt but north of Ken Doll, good ol' Wyn did *not* look inclined to approve the menu.

James handed the guy's Botoxed mother the glass of champagne to approve and followed Wyn's horrified gaze to the lumps of meat James had spent an entire week perfecting. *Meatballs*? he wanted to say. *Oh, no. Those are solid gold door knockers.* And they ought to be, given his current hourly rate and the time he'd spent on them.

Wyn didn't appear to expect an answer, however. One of those invisibility things again, James assumed. Besides, it wasn't a question so much a trap. That much James knew. But what the purpose of the trap was he had not the first clue. He tried to look both intrigued and subservient as the man of the hour went on.

"Because when I agreed to help Kate teach her wayward assistant a lesson, she assured me the food wouldn't suffer. That everything would be up to *Kate Every Day* standards."

"*Kate Every Day* standards," James echoed carefully.

The man fixed him with a patient smile. "Look. This isn't a roadside barbecue. This is an engagement party."

"Oh, darling, relax," his mother said. At least James assumed she was his mother. The matching ice-cutter cheekbones and permanently curled upper lip certainly pointed that direction. Although, James mused, it was possible they just shared a plastic surgeon. "They're just meatballs," the woman said. "Consider it a nod to your charming bride's roots."

Wyn gave his mother a quelling look. "In six weeks, she'll be a Quist, Mother. Any other roots are superfluous."

"It's not that simple, Wynton."

"Of course it is."

She regarded her son with worried eyes and pinched lips. "You know best, of course," she murmured and drained the glass of champagne. She held the empty flute off to the side in a vaguely preemptory manner. It took James a minute to understand she meant him to take it from her. He grabbed the glass.

"Tell the chef I need to speak with her," Wyn said to James, then turned and fell into muted conversation with his mother who James figured wouldn't so much as blink at a plateful of mac-n-cheese and beanie weenies so long as her champagne glass stayed full. He realized with a start that if he disappeared right now and sent some other poor guy out to deal with Wyn nobody would know the difference. The Quists had glanced at him once or twice but only saw the uniform.

He didn't know if this knowledge comforted him or depressed him.

He left the kitchen and found Bel in the dining room babying a couple of cakes into formation. One was dressed in a frothy swath of white frosting, the other in a smooth chocolate tuxedo. Bride and groom cakes, he thought. Adorable. Hand it to Bel. The girl might love her lists with a regulatory fervor, but whimsy lurked in her heart. He was sure of it.

Too bad she saved it all for her cakes. Her kiss could've used a drop or two. Yeah, take that kiss of hers, add a little whimsy, subtract the frown of disapproval and—

James blinked, startled at the direction of his thoughts. It was the frown, he thought. Bel was staring at her cakes with the same scowl she'd given James last week while he was kissing her. He'd peeked through his lashes to see how it was going over and had been taken aback at the fierceness of her expression, even with her eyes closed. He'd broken the kiss off with unusual haste and wondered if he ought to offer a written apology. Or maybe arrange for some governmental protection.

It was quite a frown. Those cakes had better be on their best behavior. God knew James had been. Though why Bel would disapprove of cakes that seemed perfect, he couldn't fathom. He shrugged. There was a lot about Bel he found baffling.

"Bel."

One last glare at the cakes and she lifted her head. Whatever she saw in his face had her bee-lining it to his side.

"The groom thinks meatballs are déclassé," he informed her.

She nodded, unsurprised. "It happens," she said. "What about the champagne?"

"Mommy likes it."

"That's all it takes." She set aside the frosting bag and wiped her hands on a rag. She strode briskly into the kitchen and presented herself at Wyn's elbow.

"Hello, Mr. Quist. I'm Belinda West, Kate Davis' chef. I understand you have a question?"

Wyn gave Bel a patronizing smile. "Why, yes, dear, I do. It seems there's been a...miscommunication."

Bel regarded him with grave eyes. "Yes?"

"Yes. I allowed a free hand with today's menu on the assumption that the importance of this gathering was understood. But based on this—" He waved what James would swear was a manicured hand toward the plate in front of him. "—I'd have to say that was a faulty assumption."

Bel's brow puckered in concern. "I'm so sorry. What seems to be the problem?"

"Well, I don't know how things are done where you're from, but around here, we save meatballs for backyard picnics and Italian restaurants." He smiled as if he hadn't all but called her tacky and gauche. "This engagement party is my future wife's introduction to the circles in which my family moves. Her first step into society, as it were. It's meant to set the tone for our entire marriage and the lifestyle we intend to pursue. So I'm afraid that this—" Again with that dismissive flick of the wrist toward a week's worth of James' work. It was starting to piss him off some, that wrist. "—is unacceptable."

Bel blinked down at the man's plate and said, "Oh, dear. Perhaps I can explain." She lowered her voice and, though the only other people in the kitchen were James and Wyn's mother, she leaned in confidentially. "Those aren't meatballs," she said. "Those are *boulettes catalanes*."

"*Boulettes catalanes*." Wyn gave the meatballs a skeptical look. Bel nodded earnestly.

"They're a Mediterranean variation on a classic tapas dish—ground veal, spiced and slow-simmered, hand rolled and skewered, then dressed in an olive and white wine sauce. I thought they'd make a lovely counterpoint on the palate to the fresh crispness of the *popiah*."

"*Popiah*?"

Bel pointed to what looked an awful lot like an egg roll to James. "*Popiah*. The *boulettes catalanes* are so rich, you know? The tender veal, the creamy sauce? I liked the juxtaposition of that against the *popiah's* bright notes of ginger and tamari on crisp shredded heirloom cabbage." She lifted elegant hands to the sides as if weighing one against the other. "Slow-simmered versus farm-fresh. Mediterranean versus Asian. I thought a fusion theme provided a lovely metaphor for marriage, where a partnership of opposites creates a single, breathtaking whole." She brought her hands together, laced the fingers and beamed. "Just like you and your beautiful bride."

"See?" Mrs. Quist gave her son a bracing pat on the arm. "The meatballs *do* represent your fiancée. Your cool to her hot. Your fresh to her cooked. Your well-bred and educated to her—"

"That's enough, Mother," Wyn said again, giving the meatballs a narrow inspection. Bel had undercut his authority with a charming, deferential precision and now it was either admit to culinary ignorance or play along. And James had a feeling this guy wasn't the type to admit a mistake.

Bel said, "If they're not to your taste, I'll certainly have them removed from the menu."

"No," Wyn said slowly. "While I certainly appreciate your effort at making a statement through the menu, my concerns are more cosmetic. The appearance on the plate, you see?"

Bel nodded. "I do hear that a lot. But it's been my experience that the more discerning and well-traveled the audience, the more this dish is appreciated. You can fool the eye, you see, but you can't fool an educated palate. Perhaps you'd like to taste one then make your decision?"

Wyn forced a chuckle, a little of his bluster restored at Bel's confidence in his palate. James eyed Bel with renewed appreciation. She was sneaky. He admired that.

Wyn helped himself to a delicate bite of meatball— *boulette catalane*, James corrected himself—and the guy's eyes nearly crossed with pleasure. An unexpected burst of pride rolled through James. He didn't necessarily care whether or not this guy liked his work but damn. He'd taken the raw materials and created a dish that made even reluctant people's taste buds do a little happy dance.

When Wyn had recovered his composure, he patted his mouth with a napkin, pretended to consider for a moment, then said, "They'll do, I suppose."

"Very good," Bel said, her eyes downcast and humble. "I'll have the staff begin plating then?"

"Fine," he said.

"Fine," his mother said and cast a regretful look at her empty champagne glass on the counter. "Now let's just hope your lovely bride gets here in time to appreciate them."

"She'll be here," Wyn said.

"She was supposed to be here twenty minutes ago."

103

Drew poked his head in the kitchen door. "The guests are beginning to arrive."

"She'll be here," Wyn told his mother again.

"Of course, dear." Mrs. Quist arranged her face in appropriately placid lines, though naked hope lit her eyes. James almost felt sorry for her. She pressed a kiss to Wyn's cheek and said, "I'll just go greet at the door until your fiancée..." *figures out how to be a decent wife to a man of your stature* "...arrives."

She sailed out of the kitchen and into, James assumed, her native habitat: the primitive, blood-thirsty, unforgiving land of DC Ladies Who Lunch.

Wyn snapped his fingers at James, whose attention had, to be fair, wandered. "Serve the champagne," he said.

"Yes, sir," James said smartly, earning himself a sharp look from Bel. But mockery from invisible people turned out to be invisible as well. James had suspected as much. He followed Wyn into the dining room and gave Drew and Will the okay to start pouring.

Then he headed back into the kitchen where Bel deftly dished up a plate with a little smattering of all the hors d'oeuvres she and James had stockpiled over the course of the week. It was gorgeous. She held it out to James and said, "Just like this, okay?"

"Sure." He started slapping food onto plates. "Hey, what did you say these were again?"

"*Boulettes catalanes.*"

"Which means?"

She flashed him a grin. "Meatballs. In French."

"Why, Bel. Aren't you the naughty one?"

She rolled her eyes at him, though dimples fluttered in her cheeks. James shook his head. "Tell you what, if I were the bride, I'd be late, too. Really late. Like *whoops, I forgot and married somebody else* late."

"I'm sure she knows what she's doing."

James snorted. "I don't know. Aside from the fact that he's really, really rich, I'm not seeing the appeal."

"You're not a woman," Bel said. "He's actually really good-looking."

James poked an egg roll into place. "He's a jerk, Bel. A hundred bucks says he couldn't pick either of us out of a line up right now." He handed the plate to Bel and she applied an artful twirl of pale green sauce to the edge.

"So?"

"So it speaks to a basic meanness of character. Geez." He wagged his head in sympathy for the tardy, unknown bride. "Poor thing."

"I'm sure she has her reasons," Bel said again.

"Yep. And I bet not one of them has to do with his sterling personality. He's not what you'd call a loveable kind of guy."

"There are better reasons to get married than love," she said, her mouth prim.

"Better?" James stared at her. "Name one."

"Security," she said. "Trust. Affection. Compatibility."

"Well, sure. If you're marrying your lawyer."

She flinched almost imperceptibly, then finished swirling sauce onto the plate James had just handed her.

He closed his eyes. "Please tell me Ford wasn't your lawyer."

The silence was damning. He touched her sleeve, and her arm was warm and vital inside it. She always looked so cool. It constantly surprised James to find her so alive under his touch. "Bel—"

I'm sorry, he wanted to say. Not that he'd done anything to be ashamed of. He still felt no guilt over being the catalyst Bel's fiancé and her assistant needed to act on their emotions. But until just this moment, he hadn't realized that Bel might've been hurt. She'd taken the whole thing so stoically, and argued with such eloquence for keeping her heart out of big decisions.

Before James could think of just what he wanted to say, Drew poked his head into the kitchen again. The combination of joy and panic on his thin face had the plate in James' hand clattering onto the countertop.

"Good lord. What?" James asked, his stomach tight.

"The bride," Drew breathed, eyes wild. "She's here."

CHAPTER THIRTEEN

Bel breathed a sigh of relief. The bride had arrived. Thank God. The last thing she needed right now was another wedding-related disaster on her résumé. She was going to get a reputation. Plus the Quist family had owned most of DC and a great many seats in both the House and the Senate since time immemorial. If there was going to be a family kerfuffle, Bel wanted no part of it. When giants fought, little people took shelter.

"Great," she said. "I'll go see about the—"

James put his hand on Bel's arm, and she dutifully ignored the slow roll of awareness that moved through her. God, she was tired of that. Hadn't she made a rule about touching?

She gave the hand on her sleeve a pointed look but James' eyes were fixed on his brother with an intensity that had Bel looking back to see what she'd missed.

"Drew," James said. "Who's the bride?"

"You'd better come see."

Five seconds later, the three of them were stacked on top of one another like the Three Stooges, one eye each to a crack in the kitchen door. Bel, by virtue of being the shortest, was on her knees with James's body curved over her own, his chin all but nestled in her hair. She could feel his breath as it fluttered the strands behind her ear. She suppressed a delicious shiver.

"I can't see anything," she whispered.

"Me, neither." James' voice was an intimate rumble and at such close range it sent a zippy little vibration through her. She squeezed to the side, putting another precious inch between her traitorous body and temptation.

"Patience," Drew said. As the tallest guy in the room, he was the top of the totem pole and Bel envied him with her entire heart.

She watched the glittery swirl of DC matrons for a few more ticks, then said, "Seriously, I can't see anything. I'm going to—"

And then the crowd broke and Bel caught a glimpse of moonlight colored hair. She saw a demure suit over an eye-popping set of curves and a pale, vulnerable expanse of inner wrist, terribly thin and oddly exposed, when the woman reached out to shake hands with somebody.

Bel's entire world constricted to that image, that single slice of the whole picture she'd been provided.

She'd seen that hair before. Those curves. That thin, fragile wrist.

"Oh my God," Bel breathed, easing back from the door.

"Exactly," Drew said.

"What?" James asked.

Bel sat on her heels and tried to think. Tried to force her brain to deliver some alternative to the disaster before her. "Where's Will?" she asked Drew.

"Serving champagne."

"Has he seen her yet?"

James shifted his gaze to Drew. "Seen *who*?"

Drew ignored him and answered Bel. "Don't think so."

"Has *she* seen *him*?" Bel asked.

"Has *who* seen Will?" James asked, through his teeth this time.

"She hasn't screamed the place down yet," Drew said. "So probably not."

"Good. Get him in here."

Drew disappeared and James planted himself in front of Bel, arms folded. "Bel. Who the hell is the bride?"

Bel sucked in a deep breath, closed her eyes and sent up a little prayer that Drew was both fast and lucky. Then she opened her eyes and said, "Remember that little waitress Will harassed out of a job at your big underwear shindig last weekend?"

James' brows disappeared into the sunny mess of his hair. "No way."

"Way."

Drew burst back through the kitchen door, dragging Will by the sleeve.

"For God's sake," Will said. "What?"

"Blake brother powwow," Drew informed him. Will lifted one sandy brow and turned his attention to James. James nodded toward Bel. Bel clasped her hands together and prayed for guidance.

"We have a small situation," she said. "The bride has arrived."

"Good for her," Will said. "I understood there was some danger of a no-show."

"Well, that's not a problem anymore. Now the problem is that you've met her before."

Will turned an unsurprised gaze on James. "Ah. The bride's a former, ah, fan of yours?"

"No," Bel said. "Nothing like that." She checked the event sheet on her clipboard and said, "Her name is Audrey Bing. She's the waitress you got fired last weekend."

Understanding dawned on Will's sharp face and he glanced toward the door, as if he could see through it to the scene on the other side. "Ah," he said softly. "Interesting."

James frowned at his brother. "What does that mean? *Interesting*?"

Will lifted his shoulders and managed to make even a vinyl tux look elegant. "The girl's got balls," he said. "I'll give her that."

Drew stepped forward. "Meaning what?"

"Meaning she took a hit last week—lost her job, lost her shot at James. But I'll give her credit, she didn't back down, did she? She got right back on the horse. And now—" He nodded toward the kitchen door. "—she's hooked herself a real golden goose. And not just temporarily, either. She grabbed the brass ring this time." He smiled. "Or should I say the gold ring? Hell, if everything I hear about the Quist fortune is true, she's probably in for several carats on a platinum band, easy. Hats off to you, Aubrey."

"Audrey," Drew said.

"What?"

"Audrey. Her name is Audrey."

"That's what I said."

"No, you didn't."

Will shrugged easily. "Okay."

Bel considered him. "You're all right with this?"

"With what?" Will asked. "It's her call. She's the one who's going to have to sleep with Mr. Important for the rest of her life. Why should I care?"

"You had a pretty big problem with her the other night."

"That was different." Will's smile was sharp and dangerous. "The other night she'd insulted one of my brothers. And you know what we say."

"Family first," Bel said. "Yeah, I've heard. But just so we're clear, you're going to go back out there, pour champagne and pretend you've never laid eyes on that girl before in your life?"

"Yes, ma'am." He snapped her a smart salute. "Now if that's all, my audience awaits." He flipped a crisp white towel over his forearm and disappeared into the dining room to wield a bottle of champagne.

Drew turned troubled eyes on Bel and James. "She wasn't wearing a ring last week," he said.

"So?" James asked.

"So Wynton Quist is an ass."

"Again, so?"

Drew shook his head. "*So*, what if she doesn't want to marry this guy? What if she's doing it for the money?"

James lifted his shoulders. "That's not our business, Drew. She's a grown woman. It's not our place to tell her what to do with her life."

"It is if she's doing it because of us."

James stiffened. "What?"

"James is right," Bel said quickly. "She's a grown woman who makes her own choices. There's no reason to think—"

"Seriously." Drew cut her off, spoke to James. "What if she's marrying this guy not because she's some heartless

109

gold digger but because she's desperate? I mean, we already know she's working at least two jobs, right? The strip club and the conference hall? Who does that if they aren't desperate? What if she was just making it and Will's little scene last week was the last straw?"

"Drew, come on," Bel said. "This isn't some marriage of convenience romance novel. This is real life. Women in tough financial straits have options. They don't have to—"

James cut her off this time. "You're really worried about this?" he asked his brother.

"Yes," Drew said, his mouth set in a stubborn line Bel hadn't seen before. "I am."

"What's it going to take to ease your mind?" James asked.

"We need to talk to her," he said.

"Oh, no," Bel said, throwing her hands up like a couple of desperate stop signs. "You two are *not* tag teaming the poor girl at her own engagement party."

"And ask her what?" James said, ignoring Bel with an ease that had her molars grinding.

"If she loves him," Drew said promptly. Bel groaned. This was not happening. Please God let this not be happening.

"Love is not the only reason to get married," she heard herself say. "There's trust, compatibility, mutual goals, shared ambitions—"

"I'll talk to her," James said.

"You absolutely will not," Bel told him.

"Thank you," Drew said. "I couldn't sleep at night if I thought we'd had a hand in some poor girl having to sleep with that guy for the rest of her life if she didn't really want to."

Drew draped a white towel over his forearm, picked up a fresh bottle of champagne and disappeared. Bel turned disbelieving eyes on James.

"You're seriously going to go out there and ask her if she's in love with her fiancé?"

James rolled his eyes. "Give me a little credit, huh, Bel? I can be subtle."

"You can?"

"Sure." He gave her a grin. "We call it sneaky where I'm from."

"That I can believe. But come on, okay? I know Drew's your brother, but do you really believe—"

"It doesn't matter what I believe," James said. "Drew's our conscience, our heart. If he thinks we have a responsibility here, I'm going to check it out. No—" He lifted a hand as Bel opened her mouth. "—questions asked."

Bel closed her mouth. "Fine," she said darkly. "Great. Just remember, this is your career we're trying to save here."

"Yours, too."

"Thanks for reminding me."

"Careers, if I may be so bold, that aren't worth a damn if we're behaving in a way that ruins other people's lives."

Bel glared at him. "I didn't have anything to do with that girl losing her job."

James returned the glare with an even look. "I did," he said.

Bel opened her mouth to deliver a stinging retort then shut it again. He was right. He personally hadn't gotten Audrey fired but he'd had a hand in creating the situation. Now he was going to take responsibility for it. How could she argue with that?

"I hate it when you do that," she said.

"Do what?"

"Blow through life all happy-go-lucky and ignorant then suddenly decide to do the right thing."

He nodded seriously. "I can see how that would be annoying."

"Shut up," she said. "Go be subtle."

"Right." He draped a white towel over his forearm, picked up a bottle of champagne and squared his shoulders like he was heading into battle. He turned to her with the devil dancing in his sea-green eyes. "A kiss for luck?"

"You're pushing it, James."

"Right. Okay. I'm out."

And then he was gone, leaving Bel alone with twenty-five gorgeously arranged plates. She only prayed the party would last long enough for the guests to taste them.

In the end, the party lasted through hors d'oeuvres, but didn't make it all the way to cake.

Bel was head down in the industrial-sized ice maker replenishing the champagne buckets when she first heard the raised voices. She couldn't understand the words but the tone said everything she needed to know. She scrambled out of the ice machine and raced for the kitchen door.

"What's the meaning of this?" Wynton Quist demanded, staring at James like an enraged peacock, all puffed chest and ruffled feathers.

James ignored Wynton. He kept his voice low and his gaze steady on Audrey as he said, "Please. I only want to talk to you."

"I don't want to talk to you," Audrey said, her face stiff and white. Her arms were folded tight under her bosom, her hands fisted in each elbow as if she were keeping them safe but at the ready.

"Come on, Audrey," James said. "The last time we saw you, things were...messy."

Wynton's black stare swung toward Audrey. "The last time he saw you? You know this person?"

"No," Audrey said.

"Yes," James said at the same time.

Audrey glared at him. "We've met," she told her fiancé. "I don't know him. And I don't care to start now."

"Fine." Wynton placed a proprietary hand on Audrey's elbow and drew her into his side.

She flinched.

Not a lot. Bel saw that. Not like she was afraid. Not like she was hurt. It was more an unintentional grimace of distaste. Probably not for the guy, she told herself. More for the gesture. There was definitely a whiff of caveman to it. Sort of a *this woman is mine, all unworthy beta males can go blow* vibe. It had to be a little demeaning.

But seeing that tiny involuntary wince wasn't what had Bel's stomach leaping into her throat. It was the fact that James saw it, too. Bel saw it register on his face. Saw his jaw go rigid, saw his shoulders square up. He wouldn't back down now. Not with this tangible piece of evidence that Audrey's marriage might be anything less than a love match.

Bel broke into a trot.

"Don't manhandle her," James said, and though his voice was low there was a menace in it that carried clear across the room. Conversations died and all eyes turned toward the little scene playing out at the head table.

"Excuse me?" Wynton's lip curled.

"You heard me," James said. Bel's desperate glance around the room revealed Drew and Will plowing through the crowd to get to James' side. *Your fight is our fight*. She could practically see the Blake brothers' battle cry in cartoon bubbles over their heads.

She picked up the pace. She had to get there first. She at least had to beat Will.

"I'm sure the lady can move under her own power," James said. "There's no need to put the leash on her. Unless, of course, you don't think she'd stay if you let her go."

"Why don't you go pick up your check?" Wynton suggested, his tone icy. "I'm sure we can manage the rest of this afternoon without your assistance."

Bel bounced off a particularly sturdy woman who'd planted herself in the aisle and was craning her neck for a better view. "Pardon me, ma'am," Bel said, then stuck her elbow into a stout flank.

The woman didn't budge. "Like I'm going to miss even a word of this," she said. "Get your own spot."

Bel lunged to the left and was hurdling a chair when she heard Will say, "Hey, James." His raised voice sang into the tense air. "Hey, Audrey. Nice party. Looks like you fell into the honey pot since we saw you last."

Audrey blanched. Wynton glanced at her. "Have you met the entire catering staff, then?"

"Of course not." She tilted her chin up, and gave Will a ferocious stare. He smiled at her.

113

"Aw, now, don't be like that. There's no call to be unfriendly." Will turned his smile on Wynton. "We're your girl Audrey's best customers."

"Customers?" Wynton said. He glanced at Audrey and eased his grip on her elbow.

"Sure," Will said. "She was our favorite—"

"Will." James cut him off. "Enough." He reached an open hand toward Audrey, as if she were a skittish mare. "Please," he said. "I just need to ask you a question. One question.

Audrey grabbed Wynton's sleeve and turned huge, pleading eyes on him. "Please," she said. "Can we just get them out of here?"

Wynton gazed down at Audrey's pale, perfect face for a long moment. Then he turned his narrow gaze on Will. "Audrey was your favorite what?"

Audrey dropped her head in defeat. Bel shoved aside the chair she'd been wrestling and threw herself into a gap in the gathered crowd. "Nothing!" she shouted.

But she was a beat too late.

Because Will had already said, "Stripper. Audrey was our favorite stripper."

CHAPTER FOURTEEN

"You," Bel said to James as they hauled trash bags to the Dumpster, "are like kryptonite for weddings."

"Hey." He heaved a giant bag over the edge without even a grunt of effort. "I was doing fine. How was I supposed to know Will was going to go all bad cop on the girl?"

"Because," Bel said. "That's what Will does. In case you hadn't noticed."

"He seemed fine in the kitchen. I thought your speech was very well received."

Bel glared at him. "No speech is well received enough to squeeze between Will and a brother thwarted, and you know it."

He hunched his shoulders. "I'm sorry, okay? Things didn't turn out the way I'd hoped. It's not like I set out to purposely embarrass anybody."

Bel stared at him. "I don't think embarrassment is the big problem here." She jabbed a finger toward the steel door between them and the kitchen. "There's a woman in there right now whose life is in total disarray because of you. Her engagement is broken, her life plan shattered. And you're sorry she's embarrassed?"

"Well, yeah," he said. "It's not like Wynton Quist was any big loss." His brows came down. "I didn't care for the way he laid hands on her."

Bel's mouth dropped open. "How a man touches his fiancée is *none of your business*, James! If she didn't like how he touched her, she could tell him that. It's got nothing to do with you!"

"Unless it does," he said. "I know this wasn't how you wanted today to go, Bel, but I did the right thing."

"Oh my God." Bel cast her eyes heavenward. "Now we're back to the marriage of convenience theory?"

"There's only one way to find out," James said. He brushed past Bel and headed for the door.

Bel jogged after him. "Oh, no, you don't. You leave that poor girl alone. Haven't you done enough?"

"Not nearly. By my lights, I'm only halfway there."

"What?"

"Seriously. I mean, at this point, the damage is already done, right?" He paused, hand on the door. "I'll be damned if it's for nothing. I'm getting my answers."

He disappeared into the kitchen. Bel ran after him.

Audrey Bing sat on a kitchen stool, staring at the untouched bride and groom cakes on the counter in front of her. She looked like a sculpture, Bel thought. *Bride and Fury*. Skin like marble, two hectic splotches of color riding high on each elegant cheekbone the only signs of life. Otherwise, there she sat, her heels hooked over the rung of her stool, her knees pressed together, her elbows jammed hard against her stomach, her fingers twisted together so hard Bel worried they might snap off.

She didn't look up when James pulled out the stool beside hers and sat down.

"Hi, Audrey," he said. She continued to stare at the cakes. She hadn't spoken a word since Wynton had dismissed her from her position as The Future Mrs. Quist nearly an hour ago. She'd simply walked into the kitchen and sat down. Bel had put a cup of hot tea at her elbow and let her be.

James pried gently at Audrey's fingers until they untwisted and he took her hand in his. She didn't flinch or pull away. Bel wondered if she was beyond caring who touched her at this point, or if she'd simply rededicated herself to hiding her tells since her slip up with Wynton this afternoon.

"Listen, Audrey," James said. "I'm sorry about today."

The silence stretched out. Bel didn't know if the girl had even heard him, but James soldiered on.

"You have every right to be angry with me," he said to her. "Ending your engagement should have been your choice, done on your schedule. But it needed to end, Audrey. Didn't it?"

He dipped his head to get a better look at her face, and the depth of kindness in his eyes startled Bel. Not that she didn't think he was a nice enough guy. Maybe he let his brothers lead him into occasional bouts of madness, but in general, he seemed pretty decent. It was more that the range of emotions he'd displayed thus far—happy, hungry, mischievous, bored, horny—weren't exactly deep.

So it was understandable, wasn't it, that the sudden appearance of this vast well of compassion would take Bel aback? *Of course* she'd be unable to tear her eyes away from the sight of his pirate's face soft with empathy and concern. *Of course* her heart would flip over in her chest. It was like watching a toddler recite Shakespeare. Unexpected and bizarre and compelling. But it didn't mean anything.

But Audrey, Bel noticed, didn't seem at all interested in James' remarkable transformation from fraternity boy to man of unexpected depth. She simply stared at Bel's cakes as if they held the answers to life, death and everything in between. James didn't push her. He simply sat there, undisturbed by the silence, as patient and companionable as a man keeping vigil at the bedside of a beloved friend.

Bel cocked a brow at James who gave her a beatific smile in return. She turned away.

Will and Drew, with a shocking lack of complaint, helped her scrub the kitchen until she could see her face in every stainless steel surface available. They packaged leftovers and loaded the van while Bel boxed the cakes and locked the doors. When there was nothing left to do but turn out the lights, Bel went back to the counter where James and Audrey still sat.

"Ms. Bing," she said, touching the girl's shoulder. She might as well have been carved from stone inside that pretty powder blue suit and Bel glared at Will over her head. He lifted one shoulder and walked out to wait in the van. Drew followed, guilt bowing his shoulders.

"Ms. Bing," Bel said again. "It's time to go. Do you have family? Somebody I can call for you?"

Bel searched the girl's perfect face for some sign of life and for a long moment found nothing. She flicked her eyes to James' and lifted her brows as if to say *now what, super genius*? Then Audrey spoke.

"You," she said to James, her voice clear but flat. She turned her gaze on him and it was the same. Precise, focused but utterly without inflection or heat or heart.

"Oh, thank God," Bel breathed. Audrey Bing was back from beyond. "Ms. Bing? Is there anything we can—"

"Yes," she said.

James gave her his instant and complete attention. "What do you need, Audrey?"

"A job," Audrey said. "That's two you owe me." Bel shivered. Because since when was being somebody's fiancée a job? "But I'd be willing to settle for one, provided it pays well."

Kate Davis presided over Sunday dinner in the Blake House the next night like the feared and honored matriarch she was. She stood at the head of the table, dealing out slices of pot roast and mounds of mashed potatoes with a firm but generous hand. Bob held down the foot of the table, watching Kate with his usual combination of mild amusement and bemused affection. One one side of the table sat Drew and Will in nearly identical sweaters and ties. On the other sat Bel with James—also combed and pressed—to her left, and Audrey—pretty and perfect—to her right.

They could have been a Norman Rockwell painting, Bel mused. Except for the fact that, after yesterday's fiasco, Kate's judgment dangled over all their heads like the Sword of Damocles as envisioned by Liz Claiborne. There was also the fact that Will's wine glass was being drained and refilled at an alarming rate. And that James' brand new personal assistant Audrey Bing was, in lieu of eating, arranging tiny cubes of roast beef into precisely ordered ranks on the edge of her plate where they would, presumably, stage a flanking maneuver on Mt. Potatoes via Lake Gravy.

Okay, so maybe they were Norman Rockwell as interpreted by Jackson Pollack. Bel forced herself to fork up a mouthful of potatoes, chew and swallow. If Kate's example was anything to go by, pending unpleasantness was no excuse to ruin a perfectly good meal.

After a decent interval, Kate mercifully laid down her silverware. "Belinda," she said. "Shall we have coffee?"

"Of course." Bel leapt to her feet to clear the table. She laid out a platter of pretty cookies and dealt out tiny china cups of strong black coffee, then sat down and willed her heartbeat to level out so she wouldn't pass out and miss Kate's forthcoming speech. From a purely clinical perspective, it was bound to be a doozy. Not to be missed.

On a personal level, she'd rather have a root canal sans Novocain.

"I understand we have a new addition to the household," Kate said, smiling benignly down the table at Audrey. Audrey kept her eyes glued to her coffee cup. Smart girl, Bel thought.

"Yes," James said. "You've met Audrey Bing. My new personal assistant."

"Lovely to meet you," Kate said.

"Thank you, ma'am," Audrey said, studiously ignoring Drew's bolstering smile and Will's open sneer.

Kate turned back to James. "Whatever prompted you to hire a new assistant? Was Bel not adequate to your needs?"

"Bel's doing fine," Drew piped up loyally.

"You bet," Will said. He gave Bel a broad wink. "Bel's the cat's pajamas."

"But?" Kate's smile crystallized, its edges suddenly razor sharp.

"But I owed Miss Bing a job." James smile was steady and, at least to Bel's eye, sincere.

"Why is that?"

"There was an incident a week or so back. My brother Will, in a fit of misguided loyalty, made a scene at Miss Bing's place of employment."

Will raised his glass in silent salute to Audrey then tipped a good ten ounces of wine down his throat. Audrey's

119

army of meat cubes advanced inexorably on her mashed potatoes.

"Yes?" Kate rested her chin on her folded hands and blinked attentively. "Go on."

James lifted one shoulder in an easy shrug.

"Said scene resulted in Miss Bing's being dismissed with some abruptness. When I ran into her again yesterday, I felt fate was reminding me of my duty to make amends."

"Surely Miss Bing's engagement into one of our state's more prominent families assured you of her wellbeing?"

James' brows came down. "I don't like to talk out of school, Ms. Davis. You'll have to ask Miss Bing about her engagement."

Kate turned to Audrey.

"My personal life is none of your business," Audrey said, her voice flat and final. "I won't talk about it with you or anybody else at this table."

"She will, however, let the occasional big tipper have a gander down her shirt," Will said. Audrey ignored him without effort.

"All right, dear," Kate murmured to Audrey, a spark of approval in her dark eyes. "That's fine." She turned back to James. "So we'll just take it on faith, shall we, that your motives for airing Miss Bing's dirty laundry to the point of forcing her fiancé to abandon her were pure?"

James cast a dark look toward Will. "I won't say I approve of the methods, but I can't argue with the outcome. We were worried about Miss Bing and wanted to make sure we hadn't done her any lasting damage with our stupid antics last week. But nothing we saw or heard yesterday eased our minds on that score. My attempts at private conversation dead ended, so Will got involved and the conversation went a bit more public."

Beside Bel, Audrey stiffened, the tendons in her neck visible from the corner of Bel's eye. She wanted to pat the girl's hand and say *I know. They're unbelievable, aren't they?*

"A bit more public?" Kate said. "What a charming euphemism for a public shouting matching that ended in a broken engagement."

James inclined his head. "Thank you."

"Am I to understand," Kate said, "that you're pleased with your performance?"

James cast a glance toward Audrey who ignored him. *Good for you*, Bel thought. *Let him twist a little.*

"Like I said, I'm sorry for the discomfort I've caused, but I do believe I did the right thing."

"And that's enough for you?" Kate asked. "Doing the right thing?"

"My conscience is clear, Ms. Davis."

"Of course it is, dear. But what about the burden clearing it places on others?"

"What do you mean?"

"I mean your stubborn insistence on *doing the right thing*—" She bracketed the words in finger quotes. "—comes at a heavy cost to everybody else. A cost which you've blithely failed to consider. Your conscience is easy, but at what price to your loved ones? Or even strangers?"

"I don't know what else you want from me, Ms. Davis. I mean, I know it doesn't always show, but my folks did raise me to be a gentleman," James said. "When it comes to women, I open doors, I say ma'am and do whatever's in my power to protect them from harm."

"Including driving off a man whose proposal of marriage she'd already accepted because you didn't approve?"

James waved a lazy hand through the air. "Proposal, hell. The girl was auctioning off her hand in marriage to the highest bidder. If her heart's broken, you can call me David Beckham."

Will jabbed his wineglass toward Bel. "And she can be Posh."

Kate ignored him. Will shrugged and drained the glass. He reached for the wine bottle but Audrey reached out and knocked it over.

"Oops." She gave him a sticky smile as wine bled into the white tablecloth. "I'm so clumsy." Her movements were a minor miracle of grace and efficacy when she snatched the empty glass from his fingers and replaced it with her own untouched cup of steaming coffee. "Here. It's fresh. Have a cookie." *And shut up*. The subtext rang loud and clear for Bel. She gave Audrey a grateful glance but the girl had already gone back to silent tablecloth gazing.

Bel pressed her napkin over the spilled wine and made a mental note to hit it with soda water as soon as Kate stopped dancing around and delivered the death blow.

"Such concern for womankind," Kate said to James, her voice a low coo of admiration that had Bel's stomach twitching. *Yep*, she thought. *Here it comes now*. "So rare and commendable."

"Thank you," James said, his eyes wary.

"Your parents must be so proud."

"If they were still alive, I'm sure they would be."

"Your parents would have approved, then, of the series of high-profile one night stands you've indulged in these past dozen years or so? In which you've been partnered by a string of anonymous women who want nothing more than to bask temporarily in the glow of your fame and the luxury of your money?"

"Hey!" James sat up, stung. "I'm no Boy Scout, but I do *not* pay for sex."

Kate laughed lightly. "Of course you do. Not in an actual cash transaction probably, I'll grant you that. But you think those women aren't getting paid? You don't think they're getting something they need from you? Or do you think they're all just slayed by your personal charm?"

James gave her a roguish smile. "Well, I *am* a handsome devil."

Kate engaged in a polite silence.

Bel closed her eyes and covered them with her hands. She couldn't watch this anymore. It was like *Wild Kingdom* when the lions toyed with the baby gazelles. Just cruel.

Finally, Kate pushed to her feet and said, "Belinda, dear. You did everything you could with the materials at hand. The Quists were understandably angry with your overall performance but did admit that the food was outstanding. I'll give you credit for actually teaching Mr. Blake to cook, and I'll give you, Mr. Blake, credit for insisting that your brothers join you in relearning the fine art of service.

"This credit, however, is far outweighed by the utter disregard you've demonstrated for Miss Bing's intellect and autonomy. Offering her a replacement job doesn't negate the sheer, persistent self-centeredness which made it necessary for you to do so, and I'm not inclined to overlook this.

"Belinda, I'm giving you a guarded pass. But I'm not entirely pleased. However, you, Mr. Blake? You have failed."

James put a hand to his heart as if wounded. Bel sucked in a deep breath and said, "Thank you, Kate. I'll do better next time."

"I'm sure you will, dear," Kate murmured.

"What *is* next time?" James asked.

"I'm so glad you asked," Kate said, her tone indicating that rushing her was perhaps not James' wisest course of action at the present time. "Given your bent for valuing your own comfort over that of society, this is a particularly appropriate task." Her smile was wide and put Bel in mind of crocodiles. "You're going to jail, Mr. Blake."

CHAPTER FIFTEEN

Monday morning, Bel and James reported to jail as promised. The metal doors clanged shut, sealing them into the Virginia Penal system until further notice. Bel's stomach took a sick lurch and her intellect switched off just like that. Fifteen years of rummaging around her emotional closet for a party dress, she thought on a bright surge of panic, fifteen years of wearing the damn thing until it was second nature. How could all that protection, all that insulation disappear in a single heart beat?

But the hows and whys hardly mattered. Bel was thirteen again and the animal inside her she'd hoped never to see again—never to need again—was free.

"Good morning," the woman who'd buzzed them in said. She was tall but soft-looking, with dove colored curls that framed a kind face and smiling eyes. Bel wasn't fooled. The kind-looking ones hit the hardest. Or maybe it just felt harder against the illusion of mercy. Didn't matter. Bel knew better than to believe in kind eyes.

The woman gave each of their hands a brisk shake and said, "I'm Jemma Halliday, Educational Director here at County Correctional School for Girls. You'll want to see the kitchens first, I imagine?"

The animal inside her head whispered *hide* and Bel obeyed. She scraped every trace of emotion off her face, deadened her eyes and pulled her real self back as far as she could manage. "Fine," she murmured.

Ms. Halliday nodded firmly, then set off down the hall. The familiar scent of commercial disinfectant had memory snarling and snapping against the locks Bel had buried it under years ago, but her body moved automatically, falling in behind the woman.

Beside her, James tucked his hands into his pockets and tackled the hall at his usual loose-limbed amble, his running shoes a merry squeak against the dull gray tile. His shaggy head swiveled around, taking in the sights with his typical delighted curiosity. *It's reform school*, Bel thought, bitterness a vile pressure in her throat. *Not fucking Disney*.

They followed Ms. Halliday down the winding, windowless hall. Funny, Bel thought. If somebody had asked her even yesterday to name all the little tricks she'd used to get through those two hellish months she'd spent in juvenile hall at thirteen, she'd have come up empty. Genuinely empty. But those plots and charms and stratagems hadn't been lost. No, indeed. Only hiding.

Because she suddenly found herself walking lightly, her hands held loose and empty, her balance constant, her shoulders tense. She found herself failing to focus on any one object, sacrificing detail for a more acute awareness of movement and change in the entire picture. Her skin tingled with the vicious awareness of each current of air, her entire system on red alert for the tell-tale shock and crackle in the atmosphere that always preceded random violence.

"Hey. Bel." She turned and found James' eyes on her. "You all right?"

She shored up her *whatever* face. "Of course," she said.

He frowned at her but she refocused on pacing the warden. Because Educational Director, her ass. Bel didn't care what the woman called herself. She knew a warden when she saw one.

Inside her, the animal chanted. *Focus. Smell. Sense. Be aware. Be prepared. Be swift and merciless.*

Survive.

"These are our culinary arts stations," the warden said. She swiped her name badge across an infrared reader and the knob gave way with a shrill beep. She pushed open the metal door and waved Bel and James inside. Bel smiled politely and put a hand on the door behind Warden Halliday's back.

"Go ahead," she said.

The warden's smile didn't budge but something flickered in her eyes. Awareness. Recognition.

125

Good, the animal whispered. *She knows what you are now.*

James sailed into the classroom without hesitation. The warden inclined her head at Bel—perhaps in thanks, but more likely in acknowledgment—and followed him.

Bel followed them both and pulled the door shut behind her.

James surveyed the neat kitchenette. It could have been lifted right out of the little rambler where he'd grown up in West Texas, all the way down to the sparkly Formica counters. Little bitty four-top electric range, oven just big enough for a twelve pound turkey. Any bigger and Dad had to do the drumsticks on the grill in the yard.

Harvest gold sink, laminate cabinets, dorm-style fridge under the counter. Four identical set ups in each corner, connected by a big old octopus of duct work overhead. To satisfy code, he assumed, though barely. He and his brothers had built sturdier go-karts.

He turned to grin at Bel. "Hey, check this out! We used to have this exact same—"

Bel was gone.

Oh, physically, she was standing right next to him. He could have nudged her with his elbow if he'd wanted to. If he'd thought it would do the trick. But her attention hadn't wandered. She was simply *gone*. The spirit or energy or whatever you wanted to call the thing that inhabited a person's body and made them, well, *them*? Bel's had vacated the premises.

His breath caught in his throat and an exquisite sense of loss gripped him. Which was stupid. Because he'd gone nearly thirty years without knowing Bel even existed and had gotten along just fine. And suddenly, the girl tunes out for a spell and he's panicking?

Stupid.

But his lungs refused to receive that message. They stayed hot and tight, enough that he had to really reach for a normal tone when he said, "Bel?"

She turned to him, her face a polite question. But her eyes—those deep, warm eyes that never failed to entertain, to challenge, to engage—were empty and blank. "Yes?"

James flicked a concerned glance at the principal lady who'd led them in. She stood watching Bel, her face stoic, her eyes full of compassion.

"It's a little dated, I know," Jemma Halliday said. "But we're mainly concerned with domestic functionality. Many of our girls come in here having, literally, never boiled water. When they leave, most of them can manage a chicken breast and some frozen peas. The sort of level you're operating at is going to be something of a stretch for our girls, I'm afraid."

Bel turned that awful plastic face on her. "That's fine," she said. "We're not asking anybody to produce a state dinner. What I have in mind, however, is going to require a more commercial set up."

"Commercial?" The principal's silvery brows drew together but she looked more wary than puzzled. "I thought you were teaching the girls how to cook?"

"I am. But not for themselves." Bel waved a hand at the kitchenette James had enjoyed so much a minute ago. "I have a client who's expecting two hundred mini cakes—one for each place setting at her wedding—by the weekend. Your girls will be helping to fulfill that contract."

"I see." Ms. Halliday put a hand to her throat, as if she habitually wore pearls. But there was no moonlight or magnolia in her voice when she said, "I'm afraid I misunderstood. When I spoke to Ms. Davis, she implied you would be covering life skills for the girls, not using them as cheap labor."

"I *will* be teaching them life skills," Bel said.

"I fail to see how producing hundreds of tiny cakes is going to help my girls budget for groceries or prepare balanced meals for themselves and whoever else they find themselves responsible for down the road."

James had to give the woman credit. She might look soft but she had backbone. And she was not pleased at the idea that Bel might be taking advantage of an already abused population.

"Ms. Halliday," Bel said, "*your girls* don't give a crap about balanced meals."

James gave a snort of startled laughter. The principal lifted a brow his direction and he said, "I'm sorry. But she said..." He petered off. "Nothing. Excuse me. Please go on."

He shook his head. Bel West, saying *crap* to perfect strangers. Good lord, what next? Rivers running bloody? Plagues of locusts? Thunderstorms of frogs?

Bel went on as if James hadn't just suffered a minor seizure. "What your girls care about is a) getting out of here, and b) getting paid. You want to play Holly Homemaker with them, fine. I'll leave defrosting peas to you. But I'm here to give them some experience that could open doors for them that don't lead to jail, the morgue or welfare." The smile she gave the woman was the barest curve of her lips. No dimples at all. James hated that smile. "And to do that, I'll need your kitchen. The real one."

James turned to the principal to see what the estimable Ms. Halliday thought of the bite in Bel's voice and the ice in her smile but Ms. Halliday didn't look offended so much as thoughtful. She returned Bel's flat gaze with measured consideration.

"Fine," she said finally. She snapped off the fluorescent lights and led them back into the hallway. "The kitchen isn't a secure location, though. You'll require supervision."

"Will I?"

The principal gave Bel that look again, all neutral features and sad eyes. "It's for everybody's safety, Miss West."

"Of course," Bel murmured.

James wondered what the hell they were talking about.

James was no amateur when it came to sexually aggressive women. He'd survived a dozen years on the pro football tour of England and Europe. He'd been groped, propositioned, flashed and stalked by hundreds of determined women over the years.

He hadn't always said no. But despite what the tabloids printed and what Kate Davis clearly thought, he hadn't said yes nearly as often as people assumed, either.

Not that he was some kind of throw-back caveman who didn't think women should have their shot at the driver's seat. Maybe James preferred, in general, to do his own driving, but there was definitely something to be said for a woman who knew exactly what she wanted and had the brass to go after it, balls out. James had nothing against headstrong women. Turned out he liked 'em stubborn. Challenging. And, lately, extremely well-pressed.

But even James didn't know quite what to do with the six sets of hungry eyes fixed directly on him. Particularly since at least four of them—and possibly more—were well under the legal age limit.

Ms. Halliday had marched the girls in and lined them up across the wide, stainless steel island in the center of the concrete dungeon that passed for a commercial kitchen according to the state of Virginia. She'd rattled off their names but James hadn't caught them. He'd been too busy trying to decide if the lingering aroma was more powdered eggs or boiled hot dogs.

Then he was distracted by the perfect racial equity of the group. Two white girls, two black, one Hispanic, one Asian. Two were visibly pregnant, maybe three. Or maybe the little Hispanic girl just ran toward chunky. Hard to tell at this age. Damn shame if she was. Kid couldn't be more than—

He broke off in blank surprise when the girl caught his eye and trailed her tongue over her bottom lip.

What the hell? Had a chubby twelve-year-old just come on to him? He glanced over at Bel for a reality check.

"Mrs. Break will escort the girls back to their dormitory when you've finished," Ms. Halliday was saying to Bel. She indicated a hatchet-faced matron standing near the door. Bel flicked a glance at the woman, nodded once. James gave Mrs. Break a cheerful wave, grateful for the distraction from the heat of all those lustful gazes.

"Thank you, Ms. Halliday," Bel said. "I can manage from here."

"I'm sure you can, Ms. West." She gave the girls a stern look. "Do not make me sorry I extended you all this privilege," she said.

"No, ma'am," they all chorused as Ms. Halliday left.

Bel laid a stack of aprons and a box of hair nets on the counter. "Suit up, girls," she said.

The girls lined up for aprons in deference to some internal pecking order James couldn't begin to fathom. The fine-boned Asian girl was first and she dropped the apron over her head but sneered at the box. "I ain't wearing no hair net," she said to Bel.

"Fine," Bel said. "Mrs. Break? Will you please take Kira to Ms. Halliday? She's chosen not to participate."

Kira's dark eyes went wide and innocent. "Damn, girl, I didn't say that!"

"No?" Bel gave her a bland smile. "I must have misunderstood."

"Straight up." The girl gingerly pulled the hair net over her glossy black head. "Clear the wax out, heard?"

"Heard," Bel said solemnly. She pointed Kira toward a terrifying contraption with a bowl the size of a kettle drum on the floor against the wall. "Stand there."

Kira crossed the kitchen, her stride the jaunty hitch-skip James had only ever seen on MTV. She slowed as she passed him, dropped one lid in an exaggerated wink and blew him a moist little air kiss.

"Ah," James said, utterly at sea. What the hell? These girls were, what, about fifteen on average? What had he been doing at fifteen? Playing soccer six hours a day, twelve on weekends? He wouldn't get anywhere near a pucker that perfect in real life for years. Where the hell had a kid—because he didn't care what she'd done to land herself in juvie, fifteen was still a kid—learned that kind of sexual self-possession?

Bel joined Kira at the huge thing against the wall—turned out it was an industrial-sized mixer—and the rest of the girls followed her in a casual pack.

"I'm Belinda West," Bel said to the group when they'd given her their attention. "This is James Blake." Those eyes swung James' way again and he gave them a little wave.

"Hey," he said.

"Hey, baby," said one of the white girls, a hand propped on a skinny hip. Caren? Cara? Something like that. Bel would know. "Saw some of your moves on the computer last night."

A muffled snicker rose from the pack of girls. James tried a benign smile. "Yeah? You're a soccer fan?"

The girl dropped her lids and peeked out from under her lashes. "No, but we got plenty in common. I take my shirt off when I score, too."

James swallowed. "Ah huh." He cast Bel a desperate look while the snickers turned into outright giggles.

"Speaking of sex," Bel said in her usual cool tone. "Can anybody tell me what a hand job is going for these days? Nothing fancy, just a quick tug."

All eyes swung back to her, James' included. A *hand job*? Jesus lord. Bel had been body snatched. There could be no other possible explanation for this.

Silence stretched out. One beat. Two. The girls exchanged glances and James wondered, not for the first time this morning, what the hell was going on with Bel.

"Kira?" she asked, her eyes going back to the Asian girl with the x-rated pucker. "A hand job?"

"How should I know? I ain't no whore. But Jackie is. Whyn't you ask her?"

A choked laugh flew out of the crowd and dropped like a stone into the suddenly charged silence.

Whoops, James thought. *Bad move, Kira.*

The heavily pregnant Jackie said, "Fuck you, Kira. I ain't no whore neither. Ask your mama, why don't you? She gets on her knees for a dime bag, don't she?"

Later James would conclude that Kira had opted for a physical response rather than verbal. All he saw in the moment, however, was a lightning swift shift from girls standing and talking to girls whooping and cheering as Kira and Jackie rolled around on the floor walloping the snot out of one another.

But by far the most disorienting feature of the fight was Bel's utter lack of expression or distress. She regarded the mayhem at her feet with not an ounce of surprise. She simply waited for an opportunity to present itself, then reached into the violence and hauled Kira to her feet by a handful of her shiny black hair. No hand-wringing, no outrage, no lamenting the sad state of today's youth.

If anything, Bel looked bored. Resigned. As if she'd seen it all before, more times than she could count and was sick to death of it.

Kira yelped and bucked against Bel's grip but Bel didn't flinch. She shoved the girl toward Mrs. Break, who looked disappointed to have missed the opportunity to use the tactical baton tucked into her belt.

Jackie lumbered to her feet next, swiped at her bleeding nose and said, "Damn. Baby's kicking like fuck-all."

Bel nudged her toward Mrs. Break, too. "You can handle them both?"

Mrs. Break patted her baton and gave Bel a grim smile. "I can handle them."

Kira and Jackie sank into sullen silence as Mrs. Break pointed them toward the door.

"All right," Bel said to the remaining girls. "Let's get started."

"Yo, Ms. West?" Caren/Cara/Shirtless Scorer put her hand up.

"Yes, Taryn?"

Taryn, James thought. That was it. God, Bel had a brain like a frickin' Trapper Keeper.

"How come you asked us what we charge for hand jobs?"

"I don't think any of you are prostitutes, if that's what you're after."

"So why you ask?"

Bel shrugged. "We'll probably be using sharp knives later on. I guess I thought I'd light the short fuses first." She lifted a brow. "Other questions?"

The girls looked to Taryn who took her time considering. Finally she shook her head. "No, ma'am."

"No, ma'am," came the chorus.

"Fine," Bel said. "Let's get to it."

But somehow James had the feeling that Bel had already done the majority of her heavy lifting for the day. More power to her. Female social maneuvering was a mystery that, in James' opinion, smart men left alone.

His own work, however, had just begun.

CHAPTER SIXTEEN

"I don't think I should go back there," James said from the passenger seat of the catering van as they drove home late that afternoon.

Bel glanced at the speedometer. The needle hovered at a safe and respectable sixty miles per hour. Which was good. Great. Admirable, even.

Because what Bel wanted—wanted more than her next breath—was to stomp the living hell out of the accelerator.

She wanted to crush it to the floor boards, feel her old van reach its shuddering limit and know that she was flying away as fast as humanly possible. She wanted to snatch up the miles in great, greedy handfuls and shove them between her and the gaping wound today had ripped in her memory. She wanted the animal inside her caged again. Wanted to forget how necessary that animal was in a certain world. Wanted to forget that world even existed. She'd forgotten once. She could forget again.

She did *not* want to listen to James Blake whine about his afternoon.

"Seriously," James said. He leaned into his seat belt and hit her with pleading eyes. "I should *not* go back there."

Me, neither, she thought. *Please God, me, neither*.

"Nobody said rehab was easy," she told him.

"This isn't rehab," James said. "It's payback. Kate Davis hates me."

"Kate doesn't hate you."

"Of course she does. She probably hates anything with a penis. And I'm the penis-haver who took the shine off her golden girl on national TV." He shot her a quick look. "Which was, as you know, totally accidental."

"So you've mentioned."

"She's got it in for me. Sending me to a reform school for the prematurely sexually active. God."

"Don't take it so personally, James." Bel glanced at the speedometer and eased back on the accelerator until the needle dropped back a couple notches. Her knuckles showed white against her skin but whatever. She was handling it.

"Don't take it personally?" James flopped back in his seat as if she'd shot him. "Don't take it *personally*? Jesus, Bel, do you know what I've been through today? Do you know what *happened* to me in there?"

Bel kept her eyes steady on the road while her heart beat louder and fiercer inside her, until it was a primal thump in her throat, in her ears. A banging, pulsing drum beat that stretched her self control thinner with each wild strike.

"No, James," she said, her voice admirably even. "What happened to you today?"

"What happened? What *happened*? What, you weren't there? You didn't see?"

She forced herself to ease off the accelerator, to coast into a gentle curve. Look at that, she thought. Absolutely in control. "Poor James," she crooned. "Had a hard day and nobody paid attention? Come on now, tell Mama Bel all about it."

He shot her a disgruntled look and folded his arms. "What for?"

"For the pleasure of reliving the details in front of a sympathetic audience?"

He paused, considered. "There is that. Okay, fine." He settled into his seat, comfortable now, basking in the glow of somebody's undivided attention. "God. I haven't been in a game that physical since the last time we played Madrid Real. Those girls..." He gave her an aggrieved look. "They, they *mauled* me, Bel. All those porn movies about reform school girls? My brothers and me, we went through a real phase with those. Figured them for bullshit but it didn't detract from the viewing experience if you know what I mean. I never suspected it was goddamn documentary footage."

He leaned toward Bel, jerked back his head and exposed the tanned column of his throat. "Do I have a hickey?" he demanded. "The little one, Maria? She trapped me behind the big tub of flour and latched right on. Sucked like a goddamn Hoover. And the big one, Taryn? She could draw my ass from memory, she spent so much time handling it. God." He shuddered. "I went into this inclined to feel sorry for those girls. Being poor is no picnic, I know that. But Jesus. Girls like that *need* to be locked up. If not for their own protection, for the protection of the innocent male population. Hormones like that, on the loose? God only knows—"

"You think those girls *want* you?" The words shot out of Bel without warning, a thin ribbon of lava bursting from the molten blackness shifting inside her. "You think, what, they're slaves to their sexual desires?"

He flipped down the visor and inspected his neck in the mirror. He made a disgusted noise and slapped the visor back into the roof. "I don't know what they're slaves to but whatever it is, it's terrifying. And my going back there is only going to make it worse. How are you supposed to teach them anything when they're too busy looking at me and thinking—"

"What? What are they thinking when they look at you, James?" Fury sizzled through her veins. It leapt across her skin like fire and burned in her cheeks, her ears but her voice was cold and jagged. "*God, what a man! I must fuck him silly and have his babies immediately!* Is that it?"

His eyes flew to hers, wide and startled. "You—" he began in tones of genuine awe, then broke off. A brilliant grin spread across his face. "Bel. You said *fuck*."

Temper spiked higher, faster inside her. Her hands trembled on the wheel but not from fear. God, not fear. It was exhilaration. Triumph. Release. Branches arched over lush green ditches outside the van, all of it whipping by Bel's window in a verdant blur. She rocketed into light gone molten with the dying day and wished it good riddance.

James took a peek at the speedometer and the grin died. "Whoa. Maybe ease up on the gas a little, huh, Bel?"

136

She ignored him. "These girls don't want you, James."

"Uh huh. Tell it to the hickey."

She snorted. "Please. They want what you have."

"Which is?"

"Power. Money. Status. Safety. And they're willing to pay for it with the only thing they have that the world seems to value. Their bodies."

"And that's wrong." James frowned at the speedometer and surreptitiously tightened his seatbelt. "I know that. That's what I'm getting at, right? You're teaching them some real skills in there. Trying to, anyway. They ought to be focused on learning. But they're too busy throwing themselves at me to even—"

Bel punched the accelerator to the floor. The van bucked forward and James paled. She took a grim pleasure in that. "You object to women throwing themselves at you?"

"I do when they're fourteen," he said.

"And what about when they wait a few years? What about when they're of legal age but still desperate and poor? Still believe their only ticket out of hell is a hot body and a pretty face?"

He said nothing, only watched her with troubled eyes.

She shook her head, gave a bitter chuckle. "They see you coming and they think, boy, this is it. My big chance. So they give you everything you want and hope that maybe if the sex is good enough, you'll stick around. Or hell, maybe, if we're dreaming big, you'll take us with you when you go. But you don't. You get what you want, you take a shower and hit the road a happy man. But what about us? What happens to us?"

He tipped his head slowly, as if sliding pieces into place and judging the fit. "Us?"

"Them," Bel said quickly. "Us." She glanced at the speedometer. Holy hell. She jerked her foot off the gas and flexed her aching fingers. Good God. What was she *doing* talking to him this way? Spewing all her madness onto him? "Women. You know, in general. Collectively. As a species."

A doubtful silence filled the van. She stared determinedly out the windshield.

"What's going on with you, Bel?" he asked. "You've been kind of...off today."

"I'm fine." Her chest felt hollow and strange, and a dull throbbing dug into the base of her skull. She shrugged, suddenly weary. "Listen, all I'm saying is sex isn't the same for women as it is for men."

"It's not fun for women?"

"It can be, I guess. But it's never simple, okay? I'm not saying they don't want your body. It's just that they probably want something else, too."

"My money."

"A lot of times, yeah."

"So what about the girls who slept with me when I was poor? Or the ones who had their own money? What were they after?"

"Something else." She breathed in and out, nice and steady, but it did nothing to fill the echoing cavern of her chest.

"Like?"

"You want me to say true love?" She shook her head, a jagged laugh erupting from the emptiness inside. "Love's just a word women use to pretty up their motives for wanting what they want. It's a lot easier to say they were in love than to admit what they were really after."

"Which is money?"

"And security. Or escape." She lifted her shoulders. "Validation. Admiration. Novelty. You name it. They want it enough, they'll screw you for it."

"So let me put this into my own words, just to make sure I'm getting it." He tapped his lips with a finger and squinted into the sunset. "You're saying that women have sex they don't necessarily want or enjoy in the hopes that I won't be an arrogant prick who takes what I want and to hell with anybody else?"

"That's about it." She tossed him a sideways glance. "You're offended."

"Please. My ego is made of sterner stuff than that."

The urge to grin took her by surprise and blunted the leading edge of whatever was driving her. "As I suspected."

"It helps that you're totally wrong."

"Am I?" She slowed for the turn onto the macadam road leading to Hunt House and the Annex.

"Maybe not in all cases, but for sure in some."

"You know best, I'm sure," she murmured.

"Damn skippy."

Bel indulged in a long, skeptical silence.

He frowned at her. "All right, let me ask you this, then, since you're being such a font of insight into the female psyche today. Say I kissed this girl."

Bel's stomach twitched and she glanced at him, suspicious. "What girl?"

"Mouth like sin, kissed like a startled angel." His eyes went dreamy. "All soft and surprised and disapproving."

"Disapproval generally means no, James."

"But does that mean I can't try again?"

"Why on earth would you want to?" She pulled into the Annex's circular driveway and parked next to the naked fountain frolickers. She switched off the ignition with careful hands and made sure there was nothing but casual curiosity in her face when she turned to him.

"Did I mention her mouth?"

"You did."

His eyes dropped to her lips and Bel's heart stumbled into a confused patter. "It's definitely worth another shot," he said.

"*No* isn't *try again later*," Bel said. "No means no."

"She never actually said no."

"She...didn't?" Bel thought frantically. She'd said no. That night in the kitchen. She'd said no. Emphatically. Of course she had. Hadn't she?

He leaned forward, as if to impart a confidentiality. Close enough that Bel could smell him, that clean, warm scent of man mixed with melted butter and burnt sugar. Her scent, she realized with a start. Hers and his, melded together. It sent a liquid surge deep into her belly.

"She didn't," he said. "I get the feeling she was just giving the question a depth of consideration I hadn't figured on." He reached up, ran the pad of his thumb gently over her cheekbone. The breath stopped in Bel's lungs, hung there, waiting. "She's a thinker, that one. No question too casual for a deep answer."

"She doesn't sound like your type," Bel managed.

"Not my usual, no. But I can't get her out of my head."

"Oh." She stared at him, transfixed by the patient green of his eyes. His hand cradled her cheek now, warm and large and just a little bit rough and she wanted with all her heart to just lean on him. Let him take the weight of her aching head and her battered heart into those strong hands. She wanted to slide into his lap, press herself into the circle of his arms and rest there.

"Bel." His voice was low and soft, more statement than question.

"Hmmm?"

"Will you tell me about it?"

She stiffened. "About what?"

"About why you disappeared on me today."

She pulled away from his hand as if burned, yanked the keys from the ignition and dropped them into her purse. "I did no such thing."

"You did."

She made a dismissive noise and jerked open the door. She slung her bag over her shoulder and said, "I have a hundred minicakes in the back that say otherwise. Cakes that need to get into the freezer if I'm planning to keep what little employment I've managed to hang onto since I met you. So if you'll excuse me?"

She dropped out of the van and slammed the door behind her. Her feet bit into the crushed gravel drive as she stalked to the rear doors of the van. And found him there, already leaning against the back panel.

She stared at him. "What, did you teleport?" He hadn't even been unbuckled when she'd slammed her door.

"I *can* run, Bel. I do it for a living."

She lifted a skeptical brow. "So you've said. I personally haven't witnessed anything above a reluctant jog."

He smiled. "You have now."

"Color me impressed."

"I will. I'd enjoy that, actually."

The heat in his eyes had her swallowing hard and reaching for a dampening tone when she said, "Will you excuse me please? I need to get those cakes into the freezer."

"No."

"What?"

"I said no. I'm not going to excuse you."

She frowned at him. "You're holding my cakes hostage?"

"Sure."

"In exchange for what?"

"The truth."

"The truth." She turned the words over in her mouth, really tasting them. "You think I owe you the truth?"

"I think you owe me something."

"*I* owe *you*?" She shook her head in disbelief. "How do you figure that? You've been trying to destroy my career since the minute we met!"

He sighed. "You're still sore about your wedding?"

"It was *live TV*."

He shrugged. "I'd feel worse if you'd actually loved the guy."

"Love," she spat. "Love? God, James, what did I just tell you? Love doesn't exist, okay? It's a convenient excuse for people to do whatever they feel like so later on they can sigh and shrug and say *I couldn't help it*! *I was in love*!" She pressed her hands to her heart and batted her eyelashes. "Ah, l'amour. Any stupid, impulsive, selfish thing you feel like doing, go right ahead. Just tell people it was for love and all's forgiven, right?"

"Is that what happened to you, Bel?"

She went on as if he hadn't spoken. "Ditch your fiancée on live TV because you suddenly discover you're *in love* with her assistant. Or, hey, break up a waitress's engagement because you're not convinced, upon half an hour's observation, that it's a *love* match. And people will forgive you because, hey, it's *love*. God, it makes me sick."

"I'm sorry Ford ditched you on TV, Bel. But I'm not sorry you didn't get married and I'm damn sure not sorry you didn't love him."

"Of course you're not," she said. "You don't care about—"

"I'm not sorry," he broke in, "because, while it may have inconvenienced you or embarrassed you or whatever, it didn't *hurt* you. And he couldn't hurt you because you didn't love him."

She gave a muffled shriek of frustration. "So *what*? Why do you care? What difference could it possibly make to you if I loved him or not?"

"It makes a hell of difference. Because if you'd loved him, you'd think about him every time you looked at another man. Every time somebody else touched you, kissed you, held you, you'd be thinking of him." His eyes were hot now, green and intense and predatory. "And I don't want you thinking about anybody but me this time."

Bel stared at him. "This time?"

He smiled at her, and it was alive with purpose as he came off the van and moved toward her.

"You never actually said no, Bel." He closed the distance between them with a couple of those loose, lazy strides of his. "And I have half a mind to ask again."

CHAPTER SEVENTEEN

Temper snapped hot in Bel's whiskey eyes and a delighted laugh bubbled up inside James' chest. Madame Self-Possessed looked like she might do him a violence if he laid a finger—let alone his lips—on her.

At first he'd just wanted to tweak her a little. The woman had invaded his house, after all, with her massive army of pots and pans, her sheets, her Tupperware, her relentless, nonstop *efficiency*. She'd moved right in, made herself at home, and started taking shots at everything he held dear in life. He'd expected her to disapprove of his family, but taking aim at his life-long love affair with the opposite sex? That was going too damn far.

Because James liked women. All women. They were like Paris to him—foreign and strange, but at the same time so damned inviting. They were a mystery that demanded to be tasted and touched, savored and appreciated. And James wasn't one to deny his appetite. But so what? Why should he? Lucky man that he was—and he'd never denied luck's starring role in his current situation—women had always liked him right back.

Or so he'd always believed. Which was why Bel's latest blow had been particularly low. Implying that no woman had ever wanted him just for the pleasure of his company? That it was just his money or status or what have you? James was willing to admit that money was fun, but he certainly didn't believe that all the women who'd been willing to share his bed over the past several years had been interested solely in his pocket book.

Not that he'd deny the pocket book could have played into it some. But he'd lay a big chunk of that cash on the bet that there was something more to it. Something simple and

143

primal and hot. An appetite Bel claimed women merely humored in men to get what they needed.

It was an intriguing theory. One James felt like testing out. Right now. On Bel. Because if he was any judge of lust—and he thought he was—there was more than pure temper crackling in her eyes. Something more earthy and interesting.

Only one way to find out.

He took a step closer to her, anticipation a hum along his nerve endings. Her skin had been like warm peaches under his hands in the dark kitchen. He was itching to find out what she'd feel like, smell like, taste like in this golden, melty twilight.

He eased toward her the way he would a skittish colt and slipped his fingers around her wrist, nice and gentle. Her pulse bumped there, a wildly arousing flutter against his palm, completely at odds with the dark menace in her eyes. He smiled at her.

"Bel?"

"What?" She glared down at his hand, then back up at him.

"I'm going to kiss you now."

Her glare went nuclear. "I think you should."

He paused. "What?"

She nodded firmly. "I do. I think you should kiss me." She closed her eyes and puckered up those gorgeous lips. James' blood jumped up and headed south but he forced himself to stop. Think. This wasn't going the way he'd expected.

"Mind if I ask why?"

Her eyes opened. "What, now you want to talk? I said you could kiss me. Don't you want to?"

That surprised a laugh out of him. "I do. Yeah."

"But?"

"But I'm a little foggy as to why you'd want me to.

"For God's sake, James. I don't."

"No?" He rubbed his thumb over the tender skin inside her wrist. Her pulse still jumped and skittered, giving lie to her steady voice and impatient words.

"No," she said. "But you clearly don't believe a woman could possibly kiss you and not be overcome with lust. You want me to be wrong so you can keep banging your merry way through life. So you don't have to think and you don't have to change and you don't have to feel guilty about it. So why don't we just get this out of the way, okay?"

He stared at her. "Well, that's...unflattering."

She cast her eyes heavenward. "Are you going to be temperamental about this?"

He rubbed his jaw, considered. "I might."

"Great." She jerked her wrist from his fingers. Her cheeks pinked up and something elusive and lost moved through those clear brown eyes of hers as she looked away. "Fine."

"Well, geez, Bel. Can you blame me? You sucked the romance right out of it. You made it so clinical. Like some kind of transaction. Where's the fun in that?"

She gave him a significant look. "It *is* a transaction. It always has been. I just made sure you noticed for once."

She was wrong, of course. He knew it in his heart. But he couldn't quite see his way to the end of that argument so he let it go.

They stood for a moment, a foot and a half of tense and wary space separating them. Finally, Bel said, "Can I have my cakes now?"

James moved aside. He considered her while she clicked open the panel doors and unlatched the straps holding the trays in the racks. Studiously avoiding his eyes, she slid out a large aluminum baking tray full of cakes. James slid out a second and followed her into the house.

He felt...itchy. Uncertain. Unsettled. And not just in light of the completely unsatisfying argument he'd just lost. It had been eating at him for days, actually. Ever since he'd seen her glaring at her bride and groom cakes with the same intense concentration she'd given his kiss. The concentration he'd mistaken for disapproval. For an unequivocal if unspoken no.

But what if it hadn't been no? That's what was chewing at him. He wasn't by nature given to regret but he couldn't

145

stop wondering about that. What if what he'd taken for *no* had actually been more *let me think*?

Because the Bel he'd come to know would no more endure an unwanted kiss in silence than she would run her precious tea cups through the dishwasher. And James had tried to run those cups through the dishwasher once, so he knew of which he spoke.

And she damn sure wasn't the sort of girl who'd allow her body to lead her into even the most harmless of detours. If there hadn't been something real and compelling in that kiss, she wouldn't have hesitated to slap his face and demand a written apology. But she hadn't done any such thing.

Instead, she'd surfaced, slow and sweet, those ridiculously long lashes lifting over perplexed and curious eyes, those dark sharp brows drawn together in a wary line.

And what had he done? He'd given up. He'd seen *undecided* and interpreted it as unmoved, unimpressed and uninterested. And when had *that* happened? Just when had he forgotten that *maybe* wasn't *no* but *try harder*? Just when had he started to take it for granted? The applause, the success, the women, the money?

He didn't know when it had started. But he knew exactly when it was going to end.

Right now.

Bel slid her tray of cakes into the upright freezer and tried not to notice the way the very air between her and James still snapped and twitched with unspent energy. She composed her face into neutral lines and turned to take the second tray of cakes from him.

He gave it to her, his brows furrowed in a completely uncharacteristic frown. Not that she'd never seen him frown at her before—that, she'd seen, and plenty. No, this was something different. This was something new. This was James Thinking.

She slipped the second tray into the freezer with a tiny smile. She hadn't thought it was possible, but had she actually broken through? Had she actually said something to him that made a dent in that perpetual laze of his? Something that had kick-started what she suspected was a perfectly serviceable brain into action? Or better yet, a decent dose of introspection?

She clicked the freezer door shut, checked the seal and turned back to him. His eyes were on her this time, and what she saw in them was enough to have her easing toward the stainless steel door at her back.

"Hey, Bel." Not a question. Just the opening volley. She understood this the way a field mouse understands a hawk in the sky.

"Hmmm?" Words seemed to be beyond her.

"I changed my mind."

"About, um, what?" She checked her watch. She didn't know why. Was she planning to time him?

His pirate's lips curved. "Kissing you. Your theory about women and lust? I think I *would* like to put it to the test after all. If the invitation still stands."

"Oh." Her pulse scrambled madly and she groped for an excuse. God, what had she been thinking? Asking him to kiss her? Throwing it down like a gauntlet? "I, ah—"

A verbal response turned out to be unnecessary, as in the next heartbeat, Bel found herself being thoroughly kissed.

His mouth was everything it looked like—utter perfection in the unlikeliest place. But Bel had been here before. She was ready for it this time.

Last time, he'd caught her by surprise and it had been one big sensory explosion. Like a well-trained army marching on an unprepared, unfortified village. Same army this time, Bel thought, dazed, as his mouth moved over hers, still sweet with the cakes they'd baked. Excellent weaponry. But this time Bel had a little firepower of her own. And a plan. It wasn't like she'd asked him to kiss her without a strategy in place.

She just had to remember what it was.

She lifted her hands—had they really been clenched in fists by her sides?—and speared her fingers into that wild rumple of sunny hair. It was crisp and alive against her skin, and a startling bolt of bone-deep satisfaction shot through her. *Finally*, something inside her whispered fiercely. *Finally.*

She arched into him without thought, into all that solid, compact heat, and a purr rose up inside her, silent and unstoppable. She hadn't known, she thought wildly, hadn't understood that itch just under her skin. The twist of nerves, the twitch of discomfort. She hadn't known what she wanted, what she needed.

She knew now. Now, with his mouth moving over hers like glory, with her body plastered up against the square strength of his, with her fingers twisted into his shaggy hair. Now, with electricity leaping in her veins, with want sliding hot into her belly, with the scent of him deep in her lungs.

It was him. Touching him. Quenching that low and aching desire to simply feel him under her hands.

She tugged him closer, rose up on her toes and opened her mouth under his. He made some kind of noise—surprise? Hunger? Gratitude?—and suddenly Bel's back was flat against the cool freezer door. He pressed into her, his body hard and hungry, his mouth hot and avid, and everywhere he touched her she burned.

But she gloried in it. God help her, she did. She basked in his blatant want and whipped the flames higher. She slid a knee up his thigh, curved it around his hip and urged him closer. Higher. Fiercer. She wanted *more*. Needed it. Needed *him*.

One big hand slid down to cup her bottom, lifted her into him as he rocked against the center of her want. Pleasure and heat shot through her, and she dropped her head back to gasp. He dragged his lips along the exposed line of her throat in a blaze of hot, open-mouthed kisses that sent shards of pleasure dancing over her skin.

More. She needed more. More heat, more skin, more contact. Just more. Her hands streaked over him, tunneled up the back of his shirt until they found the broad strength of his bare skin. God. The animal heat of him, strong and smooth under her hands, had her head spinning, had desire leaping up mad and unruly inside her. She wanted to strip him bare,

wanted to feel that tight play of muscle against her own skin.
Under her lips, her tongue, her teeth.

She squirmed against him, against the heavy, insistent
pulse of the body that had her anchored against the freezer.
He pulled back just enough to reclaim her mouth with his
and the dark swirl of desire washed over her, dragged her
down. He jerked her up higher, until she was completely off
the floor, her legs twined around his hips, his hand under her
bottom.

His other hand slipped under her t-shirt, swept up the
ladder of her ribs and closed hot and possessive on her
breast. A gasp rushed up in her throat, died there as he
cupped her in his palm, his fingers both gentle and tense. As
if he were torn between asking permission and giving
warning.

One finger dipped slowly into the lacy cup of her bra,
brushed past her nipple. An exquisite tremor shimmered into
her center and she clapped a hand over his, stilling his touch.
It was so strange and new to her. She'd never felt anything
like it—this odd, lazy hunger that compelled her to both
squirm and rush and pant, but also to taste and linger and
savor. Little shocks of pleasure still rippled away from his
finger, that simple and amazing touch, and her breathing
hitched as they moved away, bounced back and echoed.
God. What else could he do to her, she wondered? If he
could do that with one finger?

He pulled back far enough to look at her face. Far
enough for her to see the question there. The uncertainty.
The crazy reflection of her own desire in his eyes and just a
hint of smug self-satisfaction at having caused it.

Something sharp and broken twisted in Bel, cooling the
fever in her blood, allowing shame and fear the foothold it
had been seeking. God, what was she *doing*?

Way to teach him a lesson, Bel, she thought bitterly.
*Way to keep your head and make your point. Way to protect
yourself.*

But all wasn't lost. Maybe he wasn't deep, but James
was kind. And generous. She'd give him that. How else to

explain this pause, this question, this seeking of tacit approval before pressing his advantage?

And it *was* his advantage. Much as Bel would love to deny that, honesty compelled to her admit otherwise. He'd done exactly what he'd set out to do—spark a fire inside her. A fire that had nothing to do with furthering her goals. A dangerous fire that snapped and roared and threatened to devour everything she held sacred.

But Bel was no amateur when it came to Plan B. To protecting oneself at any cost. Because God knew nobody else out there was lining up to do it for her.

Even so, she hated herself for what she was about to do. But she'd spent the last twelve years of her life pursuing one goal and one goal only—to be Kate Davis, 2.0. And she was close. She was so close. The only thing standing between her and achieving that goal was James Blake and his *laissez-faire* attitude toward...well, everything. Which would be his own business except that Bel's own career had somehow fallen under James' *everything* heading. And there was only one way to get it out.

"Bel?" Very definitely a question this time, heavily laced with want. His hand was still warm and heavy on her breast, his arousal stark and unmistakable against her belly. "Is this okay?"

She peeped through her lashes at him, forced her lips to curve into a knowing smile. "Depends."

"On what?"

"On whether or not you're planning to give me what I want."

"Which is?" His smile was powerfully carnal and had lust rippling through her belly.

For the second time that day, the animal inside her surfaced. It slid through the lust in her belly, the fear in her heart. It prowled into her head and whispered *hide*. And for the second time that day, Bel did. She stripped everything from her face, from her eyes, from her body. She pulled it all back into a tiny, safe kernel deep inside her and left a husk in James' arms.

"I want my career back," she said tonelessly. "And I need your help."

His entire body tensed as if she'd struck him. Then he eased her to the floor, stepped back carefully. The desire vanished, leaving in its wake only a cool, shuttered regard. "I see. So you'll sleep with me if I perform like a trained dog every time Kate Davis jingles her little bell?"

She was conscious of a shameful disappointment, a vague loneliness as he stepped back, but it was distant. Separate. She was untouched and untouchable. She was safe.

"Of course." She lied with perfect sincerity. It wasn't a gift she was proud of, but the ability to feel one thing and project another had often been all that lay between her and utter doom. She wouldn't apologize for doing it well.

"And that doesn't make you feel cheap?"

She absorbed the lash of his anger objectively. Considered her answer. "Not really, no. I've sweated blood for this job. I want it more than anything and I'm willing to do whatever it takes to get it."

He stared at her.

"It wouldn't be a hardship," she offered. "Sleeping with you. After what just went on here, surely you know that." At his continued silence, she forced a light shrug. "At least I don't want your money, James. There's got to be some comfort in that. But I do want something. And if you'd be honest, you'd admit that you do, too. Your wants just happen to be a little less complex than mine. Now do you want to deal or don't you?"

Say no, she thought as the moment stretched out. As he considered her, that unexpected and thoughtful light in his eye. *Please God, say no.*

She reached out with a hand that she prayed wouldn't tremble and smoothed a wrinkle in his t-shirt. A wrinkle her greedy hands had surely put there. She forced herself to linger over the touch, to make it a temptation.

He reached up, took her hand in his. The shock of his skin against hers sent a pulse of awareness clear up to her shoulder and she closed her eyes against it. She didn't want to feel that anymore. Didn't want to feel anything.

151

Then he gently removed her hand from his shirt and stepped away from her. "Ah, no," he said. "I don't think so."

She tipped her head. "You're sure?"

"Yeah. Yeah, I think so." He regarded her with still green eyes until the urge to squirm was almost unbearable. "I think I'll turn in," he said, hooking a thumb toward the stairs. "It's been...quite a day."

She nodded, relief and gratitude a vague pang in the vicinity of her heart. She didn't look forward to unpacking all the feelings she'd shoved down these past few minutes. "Yeah. Well. See you in the morning?"

"Sure."

He ambled toward the stairs, lazy and loose, as if lust hadn't just exploded between them like a land mine. Bel sagged against the door of the freezer, exhausted. Then he turned back.

"Bel?"

She jerked herself straight. "Yes?"

"I'll behave for Kate. You don't need to screw me into submission."

"Oh. Okay."

"Just so you know."

She couldn't think of a thing to say. He turned and disappeared.

CHAPTER EIGHTEEN

James forced himself to walk into the foyer and up the stairs. It wouldn't do to have Bel come winging out of the kitchen only to find him propped against the wall like a shell-shocked accident victim.

But he damn sure felt like one.

He walked down the upper hall and slipped through the door to the suite of rooms he shared with his brothers. He sank into the huge leather couch—God, was he glad he'd ponied up for the biggest one available—and closed his eyes. Drew didn't look over. He was deep into a Wii tennis match and kicking ass, but Will dropped the sports section and lifted a brow.

"How was reform school?"

"Yeah, how was it?" Drew drilled a backhand down the line. "Did they exhaust you with their endless sexual demands?"

James didn't open his eyes. "You have no idea," he said. And they didn't. Hell, *he* didn't even know quite what he'd been through. Bel had laid it all out for him in frosty, precise syllables, but then she'd kissed him until his eyes were rolling around in his head like loose marbles. And then she'd capped it all off with a monstrous lie. Which meant there was only one thing a self respecting guy could do.

"Hey," James said. "Throw me a beer, would you?"

"Hell, no," Drew said. "I'm—ah, shit, look what you made me do." He glared at the screen and James knew that unless the TV actually fell off the wall his pleas for alcoholic refreshment would go unheeded.

"You look like hell," Will said.

"Yeah, thanks." James frowned at the coved ceiling. "I feel like it."

"Oh, come on. Time was, you could spend the entire day servicing reform school girls and still go out and ogle strippers that night."

"Bel kissed me," he said slowly.

Will stared at him, his clever face for once blank with surprise. "At *reform school*?"

James scowled at him. "No, Will. In the kitchen just now."

"Oh." The surprise faded and consideration took its place. "Bel kissed you. Huh."

"Damn it, James," Drew said, reaching for a volley. "I saw her first. I *called* her."

"What are we, ten?" James rolled his eyes. "You don't call women."

"Whatever." Drew gave James a quick once-over then smirked. "Wow. You *do* look like hell." He pulverized an overhead with a grunt of effort. "Like Wile E. Coyote after he rides that rocket off the cliff."

James thought for a moment. "That about sums it up."

Will winced on his behalf. "It was that bad a kiss?"

"No," James said. "That good."

"Oh," Will said. "Uh oh."

"Damn skippy," James said.

Drew sighed as his opponent dribbled a drop shot over the net. "Crap." He tossed aside the controller in disgust and flopped onto the couch next to James. "So. It was good, huh?"

"Great," James said. "Better than."

"I *knew* it." Drew slapped his knee, delighted. "That mouth."

"That mouth," James agreed mournfully.

"Shit," Will said.

"Exactly," James said.

Drew looked back and forth between them. "I do *not* understand you two. A girl James really likes just laid an epic kiss on him unprovoked. That's a *good* thing."

"I provoked her."

"Irrelevant." Drew laced his hands over his belly. "It's still good."

"Usually, sure. But not this time." Will shook his head. "Not with Bel."

"What's wrong with Bel?"

Will and James exchanged a look.

"Bel's...complicated," James finally said.

"So?"

"So I don't do complicated."

"Why not?"

Why not, indeed? James didn't believe for one minute that Bel was prepared to follow through on that ridiculous exchange she'd demanded. But he *did* believe she'd enjoyed kissing him as much as he'd enjoyed kissed her. And he'd enjoyed the ever-loving shit out of it. He could have spent all day exploring that long, elegant body of hers. And those lips—God, her lips—full and soft and curved in wicked knowledge. Her fingers, tangled in his hair, roving under his shirt and across his skin, pulling him closer. He was getting hot just thinking about it.

So why hadn't he called her bluff?

"Because sex is nothing to mess with," he said finally.

The look Drew gave him was palpably skeptical. "That's a new one coming from you."

"I'm serious," James said. "When it comes to women, you either understand what you're getting yourself into or you end up in a heap of trouble. And I don't understand Bel. At all. She's too—"

"Smart? Pretty? Talented? Successful?"

"I was going to say complicated."

"So you only sleep with the simple ones." Drew nodded sagely. "That sounds like fun. No missed opportunities there."

"Hey, I'm a simple man," James said. "I live by simple rules. I work at family and I work at soccer. Everything else—sex included—is either easy and casual, or skipped altogether. Because between my career—which as you both know is perilously close to the crapper—and my family— chock full of troublesome bastards—I'm already up to my ass. I don't have the time or the energy for complicated, okay?"

155

"Not even the kind of complicated that kisses you stupid?" Drew asked.

"Hey, plenty of girls have kissed me stupid," James said. "I don't have Will's great big brain. It's not that hard to do."

"But not like this," Drew said. "Bel's different."

"She didn't used to be." James frowned.

"No?" Drew leaned forward.

"No. She used to be...I don't know. She was just *Bel*, you know? All that snippy attitude coming out of that fallen-angel mouth?"

Drew nodded in perfect understanding. "Entertainment in its finest form."

Will shook his head. "Will you two listen to yourselves? *Fallen-angel mouth*? Jesus."

James scowled at him but Drew kicked his ankle. "So? What's so different now?"

"Something...happened."

"The kiss?"

"Maybe." Images swamped him. That trim, elegant body twisting with desire against his, that cool, alabaster skin flushed and plump in his hands. That bullet-proof composure of hers reduced to a ragged gasp he could feel against his lips.

He shook free of the memory and willed his blood to cool off a few degrees. Jesus. "Before she was just cute, you know? Fun. Handy. Now just looking at her lights my fuse. Every damn time. And I don't particularly want to look away."

Drew laughed. "You are so screwed."

"I know," James said. "But it gets worse."

"How could it possibly get worse?" Will asked.

"I don't want her to look away, either."

Drew and Will exchanged a baffled look. "What does that mean?"

James shifted, uncomfortable. But, hell, he needed help, and these were his brothers. The Blake family credo had been designed with just such miserable situations in mind. His fight was their fight, damn it. If there was a way to shake clear of this, Will's big brain and Drew's sensitive heart were going to find it for him. Whether they liked it or not.

"She disappeared on me today. Twice."

"She ditched you?" Will's brows shot up. "At reform school?"

"Not physically, no. But she was gone all the same. It happened once at the school, and once just now in the kitchen."

"What does that mean?" Will asked. "*Not physically*?"

James shrugged and studiously avoided eye contact. "She was there. Her body was, anyway. But I swear to God, there was nobody home. It was like she'd just, I don't know, vanished."

"Vanished." Drew frowned at the blank TV screen. "Huh."

James lifted empty hands. How could he possibly explain it? Twice today he'd looked to Bel for a reality check, for guidance. And both times, he'd found nothing there. He'd gone looking for the essence of her, the heart, the soul, the endless, seeking drive that defined her and found nothing but her empty eyes.

And he'd been startled to discover how much he missed her.

"And that bothered you?" Will asked. "Because you don't want her, how did you put it? Looking away?"

"No, I don't. I want her right here with me." He didn't hesitate, didn't consider. The words just popped out of his mouth, from the same dark slice of his unconscious that he relied on to predict which way a defender was going to zig so he could zag. "She's—" This one didn't come so easily. "—necessary, I guess."

"Necessary," Will repeated, his tone flat.

"Not in any unhealthy, co-dependent sort of way," James said quickly.

Drew laughed. "Somebody's been watching his *Dr. Phil*."

James glared at him. "Okay, maybe necessary is the wrong word. But I like her. She takes shots at me. She makes me think. It's like she expects my A game and if I don't bring it, she's not disappointed so much as disgusted. Because she thinks I'm better than that." He frowned into the middle distance, talking more to himself than his brothers now. "And I like the way she laughs, all rich and free and earthy. Girl who loves to iron like Bel shouldn't laugh like that. But she does, and I like how it feels when I'm the one who makes her do it. I like the way she never lets herself cry and how she's ruthless and hard and vulnerable all at the same time."

"James." Will dipped his chin and gave him a look from under beetled brows. "What the hell are you talking about?"

James shrugged, a little baffled himself. "Well, just now, for instance. She said she'd sleep with me if I'd butter up to Kate and get her job back."

"*What*?"

"But it was such a lie. She had to disappear just to get through telling it. But I'm not going to press her on it. Not right now, anyway. I have bigger problems."

"Damn straight," Will said.

"You don't have problems," Drew said.

James considered the condition of his career and his unexpected predicament with Bel. "I don't?"

"Yes," Will said. "You do." He glared at Drew. "He does."

"He doesn't," Drew said to Will. He turned to James. "It's not a problem," he said, grinning. "It's love."

James stared at him while the ring of truth reverberated through his entire body. "Oh, Christ."

Drew laughed. "This is awesome."

Will smiled grimly. "Awesome. Right."

Bel was in the kitchen studying her latest attempt at a whole-grain braided bread wreath when the doorbell rang. She jumped as Hank Williams' "Lovesick Blues" yodeled through the house. What on earth? She glanced at the skylight. It was fully dark, and had been for the several broody hours Bel had spent trying to bake her way out of the aftermath of that kiss. Who could possibly be ringing the bell?

Some friend of the Blake brothers', she imagined. Maybe they'd dialed Strippers R Us. Well, they could just get off their lazy duffs and answer it themselves. She was busy. Plus she was still pissed. At them. At James. At herself.

Mostly herself. She could admit that now. God, she'd been so smug. She thought she'd been so ready for it this time, all the heat and skill and *attention* James poured into kissing. Maybe the first one had rocked her world a little, but she'd been prepared for this one. And forewarned was forearmed and all that, right?

Wrong.

Because this kiss, unlike the first one, wasn't just an exercise in excellent kissing as performed by an expert. No, indeed. It had still broken over her head like a rogue wave, no argument. But it was no generic, I'm-a-boy-you're-a-girl-let's-have-fun sort of kiss. This time it was personal. Unequivocally so.

This time it was *James* kissing *Bel*. Watching her, touching her, absorbing her, cherishing her. Throw that on top of what her admittedly limited experience with such things led her to believe were masterly skills, and Bel was suddenly fumbling for landmarks on a previously well-lighted path. A path that led directly to her own custom-designed happy ever after, in which Prince Charming and the fairy godmother had been replaced by a well-diversified stock portfolio and a whole bunch of job security.

And that pissed her off. She'd worked herself ragged forging that path. Who the hell was James Blake to knock her off it?

The doorbell rang again. "Stand By Your Man." Bel snorted in disgust. Stand by your man, indeed. Ha. Like she was going to waste any time or energy standing by James Blake. Hadn't she just spent an hour this very afternoon explaining to him that his casual, no harm/no foul, we're all grownups here approach to sex was wrong? That it hurt vulnerable women? What possible excuse could she have for wanting to be one of those women?

159

The doorbell rang again—"I Fall to Pieces," fabulous— and Bel stomped out of the kitchen. First thing in the morning she was having a come to Jesus meeting with James and his brothers in which they would be made to understand that she was not their damn butler. She strode down the short hallway into the soaring foyer, still shaking her head in disgust, and pulled open the door.

Audrey Bing stood on the porch.

"Audrey?" She checked her watch. Ten past midnight. "What are you doing here?"

She gave Bel a grim smile. "Can we come in?"

We? Bel glanced down and found a suitcase at Audrey's knee and a little girl holding her hand. The girl gazed up at Bel, her face round and expressionless. No, Bel realized, her heart clutching. The kid had expression. She just didn't have any expectations. She watched Audrey and Bel with a dispassion that spoke of a lifetime—albeit a short one—of disappointed expectations and adults that didn't behave.

Bel looked back at Audrey and saw a bewildered, hunted weariness behind the perfect bones and the brash courage. She smiled at them both and reached for Audrey's suitcase.

"Of course," she said, leading them into the kitchen. She deposited them both on stools on the far side of the massive island counter. Audrey sat carefully, as if worried she might shatter if she moved too quickly. The child simply followed.

Bel's heart squeezed as she put on the kettle and took out a couple of china plates. She tore off two generous hunks of the bread wreath and reached into the fridge for a dish of whipped honey butter she'd made up earlier. She slid the plates under their noses.

"Eat," she said, keeping her voice carefully brisk, matter-of-fact. She knew exactly how frightening overly hearty strangers were to kids with eyes like those. "I'm going to tackle these dishes, then we'll see about making up a room for you two."

She ran a sink full of hot sudsy water and slowly washed and dried her measuring cups and spoons, her mixing bowls and loaf pans. She brushed the cornmeal off her bread stone that still radiated warmth and comfort, and tucked it back into the oven. Bel had some questions that surely needed answers, but getting this child fed and into bed came first.

Then she glanced at Audrey, whose head drooped on her slender neck like a flower after the rain.

She'd get her answers in the morning.

CHAPTER NINETEEN

Will missed the old days. He held the memory of them in his heart like a warm pebble, heating him up from the inside out as he padded down the chilly stairs in the half-light of early morning. The days when they all rolled out of bed at the civilized hour of ten and a motherly housekeeper with a tidy British accent had mugs of coffee steaming in their hung over hands by 10:05.

God, he missed that housekeeper. Mrs. Brimley. Now *there* was a domestic diva. Somebody sweet and round and unflappable. Somebody who didn't frown or criticize or judge or *fix*. Somebody who wouldn't balk at meeting last night's stripper over this morning's breakfast.

Somebody who sure as hell wouldn't go around kissing her clients. Bel could take a memo on that one. Because whatever she'd done to James yesterday had him twisted up but good. Good enough that he'd been up at dawn, banging around in his room for several extremely loud minutes before finally (to Will's everlasting relief) locating his running shoes and trotting off down the drive.

Not that Will believed Drew's bullshit about love for one minute. It wasn't love. That was fairytale foolishness. But it *was* something. Something worrisome enough to have a full two-thirds of the Blake brothers up well before their preferred hour.

And Will knew exactly where to place the blame.
Bel.

The least she could do was be awake and in the kitchen when he got there. Preferably with a pot of coffee already brewing, because he hated to yell at people first thing in the morning without the benefit of caffeine.

He idly calculated the odds of this happening as he hit each chilly step with his bare feet. The probability that she was already awake times the probability that she was in the kitchen times the probability that she, as a tea drinker, would have thought to brew a pot of coffee. It wasn't a complex equation but the results were damned depressing.

He pushed through the swinging door into the kitchen. At this point, he'd settle for opening the pantry and finding some Lucky Charms. The cereal shelf had become decidedly fiber-focused since Bel's arrival. He'd have to speak to James' new assistant about that.

He smirked to himself in the dimness. Assistant. Ha. He had to hand it to James. He had a knack for lining up the pretty women to do his bidding. Too bad he was so twisted up over Bel. Shame to put the curvy little stripper on the back burner. He'd take a crack at her himself except that she was what, twelve? And the fact that he'd looked closely enough to notice had him feeling more than a little skeevy. And every one of his thirty years.

He slowed as he approached the island counter. A cloth-covered basket sat in the center, with a note pinned to it that read *Eat Me*. Will squinted at Bel's clean, elegant printing. Obvious reference to Alice in Wonderland, yes, but also a sneaky little kiss off to the next guy who stomped into her kitchen looking for a fight.

Eat me. An unwilling smile tugged at the corners of his lips as he uncovered the basket. Bel might be a pain in the butt, but she was sharp. He'd give her that.

And, he was suddenly willing to admit, she was damn good at what she did. The scent of sugar and butter and cinnamon rose up and curled around him like a lover and he helped himself to a cinnamon roll the size of his fist.

He chewed blissfully, his mood going the same direction as his blood sugar. He was headed for the coffee maker when a tiny noise had him turning to peer into the shadows behind the kitchen door. When he registered what he was seeing, shock had him accidentally swallowing an uncomfortably large chunk of half-chewed sweet roll. Because, damn and what the hell, there was a *kid* over there.

She sat in what Bel called the breakfast nook—a sort of built-in bench-and-table deal in the space behind the

163

swinging door. Nobody used it because the island counter was so much more appealing, but she'd squirreled herself away back there. Barricaded herself, actually. It was as if she'd made herself a little fortress of it and stared at him from the safety of its walls.

"What the hell?" Will said. She gazed at him with enormous eyes, the fragile bones of her face pressed tightly against parchment paper skin, a pair of delicate hands frozen above another of Bel's gooey hunks of cinnamon goodness. He pressed a fist to the wad of dough lodged in his chest and tried to think of something more appropriate to say. Because judging from her silence, the kid wasn't biting on his opener.

"Who are you?" he finally managed. It seemed like an appropriate if not particularly polite question. "And what on God's green earth are you doing in here?"

She continued the silent staring but her hands flew into action like startled birds. She folded up the edges of the paper napkin she'd been eating from, bundled away the remains of her roll and deposited it neatly on the edge of the table, ready for trash pickup.

Will watched, struck. Those hands. Those skinny wrists. He frowned at her. "Do I know you?"

She shook her head hard and scooted off the bench.

"Hey, wait!" Will scrambled around the island counter and caught her by one bony elbow before she could disappear. "You're not going anywhere. Not until you tell me who you are and what you're doing in my kitchen."

She turned and glared at him, fury and terror and hate exploding behind those giant eyes and a shock of recognition stabbed through Will, all the way to his bare toes.

He wasn't at all surprised when Audrey Bing flew through the door next, a raggedy t-shirt skimming high on a pair of gloriously naked thighs. A t-shirt that barely—sadly—covered her world-class backside. And yeah, Will felt like a lech for even noticing. He ought to be several years past lusting over women who couldn't legally drink.

"Let go of her!" She snatched the child out of Will's already slack grip and glared at him. Which made two pairs of matching violet eyes drilling him with their laser beams of anger and dislike.

Will held up his empty hands in surrender and backed away slowly. Audrey pressed the kid to her chest—a pang of envy Will would have preferred to skip raced through him at the sight—then pulled away and looked down into the child's face. "Are you all right, honey? He didn't hurt you, did he?"

The kid shook her head slowly and Audrey brought a hand up to her thin cheek. "Just scared you, then."

The kid glanced at Will, assessing this time. She turned back to Audrey and rolled a shoulder as if to say *nothing serious*. Audrey tucked the kid under her arm and turned contemptuous eyes on Will.

"Don't you ever," she said, each word flash-frozen and carefully enunciated so as to prevent any possible misunderstanding, "*ever* put your hands on this child again."

Will stared at her. He'd been well aware that Audrey Bing was an ethereally, incandescently beautiful woman. No surprises there. And while some women became exponentially less attractive when pissed, Audrey, sadly, wasn't one of them. Will had learned that one first hand on a few different occasions now.

But he'd never seen her in a killing fury before. Not like this. Logically, a woman gunning for blood ought to put a guy off. At the very least, it ought to dampen a smart man's libido. And while his brain had never failed Will before, it failed him now.

He opened his mouth to respond but nothing fired. No words presented themselves, no dry, cutting rejoinder the likes of which he'd always prided himself on. He couldn't look at her and think all at the same time. It was too much.

He finally tore his eyes away and muttered, "I wasn't molesting her. Jesus." He winced inwardly. God. Could he possibly sound any sulkier or more defensive?

"I'm serious," Audrey snapped. "You don't touch her. Not for any reason."

He forced himself to focus on tiny imperfections in her face and figure. The imprint of the sheet on her cheek. The weed whacker scramble of her moonlight hair. Anything to lessen the monstrous impact of standing two feet from her barely covered curves and the terrible beauty of her face.

"My apologies," he said, a deliberately mocking edge to his voice. "I wasn't aware that we'd experienced an infestation of free-range children over night. She surprised me." He shifted his gaze to the child. God, how old *was* this kid? She was tiny but those eyes were ancient and wise and incredibly sad. "As I'm sure I did her."

Again, the thin shoulder twitched up and down, an acknowledgement or possibly a non-verbal *whatever*.

"But I'd still like to know who she is and what exactly she's doing here." Will brought his eyes back to Audrey's, prepared this time for the breath-stealing punch of that face of hers. "And you. Last time I checked, you were an hourly employee. When it comes to making our lives a regimented and nutritionally sound snoozefest, Bel has the night shift."

Audrey gave that same impatient shoulder twitch, one more nail in the coffin Will was building in his head. "Things have changed. I'll be discussing my new terms with your brother this morning."

"Interesting," Will said, careful to ensure that his tone would imply just the opposite. "And this?" He gestured to the child.

"This," Audrey said, her chin hiked into the air, disdain oozing from her perfect pores, "is Jillian. She's eight years old and she's—" She broke off, glanced down at the child and lightly fluffed her silvery hair. Hair only a few tones lighter than Audrey's own. She looked back at Will and said simply, "She's mine."

"Yours." In spite of everything—the hair, the eyes, those bony, fragile little wrists—he mustered up a skeptical look. "And you're how old?"

She gazed at him, temper still licking in her eyes but banked now. Under control. "Twenty-two."

He'd always liked math. It was so rigid, so predictable. So unflinching. Emotion simply didn't factor in. Or so he'd always thought. Right up until he did the inevitable calculation—the one she must've seen in thousands of eyes over the years—and arrived at the conclusion that she'd given birth at fourteen.

He knew it happened. It was a sad story, no question, but one he'd heard before. What shocked him was the dark stab of helpless fury that lodged itself in his gut. The miserable, impotent rage of knowing that some sick bastard had taken such vicious advantage of a child. Any child, of course. But the child Audrey must have been? Her body slim and unformed and graceful, her face already glowing like some kind of fucking star?

"Mine," she said firmly. "Any other questions you want to ask that are none of your business?"

"I do have a few," he said, but broke off when Bel burst through the door. Even panting and flushed from what he assumed was her sprint down the stairs, she still managed to exude an air of calm competence.

"Good morning, Will. I see you've met Jillian," she said, her voice as smooth as her glossy ponytail.

"Yep," Will said. "Audrey and I were just talking about how exactly she came to have an eight-year-old—"

He broke off again as James shoved through the door, red-cheeked and sucking wind. "Good lord," he said, and bent at the waist. "It's a party." He patted Bel on the leg. It was all he could reach, Will could see that. Nothing personal but Bel still jumped about out of her skin.

"Water," he said. "Please."

Bel moved toward the sink with an alacrity that had a grim satisfaction moving through Will. Maybe she'd tied James up in knots, but at least she wasn't enjoying it. Looked like she had a few knots of her own to untangle. Which she deserved.

She thrust a glass of water into James' seeking hand. He straightened up, drained it in one long swallow and plopped down on the tile floor to stretch.

"God," he said, going to work on his hamstrings. "When did I get this old? I used to run ten miles for fun. I got to six today before I decided I didn't feel like barfing before breakfast."

He grinned up at the assembled crowd. "Hey, Audrey," he said. "You're early today." He turned his attention to Will. "You, too. What's got you out of bed at this hour?"

"There was this ungodly racket in the room next to mine about an hour ago," he said. "You can't imagine. Impossible to sleep through."

James' grin widened. "How rude. You ought to speak to the management. She's up early, too."

Bel put up her hands. "Not my issue. I don't deal with that wing of the house."

James stood and grabbed the island counter for balance while he worked on his quads. "Out of luck, I guess. Too bad." He turned his attention to Jillian. "Hey, who's this?" He gave her his usual high-wattage smile, as if finding a silent eight-year-old in his kitchen along with half his family and most of his staff at seven a.m. was par for the course.

Audrey drew the child closer to her side. "This is Jillian."

"Hey, Jillian." James switched legs. "I'd shake but I'm disgusting. Did I mention I ran six miles?"

Will rolled his eyes and Jillian nodded, a faint smile flickering at the corners of her mouth. Audrey knelt down and took her by the shoulders.

"Jillian, do you mind going back upstairs with Bel for a few minutes? I need to speak with James."

The little girl glanced at Bel, who smiled encouragingly at her. She kept her hands to herself, though, Will noticed. Something he kind of wished he'd done himself, now. The kid's wide-eyed silence was starting to put another kink in his stomach, the kind he'd felt when he'd done Audrey's math a minute ago. What had happened to this kid? And why the hell hadn't her mother, who by God ought to know better by now, protected her?

"I need to get dressed," Bel said to Jillian. "You want to help me pick out something to wear? I can never decide."

Jillian turned uncertain eyes on Audrey who nodded firmly. "Bel's okay," she said. "She'll take good care of you. I'll be up in a minute."

Jillian gave that one-shouldered shrug again and followed Bel out the door. Bel caught Audrey's eye as they left and gave her the same smile she'd just given the child, a smile that said *courage*. Will wondered what the hell was going on.

Then Audrey turned cold eyes on him. "Do you mind?" she asked. "I'd like a word with your brother in private."

Will had expected that, but it still stung. He'd beaten James into the world by two years and had spent the next twenty-eight coming in second. With sports, with women, with success. James was, he willingly admitted, a more likeable, talented guy. He'd accepted that long ago. So why did it suddenly chafe just because a pretty teenaged mother shoved his nose in it?

Will didn't have an answer for that one, nor did he want one.

"I don't think so," he said. "As James' manager, I'm required to sit in on all negotiations concerning terms of employment."

Audrey looked to James, who shrugged easily. "It's true," he said. "I know you and Will haven't exactly gotten along in the past, but you're both part of Team Blake now, so we're going to have to put all that behind us. Time to cowboy up."

Audrey cut her eyes back to Will, a clear *yeah, right* in her face. Will smiled at her.

James finally stopped stretching. "Damn. I'm going to be one sorry son of a bitch tomorrow morning when my muscles figure out what just happened." He spotted the basket on the island counter and his eyes lit up. "Are those Bel's cinnamon rolls? Hot damn and don't mind if I do. Because I ran six miles today. Did I mention that?"

He pulled out a stool and applied himself to a sweet roll. "Now," he said. "Audrey. What's going on?"

CHAPTER TWENTY

James watched an epic struggle play out over Audrey Bing's pretty face while he chewed thoughtfully on a big hunk of Bel's incredible cinnamon roll.

"Can I take five minutes to get dressed?" she finally asked.

"Not going to help," James said. "Take it from a master procrastinator. Better to just get it out." He glanced at his brother, who stood glowering at the poor girl. What on earth did Will have against this woman? He'd have to press him on that later. In the meantime, he didn't mind evening the playing field a little.

"Will," he said, "give Audrey your robe, would you?"

Will frowned at him. "What?"

"Your robe," he said. "Give it to her. She's clearly got a lot at stake here and is feeling vulnerable in her nightie. You've got flannels on, I can see them from here. Give the girl your robe."

Will set his jaw and peeled off his robe. Audrey stared at it like it might bite her.

"Go on," James said. "It ought to cover you straight down to your ankles. Then we can talk."

Audrey grabbed the robe and stuffed her arms into it, like a kid bolting down a dreaded mouthful of peas. Will watched her, his arms folded across his bare chest, something between distaste and fascination in his eyes. James suppressed a smile. Wasn't that interesting? Will, eternally cool, urbane and self-possessed Will, with that kind of confused emotion kicking around inside over a pretty little waitress?

Audrey cinched the belt tight around her waist and stuffed her hands deep into the pockets. "I need to change the terms of my employment," she said.

"You're not happy?" Will arched a sardonic brow.

She glared at him. "Working here was, as you well know, a last resort. One I was forced into by you and your spoiled, selfish behavior."

"Point taken," James said.

Will smiled. "I'll rephrase. You're not happy with the terms we worked out to our mutual satisfaction just last week?"

Audrey fixed her eyes on James, ignored Will completely. "Circumstances have changed," she said. "I'm requesting room and board for me and Jillian. With a correspondingly adjusted salary, of course."

"Of course," James murmured. "Do you mind if I ask why?"

"My previous living arrangements recently became...untenable," she said.

"Untenable how?" Will asked. Damn, James thought. With the bare chest and the air of command, his brother was coming perilously close to the territory Yul Brenner had staked out in *The King and I*. But it was a fair question, so when Audrey looked to him, he let it stand.

"We were staying with a woman I worked with at the strip club you guys like so much, but her boyfriend...didn't care for the arrangement."

Interesting, James thought. "Didn't care for your not sleeping with him?" he asked.

Audrey gave him a grim smile. "Something like that."

"I know what James is paying you, Audrey," Will said. "Don't tell me you can't afford not to shack up with strippers and their scumbag boyfriends."

She cast him a disdainful look. "There are extenuating circumstances."

"Such as?" There Will went with the eyebrow again. Audrey looked like she wanted to tear it off with her bare hands. But again, it was a good question so he let it go.

"Jillian has...special needs," she finally said.

James tipped his head. "Looked bright enough to me."

"She is. More than enough. Way more. Her IQ is in the 180s, which in case you were wondering is about 40 points north of genius."

"But?"

"But she doesn't talk."

"At all?"

Audrey shook her head. "She used to. She still writes and reads, though. Lord, does she read. She blew through the entire Harry Potter series in about an hour last week." She hunched her shoulders. "But she doesn't talk."

"Why not?"

"I don't know."

"How could you not know?" Will asked. James looked up, surprised at the harshness of his tone. "I mean seriously," he went on. "An eight-year-old kid with a genius IQ suddenly stops talking and you don't know why? You don't know what happened? You were too busy slinging drinks to *notice*?"

"Jesus, Will," James put a hand out toward Audrey. "I'm so sorry, Audrey. I don't know what gets into him sometimes. You'd never know it to look at my brother here but we were raised better than that. Will, I think you owe the lady an apology."

"Hell, no," Will said. "I'm on the kid's side on this one. If anybody's getting an apology, it ought to be her." He fixed Audrey with a hard look. "And it ought to come from her mother."

"You're damn straight," Audrey said, her eyes bright and burning. "The minute I find her, I'll demand one. Until then, do you think you could keep your judgment to yourself for ten stinking minutes so I can deal with your brother on getting the child a more stable home life?"

"I think," James said into the vibrating silence that followed, "we'd best start at the beginning."

The following Sunday evening Will watched Bel carry a roasted chicken into the formal dining room where Team Blake/West would receive its weekly judgment. She set it on the table with an air of reverence, as if a well laid table and a platter full of meat was something sacred.

Which, okay, it probably was. Especially a chicken like this one. Dark and glossy with some sort of maple glaze, giving off a smell that was hospitality itself, it practically demanded that a guy sit down, give thanks and dig in. It was invitation, welcome and generosity, all wrapped up in one delicious, oven-roasted package.

A package Will would have accepted quite happily had it not been for the palpable disdain being laser beamed across the table toward him by Audrey Bing. A disdain that should have completely and mercifully erased the awful want this woman had stirred up in his gut. Should have, but didn't.

At all.

Evidently, she was still pissed about his assumption that she was not only a mother but a crappy one at that. And unfortunately for Will, she was turning out to be a world-champion grudge holder.

Well, screw that. Given the evidence at hand, any rational, thinking person would have jumped to the same conclusion.

Except James, said a little voice in his head. *James didn't*.

James. Will mentally rolled his eyes. Of course James didn't draw conclusions or make assumptions. He didn't have to. All James had to do was put the ball in the goal and he was a goddamn hero. At least you'd think so, judging from the way Audrey gazed at him, all limpid-eyed and grateful.

Will gazed at his empty wine glass and wished like hell Bel would just hurry up and serve the bird so he could have a damn drink.

Jillian walked into the dining room after Bel, her tiny face grave with the responsibility of transporting a heaping bowl of golden mashed potatoes. She slid them onto the table next to Kate, who blinked at the child in mild astonishment.

See? Will thought. *The kid's surprising when you're not expecting her*. He hoped Kate would say something inappropriate, just so he could feel better about his own trip down foot-in-mouth lane.

Bel glanced at Kate's face and said quickly, "Oh, darn it, I forgot the rolls. They're in a basket on the counter. Could you grab them, please, Jillian?"

The girl returned to the kitchen and Kate lifted her brows at Bel. "When did you resort to child labor?"

"I didn't," Bel said.

Kate turned to James. "Have you been hit with a paternity suit, then?"

"No, ma'am," he said. "Though you aren't the first one to mistake the girl's parentage." He smirked at Will, pushing the rage and shame that had been simmering in his chest for days up to a rolling boil.

Will picked up the wine bottle and the cork screw. "I'll just let this breathe," he said to nobody in particular. Nerves danced in his blood, hummed in his veins. His glass was empty and his chest was full and one of those two situations needed changing. Since leaking off some of that frustration and regret and that stupid unwanted *want* wasn't really a viable option, he was going to open the damn wine. Then drink it all.

"Jillian's mine." Audrey folded her hands in her lap and gave Kate a cool gaze.

"Mmm hmm," Kate said. "Your what, dear? Because while I can certainly see the resemblance, I'm not prepared to believe that you gave birth in elementary school."

"No," Audrey said. Will didn't have to look up to know her eyes were on him, hard with dislike. "I didn't. Thank you for the benefit of the doubt."

The cork popped free of the bottle, sending a surge of relief through Will. Salvation was at hand. Or at least oblivion.

"Jillian is my niece," she said. "My sister's daughter."

"I see." Kate smiled politely. "And she's visiting you?"

"No. She lives with me. My sister isn't what you'd call—" Audrey indulged in a brief, speaking pause. "— stable."

Kate's eyebrows headed for her hairline. "I see," she murmured again, her tone making it clear that Jillian's mother must be some kind of unholy mess if a twenty-two-year-old cocktail waitress was more stable.

Exactly, Will thought. *And I'm the bad guy for saying it out loud?*

But he hadn't just said it out loud. He'd said it out loud to Audrey. And he hadn't stopped there. He'd gone on to lay the blame for Jillian's current emotional crisis at her feet. Pile that on top of his earlier determination to fuck up her job prospects just because he was feeling bitter, and he had to admit it. He'd earned it. He'd earned every bit of the hate that blazed in her eyes every time she looked at him. Which wasn't often. She avoided it when she could.

"I asked Audrey if she'd consider a live-in position," James said to Kate. "I didn't think I'd care for live-in help but then Bel moved in and I decided I liked having round-the-clock access to her."

"That's true," Will said. "He speaks quite, ah, warmly about their midnight meetings in the kitchen." He gave Bel a toothy smile. She glared at him, but a flush crept up her cheeks.

James shrugged easily. "And with Audrey, I got a bonus." He beamed at Jillian as she returned with the bread basket. "Two handy girls for the price of one."

Jillian ducked her head, shyly pleased, and put her basket on the table. She took the chair between Bel and Audrey, who sent James a grateful glance. A sliver of jealousy wedged itself deep into Will's chest. James the hero. Again.

"Let's be grateful," Bel said and heads bowed all around the table for grace.

Definitely time to pour the wine.

"I have to admit," Kate said after Bel had cleared the table and filled her coffee cup. "You two have stepped up your game considerably since last week."

Her approval didn't ease the tension in Bel's stomach but James said, "Thanks. We can't take all the credit, though. The girls really outdid themselves on the cakes, didn't they, Bel?"

Bel gave him a wooden smile. "You bet." Because they had. Right after they'd stopped trying to kill each other and/or trap James into a compromising position behind the mixer. "The new Mr. and Mrs. Hartford were extremely happy with their work."

"Who would have guessed it?" Kate said, a light smile on her lips, something faint and displeased in her eyes. "That a team that fell apart serving cake to society matrons would hit its stride at reform school?"

Bel's stomach clenched even tighter. Kate hated it when reality failed to conform to her expectations, whether for better or worse. She'd clearly expected Bel and James to flame out with even greater drama at the reform school than at the wedding hall and was not at all pleased to find that she'd failed to accurately predict an outcome.

Which meant, Bel feared, that they'd won the battle only to have it cost them the war. Or at least set them up for an epic battle from which they would never recover. Her mouth went dry and she twisted her fingers together in her lap as she waited for Kate to just drop the bomb already. What on earth could she have waiting for them that would top spending a week in reform school?

Audrey stood up abruptly. "If you'll excuse us?" she said. "Jillian really ought to be in bed."

"Of course," Kate said. "Good night, dear."

Bel breathed a sigh of relief as Audrey disappeared up the stairs with Jillian. Not that Bel didn't like Audrey, but having her and Will at the same table was like trying to eat a nice supper around a downed electrical wire. Between their silent hostility, waiting for Kate to render a verdict, and Will's customary headfirst dive into the wine bottle, Bel's nerves were about shot.

"So," Kate said, setting down her coffee and folding her hands. "You've pulled it off. Passing marks for you both. Bravo."

"Thank you," Bel said. She lifted her coffee cup to her lips, though she couldn't force a single bitter swallow down her throat.

"Thanks," James said. "But again, those girls were something else. Really brave and strong and determined to do whatever it took to better themselves."

"Or whoever," Will mumbled.

"Exactly," James said. "Those girls would do anything—or yes, anybody, Will—to improve their circumstances, no matter how unpleasant. It was a privilege to help them redirect that determination into healthier channels."

Kate gazed at him in surprise. "That's very insightful, James."

"Not my insight." He patted Bel's knee under the table, sending an unwelcome shock straight up her thigh. She gave him a tight smile and shifted away from his hand. "Bel's. We had a pretty heated exchange after that first day at the school and it really gave me a—"

"Hard on," Will said.

"Oh my God," Bel said, closing her eyes while shock and humiliation piled onto her already strained system.

"Fresh perspective," James said to Kate. He ignored Will with the ease of long practice. "I was going to say fresh perspective."

"Of course," Kate murmured.

"Right." Will slouched in his chair, his wine glass cupped in a protective hand, his smile hard and bright. "Didn't I say that?"

"You can shut up now," James told him mildly.

Will held up a hand in surrender. "Sorry. Bad habit, telling the truth all the time. I'm working on it."

"Work harder." James turned back to Kate. "As I was saying, Bel really opened my eyes. She has such an empathy, an honest and personal connection with those girls. Almost

177

like she felt what they felt, had been where they are. Seeing them together was a real revelation."

James' thoughtful green gaze rested on her and the knots in Bel's stomach twisted unbearably as she finally admitted it—she'd been suckered. That happily shallow vibe he cultivated? A total sham. Granted, he'd raised it to an art form—those pulled-taffy vowels, that lazy amble, that wicked smile—but still. Bel had clawed her way out of chaos and neglect through hard work and attention to detail. Seeing what other people didn't was practically her religion. So how on earth had she failed to notice a dangerously perceptive man playing dumb?

"I can't take credit for James' work," Bel said, giving him a small, grim smile. She switched her gaze to Kate and amped up the wattage. "He's really taking his responsibility as an adult and a role model seriously. He demonstrated an unexpected and remarkable ability to downplay his celebrity and put the focus on the skills. I think everybody was really enriched by the experience."

She forced the words out, barely managing not to gag on them. Because while she believed this past week actually had enriched James, forcing him to behave like the man she suspected he really was, it hadn't enriched Bel. Just the opposite, in fact. All her reserves of strength and self-control had been used up just walking into and out of that place every day. She had nothing left to pour into the effort it took to resist this uncontrollable fire James had set within her.

Because the kiss she'd been stupid enough to ask for had ignited something inside her. Something awful and dangerously hungry. Something that lit her up like a lightning strike on the rain-starved prairie, a brilliant slash of light and color, and then the raging, consuming flame. She'd exhausted herself digging trenches and firebreaks all week, but the fire just kept leaping ahead of her defenses.

But lust wasn't the big problem here. Bel knew that. It was more that the lust was all tangled up with this odd, restless yearning she'd never experienced before. A hunger, maybe. No, a craving. An intense and unbearable craving that she had to satisfy or lose her mind.

A craving for James. Not for his body, either. No, it was worse than that. She didn't just want his touch, his kiss. She wanted his company. His companionship. His friendship. His...affection? Oh lord. A cold sweep of knowledge rushed through her.

His heart. She wanted his goddamn heart. The girl who believed love was nothing but a pretty excuse for being irrational wanted his love.

She resisted the moan of distress that edged up her throat. Good lord, what was *wrong* with her? What was she *thinking*? She was going to take her eye off the ball she'd been chasing since high school because she was experiencing warm feelings toward a charming athlete?

She gave herself a stern mental slap. *Get it together, Bel. You're so close. Just...focus, all right? Get it together and finish it out.*

She fixed her eyes on Kate's and said, "We're really pleased with our performance and hope you are, too."

"I am," Kate said, reluctant approval curving her lips. "Surprisingly so. As I said, I didn't expect this level of self-awareness from Mr. Blake, nor this show of flexibility from you. But I trust you'll find both those qualities quite handy during this final challenge."

"Final challenge?" Bel lifted her brows in polite expectation though anxiety did a little dance inside her chest. "I thought we had two more tasks to go."

"Technically you do." Kate folded her hands with satisfaction and Bel's muscles tensed warily. James' hand found her knee under the table again, gave it a warm, reassuring squeeze that, interestingly, dampened the flutter of nerves instead of causing them. She wondered vaguely how that was possible. "However, given the scope of the challenge I have in mind, I'm inclined to give you double credit for pulling it off. Plus you'll likely need a full two weeks to prepare and execute."

"Yeah?" James kicked back, hooked an elbow over the back of his chair and gave Kate a slow, lazy smile. "So what is it? Are we parachuting into Iraq with fresh muffins for the troops? Baking bread with orphans? Producing

Thanksgiving dinner over a barrel fire with some homeless guys?"

"No," Kate said, her smile cold and sharp. "You'll be throwing a ball."

CHAPTER TWENTY-ONE

James blinked at her. "We're what?"

"Throwing a ball." Kate gave him that icy smile of hers and took a sip of coffee. "It's a fancy party involving dancing."

"Thank you," James said. "But I understood the word."

Beside him, Bel cleared her throat. "You want us to throw the Fox Hunt Ball." It didn't sound like a question.

James frowned at her. "The what now?"

Kate beamed at Bel. "Clever girl. Indeed I do."

"A little help?" James turned baffled eyes on Bel.

"The Fox Hunt Ball," Bel said slowly. "It's a tradition in this part of Virginia—hunt season opens with a black tie ball."

"Hunt season?" James rolled the words around in his mouth. "As in red coats and panting dogs and horns and horses all pounding through the woods after some scrawny little fox?"

"Yes."

"Great," James said. "Good thing I left England."

"It's an annual tradition dating back hundreds of years," Kate said. "It's the premier social event of the season in this part of the country and it raises a great deal of money for charity."

"Kate throws the ball at Hunt House," Bel told him. "She's been doing it for years."

"Which means that the bones of the event are already in place," Kate said. "All you and James need to do is fill in the blanks."

"Which are?" James asked.

"Well, the catering, of course. We've contracted with our usual company, but menus need to be finalized, servers instructed and trained, personal touches." Kate waved a vague hand. "You know, details."

"I do know," Bel said with a grimness that made James wonder if she'd actually been the one handling them in years past.

"I'm sure Bel will see to them with her usual efficiency. You won't need to worry about that piece of it."

"Well, that's a relief," James said.

"Then there's usually some kind of act or entertainment. A raffle or a silent auction or, goodness, anything really." Kate smiled serenely. "As long as it's in good taste and valuable enough to inspire loosened purse strings."

"Uh huh." James looked across the table at his brothers, then down the table at his agent who'd been absolutely and uncharacteristically silent all evening. All three of them regarded Kate with varying degrees of wariness. Yeah, James kind of got that vibe himself. "And who's in charge of coming up with that bit?"

Kate sparkled at him. "Why, you are."

"I am?"

"Of course. And I'm sure you'll do it marvelously. You're quite a remarkable young man, James."

Will made an abrupt noise of disgust. He threw back the last of his wine and rose. "And that's about all the James worship I can take for one evening. My stomach, you know. It's sensitive. You'll excuse me." He shoved in his chair and stalked out of the room. James frowned after him. Will had always been prickly but this was getting uncomfortable. He glanced a question at Drew, who lifted his shoulders.

"You're a bit spoiled, perhaps," Kate mused, unconcerned by Will's sudden departure, "but that was to be expected, given how early and easily success has come to you."

"I don't guess I ever thought of it as easy," James said.

Kate went on as if he hadn't spoken. "The benefit being, I suppose, that you have time to grow out of it. Especially if you continue to force yourself into the occasional bout of introspection."

James glanced at Bel who studied the tablecloth with ferocious concentration. "Or hire somebody who forces me into it."

"Whatever works." Kate patted his hand briskly. "That insight along with your athletic ability and your undeniable..." She squinted thoughtfully at him. "I suppose *charm* is the word I'm looking for."

"Thank you, ma'am," James said humbly.

She gave him a sharp look. "Neither of which you earned, both of which you've been content to employ solely to indulge your and your brothers' every whim."

James wiped the grin from his face and tried to look appropriately remorseful.

"What I am providing you with, James, is the opportunity to take the gifts God gave you and for the first time put them to work for somebody other than yourself. I'm offering you the chance to be not just a decent man but a good human being. To have a positive impact on the world, to connect with real people in a meaningful and lasting way. I do hope you'll take this seriously."

"Yes, ma'am," James said. He glanced at Bel, her gorgeous mouth pursed into a worried little knot, the light from the chandelier playing on her bent, shiny head. The urge to cup his palm around the back of that slender neck, to bring her lips to his, to soothe away that stiff unhappiness was nearly overwhelming. "I plan to."

After dinner, Bob saw Kate back to Hunt House like the gentleman he was. He walked beside her along the crushed shell path that edged the pond while the moonlight limned her pale hair. They climbed the gentle rise toward Hunt House, and that moonlight just kept sliding down. It touched her sharp cheekbones, the straight length of her nose, the delicate curve of her lips.

"You're perfect," he said.

"Excuse me?" She turned to him, one brow arched in pleased surprise.

"You are," he said. "In the moonlight. That face of yours. It's like you were made by a master craftsman."

"Why, Bob. That's lovely."

He shook his head and continued walking. "Good thing, too. You're no spring chicken, but the camera still loves you."

She laughed and fell in beside him. "And here I thought you were getting sentimental in your old age."

He shrugged. "I am. Didn't I just tell you you were beautiful?"

"You did."

"There you go, then."

They walked on in silence, the night air moving gently in the leaves overhead. Kate stopped at the French doors that opened from her office into the back yard. She cocked a brow, her lips curved with a faint wickedness.

"Should I invite you in?"

Bob shook his head slowly. "You know where I stand on that."

"Oh, for heaven's sake." She rolled her eyes. "Not this again."

"Yep. Just old fashioned, I guess."

"You," Kate said, wrapping her hands in his lapels and pulling him in for a slow, lingering kiss, "are the furthest thing from old fashioned that's ever made a mess of my bed."

Bob swallowed hard and gathered up the scattered ashes of his resolve. God, that mouth of hers. "I'm getting too old for sex without commitment, Kate."

"I gave you a commitment," she said. "When I retire, we'll be together."

"Invite me in again when you retire, then. I'll say yes. Until then?" Bob stepped back from her greedy hands. "I can wait."

She followed him, slid one warm hand up the plane of his chest, her pout heart-stoppingly close to his mouth. "What if I can't?"

He took her hand off his chest, held it in his. It felt nice there. Not as nice as it had on his chest, but still good. Like he was courting her. Because, damn it, he was. Even if it killed him.

"So," he said brightly, "Bel and James seem to be making good progress. It was a rocky start but it looks like they're going to make it after all."

She frowned. "Well, I certainly hope so." But Bob wondered. Was that a trace of reluctance under her customary briskness?

"You have doubts?"

"Well, no. Of course not." She fluttered an impatient hand. "When Bel finishes up this last task to my satisfaction I can retire and we can be together. I want her to succeed more than anybody. You know that."

Bob gave her a shrewd look. "Do I? You've been testing her mettle for three years now and don't look any closer to retirement to me. Anybody else would have told you to stuff it by now."

She drew herself up. "Are we still talking about Bel?" she asked stiffly. "Or has this conversation taken an ugly and unnecessary turn?"

"But Bel," Bob went on patiently as if Kate hadn't spoken, "she wants this. She wants it more than anything. It's all she's ever known how to want as far as I can tell. You've been hinting at an imminent retirement for three seasons now. It's time, Kate. For you to pull it away now?" Bob spread his hands. "It's approaching cruel."

She lifted one shoulder. "It's not up to me," she said. "She either earns it or she doesn't."

Bob gave her an intimate smile. "Then let's hope she does."

"Let's do," Kate said. Her answering smile was warm but not warm enough to hide something fierce and hunted in her eyes. Bob recognized his cue to back up and shut up.

"Good night, Kate." He forced himself to stroll off into the night as if he had all the time in the world to wait. As if it didn't kill him to waste even one night they could spend together.

Patience, he told himself. If there was one thing he knew it was that no good ever came of rushing her. Woe to the guy who backed Kate into a corner.

185

He just prayed to God she came around soon. He didn't know how much more time he could afford to give her.

Bright and early the following morning, Bel hung a cork board the approximate size of a compact car on the kitchen wall. Then she pulled out a well-thumbed stack of recipe cards and got down to the business of planning a menu that would send every man, woman and child in attendance at this year's Fox Hunt Ball into raptures of culinary delight.

Several hours later, her corkboard still largely empty, she slapped her hands down on the countertop and shot to her feet with a muffled noise of frustration.

Bel believed with an almost religious fervor in the power of persistence. But even she had to acknowledge that sometimes, particularly when it came to food, persistence wasn't enough.

Sometimes it took magic.

Just admitting that offended every principle around which Bel had organized her life, but denying it did no good. The sort of home-run Bel was looking to hit was going to take more than rigorous practice and attention to detail. It was going to take magic. Inspiration. A stroke of genius.

None of which could be forced. Magic had to be invited. Nurtured. Courted. Which ordinarily she wouldn't mind. But with only the two measly weeks Kate had allowed them to pull together the state's most lavish event of the year, Bel didn't have that kind of time.

What she needed was a trip to the farmers' market. A stroll down a leafy aisle, the air rich with the scent of soil and what came out of it. She needed to fill her hands with round, lush, late-season tomatoes, to pull the tangy scent of them deep into her lungs. She needed a bag of onions with the dirt still clinging to them, and maybe a curvy, flirty little squash. A pattypan or something equally adorable.

She needed inspiration.

But she'd settle for James getting his lazy self out of bed so they could at least put together a game plan. Maybe if she knew what direction he was going with the program, the magic would get on board.

She glanced at her watch. Where on earth *was* he? He wasn't an early riser by any stretch of the imagination, but in general he could be counted on to have rolled into the kitchen by *noon*.

She could go upstairs and wake him. An unwelcome spark shivered through her at the image that flashed into her head—James tangled up in warm sheets, bare-chested and sleep-rumpled, his beautiful mouth soft and inviting.

She sat down at the stool in front of her stacks of rejected recipes with a deliberate calm. She would rather continue to unsuccessfully force the magic, she told herself firmly, than successfully wake James. And if a tiny, rebellious piece of her soul howled a protest, she didn't flinch. She simply channeled the energy into righteous indignation.

Because it wasn't right that she should sit down here and slave away over work they should both be doing. It wasn't right for her to shoulder the entire burden of worry while he snored away like a Roman soldier after an orgy. It wasn't right that he should be able to sleep at all while she scrambled fruitlessly around for a scrap of *magic*, of all things. Magic was *his* damn department, and if he couldn't be bothered to turn up by *noon*—

"Hey, Bel." James ambled into the kitchen. He plopped down on the stool next to hers and gave her a hopeful look. "There wouldn't happen to be any coffee handy, would there?"

"There was three hours ago," she said coolly, sifting through a pile of recipes she'd rejected four times already. "I threw it out."

"Aww." His face fell. "Before you got here, we used to just scrape the scum off the top and throw it in the microwave."

"Forgive me for having standards." She slapped down the stack of cards and lifted another.

"I have standards," he said. "It's just that they mostly pertain to the necessity of caffeine in the a.m."

"Then you ought to get up before noon," she snapped.

He peered at her from under a worn Manchester United ball cap. "Something, ah, wrong?"

"Certainly not." She tossed down that stack, offended that it was *still* full of non-starters, and snatched up another. "What makes you ask?"

He lifted his shoulders in a wary shrug. "You seem a little...testy."

"Testy?" She rounded her eyes in a parody of offended shock. "Why on earth would I be testy? Just because we have two short weeks to pull together the most complex event I've ever worked on, let alone run, and my partner—" Here she paused to deliver a killing glance. "—when he deigns to turn up at all, does nothing but complain? What kind of miserable shrew would get testy over something like that?"

"I have no idea," he said slowly. "Maybe you could, I don't know, enlighten me?"

She slapped her hands down on the table. "For goodness' sake, James! What do you expect? A parade for dragging yourself out of bed? I've been down here for hours, working myself into a frenzy trying to make this stupid menu *work*, and it won't and I'm frustrated and worried and angry and you're not here. I need help and you're not *here*."

She shot to her feet and walked a few paces away, horrified at the raw hurt in her voice. God. No wonder he stayed away from her. It was bad enough that she felt crazy. Did she really have to act crazy, too?

"Hey." He spoke softly, his voice shockingly near her ear. Why didn't she ever hear this guy move? "I'm here now, okay?" His hands came to rest on her shoulders, warm and strong and comforting. It took every ounce of self-control she possessed not to lean back into the solid heat of his body and let somebody else do the worrying for a minute or two.

"I could have used you a little earlier," she said instead.

"Ah, Bel." He pulled her back into his arms. She closed her eyes against the treacherous wave of contentment that slid through her, the same way she ignored the shimmer of awareness at the way their bodies fit. "You've really had a morning, haven't you?"

The hot prickle of tears in the back of her throat caught her off-guard and she tossed off a bad-tempered shrug. He pressed a quick kiss to her temple, turned her to face him and held her shoulders in those big, capable hands. He bent a little, to look at her eye-to-eye.

"I didn't abandon you, Bel," he said. "I know I haven't been the best partner to you these past weeks, but I told Kate last night I was taking this seriously and I am. Now that's for me, sure. I'd like to get my career back one of these days, too. But it's also for you."

"For me?" She blinked at him, struggling to get past the sight of those gorgeous, earnest eyes and that wicked mouth so close to hers.

"For you." He smiled at her and Bel's system took another hit. A hard one. She wanted to lean forward and press her mouth to his, to be the one to close the distance between them herself for once, but he suddenly dropped his hands and stepped back. Those lips curved into a smile, but it was a polite, arm's-length parody of the real deal. "You've given this thing—and, by extension, me—all you've got, Bel. I don't think you know how to operate any other way. It's pretty amazing, and kind of humbling, to tell you the truth. You deserve a better partner. You've earned it."

Bel's shoulders drooped under a swift pang of dismay. What, was he leaving her? Surrendering? "It hasn't been that bad, James. I could use a little lightening up from time to time—"

"Well, yeah." He grinned at her. "But that's no excuse for my playing fast and loose with your career. Which is why I spent this morning at the library."

"The library?" She frowned at him, then down at his ratty track pants and faded t-shirt. "In your pajamas?"

He looked down at himself. "I don't wear pajamas."

"Oh." Her cheeks burned and he laughed.

"Most people don't iron for a day at the library, Bel."

She shrugged, still hung up on the image of James wearing nothing but all that taut golden skin of his and a sheet.

"But I did shower before I left. A nod to basic civility."

"I'm so glad to hear it," she said.

He beamed at her. "Don't you want to hear my idea?"

"For what?"

"For the Fox Hunt ball."

She shook her head. "I think I might put that pot of coffee on after all. You don't make sense sans caffeine."

"You're an angel," he said. "I'll start again once I'm caffeinated. I think you're going to like this once I explain it right."

"Where did you get these?" Bel asked, her fingers moving reverently over the original architectural drawings of the Hunt Estate.

"The local library had them," James said, cradling a steaming coffee cup like it was manna from heaven.

"You have a library card?"

"Sure. First thing I get every place I live."

She tore herself away from the plans long enough to throw a skeptical glance over her shoulder. "Really?"

"My mom always said there was nothing wrong with this country that couldn't be fixed by turning half the churches into libraries."

Bel grinned. "Bet that made her popular in small town Texas."

"All the ideas in the world, free of charge and open to the public," James said. "What's so unchristian about that?"

"Not a thing," Bel murmured, tracing the outline of the Dower House's sweet front porch and tidy kitchen windows. A pang of loss washed through her, bittersweet and sharp, and she flipped the page. No sense in dwelling on the past, she told herself firmly. She'd find a new place to park her eggs and butter. A new kitchen to love. Just as soon as she finished up here.

Another unexpected pang of loss echoed through her at the thought but she forced herself to ignore it. To focus on the page before her and not the vast, gorgeous space she was currently parked in. The heart of James' house in which she'd made herself completely at home.

She turned the page and found herself looking right at the very kitchen in which she sat.

"Isn't it cool?" James came to peer over her shoulder, excitement warming his voice. "That's the Annex." He leaned forward to lay a finger on the drawing. "That's us. Did you know the Annex was originally part of the Hunt estate?"

"Well, yeah." She shot him a look. "That's why it's called the Annex. Because it was *added on*?"

"I know what annex means, Bel." James gave her a friendly elbow shot and jerked his chin toward the yard. "But that hedgerow out there has to be nearly as old as the house."

"Nearly."

"So why would you build a huge beautiful house then hide it behind a wall of shrubs?"

"Think of it as a glorified spite fence." Bel leaned down to squint at some tiny printing on the scrolled paper.

"Spite fence?"

"Mmmmm. The result of a family squabble, or so local legend has it."

"Must've been some squabble."

"I think a woman was involved."

"Isn't there always?" She shot him a narrow look. He smiled innocently. "How do you know these things, anyway?"

"Kate." She shrugged. "It's her mission in life to restore the Hunt estate to its previous glory. She's got Hunt House and the Dower House about where she wants them but she's never been able to get her hands on the Annex." Bel cocked a brow at him. "It really burned her toast when the owner sold to you instead of her. She took it as a personal affront."

"As well she should. The lady I bought it from had no love for Miss *Kate Every Day*, if I recall. Thought she was arrogant and snotty and holier-than-thou." His eyes twinkled at her. "And that's just what she felt comfortable saying in front of the pretty little real estate agent who showed me the place. The rest doesn't bear repeating. Plus I could never hope to do it justice, considering its original delivery by a half-deaf, ninety-year-old woman."

"Miss Farnsworth." Bel smiled. "She and Kate were...cordial."

"That's a lovely and southern way of putting it."

"Isn't it?" She flipped the page and caught her breath.

He bounced on the toes of his sneakers and beamed. "It's the original landscaping plan. For the whole estate. I couldn't believe they had it."

She blinked and leaned in, traced a finger above the spidery lines. "My God, James, look at this! Without that big old hedgerow dividing the property you can really see the way the houses were designed as three parts of a single whole. The way they're angled to face the pond but also each other. The way they curve around to create a commons, sort of. With—is that a garden in the center?"

"Yep." He flipped another page with a dramatic flourish and Bel lost her breath completely. "I give you Hunt Gardens."

"With a capital G. Good lord, James." She traced the pretty little pathways curving amidst beds and groves and arbors and nooks. "It's like something you'd read about in a historical romance novel—all those alcoves, the statuary and promenades."

"You, uh, read a lot of romance novels?"

There was a laugh in his voice and Bel turned up her nose primly. "Enough to know that Lord Thus-And-So will be much tempted to take certain liberties with Lady What's-Her-Face right here—" She tapped the drawing and squinted to read the archaic printing. "—by the fountain."

James laughed. "He will if all goes according to plan."

Bel turned slowly. "Plan? You have a plan?"

He grinned at her. "What would you say if I told you I'd decided to restore the grounds?"

"The grounds?" Bel stared at him. "You mean, like, plant this garden?"

"Yep."

"But there's a thirty yard long hedgerow out there between here and Hunt House. And half this garden lies on Kate's property. And even if those things didn't matter—which they do—we have two weeks to plan this party. There's no way on God's green earth you could possibly get all this—" She stabbed a finger at the paper. "—done in two weeks. Why, you probably couldn't even get a nursery to come out to consult in that time frame, let alone—"

"The bobcats will be here in an hour," he said. "Kate's already given the okay. I stopped by Hunt House on my way home from the library to speak with her."

"Oh." Bel felt a little faint as she struggled to process the new ground rules under which her party planning would take place. Change had never been great for her. "So your plan is to tear the entire estate to shreds for the full two weeks prior to hosting a huge annual event?"

"Yep." He took her hands in his. "I have this idea."

"Oh?"

"We're going back to pre-Civil War Virginia," he said. "When men were gentlemen, ladies wore hoops and everybody rode to the hounds. When courtship had rules, manners reigned supreme and throwing a decent ball was a skill young ladies learned at their mothers' knee."

She stared at him, at the utter earnestness lighting his pirate's face. And something sparked inside. An answering flicker. A lick of...magic.

"When the entire world ran according to the agricultural clock," she said slowly. "When people ate only what could be sowed, tended and reaped with their own hands."

"That's right." His grin was a beacon of heedless enthusiasm. Bel would have laughed if she hadn't known a similar one was spreading across her own face. "That's exactly right. I knew you'd get it, Bel."

The spark inside her glowed hot, then burst into a lovely, vivid flame. "I have to get to the farmers' market," she said. "Right now."

He laughed. "I figured. Go on. Do your thing. I'm going to wait for the landscapers."

She started for the door, then, halfway there, turned and came back. "Thank you," she said, and pressed a hard, smacking kiss to his lips.

He froze under her hands and when she drew back, he touched a finger to his lips and said warily, "Ah, okay. For what?"

"For understanding what I needed," she said. "For giving it to me."

He nodded. "Uh, sure. No problem."

She laughed. "Are you blushing, James?"

He shoved his hands into his pockets. "Geez. No. You just, I don't know, surprised me. I'm usually the one kissing you in here."

"You surprised me, too," she said. "I guess that makes us even."

"Good," he said gruffly. "Fine. Now go."

She snatched up her purse and sailed out the door, too preoccupied with heirloom tomatoes to notice that James hadn't kissed her back. Or to wonder why.

CHAPTER TWENTY-TWO

"For the love of Pete, Bel! Would you get out of here?" The caterer flapped an oven mitt at Bel, shooing her away from a tray of pumpkin pecan tartlets cooling on the counter. It was the night of the Fox Hunt Ball and Bel's nerves had drawn her irresistibly to the kitchen. "You're going to ruin that pretty dress of yours and I won't have it on my conscience."

Bel snatched her hands back from the tray with a guilty start. There was no reason, aside from observing her staff operate with a gratifying efficiency, for her to be here. Every inch counted in a working kitchen and, given the amazing circumference of her vintage hoop skirt, Bel was taking up considerable acreage that wasn't hers to waste.

"Oh, Lillian, I'm sorry." She forced a little chuckle. "I'm making a nuisance of myself, aren't I?"

"Oh, honey, no." Lillian laughed, her round, lived-in face merry. "Jim and I were just saying last night how wonderful you've been to work with."

Lillian gave her husband a fond glance across the kitchen as he shouldered an enormous tray of thin-shaved Virginia ham, country cheese, and pickled beans and made for the door. He winked at his wife, who swiped her oven mitt at him this time.

"We know it must be killing you to turn over control of your kitchen to somebody else when the pressure's on. Lord knows it would kill me. The kitchen is the heart of your house. It's where you live." She gave Bel a sympathetic smile. "It's hard to walk away from your heart, even temporarily."

"Oh, this isn't—" *My kitchen*, she was going to say. *This isn't my kitchen*. But her heart snatched the words out of her mouth and tore them into tiny pieces. This *was* her kitchen. Her heart had sunk its thirsty roots deep into the soil of this place and made it her own. It was hers. She loved it.

"Of course it is, dear." Lillian bent to pull a tray of ham and egg pastries from the oven, blissfully unaware of the reeling shock she'd just delivered. "You don't bake someplace every day for any length of time without leaving a good chunk of yourself behind. It belongs to you as much as you belong to it."

Bel stared at her, denial an anxious beat inside her head. "But I don't—" *I don't want to love it*, she thought. *I don't want to love* him.

"Doesn't matter," Lillian said cheerfully as if she could read Bel's panicked mind. "That's just how it is for people like us." She slid the tray onto the counter and fanned herself with the oven mitt. "Now, go on. Guests are due to start arriving any minute. We have dozens of servers and all systems are go. Leave this up to Jim and me."

Bel looked longingly at her apron hanging on a peg behind the door. Suddenly she wanted nothing more than to slip it on and bury herself elbow-deep in some bread dough. "Are you sure? Maybe I should—"

"Bel." Lillian gave her a stern look. "We've been at this since before you were born. We know what to do. Besides, a hot kitchen is no place for a lady in a hoop skirt and a corset. You're going to set yourself on fire or something and I'll have no idea how to get you out of that thing."

Bel fingered the heavy cinnamon-colored velvet of her skirt. "Yeah. Me neither. It took me nearly half an hour just to figure out how to put it on." Even so, a swish of giddy pleasure swirled through her at the rich fabric against her skin.

Lillian smiled. "Go find your young man and have a glass of champagne. Jim just finished pouring on the patio."

"Right," Bel said, stretching her lips into something resembling a smile. "Of course. I'll just...get out of your way."

"Have a nice time, dear."

Bel walked in her soft dancing slippers—which went a long way toward making up for the corset—down the short hallway from the kitchen to the foyer. She *should* go out to the patio, she thought. One last time before people arrived. She could make sure the champagne was properly chilled and the hors d'oeuvre stations were spaced adequately to encourage mingling. Because the last thing she wanted was for people to clump together or, God forbid, stay inside. After all the work James had gone to putting the gardens back together, the least people could do was—

She faltered at the foot of the steps, her thoughts scattering like autumn leaves as James came bounding down that grandly dramatic staircase two risers at a time. He was...good lord, he was beautiful. For once his hair seemed to have obeyed orders rather than chewing up and spitting out the comb. A few thick golden waves tumbled over his forehead but the majority had been confined to a civilized queue at the nape of his neck. Black riding boots polished to a mirror-like finish hugged muscular calves while a pair of buff trousers clung to powerful thighs and narrow hips. A deep blue jacket stretched without a wrinkle over shoulders that looked about a yard wide, while snowy white lace bloomed at the collar and wrists.

He moved like a thoroughbred pacing the track, all lean lines, smooth muscles and easy confidence. This was a man who'd found his way back to the top of his game, and everything in Bel yearned for him the way she'd yearned for the damn kitchen two minutes ago.

She laid a hand over the sudden aching void in her chest. God. She was in big trouble. Because after tonight, it was over. Her time here. Her time with James. It was all over, and she was a fool for thinking that it was the damn kitchen breaking her heart.

"Hey, Bel." He stopped short on the bottom step, his eyes bright and shrewd as they raced over her. "Well, my goodness. Look at you."

She fingered the trio of fat curls gathered at the nape of her neck, suddenly aware that while an extravagant amount of spice-colored fabric had been dedicated to her skirt, considerably less had been expended on her bodice. And courtesy of Audrey's merciless assault on her corset laces—

she'd been forced to cling to the bedpost like Scarlett O'Hara—an unprecedented percentage of her bosom now rose cheekily above the neckline.

In the privacy of her bedroom, she'd actually admired the effect. For a woman more used to angles than curves, it was something of a miracle to see cleavage manufactured out of thin air.

But now, with James' eyes hot and assessing on her...well, on her *everything*, she wasn't so comfortable.

"Too much?" She plucked at the folds of her skirt. "I'm more used to being in the kitchen at stuff like this, but Lillian kicked me out and I—"

"It's perfect." He took that last step and caught her hands up in his. "You're perfect."

She laughed, his approval seeping into her bones like summer sunshine. "I'm hardly perfect."

"Any more perfect and I'll have to dig up a set of dueling pistols to defend your honor after some jerk tries to take liberties at that damn fountain."

"It's not my fault you moved the naked frolickers into the garden. I told you it would give people ideas."

He tucked her hand into his elbow and began a slow stroll toward the patio. "Which, under normal circumstances, I'd be fine with." He patted her hand. "Then I saw you in that dress."

She shook her head, ridiculously pleased. "You're looking pretty good yourself," she said. "You'd never know you used to have a Whopper habit."

He gave her a pained look. "I still miss them."

"With the way I feed you?"

"I know," he said. "It's a terrible weakness. It makes no sense. I'm appropriately ashamed."

"Don't sweat it. We all have our little foibles." She hesitated, then leaned into him and whispered. "I like instant cocoa."

"Seriously?"

She shrugged. "I can't understand it." She thought of the kitchen that wasn't really hers. Of the man that wasn't hers either. "Sometimes the heart wants what it wants."

"Yeah, but your heart doesn't even acknowledge the existence of processed food. What's next? Velveeta?"

She shuddered. "Not in my kitchen."

He laughed, a full-bodied peal of amusement that rang up to the ceiling and warmed her from the inside out. "I do like you, Bel."

Something hungry and persistent inside her gobbled up the words and cried for more. Like wasn't enough. Not anymore.

She shrugged it off and squeezed his arm.

"I like you, too, James," she said. "But the DC Statesmen have dibs. They're going to be proud to have you back, you know."

"I know," he said. "They ought to be. I haven't been in shape this good—mind, body or spirit—since I was fifteen." He turned to her, his eyes green and intense. "I owe it all to you, Bel. You've been...good for us. For me."

Want twisted in her gut, mixed with the horrified certainty that if he tried to say goodbye right now she would humiliate herself by bursting into tears.

"I got something for you," she said abruptly. Better to seize control, right? If she couldn't avoid the punch, at least she could get herself into the best possible position to take it.

"You did?" Surprised pleasure raced across his face.

"I did." She reached into the little crocheted reticule dangling from her wrist and withdrew a small box. "This is just one of them. I left the other two upstairs, one for each of the Blake boys."

He gave her a mystified smile, then pulled off the silky bow and cracked open the little velvet jewelers box. Bel held her breath as he frowned down at the contents for a long moment.

"They're cufflinks," she said, unable to bear the weighted silence another second. "See? It's the Blake family crest." She pointed to a small coat of arms etched into two of the four heavy gold circles.

James ran a gentle thumb over the raised printing on the other two circles. "And this?" he asked, his voice quiet.

"*Clann thar gach ní*," she said, unease heavy in her chest. "Blake's a traditionally Irish name so I went with Gaelic. It means Family First. At least I hope it does. I went to a professor of Irish studies for the translation but he was about six hundred years old. It could be verse ten of "Molly Malone" for all I know. He looked like the sort of guy who might have one over on me."

She was babbling. She knew she was babbling but had no idea how to stop herself. The longer he stared into the box, not moving, not smiling, not even breathing as far as she could tell, the faster the words bubbled out of her.

"You don't have to wear them," she assured him quickly. God, she was a fool. What had she been thinking? Unless a guy was yours by either marriage or blood, you didn't give him *jewelry*. Wasn't that a rule or something? If Miss Manners hadn't written it down, surely Kate had. How could Bel have flaked out on such a basic piece of etiquette? "I won't be offended. I know your daily life doesn't have much call for cufflinks. It was just, I don't know, an impulse. It doesn't mean anything. I only wanted to—"

"Bel." His arms came around her with a swiftness that took her breath away, and then she was crushed against him, enveloped in the strength and heat of him, her chin hooked over his shoulder, her arms wrapped around his broad back. He lifted her nearly off her feet, buried his face in the crook of her neck. "Thank you." The words were rough and low against her neck. "Thank you."

He finally set her down, pulled back far enough to gaze down at her with something heart-stopping and searching in those deep green eyes. His mouth hovered inches from her own, and everything in Bel yearned to rise up on her toes and press her lips to his, to obey the snapping desire he'd ignited in her that he'd been oddly unwilling to feed these past two weeks. She could count on one hand the number of times he'd touched her of his own free will since their last dinner meeting with Kate. And on the few occasions he had, he'd leapt away from her the instant he realized what he'd done, as if she'd burned him.

For a moment, she thought the fast was over. Inside the loose circle of his arms, she watched him sway toward her, his beautiful mouth so close she could feel the sweet wash of his breath against her cheek. She leaned into him, a yearning heaviness low in her belly.

He startled and hopped back a few feet. Bel swayed, caught off-guard by the move, and he snatched up her hands. He held them between their bodies like a life preserver and gave the wrinkles he'd put in her skirt a rueful smile.

"Sorry about that," he said. "I got a little carried away."

"No, you didn't," Bel told him with painful sincerity. "You definitely didn't."

"It's just, I was surprised. This—" He tapped the cufflinks lightly against her knuckles. "—was such a beautiful gift, it...I guess—" He pulled in a breath, seemed to search for words.

"Oh, my lord." Her cheeks flamed. "I didn't mean to embarrass—"

"No! Geez, Bel, no. You didn't embarrass me. You touched me. I mean, keeping my family together has been my life's work since my parents died. It's been all our lives' work, I guess. Will had a full ride to UCLA but he gave it up to take on legal guardianship of me and Drew. I took early graduation after landing a contract playing ball for a third-tier club outside London because it was our best bet for staying together. I played my ass off, Will took whatever work he could find and dedicated himself to managing me into the money."

Bel cleared the ache from her throat and asked, "How did you lose your folks?"

"Car wreck. I was sixteen."

"Which made Will, what, eighteen?"

He nodded. "Drew was twelve. I don't know how he turned out so well. God knows Will and I didn't spend much time raising him. Honestly, sometimes I think he raised us." He shook his head. "None of us ever learned to cook—"

"Don't I know it," Bel murmured and earned a quick half-smile.

"But Drew handed us each a sack full of peanut butter sandwiches on our way out the door every morning before taking his and walking to school. So I know it's hard for people to understand why we are the way we are, especially Will sometimes. But we know what's important. We know that family is precious, that love is rare, that fate is unkind. We learned those lessons the hard way, and it taught us how to protect what we love against anybody and anything that threatens it."

He pressed her hands between his and dipped his head to look her straight in the eye. The warmth and regard she saw there had tears prickling hot and insistent in her throat again.

"And I can't tell you," he said, his voice low and warm, "what it means to me that you understand who we are. Who I am."

A great surge of love rose up and clenched itself around Bel's heart like a fist. "I do," she said softly. "I know who you are, James. And I—"

Love you. I love you.

The words caught in her throat. Thank God. Because about the only thing worse than giving an inappropriately intimate gift would be exposing a wildly inappropriate emotion.

He gazed at her, his brows drawn and concerned. "You what?"

She squeezed his hands, and gave him her biggest, brightest smile. "I think we ought to have a glass of champagne, because we're about to knock this party out of the park."

CHAPTER TWENTY-THREE

Will planted himself in front of the bar. He felt like a perfect fool in this get up. He was one tri-corn hat away from being mistaken for Patrick Henry and if that didn't earn him a double shot of whiskey, straight up, he didn't know what would.

Well, that wasn't precisely true. Watching James charm the breeches and hoop skirts off every idiot in the room was enough to drive anybody to drink.

He glanced into his rapidly emptying glass and wondered how long he ought to force himself to wait for a refill.

"Hey."

Will turned and found über-agent Bob at his elbow. "Hey, yourself."

"Tonic water, twist of lime," Bob said to the bartender.

Will snorted. "What, you give your balls to your girlfriend for the night?"

Bob smiled placidly. "I stopped measuring my balls with a shot glass years ago. It was liberating. You might look into it."

"Yeah, sure." Will treated himself to a burning gulp of his whiskey and considered Bob's hollow cheeks and the tinge of grey underneath his skin. Some health kick. "I'll do that. Tomorrow."

Bob picked up his non-drink and took the stool next to Will's. Damn it, why couldn't anybody just let him drink in peace these days?

"World Cup qualifiers are wrapping up," Bob said, his eyes following James' stupid golden head around the room. "Looks like the U. S. Team is going to make it."

"Yep."

"With James back in action, they're going to have a damn good shot at making the quarter finals at least."

"Yep." A bitter pit opened in his gut, the kind there wasn't enough whiskey in the world to fill.

"The U. S. team hasn't made it to the quarters since...when?"

"2002," Will said automatically. "And that was our best showing since a 3rd place finish in 1930." He cut Bob a look. "Not exactly an impressive track record."

"A track record your brother is looking at chewing up and spitting out."

Will gave him an elaborately careless shrug.

"Seriously, Will. He's in good shape. The best I've ever seen him in, and I'm talking physical and mental. He's fit." Bob shot him a smug glance. "Bel's been good for him."

"Whatever you say."

But a great swell of resentment rose up, nearly choking him. God, where did it end? Not only did James get all the family talent *and* first crack at all the pussy but then he lucks into some kind of *magic* pussy that solves all his problems? What kind of greedy fuck *was* he?

Bitterness backed up in his throat but Will forced it down with a swallow of whiskey. Because that was bullshit, and he knew it. James was a lot of things but he wasn't greedy. James believed without question or reservation that his success was their success. His, Will's and Drew's. That his money was their money. The house, the food, the cars, the clothes and the fans were all common property as far as he was concerned.

The only person tallying accounts and holding grudges was Will.

Disgust was an uncomfortable weight on his shoulders, and he wished he could dredge up even an ounce of the righteous resentment that had been fueling him these past months. Because sitting here at the bar, stone-cold sober, looking down the barrel of the truth was damned depressing. Without that protective layer of anger, he was starting to get an awfully clear picture of himself, and it wasn't pretty. He was seeing a lot of poor judgment, a wide streak of spoiled and ungrateful, and a hefty dose of self-pity.

Props to Audrey, he thought bitterly, lifting his glass toward her shiny blonde head. He seemed to be able to locate her in any room at any moment, much to his disgust. She'd called it. He was an ass.

Which seemed like all the reason a guy would need to have another drink.

Two hours into the party, Bel wasn't quite so thrilled with her corset anymore. She was still pleasantly surprised every time she happened to look down her own dress—*wow, where did* those *come from?*—but she wasn't overly fond of racing between the kitchen, the gardens and the ballroom on about one third of her usual lung capacity.

James was about to start the charity auction and Bel wanted the wait staff circulating with fresh trays of champagne before he did. Alcohol went a long way toward loosening purse strings.

Not that she figured they'd need a whole lot of loosening. James had done that mysterious thing again, the one where he just sort of *understood* his target market without any apparent effort. She had no idea how he'd done it on short notice, but he'd rounded up a stable of celebrities—athletes and horsey-types from both the U. S. and overseas—and charmed them into donating to charity an hour or two of whatever magical thing they did.

Small, thrilled exclamations had been flying up like startled fireflies from the crowd all night as these luminaries walked among the partygoers, talking up their offerings. Bel scanned the ballroom with narrowed eyes, satisfaction a warm glow in her chest as her servers wound through the growing buzz of anticipation like an efficient little army. *Her* army.

Audrey appeared at her elbow. "Lillian says we're ready for the dessert buffet. We'll start laying it as soon as the auction starts."

"Perfect."

"Anything else I can do?"

"I don't think so." Bel turned to grin at her. "Things seem to be going pretty—Oh. Oh, no."

"What?" Audrey's purple eyes went wide and she followed Bel's unhappy gaze over her shoulder. "What?"

"At the bar," Bel said grimly. "Will."

Audrey looked. "What about him?"

"He's drinking."

She rolled her eyes. "He's always drinking."

"No, sometimes he just has a drink or two."

"Or eight," Audrey muttered. Bel ignored her.

"This is Drinking, capital D," she said. "This is drinking with serious intent."

"Intent to what?"

"To get wasted. And then do something foolish and/or destructive, to himself or the assembled company."

"Oh." Audrey looked closer. "Right."

"Bel?" James waited at the base of the steps leading to the podium. He lifted his eyebrows in question.

She checked her watch. It was an anachronism, she knew, but she'd be damned if she'd throw a party without her watch. She nodded at him, mustered up a bright, reassuring smile. "Go for it."

She turned back to Audrey and lowered her voice. "Can you get him out of here? Will?"

"I may not be, um, the best choice," Audrey said.

"Why not?"

"I'm sort of afraid of him."

"Everybody is." Bel watched as James took the stage and started charming a couple hundred people all at once with every appearance of ease. Love filled her chest and she looked away. "I think he likes it. Don't give him the pleasure."

"No, it's more than that." She twisted her fingers together, worry wrinkling her perfect face. "I don't even know how to explain this."

"Try."

"Wow. Um, okay. You know how it feels when you stand at the edge of a really tall cliff? And how, even though you know you'd never jump, you have the insane impulse to do it anyway? Just to see what it would feel like before you hit bottom?"

Bel shrugged. "Sure. Everybody does."

"It's like that with me and Will."

"He makes you want to jump off a cliff?" Bel asked, at sea.

"Not that I ever would," Audrey said quickly. "I'm not a suicidal fool. But it's the impulse coming up inside me like that, all strong and sharp and unexpected. It's uncomfortable. I don't like it, and I don't like him."

Bel frowned at her. "Are we still talking about cliffs here? Because it feels like we're not but I have no idea what we've moved on to."

Audrey closed her eyes and her shoulders slumped. "Never mind. I'm not explaining this very well."

"No, you're fine. I was totally following you right up until—" The dots connected abruptly in her head and she grabbed Audrey's pointy elbow. "Unless you're saying that you sort of want to..." She trailed off, disbelieving, as color raced into Audrey's milk-pale cheeks. "With *Will*?"

"No!" Her eyes went wide and panicked. "No, see that's what I'm trying to say. I *don't*! Really, really don't. It's just that sometimes, I sort of..." She lifted thin shoulders in pained bafflement.

"Do." Bel shook her head. "Sometimes you sort of do."

The fight went out of the girl's spine and she deflated right before Bel's eyes.

"Yeah. But only sometimes. When I'm feeling particularly, I don't know, fragile."

"That's a good word for it." *And I ought to know*, she thought, not looking at James. "Okay, you know what? Don't worry about Will." She checked her watch. "I've got this."

Audrey gazed at her with pathetic gratitude. "Are you sure?"

"Absolutely." She thought about James weaving his magic spell from the stage and her heart swelled. "Tonight is perfection, and I'm not going to let anybody smear the frosting. Not even Will."

207

"Right." Audrey frowned at the bar. "Good luck with that."

Will sprawled over one of the benches in the kitchen's breakfast nook and missed his whiskey like he'd miss his right arm.

"The least you could have done was let me bring my drink," he said to Bel, who paced back and forth across the opening of the nook looking for all the world like Martha Washington. If Martha Washington had been tall and tidy and quietly enraged.

"What on earth is *wrong* with you?" Her voice was low and tense. "Your brother is *this close* to climbing out of the hole you helped him make of his life, and you're at the bar drinking yourself blind?"

"Yeah, poor James." Will ran a skeptical eye over the acres of gleaming kitchen at Bel's back. "Trapped in this wretched hole."

She said nothing, only gazed at him with such open dislike that shame seized his belly like a cramp. He forced an elaborately false smile.

"And I wasn't drinking myself blind." Trying, though. Solid effort. "Unfortunately, I can still see just fine."

"Ah." She pounced on that stupid *unfortunately* and his stomach cramped tighter yet. *Shit*, he thought. *Said too much.* Bel was bright, and—worse—detail oriented. He should've remembered that. "And you're seeing something you don't like, aren't you?"

He surprised himself with a laugh, but it broke like glass so he let it go. "I sure am." And he was. He just hadn't meant to say so out loud.

"What is it?"

He snorted out another laugh. Like he was going to detail his pathetic woes for James' perfect girlfriend.

"Will." She moved forward until her dress brushed his knees. He wanted to move away but his back was already— literally—to the wall. She was inexorable. "Tell me."

"Yeah, I don't think so." He stared straight ahead at the hands she'd folded into a concerned knot at her waist. Her voice was all firm command but her eyes would be full of dislike or—worse—pity, and he couldn't make himself lift his gaze to hers.

She sighed and dropped gracefully into a crouch that brought her eyes level with his. Her skirts gave a perfumed billow, and longing hit him like a hammer. God, he wanted. Wanted what, though? Her? Sure. He was a guy and she smelled nice. Plus that corset was doing amazing things for her figure. But this want was a pale, measly thing compared to the gut-punch of lust Audrey unleashed inside him every time she so much as sneered his way.

Because Audrey? She saw him for exactly what he was—a parasite living on his brother's charity. Hating that charity, and hating himself for being too weak to reject it, but sucking it up like mother's milk just the same. But there was no pity in Audrey's eyes. Just contempt. And he wanted her anyway.

That plus Bel's pity equaled Will's very last straw.

A jagged jumble of impulses swam up his throat—run, hide, howl—but he didn't act on any of them. No, he just let them back up into his chest then take over his head where they pounded until he thought his skull would split open and spill its poison all over the kitchen floor.

Bel gazed patiently up from her crouch at his knee. She tapped his boot with one elegant finger and dipped her chin until he was forced to meet her eyes.

Don't push me, Bel. Have pity. For once, just give up.

"What are you seeing here, Will?"

He managed an insouciant shrug, but Jesus, it cost him. "Straight down your dress, for starters."

"For God's sake." She sat back on her heels with scowl that made him wish once again that he'd seen her before James had. He nearly laughed out loud at that one. Like it would've mattered who saw her first. The point was that *she* hadn't seen *him*. Nobody ever did. Not when James was in the room.

"Not that I don't appreciate the view."

"Nice try." But she tugged the neckline of her dress marginally higher. "You're not getting out of this conversation, William."

He sighed. "I'm not?"

"No." She folded her arms, which plumped up those pretty breasts until they all but spilled out of her corset. He willed himself to want her—want her for real—but it was no use. There was only one woman he wanted on her knees in front of him, and it wasn't Bel. Bitterness all but closed his throat. "But before we leave the subject? You're an ass."

"Sweet talker." But she was right. He *was* an ass, and he hated it. Hated himself. Hated what being here—in this house, in this family, in this *life*—was doing to him. Things were breaking inside him; he could feel them snapping and splintering every day. The bones of his soul were softening, and it was only a matter of time before the damage became permanent. If it wasn't already.

He needed out, but there was no way his brothers would ever let him go. He knew that like he knew his own face. Not unless... He eyed the woman kneeling in front of him. Not unless he did something utterly unforgiveable. Something that would once and for all destroy the bonds of loyalty that held him so mercilessly in James' orbit.

Some long-buried thread of gallantry reared its head inside him and insisted on fair warning.

"Go away, Bel." Was that his voice? So rough and agonized? "Please?"

"No." She glared at him with magnificent disdain. Lucky, lucky James. "We can't go on like this. None of us. It's constant damage control with you, and one of these days we're not going to be able to fix whatever it is you broke. So you're going to tell me what *the hell* is bothering you. Right now."

Resignation flooded him along with an odd, nervy energy. So be it.

"You want to know what's bothering me, Bel?" He grabbed the bench under his thighs with hard hands, gripped it until his fingers ached. "You. You're what's bothering me. You and James and your perfect, perfect love."

Her mouth dropped open, a soft *oh* of shock and guilt. "Our perfect—" She swallowed, and he watched her pale throat work while color rolled up her pretty cleavage. "For God's sake, Will, we're not—"

"In love? Oh, spare me." He wanted to wave that aside but didn't know where his hand would land if he let go of the bench. "You are so."

She blinked and came slowly to her feet. He watched as the shock cleared out of those sharp dark eyes far too soon. As that tidy brain of hers shifted into high gear and started clicking. Longing crashed over him again. He could've loved this woman. He *should* love this woman. Damn James. And damn Audrey double. "And that's a problem for you?"

"Yeah, Bel. It's a problem for me."

"Why?" She frowned down at him with honest perplexity. "Why don't you want James to be happy? Not—" She threw up a stop-sign hand. "—that I'm claiming to be his one true love and the key to all future happiness."

His lips twisted appreciatively in spite of himself. "Understood."

"But for argument's sake, let's go with it." Her hands went to those neat hips. "Why would that be a problem for you?"

He came slowly to his feet as well, and the whiskey finally kicked in. His head swam pleasantly, and thank God for that. He doubted he could've done this sober.

"Because, Bel." He lifted both hands and cupped them with careful precision over the delicate balls of her bare shoulders. "You should have been mine."

She went stiff under his hands. "I'm sorry?"

"You weren't for James." He smiled at her, almost gently. "You were for me."

"*What?*"

"I mean, come on. You, with those eyes and that mouth and that brain of yours?" He shook his head slowly and the room did one of those fun dip-and-tilt things. "You should love *me*, not my idiot brother."

211

And I should love you back, and leave the too-pretty, barely-legal waitresses with sin-to-the-nth-degree bodies to James. More his style.

"James is not an idiot!" Like that was the point.

"Oh, all right." He took advantage of her outrage and eased her a little closer. "But you have to admit, he's not what you'd call a deep thinker."

"He can't be." Her alarmed eyes dropped to his mouth. "His job depends on snap decisions, and good ones. He stops to consider his options and—"

"—and there goes the goal, I get it." He gave her a disarming smile. "I didn't say he wasn't a great athlete. He is, no question." He eased her closer yet. "But he's a rotten brother."

"A rotten—" Genuine horror. Will's disgust for himself grew and grew. "You selfish *ass*. He's given you everything!"

"Leftovers." He reeled her in another inch. Two. "Hand me downs."

"Including the women, is that right?" Her eyes went hot and narrow. "Trust me when I say you are *not* getting a doggy bag on this one."

"Oh, I do. I trust you completely." He slid a hand into the silky warmth of her hair and hated himself with a depth and passion that shocked even him. "But I'll have my taste just the same."

And he kissed her.

CHAPTER TWENTY-FOUR

Will was kissing her—*kissing her*!—when the kitchen door swung open.

"Bel," James said. "I need to—"

Bel snapped out of her paralyzed shock and gave Will a solid shove. He didn't resist, just stepped back with a smirk and a shrug. She stared at him, lungs cramped, ears ringing. She shot a numb finger at him. "You," she said, "are going to explain that."

She turned to James who was staring at her, his face set and grim. Her stomach floated into her throat but she shot a finger at him, too. "You. Hang around." Her hands were shaking but her voice was a miracle of calm. Small blessings. "Your asshole brother is about to explain why the *hell* he decided to drink himself stupid then paw me."

She shifted her glare back to Will and folded her arms. "Well?"

He sighed. "I love it when you fold your arms."

"For God's sake, Will!" Bel yanked uselessly at the neckline of her gown. "You *kissed* me!"

"Sure did." Will turned to James and dropped his head in a mockery of remorse. "Just call me Judas. I've betrayed you, brother."

James flicked a glance at his brother. "Yeah, I doubt that." He turned to her. "Bel, listen. We have kind of a situation."

"No kidding." She stared at him. "Your brother just *kissed* me."

"Yeah, I saw. Now, listen. Bel." He took her elbow with careful fingers. "Honey. I need you for a minute."

She blinked. *Honey*?

"So you're okay with this?" Will's head came up, and while the smile was just as oily and impenetrable as always, his eyes burned with a fierce desperation. Bel took an involuntary step back. "I didn't realize you were done with her already."

"With Bel?" James didn't bother to look at him, but kept his eyes on Bel's. "I'm not."

Warmth glowed stupidly inside Bel's chest—*he's not done with me!*—and she gave a little sigh.

Then Will slid a hand into Bel's free elbow and began to draw her into his arms. "Huh. I didn't know that *share and share alike* thing applied to women you were still fucking but, hey, I'm in favor. I've been waiting forever for a taste of Bel's sweet little—"

She flinched. Will used words like weapons but this was extreme even for him. James slapped a flat hand to Will's chest.

"Jesus, Will." James slid him an exasperated look. "You want me to punch your face in. I *get* it, okay? But I'm not going to do it right this minute so will you please knock it off?"

Audrey burst through the swinging door, Drew on her heels. "What the hell is going on in here?" Her wide violet eyes were very close to panicked. "The dessert buffet is laid and the auction is rolling but we still have to—" She stopped short. Drew barreled into her back.

"Geez, Audrey." He grabbed the girl's shoulders and kept her on her feet. "Give a guy some warning before you—"

She jammed an elbow into his stomach and he gave an affronted *woof.* She took in the scene before her more slowly, paying attention this time. "Oh crap. What's the matter?"

Drew gave her reproachful eyes. "Well, you put your elbow right in my bread basket for starters."

"Not you." Audrey jerked her chin toward the breakfast nook. "Them." Suspicion replaced the panic in her eyes. "Bel? What's going on?"

"I—" Bel closed her mouth. Shook her head. "I'm honestly not sure."

"James?"

"Unclear. All I saw was Will kissing Bel." Audrey's eyes went to slits and James held out placating hands. "Trying to, anyway, and not very hard from what I could see. She was fixing to slap his face when I walked in. Didn't get to it, though, and now he's angling for a good punching from me." He shrugged. "Normally I'd be happy to oblige but right now—"

Drew brightened. "You want me to take care of it?"

"No. No punching." James sighed. "Right now all I really want is a quick chat with Bel." He gave her a significant look. "It's important."

Drew raised his hand like a kid in class. "Okay, but just to clarify: We're allowed to kiss Bel now? All of us?" Drew sent her a warm, slow smile and she thought *Like this guy needs leftovers*. "Because if that's the case—"

James actually bared his teeth. "It's not."

Drew tipped his head doubtfully. "But we're not punching Will."

"Not at this time, no." James sent Will a grim look. "Rain check."

"Oh. Well, that's different." Drew turned his reproach on Will. "What were you thinking, Will? Kissing James' girl. Geez."

"I'm not James' girl." Bel felt honor-bound to point it out.

Drew scratched his head. "Are you sure?"

Bel didn't know how to answer that one.

Audrey snorted. "Well, she's not *his* girl." She jerked her chin toward Will. "I have too much respect for her taste to believe that."

"Thank you," Bel murmured while Will suppressed a flinch.

"Just quit making trouble, Will. Okay?" James took Bel's elbow again. "We actually have kind of enough."

"Besides this?" she asked, the first trickle of alarm surfacing. Had he been this grim *before* he'd witnessed Will's unauthorized kissing?

"Besides this." He gave her arm a bracing squeeze. "But I think it would be best to talk about it—"

215

Will said, "No."

James frowned. "What?"

"I said no." Will gave a jerky shrug. "You told me to stop making trouble and I'm saying no."

James opened his mouth then closed it. "Why?"

"Because I'm a shitty brother."

"True enough. And I've penciled your punching into my calendar, okay? Now shut up for two minutes so I can—"

"No," Will said again, and his voice was terrible. So hollow and grave. Goosebumps raced up Bel's arms into her hair, and she took James' hand without thinking. "For Christ's sake, James, I moved on *Bel*. I know how you feel about her and I moved on her anyway."

Bel suppressed a snort. Like Will knew how James felt about her. He thought she and James were enjoying a perfect, perfect love, if memory served.

"Yeah," James said darkly. "I got that."

"So, what, you're going to stand there like nothing happened?" He huffed out a noise that was more snarl than laugh. "For Christ's sake, James, do you love her or don't you?"

James' fingers curled around hers but he kept his eyes on his brother. "I love her."

Bel's heart hammered painfully in her chest. Well. That was unexpected. He *loved* her? Since when? Will gave Bel a wan smile over James' shoulder that said *Told you so*.

Drew muttered, "Foul. I called dibs weeks ago."

Audrey cocked a brow. "You called dibs on a *person*?"

"Sure." He gave her that knock-out smile of his. "But it's okay. Nobody ever pays attention to me. I saw you first, too. But try telling that to Will."

Color leapt into Audrey's cheeks and she rolled her eyes.

"For fuck's sake, James!" Will snapped. "If you love her, then act like it!"

"How?" James asked.

"Swing at me!" Will thrust forward his chin. "Throw me out! Fire me! Something! Anything! But, Jesus, don't *forgive* me!"

"Amen," Audrey muttered.

"I might could toss you out," James said slowly. "If I thought you meant it."

Bel frowned. "Meant what?"

"The *move*," Drew hissed. "The kiss." He had pulled up a stool and was watching the byplay with avid enjoyment. Audrey stood frozen beside him, her eyes fixed on Will, disgust written plainly on her exquisite face. "Shhh, now. This is getting good."

James went on. "And maybe I don't have your great big brain, Will, but it doesn't take a super genius to see that you don't want Bel any more than Audrey does. Not really." He cut a look at Audrey. "You don't want Bel, do you?"

She shook her head.

"There, see?" James gave him a lopsided smile and Will closed his eyes as if in pain. "Now I don't pretend to understand why you decided to move on Bel when you don't want her. But you're my brother and she's my—" He paused and Bel's heart hammered in her chest. What? She was his *what*? "—well, she's just mine. And I'll be damned if I let you make her our Yoko Ono. I don't know why you're trying to make me choose between you but I'm not going to do it."

Bel gaped at James, her fingers and toes tingling like she was considering passing out. She might do just that, actually. She was *his*? He *loved* her? Had he really said all that? Like it was nothing new? A forgone conclusion?

A brilliant joy gushed up inside her, mixed with a blinding panic and a healthy helping of dismay. What the hell did it mean, James' version of love? What was she supposed to *do* with it? She didn't believe in love. Didn't—no matter what her stupid heart might say—even want it.

"So you're not going anywhere," James said to Will. "You're staying right here and we're working this out. Just like always."

"For pity's sake." Will dropped his head and pinched the bridge of his nose. "Just...let me go, James. Please."

"No." James dug a hand into his pocket. He pulled out the jeweler's box Bel had given him earlier that night and shoved it at Will. "Here. Open it."

"No." Will shook his head and backed up. "And stop *giving* me shit."

"It's not from me." James cracked the box and put it into Will's hand. "It's from Bel. Now tell me what that is."

Will lowered his eyes reluctantly to the cufflinks in the box. "It's the Blake family crest," he said slowly. "And...is that Gaelic?"

"Yep. It says family first," James told him. "She had them made special for us. There's a set for you, one for me and one for Drew." Will stared at the box in his hand, stricken, and Bel realized suddenly how much he looked like James. They were such different people; the more she knew them, the less she saw the resemblance. But there it was— the same fair hair, the same broad shoulders, the same long legs. The same extraordinary air of fluid competence, though James' stemmed from his lean-muscled grace while Will's depended on his nimble mind.

"God," Will said finally, his voice strangled. He lifted his hands and let them flop back to his sides like helpless birds. James took him by the shoulders and kissed both of his cheeks, first one, then the other.

It should have looked weird, Bel thought. Men kissing men in the kitchen? Not something you see every day. But it didn't. It felt...biblical. Like Will really was Judas but James was reversing the traditional symbol, forgiving with a kiss rather than betraying.

"You're my brother," James said simply. "I want you to be happy. Whatever's making you so angry, so poisonous? We'll find it and we'll fix it. And the rest of it can go to hell because I'm not letting you go. Not now, not ever." He smiled that sunshiny smile of his. "But I'm still punching you later. Nobody kisses my girl for free."

And with that, Bel stopped resisting. Stopped fighting. This aching desire, this dangerous yearning? It was love—no use denying it—and she finally, finally let herself fall.

Because for the first time, she understood James. Or maybe she didn't understand him completely, but at least now she believed him. She trusted him.

This was a man who said what he believed, then lived it. Because lots of people *said* family was the most important thing in their lives. Lots of people *talked* about love like it was some precious miracle. But she'd never—not once— seen anybody actually live the words out. Not like James just had.

Will, for reasons unknown, had backed his brother into a corner and issued the perfect ultimatum: Love or family? Lust or loyalty? Bel or me? But James—good heavens— James had come up with the third alternative. He'd chosen them both. He'd declared his love for Bel while simultaneously proving his love for Will by refusing the betrayal. He simply refused to accept that Will was capable of hurting him in such a profound and fundamental way. Logic dictated, therefore, that Will must have reasons of his own—twisty and incomprehensible, yes, but reasons nonetheless—for kissing Bel in the kitchen. For some reason, he *wanted* James to reject him.

And the amazing thing? Bel thought James might just be right about that.

She gazed at him in pure wonder. He might say Will was their brain, Drew was their heart, and he was simply the muscle but now Bel knew better. James was their courage. He was a soldier of the first order, a knight in shining armor who'd pledged himself to his family and would do whatever it took to keep that pledge. To uphold his own sacred truth.

He was a throw-back. An honorable man. The kind Bel had simply assumed no longer existed. The kind she didn't think had ever really existed in the first place.

But she'd been wrong. Dead wrong. And the thrill of witnessing that kind of courage and loyalty in action had zapped clear through all the protective layers of jaded disbelief she'd accumulated over the years and arrowed straight into the vulnerable heart within her. The heart that longed to join the circle of family James was willing to protect with everything he had. Everything he was.

The heart that wanted—more than safety, more than security, more than comfort—to belong to him.

It was what she'd always wanted, honestly. To be part of a family that worked. She'd just never expected to find one. Had never expected it to look like *this* even if she did. But life was just full of surprises, wasn't it?

A thrill of optimism sparkled through her. She was going to make this work. No matter what it took, she was going to make this work.

She would have her family, finally.

And it would be James.

CHAPTER TWENTY-FIVE

"Everything all right, Bel?"

James turned to find the caterer hovering at the edge of their tense little circle.

Bel's hand twitched in the folds of her skirt but she gave the woman a reassuring smile. "Of course, Lillian. Something just...came up." She didn't so much as look at Will.

"Not the food?" Lillian asked.

"No, of course not. The food's been marvelous. Everybody's raving about it." She smiled. "Mrs. Vernon-Smithe asked for your card."

Lillian pressed a hand to her generous bosom. "Not *the* Mrs. Vernon-Smithe?"

"The very one." Bel's smile spread into something more natural. James' chest loosened a bit at the sight. That smile of hers was one of God's good gifts. The dimples just sealed the deal.

Not that the beast inside him wasn't still out for blood. But something about Bel soothed it. Soothed him. He didn't know if it was that square, serious face of hers, the smile that transformed it into something exceptional, or just her implacable conviction that decent people exercised self-control. Whatever it was, it propped up his badly shaken better self, and reinforced his determination to do the right thing.

"Anything I can do to help out?" Lillian asked Bel now. "With your, uh, situation?"

Bel shook her head. "I don't think so, Lillian. There's not much we can do tonight anyway."

"Then y'all get out of my kitchen and enjoy the party."

James smiled at her. "Smartest idea I've heard all night." He turned to his brothers. "We'll talk in the morning."

"Sure thing," Drew said. Will just shook his head.

"You, too," he said to Audrey. "This is going to be an all-hands-on-deck sort of event at Blake House."

She nodded, her exotic face drawn. "I'll be there."

"But for now," James said, "all of you need to get back out there and act like you're having the time of your life. And you—" He pointed at Will. "—avoid the bar."

"I'll babysit," Audrey said grimly.

"We'll double team," Drew said.

"House arrest," Will said. "Awesome." He threw up his hands under the weight of four different stares. "Fine. Whatever. I'll sit next to Bob. He can share his tonic water and lime and tell me about the benefits of his new fish and seaweed diet or whatever."

James watched them leave the kitchen. He looked back at Bel and found her beautiful face turned up to his, her honey-colored eyes cool and unreadable. Crap.

"So." He tried a smile. "We probably need to talk about, um—" *The fact that I just—Jesus—threw* love *on the table. Unless, of course, you're too busy running for the hills to chat it out.* "—about what happened here just now."

"James—" She bit her lip, then tumbled the words out in a uncharacteristic rush. "God, James, I'm so sorry. I swear I didn't do anything to encourage—"

"Geez, Bel, I know that." He put out staying hands. "I know you didn't. I never even thought it." Which was true. He trusted Bel absolutely. He had no idea what was wrong with Will, let alone how to put it right. But at this moment, with Bel's dear face tight with worry for him—for *him* when she was obviously the injured party—he didn't care. "We're okay here, Bel. You and me? We're good."

"We are?" The worry shifted into skepticism. "How?"

He laughed, a wary joy creeping into his stomach and crouching down alongside the throbbing anger. "Ah, Bel. You're so...dependable."

She rolled her eyes. "You sure know how to butter a girl up." She tucked her hand into his elbow. A zing shot up his arm and clear into his head. Bel, touching him? Of her own free will? God, he must look worse than he felt.

"Come on." She gave his arm a little squeeze. "We've got work to do. Let's get back out there before you turn my head with your pretty words."

"You don't want to talk about—" He circled a hand between them, then cocked a thumb at the breakfast nook and everything that had happened there.

She laughed. "God, no."

He frowned. "Why not?"

She shook her head and drew him toward the door. "That's going to be some conversation. This isn't exactly the time or place."

"Oh. Right. Of course." He told himself to be relieved. The L-word was out there way ahead of schedule but evidently she wasn't taking it any more seriously than she'd taken Will's kiss. Which was a good thing, right? Maybe he could salvage Plan A after all. So why did he feel vaguely uneasy?

He allowed her to lead him through the door and into the foyer. Then memory rushed up and James pulled back. "There's something else, Bel," he said. "And this one can't wait. I need a minute. Now. In private."

"Okay." Bel looked around the deserted foyer and cocked a brow. James steeled himself to deliver the news. *Guess who's back from his honeymoon, looking tanned, fit and in love? Two hints—he used to be engaged to you and he's in the ballroom right now enjoying the auction with his new wife, who—sorry—used to be your personal assistant until she stole your fiancé on live TV.*

He hesitated and his courage fled. "Not here."

"All right." She lifted those smooth, bare shoulders— God, he was dying to bite one of them—and said, "How about outside? The guests are all busy with the auction, and I haven't seen the gardens since they've been finished."

"The gardens? But the gardens are—"

223

She waited with perfect patience for him to finish his thought, one finger threaded through the fat curl nestled against the swell her breast. The impulse to put his mouth right there, just there where all that autumn-colored velvet rode high on the plump curve of her breast grabbed him by the throat but he battled it back.

"—dark," he finally managed. "It's dark outside."

"Yes." She nodded slowly. "Because it's nighttime." Her brows slowly rose. "Is that a problem? The gardens are lit, aren't they?"

"No. I mean, yes. I mean—" He pulled one hand down his face, shoved out a breath and ordered himself to pull it together. "Yes, the gardens are lit." And they were. With fanciful little fairy lights that would make her far too kissable. "No, it isn't a problem." Total lie. His self-control was already on the ropes. Strolling around in the fairy-twinkled dark with Bel would almost surely deal it a fatal blow.

"Well, then." She gave his arm a companionable squeeze. "Let's go. Privacy awaits."

"Right. Okay."

James concentrated all his energy on acting as if her breast weren't snuggled up to his biceps as they walked beyond the soaring foyer and out a pair of French doors onto what used to be the patio. He stepped onto the crushed oyster shell path that bisected a manicured sweep of lawn bordering the formal gardens, her skirt swishing companionably against his boots.

"You did some really extraordinary work here, James," she said as they entered the garden through an arching arbor twined with grape vines.

"Not me. I just sign the checks." But he hardly heard himself speak. He was too busy staring down at Bel.

He hadn't been prepared for this, he thought a bit wildly. To see Bel here, like this. Oh, he'd known it would suit her, the strict geometry of an English garden. She thrived here like a perfect, pink-cheeked tea rose, just the way he'd known she would.

But he hadn't anticipated the moonlight. He'd braced for fairy lights but, Jesus, the moonlight. He hadn't braced for that. How could he have? How could he possibly have anticipated the way it would steal Bel's practicality and crush it into glittery dust? The way she would glow under it with a serene, mysterious beauty?

"You always say that," she murmured. "Like other people have all the talent, and you just make the money. Like you're nothing special."

"What can I say?" He concentrated on keeping their pace, unlike his heartbeat, smooth and even. "It's the truth."

"Believing what you say doesn't make it true."

"No?"

She shrugged, and James tried to avoid the view it afforded him down her dress. God, that dress was killing him. It had nearly flattened him in the soft light of the ballroom, about undone him in the industrial brightness of the kitchen, but here in the moonlight? With nothing but the cool night air and James' embattled self-control between them?

Stick to the plan, he told himself firmly. Break the news about Ford and what's-her-name. Be a kind and loving friend. A hands-to-yourself friend. A no-crazy-monkey-sex-in-the-outdoors friend. A *friend*. Period

Not that his feelings toward Bel were at all platonic. Not hardly. James knew love when he felt it and this was it. Capital L love. The grown-up, for-real, down-on-one-knee-with-a-diamond-solitaire kind. James wanted Bel's groceries residing in his fridge on a permanent basis and wouldn't rest until they did.

Which was hardly a secret anymore, thanks to Will's big scene in the kitchen. God, was he going to enjoy the punching later. Not that it would change anything.

The bottom line was that the current state of his life would cause a girl like Bel to run—not walk—to the nearest exit. As well it should, considering that his idiot brother had gone ahead and laid a fat wet one on her without so much as a beg your pardon.

A hot sliver of rage with Will's name on it wedged itself into chest but he ignored it. He didn't have the time or energy to deal with that right now. Right now he was working the plan.

And the plan—the best he'd been able to come up with over the course of the past two weeks—involved keeping Bel at arm's length until the time was right. Until his home life was a little more appropriate, which meant straightening out this thing with Will, getting Bel her job back and taking his team to the World Cup Finals for the first time since the Great Depression.

That was Phase One. Phase Two involved luring her into his bed and keeping her there until she was too weary, too sated, too undone with sexual satisfaction to even consider leaving.

And then he could move on to Phase Three, in which he somehow transformed all that crackling lustful energy between them into something more solid and meaningful. Something more like love.

Simple, right?

But until then, he'd keep her close and work the friendship angle. Even if it killed him, which was seeming more and more likely.

"Listen, Bel." He forced himself back to the unpleasant task at hand. "I have to tell you something."

"Oh!" She broke off as the path under their feet opened up to a broad circle centered on the marble fountain that used to grace his front lawn. "Oh, James, this is gorgeous! I didn't realize I was looking for the fountain while we were walking, but I must've been. I could hear the running water, I guess, on some subconscious level. Funny how your brain works, isn't it?"

"Yeah," he said. "It is." He'd wondered himself why the original landscaper had hidden the centerpiece of the garden inside a ten foot tall ring of shrubbery, but it was just like Bel said. The sound of unseen water drew people. Called them into the mazes and alcoves, and rewarded the persistent with this lush, intimate surprise of a space. The illusion of isolation capped with nothing but the endless night sky. The sort of place where men lost their heads and women lost their inhibitions.

The sort of place he should avoid like the plague with Bel on his arm, beaming up at him with pure delight. He stared down at her, trying to ignore the way the curve of her breast pressed warm and inviting against his sleeve. The way the heat of her seeped through his coat and into his skin. The way want danced to life inside him, sparkled hard and fast through his gut.

"Dance with me?" she said.

"What?" His brain felt half-awake, sluggish. Nothing at all like the rest of him.

"Dance with me," she said, laughing. "Can't you hear it? The water?"

He frowned at the burbling fountain. "What about it?"

"It's waltzing."

"It's what?"

She laughed. "Seriously, listen." She slid her hand up to James' shoulder, seized his other hand and eased him into a gentle one-two-three sort of thing around the wide, gracious path ringing the fountain. He followed, his feet moving more out of an unconscious imperative to stay near her than any actual desire to dance.

And then he heard it. *Burble* beeble beeble, *burble* beeble beeble. The water trickled along in some primitive, gravity-driven rhythm that ticked through his veins and had him sinking his hand into the small of her back, drawing her into him and taking over the lead.

"There you go," she murmured. She nestled her cheek into his shoulder and they sailed over the path in a perfect unity of motion and spirit. And inside him, something caught fire. Want surged up, fierce and undeniable, and he didn't have an ounce of self-control left to put out the flames. He'd used most of it not kissing the hell out of Bel the minute she'd walked into the foyer in that dress. Not punching Will had finished him off.

Now he just *wanted*. Wanted with an aching, searing need that drowned out the better angels pleading for caution inside his head. And what he wanted—more than a happy

227

family, more than a successful career—was her. Bel. Her faithful heart, her tidy soul, her elegant body. All of her.

Her breath fanned against his throat, sweet and warm, and that beautiful earnest face tilted up to his. And that mouth of hers, that impossible mouth was *right there*. It pulled him and he swayed into her, dipped his head. What would it hurt? Just a taste—

He stopped. Stopped dancing, stopped breathing, stopped moving in for that kiss he could almost taste. "Bel," he said, a desperate panicky edge to his voice that even he could hear. He took her by the shoulders and set her carefully away from him. "Listen, I *really* need to tell you something—"

"No." Her mouth turned down in a sulky pout that utterly short-circuited his internal pep talk.

"No?" James gazed at her, enthralled as she stepped toward him. He shook his head. "Wait, what do you mean, no?"

"I mean no, I don't want to talk." She took another step toward him. He could feel her now, the heat of her shimmering in the cool night air.

"But I—"

"What I want—" She slid her hands up the front of his jacket. "—is for you to kiss me."

James' jaw dropped and his brain simply stopped. His conscience threw up its hands and when she took that last step forward, his arms automatically circled her, his palms cruising toward the small of her back. "You want me to, um, what?"

She rose up on her toes, put that gorgeous mouth a wish from his and slid her fingers into his hair. "Kiss me."

It was all the invitation he needed. The beast inside him surged ahead, snapped its leash, and yanked a grateful James along behind it.

He dragged her to him, let all that satiny cool skin, all those neat angles and plump curves, slide over his body like running water. He pulled the scent of her deep into his lungs, feasted on the vanilla-and-cinnamon smell that clung to her hair even when she hadn't baked in days. He plunged himself into her mouth, her hot, willing, beautiful mouth, all honey and spice and lush welcome.

Plan A could go screw itself.

CHAPTER TWENTY-SIX

Bel fell into the kiss, dizzy with success and fear and love. This was what she wanted. His hands streaking over her with undeniable want. His mouth hot and commanding on hers, the force of his desire bending her like warm wax to his will. Enclosed in the circle of his arms, safe inside his want, his need, his love.

She twisted her hands into the stiff fabric of his jacket and pulled herself higher onto her toes. More. God, she needed *more*. She opened her mouth beneath his and a trembling glory shook through her when his tongue touched hers. She dragged in a deep breath, and it was hot with the scent of him. Clean, masculine, his breath swift and sweet on her face, in her mouth.

"Bel," he said. "Bel."

She speared her fingers through his hair and brought his mouth back to hers with a greedy purpose. She didn't want to talk. She'd had enough talk to last her whole life. Now she wanted action.

Because she'd seen James in action, seen him back up all his words with an enormous act of courage and strength. And now she wanted it all for herself. All that courage, all that strength, all that loyalty and determination and goodness. She wanted it in her arms, in her bed, in her heart. In her life.

He loved her. He'd said so. And she loved him. For better or worse. She wanted to bind him to her now, before they talked and things got complicated. She wanted to give him her pledge in the most ancient and primal way possible. Not with words, but with her body. With her heart and her kiss.

She wanted her mark on him, and his on her so the entire world would see them and know they belonged to each other. That no matter what fate threw at them, they would weather it together.

Hunger like she'd never experienced ate at her, sharp and cruel. A hunger that she somehow knew nothing but his skin under her hands would satisfy. She pushed at his coat, shoved it off his shoulders with an impatient jerk. He wrestled out of it, dropped it to the crushed shells underfoot while she tugged his shirt free of his waistband.

Her hands found the warm skin of his back and streaked upward, greedy to discover all his edges and angles, to explore the supple muscle and smooth skin. She'd denied herself even wanting him for so long. To have him now hot and alive under her fingers had a soft purr of pleasure humming in her throat. He was so real—all this bone and blood and breath, trembling under her touch. Trembling with desire for her. For *her*.

Her lips curved in satisfaction and a whippy excitement crashed into her system. Had she ever made anybody tremble before? Doubtful. It was a new experience. One she could get used to.

"Bel."

His hands slid up her arms and across her shoulders, his thumbs dipping down to flirt with the neckline of her dress.

"Yes?"

She brushed her lips across his cheekbone, then moved on to explore the shell of his ear.

"Bel, are you sure?" His hand drifted down to trace a path of tingling fire across the edge of her bodice. Her thoughts fell to her feet and blew away.

"About what?"

He dipped a finger into the hollow of her cleavage and limned the inside curve of her breast. Her nipples tightened to an aching awareness and the breath left her lungs. "About this."

That finger dipped again into the cleft between her breasts. Bel's spine went to warm honey, her shoulders rounded and her lips parted on a soft, silent oh. Her bodice gaped slightly and the night air flowed cool and forbidden across the exquisitely sensitive skin of her breasts.

"Um, yeah," she said, breathless. "Pretty sure."

His clever fingers slid warm and sure into the hot velvet of her dress to cup one breast in his palm. He dragged a slow, deliberate thumb over her nipple and an electric shower of sparks exploded low in her belly.

"God, James, I—" She broke off, catching the words before they fell out and ruined everything. The way they always did.

"What?" His voice was a low rumble, amused and urgent, against her neck where he'd pressed his lips. "You what, Bel?"

She forced her eyes to open, to focus on the precisely trimmed hedge silhouetted against the night sky. *I love you*, she thought. *God, I love you.*

"Nothing." It was already perfect—this night, this man, this decision. There would be time to define it later. For tonight, she wasn't going to talk, wasn't going to think. Tonight she was going to just let herself ride out the thrilling, crazy, buoyant storm inside her.

She arched into his hand, and her bodice snapped tight again. His palm, trapped hot and hard against her exquisitely sensitive skin, sent a knee-weakening surge of liquid heat into her belly, and a small moan escaped her. But James seemed to be breathing through his teeth, so Bel let embarrassment slip away like her thoughts.

"Jesus, Bel," he said. "I want—"

He broke off to drag his mouth, hot and open, up the side of her throat and she dropped her head back to allow him better access.

"I know." Her laugh was rich and full with the jittery want streaking through her, but it cut out when his arm came around her waist like a steel band. He jerked her off her feet and bowed her into him and suddenly her world narrowed to only what she could feel.

His mouth, hot and open and demanding on hers. His fingers, clever and maddening on her breast, his heartbeat, strong and unsteady against hers.

His leg slid along hers, caging her between long and powerful thighs, and his desire pushed hard and strong against her belly. A brilliant, blinding streak of light shot through her, settled low inside her, screwed the blind, seeking hunger in her a notch higher.

She arched herself into him mindlessly. Closer. She wanted to be closer. She wanted to draw him into herself, to take all this heat, this desire, this power inside her body. She wanted to take and take and take, let him fill her until there were no empty spaces left, nothing cold or abandoned or untouched.

"More," she said into his mouth. "Please, James. More."

"Anything you want," he said. "I swear to God, I'll give you—"

"You." Her fingers dove between them, flew fast and clever into the waist of his breeches, worked the buttons there with feverish haste. "Just you. Please."

"Holy mother of—" He sucked in a harsh breath as she yanked open the last of the buttons, took him in her shaking hands. His hands fisted in the lush flow of her skirt, then danced impatiently up the back of her dress. "I can't...there's no—ah, screw it."

He gave up what Bel assumed was a search for buttons or zippers or what have you at the back of her dress and instead simply hooked his fingers in her neckline and jerked. The dress—already precariously balanced on her corset-induced cleavage—gave way without protest, and her breasts popped free.

"Oh, sweet Jesus," James said, staring. Bel had a look herself and was astonished. Her dress pooled dark and rich around her waist, her skin glowed pale and pearly in the moonlight. Her breasts spilled ripe and full—as full as a modest B cup would ever get—over the lacy edge of her corset, as if served up on a silver platter for the guy industrious enough to free them from the confines of her neckline. And James—lucky, lucky Bel—was that guy.

He plunked her down without ceremony on the wide marble edge of the fountain, dropped to his knees and cupped her with reverent hands. The cool night air flowed over her, broken only by the heat of his hands. Her skin pebbled, her nipples peaked and James slowly lowered his mouth to one aching point.

"Oh." Her head dropped back, too heavy suddenly to hold upright. She speared her fingers into all that golden hair and arched into him, into the glorious tug of his mouth, into the delicious molten glow it banked deep inside her.

One wide hand splayed over her back, holding her steady against him. As if she were going anywhere, she thought, a strangled laugh lodging in her throat. A laugh that died when he circled her ankle with long, clever fingers. Fingers that slid up her calf, danced over her knee and stole slowly up her inner thigh. Oh God.

His teeth dragged lightly over her nipple, and a pleasure lanced through her so intense it bordered on pain. His tongue laved gently, immediately soothing the sting into a punishing, achy want. A want that spun higher and tighter with each inch of her thigh he conquered with those clever, questing fingers. He toyed with the frilly edge of her vintage pantaloons for one eternal moment, then finally, *finally*, slipped inside.

A black heat filled her mind, scoured away all rational thought, leaving nothing behind but the primitive want pulsing through her entire body. A want that drove her relentlessly toward her goal. Toward him. Toward having him, marking him, taking him.

"James." She gripped great handfuls of his fine, linen shirt. "*Now*."

He lifted his head from her breast and the want inside her only burned brighter at the sight of an answering hunger in his face.

"Right." He leapt to his feet. "Now." He drew her to her feet and applied himself with vigor to the elaborate array of knots and buttons and pins holding her dress in place.

"No." She shoved him down on the wide marble slab she'd just vacated. "Now." She wriggled out of the funny little Miss Muffet pantaloons and kicked them aside. She stuffed half a dozen yards of skirt under one arm and straddled him, the marble cold and unforgiving under her knees.

"At least the corset, Bel." He smiled, his eyes hot on hers. "You'll die of oxygen deprivation."

"Then I'll die happy." She settled against the hard length of him with a sharp, indrawn breath. An answering emptiness ached inside her, throbbed for something. For fulfillment, for satisfaction, for him. For this.

She rocked into him, against him, took him into her by slow, agonizing increments until he was seated deep inside her and her breath came in sharp pants. Until his hands found her hips and clamped there, shaking and strong and urgent. The need to drive herself onto him, to slake this vicious, twisting hunger lifted her and brought her back down. But it wasn't enough. It wasn't—

"Lie back," she said. She twisted and he fell back across the curved edge of the fountain, one boot on the ground, the other stretched across the marble lip. He propped both elbows on the wide rounded edges, and clamped his hands onto her hips. She wrestled her skirt high onto her thighs and shoved most of it behind her. Then she put one foot on the ground, the other in the shallow water and rode him.

She rose and twisted, lifted and fell, climbed with the light and the heat and the hunger inside her until everything spiraled up, higher, brighter. Until there was nothing between them, nothing unspoken, nothing unsolved. Nothing broken in her, nothing empty inside. Nothing holding her back from that wicked, knife-sharp edge. She hurtled heedlessly over and pulled him behind her.

James dragged himself hand over fist back into consciousness. He didn't really want to, because the dream he'd just had was too good to leave behind. Bel. Warm, open, touchable. Her lips curved in welcome, in humor, in love. Her dark eyes narrow and glittery with heat, want, desire. All of it centered on him.

Then he realized the contented warmth wasn't coming from that dreamy, happy place he'd just visited. It was coming from Bel. She lay across him, her dress twisted around her waist, her hair tangled over his shoulders. And— sweet baby Jesus in the manger—he was still *inside* her.

He jerked awake and clamped his arms around her before she could escape. He needed to reorient himself and didn't want her to run away while he was getting his bearings. Plus if this went the way he figured it might—lots of recrimination, second-guessing and dear-lord-what-have-I-done-ing—he didn't want this part to end any too soon.

A wheezy chuckle wafted out of her. "Okay," she said, "you may have had a point about the corset. Can't...breathe..."

"Oh." He forced himself to ease up the grip. "Right. Of course. God. Are you all right?"

"Better than." She lifted her head and the smile she gave him arrowed straight into the cotton-candy center of his heart. "You?"

"I'm, ah..." He smiled back at her, totally on autopilot in the face of that smile of hers. He touched one of those silky maple-syrup curls still pooled on his shoulder. "I'm sort of confused." He closed his eyes. *Nice one, James.* The girl he loved had just screwed him into literal unconsciousness, and instead of thanking her profusely and begging her to do it again for, oh, say, the rest of his life, he tells her he's *confused*? "I'm good, too," he said hastily. "Really, *really* good. Thank you for that, by the way. I'm just, well...kind of surprised, too."

She reached up and pressed a soft kiss to his mouth. He fell into that kiss—God, who wouldn't? Mouth like hers?—and time sort of warped into something indeterminate and circular. Though clearly more for him than for Bel because when he surfaced, she was already squinting at her watch.

Then she leapt straight off him, leaving him feeling way too abandoned for his liking. "Okay, time to get dressed," she said briskly. "You hear that?"

James cocked an ear. And suddenly, he did hear it. People. Voices. Footsteps. The auction must have wrapped up while he and Bel had been, ah, otherwise occupied. And now their guests were flowing out of the house and into the gardens. "Right," he said. He leapt into action alongside her and in a disappointingly short amount of time, his lovely, wanton, deliciously disarrayed Bel was perfectly respectable again.

He had no idea how she did that. He himself felt wrinkled, rumpled and completely, bonelessly satisfied. But there she was, fresh, pressed and glowing like some kind of tidy flower.

He didn't know if he'd ever loved her more.

"Hey, Bel?"

"Yes?" She gave him those wide, dark eyes, her hands folded primly together in front of her skirt.

"You're really something else, you know that?"

She smiled at him, full speed ahead on the dimples and his heart did one of those Grinch things where it grew about three unexpected sizes. He wanted to say more but just then a couple strolled through a break in the hedge circle. Bel gave them a polite nod and James offered her his elbow. She took it and they began their own slow circuit around the fountain, as if they were seeing it for the first time.

"So," Bel said. "You wanted to talk to me?"

A guilty start rolled through him. "Oh, hell. Yeah, I did."

He stopped, took both her hands. "Listen, Bel, there's a person here tonight, and you're not going to like hearing who it is."

"All right." Her eyes went wide and wary. "Who?"

"But I'm not going to leave your side for a second, so everything will be fine."

"Thank you," she said. "But who is it?"

"Just do that stiff upper lip thing you're so good at and we'll get through this no problem."

"James." She narrowed her eyes. "Who?"

He sighed and wished Ford the ex-fiancé to the depths of the ocean with all his heart. Because, come on. He and Bel had just taken their first, tentative steps toward a future together. Okay, so maybe mind-blowing sex in the great outdoors wasn't exactly tentative but it *was* a step in the right direction. A big one. Was it too much to ask that the guy Bel had almost married not crash the moment?

He pulled in a deep breath but before he could force himself to spit out the name, a new voice soared through the night air. It was sweet and clear, like a small, expensive bell and it said, "Belinda! Darling! I came as soon as I heard!"

James watched the animation drop out of Bel's face like somebody had switched off a light inside her. She turned slowly to face a tiny woman in violet silk flying over the path toward her with quick, graceful steps—not a run exactly but certainly faster than walking. The woman threw herself at Bel and squeezed her with frantic hands. "Oh my darling, my dearest. My poor, poor lamb. Don't worry, dear heart."

Bel's hands stayed at her sides, curled loosely into the fabric of her skirt though her spine was as rigid as a two by four. The woman didn't seem to notice, just clasped Bel to her corseted bosom, rocked her side to side and crooned, "Mummy's here, now, darling. Mummy's here."

CHAPTER TWENTY-SEVEN

Bel's eyes met his over her mother's head, a stark question in them. *You knew?*

James shook his head quickly. God, no. But, geez, poor Bel. Her ex-fiancé and her mom, with whom James knew she wasn't exactly close, at the same party? His girl was taking it on the chops tonight.

"Oh sweetheart." Bel's mother drew back to gaze at her daughter. Her hands flew up like tiny birds to pat Bel's cheeks. "You're so thin! Why didn't you *call* me?"

James stepped back, the better to watch the impromptu family reunion taking place under his nose. He'd known Bel had a mother. He just had never pictured her quite like this. She was a good head shorter than Bel, to begin with. And where Bel exuded that quiet correctness that started with impeccable posture and ended with imperturbable calm, her mother—so far—was all about the dramatic flourish.

"Call you?" Bel asked with the same tone she might use to inquire about the freshness of a cabbage. "About what?"

"About *what*?" Her mother blinked in astonished horror, one little hand pressed to her frilly bosom. "About *what*? Dear lord in heaven, Belinda! Your faith in mankind was abused most cruelly. And on *live television*?" She closed her eyes and shook her head. "I cannot *imagine*. But you— you poor, *poor* dear—you simply gritted your teeth and bore up under the humiliation. My sad, strong, *darling* girl."

She clutched at Bel, trying, James supposed, to bend her into a sad, darling girl. He smiled into his collar. Not exactly Bel's style. He could see how Bel had characterized their relationship as difficult.

Her heart seemed to be in the right place, though. And she was here. That counted for a lot in James' book. The balance of family duty, as he knew from vast experience, lay

239

in simply showing up. Just being there through it all, whether your presence was wanted or not. Nobody with family—any decent family anyway—suffered alone. It simply wasn't allowed. Your family sat there with you in your misery, propping you up, renting DVDs, serving snacks and making bad jokes until you were ready to venture out again on your own wobbly legs, blinking against the sunlight.

Bel disentangled herself from her mother's arms and stepped back just as Bob and Kate strolled into the fountain enclosure. Kate, one hand threaded through Bob's elbow, chatted easily with a gossip columnist from the Washington Post. But her eyes landed sharply on Bel.

"Vivi, please," Bel said. "I didn't call you because I didn't want you here."

Vivi? James felt his eyebrows heading for the sky. She called her mother by her first name?

"Didn't want—" Vivi pulled back as if she'd been slapped. Her round blue eyes filled with hurt. "Why, Belinda, that's an awful thing to say! I flew halfway around the world to be with you and this is how you thank me?"

"I didn't want you here," Bel said again, her voice flat, "and I still don't. I never will. Please go."

James' mouth dropped open. This wasn't a difficult mother-daughter relationship. This was rejection, flat out. Bob must have sensed the sour note from fifteen yards off because he touched the back of Kate's hand and murmured something in her ear. Kate ignored him with her usual regal impatience, her eyes fixed and fierce on Bel. The gossip columnist followed Kate's gaze with the seeking focus of a blood hound catching a scent.

Kate didn't break stride but continued toward them at the same serene stroll. Bob didn't fight it but his brows were a straight unhappy line. The columnist fingered her cell phone furtively, probably cuing up the camera. James braced himself for company in about thirty seconds, tops.

He touched Bel's stiff elbow and leaned in. "Gossip columnist," he murmured. "On your six."

"Of course there is." She didn't look away from her mother. "I don't want you here, Vivi. Please leave."

James stared, alarm shifting toward disbelief. What the hell? His Bel had a real gift for polite displeasure, no denying that, but she wasn't cruel. Farthest thing from it. But giving your mom an unflinching *get lost* in front of the national press? That was cruel. Unquestionably.

"Oh." Vivi's eyes flooded with tears. "Oh. I see."

James' heart squeezed inside him and the fury he'd been saving up for Will's punching suddenly jumped the tracks. He knew real life had, at best, a vague acquaintance with justice. He didn't expect a Brady Bunch reunion here. But this woman was Bel's *family*. There was no greater good in James' world—in any world—than family. James would give anything to have his mother annoy him at a party one more time. He'd be damned if he'd let Bel reject hers right in front of him.

"Hi." He stepped forward and shot Vivi a warm smile. "I'm James Blake."

"Vivienne Pietrantoni." She held out a tiny hand and returned his smile with a brave curving of her lips. "Belinda's mother."

"Of course you are." James folded her hand gently into his. Geez, the woman felt breakable. "I see now where Bel gets her dimples."

Vivi's smile deepened. "Oh, you're sweet."

"They're gorgeous on both of you," James told her, patting their joined hands. "I'm always after Bel to smile more."

Vivi's eyes went warm and her dimples fluttered. "I am, too."

"Then we ought to be good friends, Ms. Pietrantoni."

"Vivi," she said, and hugged him. "Oh, you're a kind man. I'm so pleased my little girl has somebody like you. I worry about her, you know. She's so...alone."

James cut his eyes to Bel, who simply gazed at them. And she did, in that moment, look strikingly alone. A pale, composed woman who might have been watching a movie for all the emotion in her face.

"Vivienne?" Kate asked, appearing behind the woman's shoulder. She beamed her on-camera smile down at Bel's mom. "Kate Davis. I'm so pleased to finally meet you." She turned to Bel. "Bel, dear. Why didn't you tell me your mother would be attending tonight?"

"I had no idea she would be," Bel said. She gathered her skirts. "If you'll excuse me?"

Vivienne's head drooped and Kate gave Bel a look of genteel disapproval. The columnist hanging a few paces back snapped a surreptitious picture. James gritted his teeth. "Bel, come on. It's your *mom*, for heaven's sake."

She arched a brow that said *so*? Anger leapt hot and jagged inside him.

"We're intruding," Bob said. He took Kate's elbow firmly. "We should—"

"Which means—" James went on as if Bob hadn't spoken, his voice carefully calm. "—that no matter what the beef is between you two, you owe her at least a thank you."

Bel tipped her head, considered. "For what?"

"Well, for her concern, for starters," James snapped. "For the impulse that put her on a jet from wherever—"

"Italy," Vivi said.

"—from Italy to see for herself that her daughter, however difficult the relationship between them might be, was all right."

"No." Bel folded her hands in front of her, her face smooth, the erratic pulse in the base of her throat the only sign of life.

"No? No what?"

"No, that's not why she's here, and no, I absolutely will not thank her for it." She gathered her skirt and moved around her mother as if she were a stone in the road. "Go home, Vivi. There's nothing for you here."

Vivi made a small squeak of distress that tore at James' heart with sharp little claws.

"Belinda," Kate murmured with a significant glance at the scribbling reporter. "You forget yourself."

"No," she said quietly. "I've finally remembered myself. But I do apologize for creating a scene." She turned empty eyes on her mother. "I sincerely wish it hadn't happened. Now if you'll please excuse me."

Vivi began softly crying.

"We'll discuss this in the morning," Kate told Bel in tones of dark promise. If Bel picked up on the threat in those words she gave no indication. She simply inclined her head.

"If you like." She moved toward the gap in the hedges with a fragile dignity that had confusion twisting together with the snarling anger in James' gut. She was the one inflicting all the damage here. Why on earth should she look one stiff breeze away from shattered?

He lunged after her, closing the distance just as she reached the gap. "Jesus, Bel." He snatched at her elbow. "Would you stop for one stupid minute here and think about what you're doing?"

She stopped, her back stiff and unrelenting. Then she turned her head, slowly, until she'd aimed the point of her chin at him with the haughty grandeur of an offended queen. "What," she asked, "am I doing?"

"You're walking away from your *mother*." His chest was tight with urgency. She had to understand this. Because if she understood what she was doing, she wouldn't do it. She couldn't. How could she? Surely her heart, the heart he held as precious as his own, wouldn't allow it. No heart worth loving—no heart capable of loving—could. "Your *mother*, Bel."

"That's right," she said.

"No, it's *not* right." Frustration and fear howled inside him. This was wrong. *She* was wrong. Bel was good, loving, forgiving and patient. This wasn't her. Not the Bel he knew. Not the Bel he thought he knew, anyway. "God, why are you *being* like this?"

She gazed at him with a cool finality that only stoked the anger burning in his belly. "I'm leaving now," she said. "We can discuss this in the morning, if you'd like."

He stared at her, waiting for this cold, stony woman to disappear. Waiting for her to turn back into the Bel he'd fallen in love with, the Bel who understood what family meant.

He thought about his own mother, her quick smile, her strong, ready hug. The instant application of the flat of her palm to the back of his head whenever she considered it necessary. There wasn't a day that went by that he didn't need her. Didn't miss her.

He looked over his shoulder at the tiny, sad-eyed woman by the fountain. At the mother Bel refused to even acknowledge.

"No," he said, and his voice surprised him. He hadn't known he was going to speak. The words just leapt from his mouth like a cork from a bottle, shoved out by anger and pain. "There's nothing to discuss."

Bel gazed at him, her eyes dark and remote. "She's not even your family."

"She's yours," he said on that same wave of unconscious desperation. "It matters, Bel. And I thought, after what happened in the kitchen with Will, after what it led to right here between us—" He leaned in, locked his eyes on hers, willing her to remember every touch, every sigh, every lingering, electric taste. "—I thought you understood that. I thought you understood me." He raked both hands through his hair and huffed out a jagged laugh. "And I thought I understood you."

"But you don't anymore." Her eyes were deep and wounded. "Because of this." She waved a hand to encompass the gently weeping Vivi, Kate's arm around her shoulders, Bob hovering uncomfortably behind them.

"I don't even *know* you, Bel. I thought I did, but this woman who'd hurt and humiliate her own mother in front of an audience? She's a stranger to me."

And because the wrenching, gut-churning pain of that loss threatened to put him on his knees, he let the anger take it. Let the anger turn his pain into sharp, nasty words he could throw at her like rocks.

"Kate's been right about you all along," he said. "You don't even have it in you to be the heart of a TV show. How could I have possibly imagined you had it in you to be the heart of a family? *My* family?"

"I know exactly what it takes to build a family," Bel said softly. "And I know how to sacrifice everything I have to protect it from harm." She gave him a faint smile that stole the sharpest edge from his anger and replaced it with a thin slice of dread. "Unfortunately, no family I've chosen so far has ever returned the favor."

"Chosen?" His stomach went cold. "You don't choose family, Bel."

"Of course you do. People do it all the time. They call it falling in love."

"You—" The cold in his stomach turned to solid ice. He cleared his throat and tried again. "You don't believe in love."

"I believed in you." She gathered up her skirts with calm hands, her eyes full of pain but no surprise. "My mistake."

She turned and disappeared through the gap in the hedges. James watched her go, his heart empty and numb inside him.

Bel moved woodenly along the path. She'd burned herself to cinders tonight, she observed. Icarus flying too close to the sun. She'd been yearning for things she could never have, things that mere mortals just didn't get. Stupid. She wondered if it was possible to erase the entire last hour from her memory. Just slice it out like a surgeon would excise a tumor.

"Bel?"

At first she didn't recognize the voice. It had been too long. A life time. Then she turned and found Ford and Annie standing there, their fingers still tangled together, having just rounded the corner of the hedge maze only to find awkwardness itself lying in wait for them.

"Ford," she said. "Annie. You're back." This, she realized, was who James had been trying to prepare her to see. *But I'm not going to leave your side*, he'd said. *So everything will be fine.* Bel tried not to dwell on how very alone she was. "How was your honeymoon?"

Ford cast a worried glance down at Annie, who frowned and stepped closer to Bel.

"Bel?" she said again. "What's wrong?"

"Wrong?" Bel laughed lightly, aware she sounded more broken than amused. "What could possibly be wrong?"

Ford reached for Annie's elbow. "It's too soon," he murmured to his wife. "We'll go," he told Bel. "We're so sorry. We'll just—"

Annie shook off her husband and moved a step closer. "For heaven's sake, Ford," she said. "Look at her. This isn't about us. This is bigger than that. Way bigger." She reached out and touched Bel's elbow, her eyes warm with compassion and understanding. "Your mother found you?"

"Hmmm? Oh, yes." Bel nodded, idly wondering why this final humiliation—being confronted with her ex-fiancé, her ex-assistant and their happiness—didn't sting more. Perspective, she supposed. Her heart knew what real pain was now, thank you very much. "Yes, she did. She flew all the way from Italy the instant she heard. To comfort me in my time of heart break, you understand."

"Yes, I can see that." Annie's lips twisted. "What's difficult to see is how she managed to rustle up an authentic period costume and crash the biggest single event on the *Kate Every Day* roster when she was so busy rushing to your side. I assume there was press?"

"And Kate and Bob and James. And several strangers." Bel waved a hand. "You know Vivi."

"By reputation only. I assume the shine wore off her Italian prince or duke or whoever and she needed a little fresh juice. Some new drama."

"And then my fiancé happened to run off with my assistant on live TV." She gave Annie and Ford a wan smile.

Ford stepped forward, compassion warm in his eyes. "I really am sorry, Bel. We both are. I hope one day you'll be able—if not to forgive us—at least to understand."

Bel patted his arm and it was still solid and comforting under her hand, just like always. "I already do, Ford. We would have been a monumental mistake. I know that now."

"You do?" He glanced down at Annie, surprise clear in those straight-ahead brown eyes of his.

Annie's gaze went shrewd on Bel's face then she swooped Bel into a fierce hug. Bel sank into it for a moment, into the sheer, unlooked-for comfort of a loving touch, then Annie pulled back. "You do understand," she said, studying Bel. "It's finally happened. You're in love."

"I am," Bel said. No point wasting wishes on things that couldn't be undone. She was in love. She might never be out of it.

"Have you told him?"

Bel replayed it in her head, the horrible moment when she had all but confessed her love to James *after* it had already become apparent that he didn't love her back. Not the way she loved him. She closed her eyes against the jagged rush of humiliation and pain and wished with all the strength left in her battered heart to undo it. To take back those pitiful, plaintive words—*I believed in you.* To erase the flash of startled realization they'd put in his eyes. She could almost hear him now. *Wow, Bel. That's...I mean, geez. I'm flattered. But when I said I loved you, I meant—*

She cut off the James in her head. Couldn't bear to hear it, even in her imagination. She'd spent her entire childhood wanting too much. Expecting too much. Loving too hard. Hadn't Vivi taught her anything? Love was a game. A thrilling, entertaining rush, but it wasn't permanent. The minute it wasn't fun anymore, the minute it felt like work, it was time to move on. Time to find a new job, a new man, a new passion. Time to abandon everything—including your thirteen-year-old daughter—and seek your bliss on a new continent.

"I could've picked a better moment to share the news," she said finally.

Annie's mouth went hard. "Tell me."

So she did. Annie threaded an arm around her waist and they walked, keeping to the darkest corners of James' new garden while Bel told them everything. She started with moving into the Annex and brought them clear through to tonight. To Will's bizarre kiss and James' refusal to accept betrayal. She covered her impulsive decision to have wild, mind-blowing, ruin-her-for-all-other-men, *completely unprotected* sex with James under an extravagance of twinkly stars. Then she wrapped it up with his uncompromising position on the poison that was Vivi.

When Bel was done, she found herself on a stone bench in one of the cozy, secluded arbors overlooking the pond, her hand firmly in Annie's. She accepted a clean white hanky from Ford and mopped at her face.

"What are you going to do?" Annie asked.

"What is there to do?" she asked, forcing a bright note. "I mean, lesson learned, right? I'm going to just walk away from this whole mess. Pretend it never happened. I'm going to wake up in the morning and start fresh. Fresh heart. Fresh life. Fresh dream. God knows, I'm going to need one." She gave a shaky laugh. "I received the distinct impression that Kate's going to fire me again—for good this time—bright and early."

"The bitch," Annie said.

Bel shrugged. "People don't take homemaking advice from people whose homes are broken beyond repair, Annie. It's a fair point."

Ford shook his head. "Not necessarily. If you want to take legal action, I think there are probably sufficient grounds for breach of contract. I'd be happy to draft—"

"Oh, Ford, thank you. But no." Bel squeezed his hand and gave him what she hoped was a brave and plucky smile. "There's no point trying to hang on. It's all part of an old dream now. I'm putting it behind me. Him, too. James. The whole thing."

Even as she said the words, heartbreak gushed up inside her ugly and fresh. It flooded her eyes and swamped her fragile little boat of calm.

God, what a load of shit. Putting him behind her? Even if she somehow managed to ignore the death throes of her broken heart, she could hardly fail to notice that one leg was still soaking wet from the knee down after her impetuous decision to screw the love of her life on the edge of a gaudy Italian fountain. No, James had written himself on every inch of her skin tonight and no matter how much her heart wanted to forget, her body remembered.

"Oh honey." Annie sighed. "You are *not* okay."

"No, I am. Seriously." Bel flicked at the tears that spilled onto her cheeks and gurgled out a soggy laugh. God, that fountain. "I'm sure I'll have regrets when I look back on how I handled this whole godawful mess but walking away from a boss I can't please won't be one of them. And God knows I should but even now I can't regret James. Okay, maybe the unprotected bit was a mistake, and maybe the aftermath isn't pretty but for a minute there, it was really beautiful. The kind of beautiful I didn't know existed. The kind I thought people were making up."

Annie's hand found Ford's and Bel suffered a small but stinging slap of jealousy. She'd always cultivated the cool, empty spaces around her heart. They'd kept all threats at a safe, sanitized distance, like a well-tended moat. But James had blown past her moat like it didn't exist, had blasted right into the sacred, secret core of her as if he had every right to be there. As if he belonged.

And he had. For that brief instant, he had belonged to her and she to him. She would cherish that for the rest of her life, that sense of utter belonging. Of family.

These past weeks, she'd come to know him as a man of immense courage. Just tonight, she'd seen him give more than he had to give, lift more than he could carry, and endure beyond endurance. Now she understood why. He belonged to something greater than himself alone. He had a family.

A family to which Bel didn't belong. Maybe she couldn't force him to include her in that sacred circle, but neither could she love him with anything less than the strength and courage he'd shown her family deserved.

"Oh Bel." Annie squeezed her hand. "Is there anything we can do for you?"

Bel smiled. "I wish, but no. I think I'm probably as good as I'm going to—"

"Actually, there is something." Bel jumped—they all did—and turned to find Bob strolling across the moonlit lawn toward them.

"Bob!" She patted her thundering heart. "Where did you come from?"

"A chat with Kate." He smiled but it looked grim and hard. "An unpleasant one."

Bel shook her head. "Don't worry. I know I'm fired. Ford's already offered to take up breach of contract proceedings but I'm not going that route."

"Good. I was thinking along different lines anyway." He sat down on the bench beside her with a weary sigh. "Grab your lawyer and listen up, kid." He patted her knee. "I have an alternate proposal."

CHAPTER TWENTY-EIGHT

When the sun cracked the horizon the next morning, James finally allowed himself to head down to the kitchen. To Bel. He knew she'd be there. Knew it the same way he knew which direction a goalie would dive, or a defender would attack. He just knew it in his bones.

He forced himself not to jog down the stairs. He couldn't seem too eager. He couldn't compromise his values. But he'd spent the sleepless night after Bel's staggering confession of love—she *had* said she loved him, hadn't she? In her usual, sideways sort of way?—thinking. Really thinking. And thinking wasn't James' usual forte.

Not that he wasn't a smart enough guy, or didn't know how to think when he had to. Just that success in his line of work meant *not* thinking. There wasn't time. He had split-seconds to make decisions and the answers had to come from his gut, not his head. He couldn't think; he just had to *know*.

And what he knew right now was that, no matter what had happened between them last night, he wasn't going to let Bel walk away from him so easily. Maybe the thing with her mom was a problem but so what? Problems were made to be solved, and he was going to solve this one. He could start by learning one hell of a lot more about what would make a woman as inherently fair and justice-oriented as Bel turn such a hard cheek to her own blood. He'd bet his heavily insured right foot there was a story there. Several of them, knowing Bel. She wouldn't cut somebody off after the first mistake. Not if she could love a guy like him. God, he was such an idiot. Why hadn't he remembered that last night?

The scent of coffee hit him first, before he'd even pushed through the swinging door, and his heart lifted inside him. She was there. Bel was in the kitchen. Because who

251

else could possibly be brewing a pot of coffee in his kitchen at the crack of dawn? The smile that spread across his face felt goofy and wonderful. Bel didn't even like coffee. She drank tea. She'd made it for him.

He hit the doors at a near run.

"Look, Bel, we need to talk," he said, then stopped. Because Bel wasn't manning the coffee pot. Bel was nowhere to be seen. Instead, Audrey sat at the island counter, deep shadows under her eyes and bleak acceptance in her perfect face.

"Bel's gone," she said.

"Gone?" Dread clenched his lungs in a powerful grip. "Gone, like out for groceries? Or gone, like—"

"Gone like gone," Audrey said. "Gone like not coming back."

"That's ridiculous," James said, as much for his benefit as Audrey's.

"Did you two have a fight or something?"

"Well, yeah. But she lives here. This is her home."

"This is your home, James." Audrey spoke carefully, as if mindful she was speaking to her employer and trying not to shout. "Had you talked about her staying on after last night? Even after Kate all but fired her again?"

"No, but—"

"Or did you tell her she was a failure to you, too, and that you didn't want anything to do with a girl whose family doesn't work like yours?"

"She talked to you?" James pressed a hand to his chest. It felt like somebody had landed a punch right under his heart. He couldn't get a decent breath.

"No, not really. I surmised a great deal of it."

"That I was an ass? You surmised that?"

"It wasn't a hard conclusion to draw, James. Not looking at Bel's face when she got back here last night."

He shook his head. "Bel's used to it by now. She's got to be. I mean, I'm always popping off without thinking. It's why I'm sitting here with you now instead of helping my team kick Mexico's ass. She knows my mouth gets ahead of my brain sometimes. She's got to know that most of what I said last night was stupid, spur-of-the-moment shit."

"That doesn't mean it didn't hurt her."

He glared at her. "I know that, Audrey. Thank you."

She shrugged. "I'm just saying."

"She's angry right now. God knows she deserves to be. But this is Bel we're talking about. She wouldn't leave without giving me a chance to apologize or explain." Would she?

"She took suitcases, James. Plural."

"She'll be back." Audrey looked doubtful and he said, "Seriously, unless she took her eggs and her butter and her milk, she'll be back."

Audrey reached behind her and pulled open the fridge. "First thing she packed," she said. "The clothes seemed like an afterthought, to tell you the truth."

James stared at his refrigerator. Anybody else might've seen a well-stocked fridge but to him it was a ghost town. Because all Bel's stuff—the yeast, the capers, the fancy olives or tapenades or what have you? Gone. The farmers' market eggs, the hunks of weird cheese, the big ol' block of butter? Gone. She'd left behind *his* groceries, he realized slowly. She'd taken her own. There was no trace that Bel had ever so much as made a sandwich in his house. His stomach went cold and tight.

"Did she—" James had to clear his throat against a sudden lump of fear and pain. "Did she tell you where she was going?"

Audrey swung the fridge shut and regarded him with equal parts accusation and sympathy. "No. She just said to tell you goodbye."

"Goodbye." James pushed on the straining emptiness in his chest with the heel of his hand. "God."

"What are you going to do?" Audrey asked.

"Wake Will and Drew, would you?" James was already heading for the door. "Catch them up. I'm going to talk to Kate."

By the time he got to Hunt House, it wasn't yet 7 a.m. on a Sunday morning but he found Kate fully dressed and at her desk, as if the cameras were rolling.

He rapped his knuckles on the glass of the French doors and waited while she rose, still staring at a paper in her hand.

"James," she said, her knuckles showing white where she gripped the paper. "You heard about this?"

He glanced at the paper. "About what?"

"About Bob's retirement." She stared at the paper in her hand as if it were a snake. "Effective immediately."

"No. Doesn't really surprise me, though."

Her eyes flew to his. "No?"

James shrugged. "He's been looking tired lately. Thin. Seemed sort of, I don't know. Off."

"Off."

"I expect Will knows all about it. You can talk to him if you're overset by this, Kate." He stepped into the room and she automatically gave way, still frowning thoughtfully at the letter in her hand. "But that's not why I'm here. I'm looking for Bel."

"Bel?"

"Sure. Bel. You know—tall, killer smile, hell on cakes?"

"I had the impression Belinda was leaving town. She tendered her resignation late last night."

Fury and fear twined together inside James, biting at his self-control. But he kept his voice easy when he said, "A resignation you accepted?"

"Of course. While I liked Belinda a great deal personally, my successor's authority on family relations must be above reproach. She simply wasn't qualified for the work, James."

"Because of her mother."

Kate inclined her head but the stately regret of the gesture clashed with the satisfaction in her eyes. He thought back to Kate's avid, hungry gaze on Bel and Vivi at the fountain last night.

"You knew her mother was a problem, didn't you?"

Kate seated herself with precision on the curvy little chair behind her desk and watched him stalk back and forth on her fancy rug.

"You knew exactly what would happen if you put Bel and her mom together in front of a crowd, didn't you?" He stopped pacing long enough to rake his hands through his hair and stare at her in dawning wonder. "You set her up. You *invited* Vivi last night, didn't you? You *wanted* Bel to fail. Why would you want that?"

"Oh, for pity's sake." Kate crossed her legs. "I didn't *want* her to fail. I didn't *want* anything. It was a simple vetting process, and Belinda proved last night beyond a shadow of a doubt that she lacked a basic job qualification. An extremely important one. Possibly the most important one." She folded her hands on the desk calmly.

"A picture perfect family." James spat the words with a derision he couldn't have imagined himself using even twelve hours ago.

"They don't happen accidentally, Mr. Blake. No more than a perfect pot roast or a gorgeous party does. They all require time, effort, attention to detail, and—most importantly—an excellent recipe." She leaned forward, pinned him with that cool gaze. "That's what I sell, dear— dependable recipes for good food, good friends, a beautiful home, a happy family. And while we all agree that Belinda is a certifiable miracle in the kitchen, I think we can also all agree that her ability to perform up to *Kate Every Day* standards in other areas was...lacking."

"And you're such a paragon of family life?" He looked pointedly around the pristine space. "Where are all the pictures of your husband and kids, Kate? Your grandkids? The stray stuffed animal or dirty sock or empty coffee mug that might point toward some people actually living in this museum you call a house?"

He flopped down in the antique chair across from her desk, paying no attention to the pitiful creak as it bore up under his weight. "Oh, right, sorry. You don't actually *have* a family living here, do you? Because you don't have a family at all. And this isn't really a home."

She stiffened. "I beg your pardon. This absolutely is my home."

"It's a set, Kate. An immaculate and carefully constructed set where you create the illusion of the perfect home, the perfect family, the perfect pot roast, whatever. But nobody actually eats in your dining room. Nobody actually lives in your living room. And sure as hell nobody actually cooks in your kitchen. It's all for show. So where do you get off judging Bel for her family life?"

"Judging her?" Kate smiled at him, smooth and pleasant. "James, please. You're not angry with me for judging your precious Bel. You're angry with yourself for judging her. And more harshly, too. I only suggested she wasn't particularly qualified for my job. You suggested she wasn't particularly qualified for your heart."

James stared at her for a long moment while he absorbed the sting of that one. God. This woman had a real talent for swinging the truth like a hammer. And her aim was friggin' exceptional.

"You're absolutely right," he finally said. "I did. I was hurt and tired and pissed off that life wasn't giving me exactly what I wanted. What I thought I'd earned. And because of that, I hurt somebody I love very much. But unlike you, Kate, I'm ashamed of myself. I dropped the hatchet on Bel without even trying to understand her point of view, and she deserves more than that from me. She's *earned* more than that from me. From both of us, really. She's been feeding me since the minute I met her—body and soul. And if she's willing to give me the chance to try, I'll spend the rest of my life returning the favor."

"A worthy endeavor, I'm sure," Kate murmured.

"It is. And if you gave your viewers the chance to know her like we know her, I'm pretty sure they'd love her, too. Vivi or no Vivi."

"Yes, well. You'll forgive me if I don't agree."

"Suit yourself." James rose from the chair, a sudden, itchy energy bubbling up inside him. He needed to find Bel. Needed to share this new clarity in his heart with her. "Can I see that letter from Bob?"

Kate pushed it across the desk with one finger.

"Says here he'll be out of touch immediately and indefinitely. No email, no cell?" James cocked a brow at Kate. "Doesn't sound like the Bob I know."

"He advises me to have my lawyer handle any contract negotiations that arise until he can finalize the sale of his agency."

"Mmmmm, yeah, I see that." James frowned at the letter. "Any idea where he might have holed himself up?"

Kate blinked at him. "Why?"

"Because if anybody knows where Bel is, it's Bob."

"Why would Bob know where Belinda is?"

James glanced up from the paper. Kate looked genuinely confused. "Because he didn't doubt her," James said. "Not ever. Bob believed in Bel from the beginning and he never swerved. Bel wouldn't blow town without seeing him. It would be rude."

Kate accepted that like the manners maven she was. "I can give you his home address and a number for a land line. After that, you'll have to work with the answering service he's listed in the letter."

"Fine. Thanks." James took the sheet she tore off a monogrammed note pad and headed for the door. He stopped, one hand on the knob. Turned back.

"Are you really going to let him disappear like this?" he asked. "Without a word or a fight?"

Kate shrugged, an elegant twitch of the shoulders inside her silky blouse. "I'll find another agent," she said.

"That wasn't really what I was asking, Kate."

"I know." She picked up her china tea cup, sipped what must surely be cold tea. "Please close the door on your way out."

CHAPTER TWENTY-NINE

When he returned to the Annex, James found Drew hunched at the keyboard of what served as his computer, Audrey peering over his shoulder at the screen. As usual, the casing was off the tower and a jumble of wires and computer innards spilled out onto the floor. The man had at least half a dozen high-powered laptops to his name, James knew, not to mention the tablets and the smart phones that weighed down his pockets like spare change. But when performance mattered, Drew headed straight to his desktop Frankenstein.

"Kate says Bel quit last night," James announced. "Just *thank you for the opportunity*, etc."

"So Audrey tells me." Drew continued typing. "I'm pulling former addresses right now. Maybe she'll go somewhere familiar."

"Good thinking." James battled back a surge of hope. "Any luck so far?"

Drew scowled at the screen.

"Not yet." Audrey put both fists in the small of her back and straightened with a wince. She glanced at her watch. "All right, I think it's finally a respectable hour. Let's call Bob. I'll bet he knows—"

"Probably does." James handed over the scrap of paper Kate had given him. "Only he's in the wind, too."

"What?" Audrey stared at the paper. "What does that mean?"

"It means he left his resignation on Kate's desk this morning, too. Retirement or some such. Effective immediately. That's his answering service and home address."

"Good thing your contract's solid for another eighteen months," Drew mumbled around the pen in his teeth.

"Did we even know he was retiring?"

"News to me," Audrey said. Drew just squinted at his screen and swore under his breath.

James flopped onto the couch to stare helplessly up at the ceiling. What the hell was he supposed to do now? He was more foot soldier than general. He blew at strategy.

He sat up like the couch had goosed him. Jesus, of course! He didn't need to *be* a strategist. He *had* a strategist. World-class, too. A guy whose middle fucking name was brilliance, and who happened to owe James, major large.

He said, "Where the hell is Will?"

The frantic clickety-clack of Drew's keyboard hitched then resumed. Audrey said, "Oh. Um." James stared.

"Oh, fuck, are you *kidding* me?" Because he wasn't Mr. High IQ but his intuition was faultless. Last night notwithstanding. "He's gone, too?"

"I'm sorry, James." Audrey twisted her fingers until James thought they might snap off. "I told you I'd keep an eye on him last night but—"

James dragged both hands down his face and came to his feet. "I didn't expect you to chain him to his bed, Audrey. You're fine."

"I *hate* that guy," she muttered, and James tried for a smile.

"Don't we all? Skated out from under a good punching, too." He patted her shoulder. "Ran like a little girl from my mighty Fist of Death."

She obliged him with a smile but it was half-hearted at best. "Hey. No knocking little girls."

The chatter of the keyboard stopped dead for five full seconds and the resulting silence was louder than a jackhammer. Hope blossomed inside James for the first time since he'd discovered Audrey instead of Bel in the kitchen.

"What?" He flew across the room, grabbed a handful of Drew's sleeve and leaned in. "What did you find?"

Drew stared at the screen, his arm hardening like concrete under James' hand. "Juvie records."

"Juvie records?" James frowned at the screen. "Whose?"

"Bel's."

259

James huffed out a startled laugh. "Shut up. Bel does *not* have a juvie record." Drew's silence was grim and the laugh died. "Does she?"

"I'm about to do something relatively illegal." Drew turned flat eyes on him. "Plausible deniability would suggest you take a quick walk."

James blinked. "What?"

Audrey threaded her arm through his. "Walking!" She dragged him to the window overlooking the driveway. "What a pretty day. *Look* at the view, will you?"

He glanced over his shoulder at Drew's dark, bent head and wondered when his baby brother had moved beyond geek territory and into hacker land. Wondered what else he'd missed, because he was starting to think he'd missed plenty lately. Enough to drive three of the most important people in his life into hiding. Christ. Some instincts.

A printer hummed to life in the corner and James leapt for it. The pages were hot, the information bare-bones, and James scanned it avidly. He read it a second time more slowly, while his stomach knotted with horror and disgust. While his heart wept with pity.

Losing his parents had been the shittiest thing life had ever thrown at James, and it was the gold standard by which he judged all life's shittiness. The shittiness Bel had survived hadn't even been on his radar. He handed the papers silently to Audrey, and met Drew's sad, patient eyes.

"How the hell did this happen?" he asked. Drew shrugged.

"Kids land in the system for all kinds of non-criminal reasons," Audrey said quietly. "Your parents take a walk and there's no family to step up? Hello, juvie."

He glanced at Audrey, at the cold anger in her eyes. A pang of sick dismay edged up his throat. "Is that what happened to Jillian?" he asked. "A stint in juvie?"

"No." Her smile was faint but fierce. "Jillian has family. She has me."

"Lucky kid." He worked up a smile. "But what about foster families for those who aren't?"

"There aren't nearly enough of them, particularly not those willing to take on older kids like Bel would have been."

"But why would she need fostering in the first place?" he asked, while sick anger churned inside him. "Vivi might not have been a first rate mom but, God, she's *alive*, isn't she? I can't imagine that she'd have abandoned her own—"

"Of course you can't." Audrey handed the papers back. "People with normal moms seldom can."

He accepted that in silence, and rage prickled at the edges of his mind.

"Academic records," Drew said quietly. "Coming right up."

James didn't bother to ask how the hell he'd managed that one. He was too busy fighting the urge to break something. Because while breaking shit would be a righteous outlet for the rage boiling inside him, it wouldn't help him think. And he needed to think. Slowly, coldly, rationally. Because he simply could not grasp the idea of Bel—his beautiful, gentle *Bel* who made homes everywhere she went—living in a concrete dungeon like the one where they'd just taught those hard-eyed girls to bake.

Especially when her mother was damn well alive.

He flashed back to Bel's disappearing act at the girls' school, and a bunch of puzzle pieces fell into place. Kate had known. That canny bitch had *known*. She'd sent Bel there on purpose, same as she'd invited Vivi last night. She'd buried her landmines for maximum possible damage, but his girl had grit. Bel had walked right through with a strength and courage he could hardly imagine. A strength and courage he'd betrayed.

He didn't deserve a second swing. He knew that. But he was going to take one anyway. Or die trying.

Four hours later, James was still very much alive and no closer to locating Bel. Bob and Will were still in the wind, too. He rubbed a palm over the banging emptiness inside him and decided to name it hunger. It was pushing noon and he hadn't eaten since the night before. He could probably do with a sandwich or something. He doubted it would fix whatever was wrong inside him but it was something to do. And he desperately needed something to do.

"Hey, why don't I get us something to eat?" He leapt to his feet with an abruptness that had Jillian in the window seat glancing up from her book with a startled frown. He dug his keys out of his pocket. "I'll just run into town—"

"Are you kidding?" Audrey said. "You saw the fridge. We have enough leftovers from last night to feed a small army. It would be a crime to go buy more food."

"Oh." He forced a smile. "Right."

Of course the kitchen was full of food. Bel wouldn't have left it any other way. She'd made his kitchen the heart of his house—full of light and color, good food and laughter. And now—food or no food—it was empty as hell. And he couldn't face that.

"How about Jillian and I see what we can rustle up?" Audrey said quickly. James figured his poker face could use some work. "You should stay here in case...Well, in case." Now it was her turn to force a smile. Nice.

"Fine," James said. "Thanks."

"Come on, Jillian," she said. "Let's go see about lunch."

The door swished shut behind them and he was right back to where he'd started. Desperate to take action, no action to take. Fuck.

He laced his fingers behind his head and started pacing the perimeter. He was going to wear a track in the floor at this rate.

Drew shot him a sympathetic glance. "Have you tried her cell?"

"Every half hour since dawn." James reached the corner and hung a left. Headed for the next corner. "Complete with increasingly pathetic messages."

"Okay, that should probably stop." Drew went back to his screen. "We're going to find her and you'll get a chance to make your case face to face. Meantime? Let's not get into restraining order territory."

James stopped pacing, dug his fingers into his hair and gripped his scalp. "Drew, I was such an ass last night."

"Kind of our specialty, bro."

James dragged his hands down his face, blew out a breath. "That shit's got to change."

"Okay."

"*We* have to change, Drew." He frowned into space, struck. "You, me, Will? We've got to pull our shit together."

"Right."

"We've been boys long enough. Been a hell of a run, but it's time to grow up."

"Wait, what?" Drew finally looked up from his monitor, startled. "*You* fell in love so *we* have to grow up?"

"This is some brave new territory for the Blake boys," James mused, continuing to pace. "But Bel deserves better than—" He waved an arm that took in the Wii and the massive couch, the beer fridge and the computer guts. "—well, than *this*."

"What's wrong with *this*?" Drew looked around. "I like our *this*."

James continued as if he hadn't spoken. "Better than us, that's for sure. The drinking, the fighting, the suspensions, the scenes—"

"Hey, don't blame your shit on us. Bel was cool with me and Will. She didn't blow town until you got all judgy on her family situation."

James scowled, ashamed. "Well, that might've been, you know, the last straw but—"

"And telling me and Will you loved her before you told *her*?" Drew snorted. "What kind of asshole does that?"

He jammed his hands in his pockets, mortified. "How do you know I didn't tell her?"

"Please. I saw her face in the kitchen last night when Will outed you." He sent James a beatific smile. "She looked like you'd rapped her on the melon with that meat mallet of hers. No wonder she left."

"Oh, hell." James dropped his head. "I have *got* to stop fucking this up."

"Well, sure." Drew shrugged. "She's a peach, our Bel. You want to deserve her, you'd better man up."

"But *how*?"

"How what?"

"How do I man up?"

Drew blinked. "You're asking me?"

James threw out helpless hands. "Bob was my first choice. Then Will, maybe. But since they're both in the fucking wind? Yeah. You." Fear and love tangled messily together inside him and he rolled his shoulders, trying to settle it all. "I love her, Drew. I don't know what to do. I don't know how to be what she needs, and it's pure killing me. So if you have an idea, I wish you'd lay it on me."

"Huh." Drew leaned back in his chair and linked his fingers thoughtfully behind his head. "You're serious."

"Yeah." James shoved his hands into his pockets again and shrugged miserably. "I am."

"Well, shit."

"I know, right?"

The door flew open—hard enough to bang the wall—and Audrey appeared. "Hey, guys." Her smile was big, bright and furious. "Look what I found in the kitchen."

CHAPTER THIRTY

Drew looked at her empty hands. "Not lunch," he said dolefully.

"No." Audrey's smile was a vicious slice of fury. "Not lunch." She stepped into the room, folded her arms and aimed all that malevolence at the threshold. "I found your stupid brother."

Will appeared in the doorway, wary and rangy in jeans and a button-down shirt. He looked tired and thin, and not precisely happy to be there. James vaulted over the couch and pelted toward the door. Will's hands jerked up automatically, half-curled, then dropped. It was like his nervous system said *fight*, his conscience said *don't*, and Will himself was reaching for his better angels. By the time James hit the door, Will's hands were up again, but open and empty this time.

"James, hey. Listen, I—"

He grabbed Will by the scruff of the neck and hauled him into his arms. Squeezed the ever-living hell out of him and laughed in relief. Will had come back. His family wasn't complete—never would be without Bel beside him—but it was one hell of a lot better than it had been two minutes ago. He pulled back to grin at his wayward brother. "Hey yourself, bro."

Will arched one brow. "That's it? Just hey? No *where the hell have you been, you asshole*?"

"Nope." James clapped him on the shoulder. "You'll tell me that when you're ready, I imagine. Meanwhile, I'm just happy to see your ugly face."

"But if it'll make you feel better?" Audrey stepped up and punched Will's shoulder, hard. "Where have you *been*, you asshole?"

"Ow." He rubbed his shoulder and scowled at her. "Why are *you* hitting me?"

"We needed you here!" She hit him again. (*Ow*. More scowling.) "Do you have any idea what's been going on here this morning? Bel's gone! *Gone*, you jerk! And poor James is beating himself up thinking it's all his fault but your hands aren't exactly clean where Bel's concerned, and you know it. So instead of running off without a word like a whiny-pants jerk wad—"

"Whiny-pants jerk wad." Drew rolled the words around his mouth like a professional wine taster. "Nice."

"—you should have *been here* for him. For us! But no, not you. You were too busy doing God knows what with God knows who, probably putting down whole bottles of expensive God knows what the whole time! So if he—" She hooked a thumb over her shoulder at James, who took an automatic step back. Audrey had some temper on her and James was a prudent man. "—can find the grace to forgive you, you can pony up some goddamn gratitude!"

"You're right." Will put up those hands again. "Okay, you're right. I'm not going to argue. I deserve that."

Audrey frowned. "Well, of course you do." But it was muttered, half-hearted.

"And if you'll give me a few minutes, I'll explain everything. Where I've been, why I went, why I'm going back."

"Going back?" James frowned. "But you just—"

He shifted that gaze to James. "I can tell you about Bel, too, though I don't know as much on that score."

"You've talked to Bel?" Hope exploded almost painfully within him and he grabbed Will's arm. "Where is she? What did she say? Is she all right? Did she—"

Will gripped James' shoulder. "She's fine. Pissed at you and unhappy in general but fine. She's why I'm fine—or going to be—and she's why I'm here." He nodded toward the couch. "Sit down and I'll tell you everything I know."

James and Drew headed for the couch but Audrey hesitated in the doorway.

"You, too, Audrey." Will smiled at her. James gaped. It had been years since Will had smiled and it hadn't felt like a weapon. "You deserve to hear this, too."

"Oh, but—" She glanced toward the door.

"Jillian's fine. She's in her room with one of Drew's e-readers."

"Uh oh." Drew sat forward. "Which one?"

Audrey tensed. "The blue one. The mini-tablet?"

"Okay." Drew smiled. "That's fine, then. Porn's on the red one."

She stared for a moment. "Right. I'll remember that." She sank onto the couch with a muttered *Lord Almighty*.

Drew turned his attention back to Will. "All right. Lay it on us."

"So Bob called me last night." Will tucked the tips of his fingers into the pockets of his jeans and faced them over the coffee table. "Late last night. Well after Audrey and Drew made sure I was in bed like a good boy." James' brows lifted. The words were right, the twisted smile was as usual, but he had the feeling Will wasn't mocking anybody but himself. And that *was* unusual. But impatience prodded him with sharp fingers so he filed it away for chewing over later. "He made me an offer."

"What was it?" Drew was big on audience participation.

"His agency."

"What?" Audrey's eyes went huge.

Drew said, "He wants to give you the agency?"

"Hell, no. He wants to *sell* me the agency. Apparently he's retiring, effective immediately—"

"Yeah, we heard," James murmured.

"—and wanted to sell the agency. Wondered if I was interested."

"Just the agency?" Audrey leaned forward, eyes narrowed. "Or is he giving you the client list, too?"

"Oh, the whole thing, bait and tackle. Reasonable pricing." His lips twisted again. "But there were conditions."

"Aren't there always?" Drew grinned. "But I've seen you negotiate a contract. You eat conditions for breakfast. You clean conditions' clock! You take conditions to the—"

"I accepted them both as-is."

Drew's mouth dropped open. Audrey frowned. James said, "There were only two?"

Will nodded. "Only two."

"What were they?"

"Number one? The sale doesn't go through until I get out of rehab."

"Rehab?" Now Drew's eyes went huge.

"Thirty days, in patient."

Drew considered that. "I don't know, Will. You drink a fair bit but rehab?"

"Yes, rehab," Audrey snapped. "It's where you go when drinking moves beyond a hobby and into a lifestyle. Now shut up."

"Yes, ma'am."

James hadn't shifted his gaze from Will. He didn't know how Will felt about rehab but if he was willing to do it in order to make this move, then fine. His decision. Wouldn't hurt Will a bit to lay off the drink, and everybody knew it.

But he hadn't mentioned the second condition yet, and James had an idea he was gathering his courage. So he waited.

Will said, "Bob even had a rehab facility in mind already, some place he's sent clients before. Evidently, when you're in the business of making multi-millionaires out of twenty-year-olds, you develop resources that way." He shrugged. "I filled out the paperwork this morning. I check in tonight."

"That's wonderful, Will." For once, Audrey sounded absolutely sincere.

"I fucking hate everything about it."

"But you're going."

"Oh, I'm going, all right." He huffed out a short laugh and dropped his head. "She didn't leave me a choice."

"She?" James' stomach dipped suddenly.

"Bel." Will lifted his head and met James' eyes straight up. "Evidently, it was her idea."

"Of course it was," Audrey murmured. "That girl is something else."

"No kidding." Drew's tone was awed. "I've been tempted to kiss her in the kitchen myself. Nobody scrambles an egg like Bel. Glad I remembered myself now." He whistled. "Rehab, Jesus."

"What, you think this is some kind of petty revenge?" She made a disgusted noise. "This isn't for her. It's for *him*." She jerked her chin at Will. "You think he was Bob's first choice to buy his agency? Please. Bel's just made Will the world's prettiest bed, not that he deserves it. All she's asking is that he lie down in it sober."

Will's head stayed down and James imagined he was concentrating all his energy on leashing that sharp tongue of his. Will was a stubborn bastard but he wasn't stupid. Audrey had a point.

"Hey, where is this place?" James asked. Rehab was one thing—likely a very good thing—but he didn't want Will disappearing again. "Will we be allowed to visit?"

Will gave a jerky shrug. "Not for the first week, I don't think. But after that, sure. It's in Virginia. Not too far. Pretty country."

"Okay." He sat back, but his hand crept to his heart, to the hollowness still banging away there. "All right. Now for God's sake, what's the second condition?"

Will paused, and James' heart banged harder. "The second condition is that I pass along a message and extract a promise."

"A promise?"

"Yeah. To Bob."

"God." James scrubbed both hands through his hair and put his elbows on his knees. Drew's hand found his shoulder, gave it a bracing squeeze. "Okay, I'm ready. Hit me. What's the message?"

"It's not word-for-word," Will warned him. "So don't try to read between the lines or anything. Bob said to tell you that Bel's sorry she left without saying goodbye but she'll be back."

"She's coming back?" James shot to his feet. "Oh, thank Christ. When?"

"Christmas." Will rocked back on his heels. "Bob's launching some *new venture*—" He put the words in finger quotes. "—and he's apparently hired Bel as his personal assistant." He threw up a flat hand. "Don't ask me what or where it is because I have no idea. Bob didn't say and I didn't ask. I only know that they'll be on-site with it until Christmas at which point they'll come home and Bel will come see you."

"Christmas," James breathed. "That's, like, six weeks from now."

"More like seven. You ready for the rest? The promise?"

"Anything."

"While she's away? Leave her alone."

He flinched like he'd taken a punch. "She said that?"

"No, Bob said that but I don't think she disagrees." He took a seat on the edge of the coffee table facing James. "You've just got to wait this one out, bro. She's calling the shots now." His mouth was grim, flat. "On all of us."

"For God's sake, listen to yourselves!" Audrey shot to her feet, fists on her hips. "All Bel's asking for is your patience and your trust. Maybe enough time to come to terms with the fact that she didn't have either of them last night." She gave James an accusing look. He held it bravely. Girl had a point. "If she's your family now—"

"She is."

"—then for the love of Pete, act like it. Earn her."

"That's what I said!" Drew slapped his knee, delighted. "Just before you guys came in, I was like *Dude, Bel's a peach. You've got to earn her*. And James was all *Dude, how?* And I was all *hell if I know* but it sounds like Bel's delivered the step-by-steps." He sighed happily. "I love that girl. I had dibs, you know."

Audrey rolled her eyes and went on. "And in case you were unclear, earning her means abiding by her wishes in this, James. So stop mucking around and just let it unfold."

270

"It's just like you said to Ford the ex-fiancé," Drew said. "Remember? Right before he ran off with the ex-assistant? Something about not forcing shit, just letting it sing?"

"Flow," Will supplied bitterly. "He said love should flow."

"There you go." Drew sat back, satisfied. "You got to let this one flow, son."

"Flow." James clenched his jaw so tightly he feared for his molars. Everything in him howled in protest. He wasn't built to sit and wait. "Sing." He shifted his eyes to Will for a long moment. "Christmas. You're sure?"

He lifted his shoulders. "That's what Bob said."

James thought about his still, quiet kitchen. He thought about six—no, seven—endless weeks of cold silence from the other half of his heart. He thought about what kind of guy Bel could love, and wondered how long it would take to make himself that guy.

"Guess I've got my work cut out for me, don't I?"

CHAPTER THIRTY-ONE

Three weeks later

Bel loved autumn. Really loved it. Oh, there were plenty of people who loved fall, she knew. Who enjoyed the smell of wood smoke on the crisp night air, who appreciated the way brilliantly colored leaves turned up their noses at gravity to dance across breezes gone all swirly and quixotic. But her love went beyond these simple pleasures. She loved autumn the way other people loved newborn babies or baseball season—with a deep, primal, possessive devotion.

Because autumn, to Bel, was harvest season. It was that most wonderful time of year when the earth reveled in its own fertility and the bounty at the farmers' market made her want to weep with joy. When she descended into her kitchen for weeks on end, indulging in a frenzy of glorious, exhausting labor that ended only with Thanksgiving dinner, Bel's own personal high holiday.

Which was why normally today would have sent her into a tailspin of giddy delight. Not only had it dawned sharp and bright, bringing to life a sky so perfectly blue it looked like a movie set, but it was also the Monday before Thanksgiving. It was a day custom designed to meet or exceed Bel's personal specifications for perfection.

But just now, standing on the massive front porch of the Annex with a bag of groceries in her arms and her heart lodged in her throat, she couldn't work up any enthusiasm for it.

Ring the damn bell, she told herself. *There's no time for nerves.*

Which was true, she thought, a wave of grief breaking inside her. There was hardly time for anything anymore.

She sucked in a deep breath and punched the doorbell. "And I Will Always Love You." The Dolly Parton version, she had to assume. God. Hope-laced terror rose inside her, crested then crashed into disappointment when Audrey rather than James answered the door.

"Bel!" The young woman stared, then launched herself over the threshold. She threw her arms around Bel, groceries and all, squeezing her with a joyful strength that had Bel blinking back tears. "Oh my God, you're back!" Audrey drew back to beam into Bel's face, and what she saw there had the welcome fading into caution. "*Are* you back?"

"I don't know," Bel said honestly. She glanced beyond Audrey's shoulder into the house. "Is James here?"

"No." Audrey pulled her inside and closed the door behind them, as if afraid Bel might escape. "The Statesmen are done for the season, but the US Team starts World Cup training camp in January. He's been doing two-a-days these past couple weeks. Wants to make sure the whippersnappers respect their elders, or something like that."

Bel tried to smile but it trembled around the edges. Audrey had the courtesy to ignore that small fact. She nudged Bel toward the kitchen. "I'll go make up your room, just in case," she said. "Why don't you park your butter and eggs?"

James tramped into the house and dumped his disgusting practice bag in the corner. Every muscle in his body ached. Every ligament, every tendon, and every twenty-eight-year-old joint made a point of expressing its displeasure at James' callous treatment as he headed toward the kitchen.

So, okay, two-a-days weren't exactly fun but if that was what it took to fall into an instant, dreamless sleep the minute his head hit a pillow, he'd deal with the physical pain, and happily. Because thrashing around alone in his bed, torturing himself with wondering what the hell Bel had found out there that was better than coming home to him? Yeah, he'd had about enough of *that*.

Fuel, he thought, shaking off the melancholy that dogged him whenever he stood still more than a minute or two at a time. He needed fuel. And about a gallon of orange juice. Because after three hours of hard-core drills and another half an hour in a steamy hot shower, he felt about ready to dry up and blow away. Which meant he needed to zip through the kitchen.

That was how he'd trained himself to think of the kitchen lately. A pit stop. He'd taken to making himself plates of food and taking them upstairs to eat on the couch in front of the TV with Drew rather than try to endure the cold, empty kitchen Bel had left behind. Audrey tried, God bless her, grilling the occasional cheese sandwich, slapping together an adequate meatloaf every now and then. But she wasn't Bel.

He shoved through the swinging doors, allowing himself to think of nothing more than the ham sandwich he was about to create, then froze. Just stopped dead, like he'd been shot or stunned. Because unless countless fantasies had suddenly obliged him by taking corporeal form, she was here. Bel was *here*, moving around his kitchen with that efficient grace and serene purpose, tucking those fancy little packages of unidentifiable foodstuffs into his refrigerator as if she'd never left.

A wild joy exploded inside him, sang through his veins and electrified muscles that, two minutes ago, would have sworn they couldn't move one more inch. The urge to go to her geysered up within him, hard and strong. He wanted to gobble her up, gorge himself on the smells, the textures, the sweet small pleasures of her that he'd missed like he might miss air or sunshine. The smell of her hair. The sound of her laughter. The taste of her kiss. God, he'd been starving for so long.

But no. He forced himself to stop, to take a minute. To wait. To watch. To *think*. He needed to think. This was Bel, and he'd already screwed up so many times. He needed to get this right.

"You're thinner," he said, surprising himself with a perfectly normal tone of voice. Then he closed his eyes and cursed himself for an idiot. *Way to think before you talk, James.*

She spun, a stick of butter clapped to her chest, her beautiful mouth a soft *oh* of surprise. "James!"

"Hey, Bel." He drank in the sight of her with hungry eyes. "Putting up your perishables?"

She dropped her eyes to the butter. "This looks bad, doesn't it? Presumptuous." She set it aside, then came to the island counter. She braced the flats of her palms on the granite as if preparing to make a stand.

"Your room is just like you left it," he said. "I hope you'll stay." He forced his shaking hands to unknot, forced his feet to stay planted, tried to blank the naked hope and need out of his face. "I've missed you."

She stared at him. "Are you *kidding*?" she asked, and James' heart dropped into his stomach. He'd screwed up. Again. How, he hadn't the faintest, but there was no mistaking the disbelief in her eyes. Exhaustion chased the hope out of his heart and he didn't have to work so hard to stand still anymore.

Okay, so maybe this wasn't exactly the fantasy he'd hoped for. But she was here, and that meant something. He'd be damned if he'd let her disappear again before he had a chance to tell her how he felt.

Bel stared at him across the island counter. He looked...different. He'd honed his body down to the absolute essence of speed and strength, and though every line spoke of weariness and wear, his eyes glowed with determination and something else. Something warm and forgiving and utterly foreign.

Welcome, she realized with a dull shock and a hefty side of confusion. It was unconditional welcome. How could that be?

"Listen, James," she said, nerves and fear putting an unfamiliar edge on her voice. "I bolted three weeks ago with a pretty firm *leave me alone.* Now I turn up out of the blue without even a phone call and you're all *there's the fridge, here's your room*? Aren't you angry with me? Don't you want an explanation?"

He shook his head, a small smile kicking up one corner of that beautiful mouth. "You're home, Bel. For now, that's plenty."

Home. She backed away from the counter, the confusion in her gut twisting into something she didn't recognize. Something with wings of hope and streaks of joy and a black shadow that said *it's a trick, there's a price, there's always something*.

"My mother—" she began, then broke off, something ugly and choking in her throat. She shook herself, cleared it away and forced herself forward. Maybe she was going to look like a fool when this was over but she'd be damned if she'd shirk the work of loving him. Maybe Vivi was in her, but Vivi wasn't *her*.

"I know about your mother," James said, taking a step forward, then stopping abruptly, as if catching himself. "You don't have to tell me anything if you don't—"

Bel shook her head. "No, please. I need to say this. I need to understand what this is, this thing you're doing."

"Okay," he said, his eyes so kind and patient that Bel had to clear her throat again.

"My mother was—*is*—dramatic," she said finally. "She needs high drama, big emotions, constant chaos. She can't function any other way."

"Yeah," James said. "I got that."

"She wasn't really suited to raising a kid like me."

"A kid like you?"

"Serious. Steady. A perfectionist."

He smiled at that. "No. You?"

"I know. Hard to believe."

"I'm agog. Go on."

"She didn't ignore me or abuse me," Bel said, searching desperately for the right words, "if that's what you're thinking. I just wasn't enough."

"Enough?"

"Enough to keep her entertained on a daily basis. But every now and then—between boyfriends or blow-outs with her friends at the yacht club or whatever—she turned to me to fill in the gaps. She lavished all that energy and love and attention on me. She loved me with this ferocious focus until I loved her back." She smiled wryly. "It never took very long."

"And then she fell in love with somebody else," James said quietly. "And she broke your heart over and over."

Bel lifted her shoulders. "By the time I was ten I'd figured things out. Or so I thought. Love didn't exist. It was just an excuse to do what you wanted to do and damn the consequences. A socially acceptable get-out-of-jail-free card she could play every time she forgot to come home. Every time she wandered in at dawn while I was fixing myself breakfast and getting myself ready for school. Every time she hopped up on the counter, reeking of cigar smoke and whiskey, all bright-eyed and breathless, telling me she was in love again and she'd be speaking to my principal about transferring my records to a new school. Again."

Bitterness welled up inside her at the memory but she pushed it aside. That wasn't her point.

"She didn't like that, I'll bet," James said, encouragement quiet in his voice. "Your cottoning on to her game. Refusing to play."

"No." Bel tried a smile. "No, she didn't. Maybe I hadn't been enough to hold her attention in the long term, but she sure liked having an adoring audience handy when she needed one. And once the adoring part dropped out of the equation, well. Vivi does need her scenes, regardless of whether they're positive or negative."

"How negative?" James asked, concern darkening his eyes to the ominous green-gray of an unsettled sea.

"Let's just say that if I'd ever pulled anything on her remotely like what I just pulled on you, there would be no way on God's green earth I'd have gotten an invitation to put away my groceries and go visit my old room. There would've been endless tears, hours of recriminations, days of deliberating over whether to accept my apology and take me back, at least conditionally. So this whole thing?" She twirled a finger in the air to sum up everything that had happened between them in the past twenty minutes, the forgiveness, the mercy, the incomprehensible, radical welcome. "This is foreign to me and I don't know what it means."

"What do you think it means, Bel?"

"I don't *know*!" She fisted her hands beside her ears, as if she could reach inside her head and pull out the tangled thoughts and emotions and straighten them out. "I know I love you, and that makes me totally unreliable when it comes to figuring out what you're talking about." She drew in a shuddering breath and forced what was inside her out. Forced herself to form the words that would push her over the edge into complete, bald vulnerability.

"I want so badly for this to be what it looks like, James." He moved toward her, but she shot out a hand, stopped him there. She needed to say it or it would never come out. It would lie between them always, unresolved, a question she needed to ask now before the price of honesty skyrocketed. "I want that, more than I can tell you. But I also know I've done nothing to deserve it and nothing in my experience says I should expect it, so if there's something else going on here, if there's a price I need to pay, if you need your pound of flesh or whatever before you take me back, will you please just *tell me*? I'll pay it, I'll do anything you want, but please don't make me guess what it is."

He stared at her in silence, but she forced herself not to run. Not to hide. Her heart beat wildly inside her, but she stood before him, raw and naked, his to take or leave, to punish or forgive.

For an endless moment, they stood frozen in the shadow of that tense, brave question. Then time shot off the mark like a world-class sprinter, and before Bel could think or blink or breathe, James was there, his arms locked around her, the good, dear strength of them filling something aching and needy in her soul, the clean, freshly-showered scent of him making her lightheaded and giddy.

"Bel." He breathed it into her hair, like it was a prayer or a song. Like she was something sacred and valuable and treasured. It sparked a small, quiet flame inside her, a flame that both destroyed and healed. "Bel. My God."

"I love you, James." It was her own prayer, a song of thanksgiving and gratitude, of humbled astonishment. "I do. It's real and I know now how to tell the difference. I thought love only existed the way Vivi did it, but now I know—"

He made a noise, anguished and deep, then slipped from her arms onto his knees on the hard tile floor. She gazed down in astonishment at his bent, golden head pressed to her belly. She touched a tentative hand to those unruly curls. "James?"

He jerked back and gazed up at her with wild green eyes. He seized her hands in his with a fierceness that both startled and thrilled her. "I thought you'd left me, Bel. God. I thought I'd finally done it. Driven you off with my stupid temper and my stupid mouth. I thought I'd lost you."

"Oh, James," she whispered. "Never. Things just got—"

"No," he said. "It doesn't matter. None of it matters. Not where you've been, not my being a judgmental ass about Vivi. All that matters is that you're here now. *We're* here now, together. All that matters is that I love you more than my heart can stand, and that I'll do anything, *anything*, to keep you here with me." He dropped his forehead to her hands. "You're my family now, Bel. You're my heart. Without you, I'm as empty as this damn house. And I *hate* this house without you in it. Stay with me. Please."

Bel's knees went watery, and she didn't fight them. She simply joined him on the floor and threw her arms about his neck, her heart singing inside her like a wild bird, simply for the joy of the song.

"You're my home," she said. "My family. I don't want to be anywhere but with you. I'll never leave you, James. Never again. I hated being away from you. I didn't want that, never wanted it. I hadn't been gone two hours before I wanted to come back but things got—"

She broke off, a surge of familiar grief tempering the incandescent joy. He pulled back, searched her face with serious eyes. "Got what?" he asked gently.

"Complicated." She hesitated, bit her lip. "I know you said you don't need to know where I've been but I need to tell you about it. It's...important." She took his hands in hers, those dear, warm hands. God, she'd missed him. She didn't know if she'd ever get enough of touching him just because she could, because he was there. "But before I do, I need you to understand something. I need you to believe that, had it been up to me, I'd have been back here practically before I left. I would never—will never—leave you like that." Tears swam into her eyes and she blinked them back. "I spent every minute of these past weeks hating what I was doing, hating that you might think I would be so brutal, so vindictive as to make you pay like this for some stupid argument. It was—" She shook her head. "It was awful and it wasn't me. I would never—"

He pressed his lips lightly to hers, a sweet, uncomplicated touch that had the tears spilling over. "I believe you."

She gawked at him in wonder, because he did. He absolutely believed her. It radiated from him like heat from her ovens on baking day, and it touched something inside her, thawed some distant corner of her heart that had been frozen so long she'd forgotten what it was like to feel anything there.

She smiled at him. It was a little off-center but not bad for a girl who really wanted to bury her face in his shirt and weep for the next hour or so. But she didn't have time for that. Thanksgiving was only three days away and she had a miracle to perform.

"Now," he said, eyeing her mouth with a purposeful light in his eye, "tell me about complicated. Before I forget to be interested and try to talk you into other things."

Bel felt the corner of her mouth quirk up in spite of the press of sorrow on her heart. "Other things?"

"Like the pleasures of making love indoors, on clean sheets. Hell, on a mattress rather than a foot wide strip of marble."

"You have a problem with *al fresco*?" Bel asked, willing to be distracted.

"Hell, no. But I do like my variety and I've been making a list."

"A list." Bel eyed him, intrigued.

James shook his head and climbed to his feet. "Nope. First, we talk about complicated. Then you can see the list." He held out a hand for her and she sighed but allowed him to pull her up. God, she didn't want to do this.

"Sit," she said and pointed her chin at a kitchen stool. She ran her eyes over his frame with a weird combination of worry and lust. "You haven't been eating right while I've been away. You look like you're about to fall over."

He scooped her into his arms and regarded her with delighted eyes. "Bel. Darling. Light of my life. I hesitate to ask because it seems presumptuous and rude, and your answer in no way affects my desire to love you for the rest of your life, but...are you offering to feed me?"

She frowned up at him. "No, I thought we could ride bikes. Of course I'm offering to feed you."

He pressed a hard kiss to her mouth. "I love you."

She blinked away the spinny after-effects of that kiss. "You're just saying that because I have groceries."

He grinned at her. "Honey. Groceries are part of who you are. I couldn't love you if I didn't love your sixteen teeny-tiny bottles of mustard, too."

"Mustard that's going to make you one kick-ass club sandwich on rustic sourdough with a side of baby field greens dressed with a balsamic-walnut oil vinaigrette."

"Did I complain? I did not. I love your mustard." He released her and plunked himself on the stool. "Get to work, woman. And tell me about complicated while you're at it."

CHAPTER THIRTY-TWO

The next morning Bel walked into Hunt House through the open French doors in the rear just as she had nearly every morning of the past three years. Used to be that she'd scurry along the garden path from the Dower House without even seeing it, her head stuffed with to-do lists, her hands full of recipes, her heart a deliberate numbness inside her. But today was different.

Today, she walked slowly, her head clear, her heart alive with worry and grief and joy, and her hand tucked safely into James'.

A green light blinked in the hallway outside the kitchen and Bel said, "They're not taping. I should go in."

"You want me to come with you?"

"No." But nerves had her rubbing a palm down the seam of her jeans. "I think I should do this alone."

He nodded, then tipped up her chin with a thumb. He pressed his lips to hers, warm and solid and certain. "You'll be fine," he said. "I'll be sitting right here." He eyed the concerningly frail antique bench beside them, sighed deeply and put his shoulder blades to the wall. "I'll be *standing* right here."

"Right. Okay. Good." She kissed him back, put all her love and gratitude into it. "Here I go, then."

He gave her bottom a companionable pat, then she turned and marched grimly toward the kitchen.

She checked the light to make sure the cameras hadn't started rolling—nope, still green—then slipped through the door. Habit had her stepping carefully over the thick cables that snaked across the floor, then she squinted toward the enormous island counter broiling under the glare of a dozen or more canister lights.

Kate was there in a pristine white oxford and a pretty bib apron, her hair gleaming, her makeup perfect and camera-ready. She frowned down at a huge raw turkey in front of her while a kitchen tech grabbed the drumsticks and demonstrated how to poke her hand down into the cavity at the best angle for the camera. Bel half smiled at Kate's expression of mild disgust. The kitchen had never been Kate's favorite part of the show—she was more of a gardener than a cook—and Bel knew she was weighing whether or not she could get away with using gloves to dig out the bag of giblets.

A quick pinch of sorrow surprised Bel. She'd spent the past few weeks forcing herself to grieve for this, for the old dream. Forcing herself to let it go so she could build a new dream, a new vision for her life, for success. She thought she'd prepared herself, thought she could walk onto this set without regret, ready to say what she needed to say to Kate and move into that future she'd worked so hard to envision.

But somehow it still hurt. It still hurt that she would never do this job she'd loved for so long. A new generation of women was at this very moment struggling to find meaning in the work of making a home and feeding their families. Or at the very least, they were struggling with an enormous raw turkey. They needed help, and Bel had been so proud to be the one they turned to.

Kate looked up, saw Bel there and scowled. Actually scowled. Bel sighed and bid her final farewell to the old dream. She would *not* be assuming the role of Kate 2.0, not now, not ever. Not while Kate was alive, kicking, and actively against the plan.

Bel threaded her way through the maze of cameras and staffers until she landed at Kate's elbow. "Hi, Kate," she said.

"Belinda." Kate betrayed not an ounce of surprise, only inclined her head with her usual frosty good manners.

Bel nodded at the turkey. "Ambitious," she said. "That's got to be a twenty-five pounder. You'll roast breast-down for the first hour, I hope?"

Kate lifted her chin. "Please tell me you're not here to discuss recipes."

"No. But I do need to talk with you."

"Oh, dear." She offered a thin smile. "I worried this might happen. Please, Belinda. Let's avoid an ugly scene. My judgment on the matter of your employment is final."

"Your judgment blows," Bel said. "That's part of why I quit, if you'll recall." She returned the smile in the spirit in which it was intended. "But I'm not here to talk about my employment. I need to talk to you about something else."

"What else could we possibly have to talk about?"

"Bob."

Kate's lids twitched faintly, as if suppressing a flinch. "Bob." She gave a delicate sniff and turned her attention toward the massive, naked bird in front of her. "What, is he back from vacation? Did retirement not suit him? Is he hoping to reconnect with some old, lucrative clients? Because if that's why you're here, you can just—"

"He's dying, Kate."

She blinked, her face perfectly devoid of emotion. "Excuse me?"

"Pancreatic cancer," Bel said. She forced the words out past the gummy lump of rage and grief in her throat. "He's been in treatment off and on for the past year, everything from chemo to weird dietary stuff. He finally ran out of options."

"Ran out of options?" Kate echoed the words, her voice crisp and precise as always. "What does that mean?"

"It means that he decided to sell his agency and go see the pyramids, the rainforest, the south of France. Machu Pichu. You know." She circled an encompassing hand. "The stuff you don't do until the clock starts winding down."

"Machu Pichu." Kate's face was utterly blank.

"Right. I surmised he intended to do those things, see those sights with you. Then you used the Fox Hunt Ball to make very clear that such wasn't the nature of your relationship going forward. You wiped out my future plans with the same well-placed stroke." She smiled coldly. "You always were a good multitasker. Inviting Vivi was inspired."

Kate canted a single brow. "Your point, Belinda?"

Bel stared. Didn't this woman feel anything? Her lover of the past twenty years was *dying* and the best she could do was mild impatience? Suddenly Bel was glad she'd never be Kate 2.0. No, *screw* glad. She was delighted and relieved. Nobody should grow up to be...this.

"He hired me on as a personal assistant," she went on with careful precision. "To take care of his travel arrangements, keep track of his meds, cook when he wanted to eat in, accompany him when he wanted to eat out. Nothing demanding, just general Girl Friday stuff. He didn't need me. Just wanted the company, I think. He hadn't planned to travel alone, you understand."

Kate did flinch at that, and Bel felt only a savage sort of joy. Finally. Bob deserved at least that. He deserved a hell of a lot more, actually. Kate's flinch was just the start of what she owed him. "We didn't even get through the first stop— an African safari, if you were wondering—before his kidneys went."

"Kidneys?" Kate's lips were white, pinched.

"Yeah. Then the liver. It's all of a piece when it comes to pancreatic cancer. I told him we should have started with the south of France." She shook her head. "He thought it would be his favorite, though, and I guess he didn't want to peak too soon." She lifted a shoulder. "I offered to make it happen anyway—there are excellent end of life facilities there—but he wanted to die at home. So I brought him home."

Kate's eyes flared with panic. "Here?" A hand crept to the pearls at her throat and she glanced at the ceiling, as if Bel had managed to stash Bob in the attic while she wasn't looking. "He's here?"

"What, in Hunt House? Hell, no. This isn't his home. You're not his family. He offered you that job and you turned it down, remember? In favor of—" She cast a scornful gaze around the kitchen that produced for the cameras and nobody else. "—this ridiculous sham of a life. Crappy choice, you ask me, but that's as may be. No, Bob's my family now. I brought him home with *me*."

"Oh, dear. This is awkward." Kate smiled politely but something furious and malicious flickered in her eyes. "I'm afraid your home is no longer yours, Belinda. You see, Vivi needed a place to stay and the Dower House was standing empty—"

Bel gave a short bark of laughter. "My God, you're amazing. I have to assume you think that's some kind of blow to me?" She tipped her head and gave Kate a searching look. "You do. Lord have mercy." She shook her head. "Oh, Kate. The Dower House is beautiful and I loved it there. But it's not my home. It never was. It belongs to you and you're free to do whatever the hell you want with it." She smiled fiercely. "My home is the other direction. I live at the Annex now, with James and his insane brothers and his housekeeper—"

Kate's lip curled. "The stripper?"

"—and that precious little girl who came with her." She folded her arms and gave Kate some good, solid eye contact. "And Bob. Make no mistake about it, Kate. *I'm* Bob's family now. He believed in me when I had nothing. Thanks to him, I have plenty now. A decent savings, a nice résumé and a whole boat-load of love and gratitude for the guy who saw something in me that nobody else ever did. I owe him for that. More than I can ever repay, and that's the only reason I'm here."

"How is being radically unpleasant to me a favor to Bob?"

"Oh, the unpleasantries aren't from Bob. They're from me. The invitation is from Bob."

"What invitation?"

"Didn't I mention? Bob's proceeding with his death a little non-traditionally. He wants his will read while he's still around to hear it. And he wants you to hear it, too." She smiled coldly. "Ford will be doing the honors tonight at the Annex."

Kate stared. "Pardon me?"

"Tonight. Will reading. Six o'clock. And you'll want to be punctual. Bob doesn't have time to waste these days." Bel turned her back on her old boss, her old job, her old dream and walked out the door.

Bob's room in the Annex was right across the hall from Bel's. If she left her door open, she could see his bed from her own. She hadn't gone so far as to set up a formal sitting schedule but somehow Bob was rarely alone. And by six that night, he'd packed in a crowd.

Bel sat in the recliner James and Drew had hauled from their common room to Bob's bedside, pie recipes spread across her lap, James sprawled at her feet. Drew had dragged in some folding chairs for himself and Audrey, and a bean bag chair for Jillian. The girl curled up in it like a cat and read while Ford opened his attaché case at the foot of Bob's bed.

Kate appeared at precisely the stroke of six. She stopped in the door jamb, her face white, her eyes stricken. She stared at Bob. At the hospital bed, the morphine drip, and the small army of beeping machines that tethered him to this world. That fierce joy surged through Bel again. *Good*. She wanted Kate to hurt. To hurt like Bel was hurting. To hurt *more*. But that vindictive joy was laced with pity. With empathy. Bel knew how easily selfishness and fear could put love on the ropes. She and James had come perilously close to going down that road themselves.

James leapt to his feet like the southern gentleman he was and Bel followed suit. She gathered her recipes and silently offered Kate her chair. Kate glided across the room and sank into the battered old recliner. Bob smiled faintly and stretched out a hand. Kate took it between both her own, though her face could have been carved from marble.

Bob closed his eyes and nodded to Ford, who cleared his throat, and intoned some barely comprehensible lawyer-speak for a few minutes. Finally he said, "It is Bob's wish that I now read to you the following, which he himself wrote and I witnessed one week ago."

He adjusted his reading glasses, cleared his throat again and began reading from a single sheet of paper.

"I, Robert Daniel Beck, being of sound mind and shitty health do hereby ask that Belinda West be named the executor of my estate, such as it is. As my defacto family—and the daughter of my heart—I hope she won't mind taking on this one last task of sorting through what I've accumulated in my life, giving away what others might need and keeping whatever speaks to her for herself. Aside from those items which I will now detail, I leave her everything, including my love and thanks for her astounding generosity of spirit. I also bequeath James a swift kick in the ass if he doesn't pony up a ring ASAP. A nice big one, as I know what he gets paid."

Bel managed a watery laugh. James twined his fingers through hers and she leaned into his shoulder.

Ford read on. "I leave my agency, my client list, and all accounts, events, agreements, licenses, etc., attached to it to William Yeats Blake."

Audrey leaned around Drew and gave James big eyes. "*Yeats?*"

"Mom liked her poets." James smiled. "Just ask Andrew Shelley Blake beside you."

Drew flipped him a lazy middle finger. Even Bob smiled.

"Like the previously negotiated and now voided sale before it," Ford continued, "this gift is contingent upon Will's successful completion of the in-patient rehab program to which Bel sentenced him. The gift also assumes that he will apply his lazy ass for once. Because I swear on all that's holy that if he drives my life's work into the ground I'll haunt him for eternity."

Drew grinned. "Fun. I'll let him know."

Ford consulted the paper. "Also, tell him to get a damn good administrative assistant and pay her double what he thinks she deserves. Trust me."

Audrey considered that. "I'll round up a pool of candidates and start interviews this week."

Drew gave her a startled look. "You want to help *Will*?"

She shrugged innocently. "If by *help* you mean hiring him a schedule Nazi with ideas about healthy eating and an

288

iron-clad five year employment contract before he busts out of rehab, then yes." She gave a happy sigh. "I want to help Will."

"Audrey, that's terrible." He grinned brilliantly. "Are you *sure* you don't want to marry me?"

"I'm sure." She patted his knee. "Please stop asking."

"Hell, no. One day you might say yes."

"Yeah, I don't think so." But her lips twitched.

Ford waited for Drew and Audrey to refocus, then said, "And last, for my beautiful, stubborn, terrified Kate."

Bel turned to look at Kate, but the woman didn't so much as blink.

"To Kate, I leave the ragtag bunch of idiots sitting around you right now. They'll be your family if you'll let them. Start with Thanksgiving. I told Bel not to serve unless you're here, so don't be late."

James shot Bel a *really*? face. She shrugged.

"Three o'clock," she told Kate. "You could bring a bottle of wine. Red would be nice."

Kate gave one small nod but otherwise stayed still and composed, her eyes fixed on Ford who read on.

"There's also the diamond wedding ring I'd planned to give you upon your retirement, and an open-ended plane ticket to the south of France. I know better than to rush you, but one day you'll wake up and you'll be ready. When you are, go. And be happy, Katie. I love you."

Bel's throat closed. She reached over and touched Kate's knee, but the woman simply gazed at the far wall as if the room and all its inhabitants had ceased to exist. Bel looked up at Ford.

"Is that it?"

He laid the paper down. "That's it."

She glanced again at Kate, who didn't appear to be even breathing. "Kate?" She stood and put a tentative hand on the woman's shoulder.

"Could I have a moment please?" Kate's voice was as composed as her face. "Alone?"

"Oh. Um, sure." Bel turned to the assembled family but they were already on their feet and pelting toward the door.

Evidently Bel wasn't alone in her wish to avoid witnessing whatever came next between those two. But once she gained the hall, she paused. Glanced back and watched with a dull pulse of surprise as Kate—cool, aloof, no-nonsense Kate—toed off her Italian leather pumps and climbed into the bed beside Bob. She laid herself alongside him, taking meticulous care not to jostle the morphine drip, slipped her hand into his and pressed her face into his shoulder.

Bob didn't open his eyes, but a smile ghosted over his dry lips. A smile so peaceful and resigned and grateful that it hit Bel like an unexpected punch. Tears sprang into her eyes and she all but fled down the stairs.

CHAPTER THIRTY-THREE

An hour later, Bel was scooping pastry flour into her favorite mixing bowl at the island counter. Across from her, James pitted a small fortune of off-season cherries. "God, that guy's fast." He nodded at his iPad and Team Argentina's star defender.

"Fast as you?"

"Well, I'm ten years older than he is," James demurred.

"Ten years sneakier."

"Well, yeah." He grinned. "I'll be taking this young sir to school shortly. But it still pays to know which way he likes to zig when a striker zags."

Kate stepped into the kitchen, silent and pale. James leapt to his feet. "Hey, Miss Kate." He wiped his hands on a dish towel. "You and Bob have a nice chat?"

"No. He's dying."

James shot a swift look at Bel. "I know it, ma'am. And I'm sorry."

"He won't make it to Thanksgiving," Kate said calmly. "I doubt he'll make it through the night."

James lifted a brow at Bel. She shrugged back. She'd had the same feeling. They all had. And now that Kate had paid her respects, it was likely that Bob would just let go. She'd heard of things like that happening.

"I think Bob was pretty clear about his wishes," Bel said carefully. "Thanksgiving is on whether he's with us or not. And he expects you to be there."

"I know." Kate smiled and Bel had never seen anything so devoid of humor.

"You'll honor the invitation then?"

"Of course. To do otherwise would be rude." Kate walked briskly into the kitchen and flicked an apron off the row of pegs next to the stove. "Now, what are we doing here?" She lifted a brow at the sprawl of ingredients covering the generous island.

James caught Bel's eye and looked a question. She gave him a tiny nod toward the door and he all but sprinted for it.

"Sour cherry pies with an almond-scented crust," Bel told her as the door swished shut on James' hasty escape. "Bob's favorite."

"Oh?" Kate slipped the apron over her head and Bel stared. How on earth did a woman share a man's bed for twenty years without knowing what kind of *pie* he liked? "Heavens." Kate eyed the mountain of cherries James had half-pitted. "How many people are coming on Thursday?"

"I'm not baking for Thanksgiving." She met Kate's gaze evenly. "I'm baking for the wake."

"I see." Kate didn't flinch and Bel wanted to slap that serene composure off her face. "How many mourners are you anticipating?"

Bel shrugged. "Hell if I know. Bob knew a lot of people. I'm just going to bake until I feel done." She jerked her chin at James' vacated seat. "If you want to help, pit the rest of those cherries. If you don't, there's the door."

Kate approached the mountain of darkly glistening cherries and took up the pitter. Bel checked her recipe, surveyed the mound of flour in the bowl, then made a vague attempt at mental math.

"Which recipe are you using?" Kate asked as her hands began the swift, economical ballet of cherry pitting.

"That one." Bel nodded toward a stained and tattered index card under a magnet on the fridge. "We used it on the summer harvest show two years ago, remember?"

Kate squinted at it, then glanced at Bel's bowl. Her brows shot up as she took in the sheer amount of flour. "Good heavens, you must be tripling the recipe!"

Bel shrugged. "At least."

Kate shook her head. "Belinda. You know how touchy recipes can be about doubling, and this one in particular is—"

"It'll be fine, Kate," Bel said. "Trust me. I've done this before."

Kate went back to pitting. "As you like."

"Thank you. I like it fine."

Bel grappled with ratios for a few more seconds but her brain just wasn't up for the work out. So she tossed in some salt, cut in what felt like enough butter and an equal amount of shortening. A pinch of baking powder. She finished it off with a single drop of white vinegar and the merest dash of almond extract. Just until it smelled right.

Then she dribbled in a little cold water, folded gently until it came together, then set aside the wooden spoon to work it bare-handed. After a few minutes she dashed a stray hair out of her eyes with a floury wrist, then gave the dough an experimental pat. She hefted it out of the bowl and held it up to the light.

"Good," she muttered to herself. "Nice texture, good marbling." She offered it to Kate for a pinch. "What do you think of this? Too soft? I don't want it to tear, but I need a good drape in the pans."

Kate frowned at her. "If you'd simply followed the recipe as written, Belinda, you wouldn't have to ask."

Bel ignored her. "A little more flour, I think. A dusting." She shook a fine sprinkle of flour onto her marble-topped pastry board and gently worked it into her crust, careful not to over-exert the dough. Too much handling developed the gluten fibers and the next thing you knew you were chewing your crust like a cow chews cud. It should melt, like angel wings, in your mouth.

And then she felt it. That perfect combination of give and spring under her hands, that elusive melding of resilience and delicacy. "There," she said to Kate, beaming. "Perfect. It was touch and go there for a minute but—"

"This," Kate said, her voice sharpened to an icy edge, "is exactly why you will never take over my show."

Bel turned to stare, triumph forgotten. "Excuse me?"

"This." Kate waved an elegant hand at the entire scene before her—the ball of dough on the counter, the flour streaked across Bel's face, up her sleeves. The gluey crud under her fingernails and crusting the face of her watch. "You do this all the time."

"I do what all the time?"

"Improvise." Kate dismissed the whole of what Bel had just accomplished with a single, disdainful word.

"Hey, a perfect pie crust is nothing to sneeze at," Bel said, stung.

Kate looked away from the lump of dough on the counter. "I'm sure it's lovely," she said. "But I don't sell improvisation. I sell recipes. Exact, time-tested, bullet-proof formulas that women can count on to work *every single time* so long as they respect the recipe."

"But, Kate," Bel said, baffled. "No recipe is that good. Flours are like fingerprints. I mean, at first they all look the same but when you get into them, they're so different. All those different strains of wheat, all the different grades of grind? Different tolerances for liquid, for acid, for heat, for fats? A recipe—I mean, it's a great place to start, but eventually you have to trust yourself. You have to give yourself permission to believe what your hands are telling you above what the recipe says."

Kate shook her head hard. "No. It's better to accept small deviations in quality than to risk ruining the whole effort."

"But why?" Bel spread her floury hands. "Why should we teach people to accept tough crust when all it costs to be wrong is a few cups of flour and a stick of butter?"

"It's not about flour, Belinda. It's about consistency," Kate said coldly. "It's about delivering a dependable product. It's about *trust*."

Bel gazed at her with dawning realization. All these years, she thought in wonder, all this time, she'd had Kate totally wrong. She'd assumed Kate's beautiful manners, her exquisite taste and unshakeable calm were an outward expression of an inward serenity. A serenity Bel had envied with her whole soul. But it was just the opposite.

"This isn't about your brand," she said slowly. "It's about control, isn't it? It's about imposing order on a disorderly world. A world of chaos and hurt and terrible danger. A world where—"

A world where cancer could defeat a guy like Bob.

But she didn't say that. She didn't need to. It lay between them like the Grand Canyon. Neither of them missed it.

She took a half-step forward. Good God, how had she missed this? Hadn't she spent her entire life trying to accomplish the same thing? Trying to wring the risk out of an impossibly threatening world? How had she not recognized that same desperate effort in Kate?

"You're afraid." She put out a hand toward the older woman. "Oh, Kate, you don't need to be—"

"Yes, I do." Something tense and leashed vibrated in Kate's voice, something that had Bel's hand freezing in the air between them. Then whatever iron-clad control had held her together all these years in such prim, proper order snapped. A black rage seeped through the cracks and Bel could feel the molten heat of it on her own skin. "I absolutely do, and do you want to know why?"

Bel nodded, gazing at her in mute fascination.

"Because Bob's dying. He's *dying*, Belinda. He'll be gone by morning. But all this?" She waved her hands in a tight circle, taking in Bel didn't know what. Everything, she supposed. Hunt House. Her career. Her health and the thirty or more years she had left to enjoy it all by herself. "All this is still right here. I was *right*." She fired the word like it was a bullet, a weapon she could wield against the grief. "I was *right* to choose it over his goddamn *ring*. I was *right* to stay here instead of flying off to the south of fucking *France*." She gave a jagged chuckle and shook her head. "France. My God."

Then her eyes went hot and narrow, and she took a menacing step toward Bel. "So you can sit here and *improvise* all you like. I prefer recipes, and I won't apologize for that. Not to you, not to *him*—" She stabbed a finger at the ceiling, toward Bob and his death bed. "—not to anybody. I have nothing to apologize for. I made my choices and I'm *satisfied*."

"Are you?" Bel asked softly. "Are you really?"

"Yes." She jerked at her apron strings until they gave and she yanked the thing off over her head. "Good night, dear."

CHAPTER THIRTY-FOUR

As usual, Kate had been right. Bob didn't see Thanksgiving. He passed away quietly and without drama on Wednesday morning, Bel holding one hand, James holding the other. Drew and Audrey took turns keeping Jillian otherwise occupied, and Will, in deference to Bob's wishes, refrained from breaking out of rehab. Barely.

Kate paced the gardens between their houses, unable or unwilling to bear witness.

Bel served Thanksgiving dinner the following day at three o'clock, exactly as Bob had wished. They all sat down—Kate included—to a meal nobody wanted, capped with picture-perfect slices of sour cherry pie with the almond scented crust.

The next morning, Bel embarked on the business side of death. She wasn't surprised to learn there was one. Everything was business in the end, wasn't it? Kate would have told her that, and happily. But she *was* surprised at how grateful she was for the work.

Because, despite the solid anchor of James' love, she still felt disconcertingly adrift. She'd let go of the old dream—*Kate Every Day* was off the table and she was okay with that—but she hadn't fallen in love with a new dream yet. Wasn't really ready to, if she was perfectly honest with herself. So she stayed busy and thanks be to Bob for the one last gift.

She spent her days sorting and filing, calling and emailing, making lists and checking items off them. And every night she baked. Christmas cookies, mostly. 'Twas the season, after all. She baked cookies by the dozen, everything from humble Russian tea cakes to elaborately decorated sugar cookies to deep fried Norwegian rosettes. She grieved in her kitchen, and everything she baked tasted of love and sorrow. Which—to Bel's mind—suited Christmas completely. She'd always thought the Jesus story was sort of a mixed bag when you got right down to it.

And when it was finally over, when she'd filed the last paper, signed the last form, and closed the last account, she brewed up gallons of the strongest, blackest coffee she could find. (Unless it supported a spoon at a perfect vertical, Bob hadn't considered it coffee.) She bought half a dozen antique platters with gold edges and tiny roses, and piled them high with the most perfect cookies of her hundreds. She sliced into her sour cherry pies. Then she flung open the Annex doors to everybody Bob had ever known, met or worked with.

The doorbell rang for hours—Johnny Cash's "Wayfaring Stranger" which Bel didn't know but James assured her was perfect. She accepted hug after handshake after air kiss, many from people she'd never even met but who had loved Bob and needed somebody to console. Finally, when her throat was too tight to even murmur *thank you so much for coming*, she snatched up an empty cookie platter and escaped to the kitchen.

She was deliberating over the placement of the Russian tea cakes when James pushed through the kitchen doors.

"Hey, Bel."

"Hey." She smiled sheepishly. "I ran away."

"No shame in it." He ambled her way. "Some crowd."

"Bob was a popular guy."

He hooked a warm hand around the nape of her neck and comfort slid warm into her veins. He pressed his forehead to hers and she released her first full breath in hours. "How you holding up, hon?"

She shrugged against the now-familiar swell of tears. "I miss him."

"Me, too."

"Kate didn't show."

"Did you expect her to?"

Her throat was too tight to even sigh. "I don't know. I hoped."

The doorbell pealed yet again and James smiled. "Ah, the man in black."

She sighed and pushed the platter of cookies into his hands. "Here we go again. Put those on the sideboard, would you?"

"Yes, ma'am."

Bel excused herself through the crowd while James offered his platter left and right in her wake. She finally reached the door and pulled it open. Then she simply stared.

"Belinda!" Vivi sailed in, draped beautifully in black. Her hat was massive and airy all at the same time, a mournful wedding cake of lace and tulle. She flung her arms around Bel just like she had at the Fox Hunt Ball. "Oh you poor, darling girl! Look at you! You're so *gaunt.*"

James handed his platter to a startled hockey player and arrived at her side within split seconds. "Hey, Ms. Pietrantoni," he said with that easy charm of his. Bel's lips were too numb to force out a single word.

Please, it's Vivi." Her mother gazed gravely at him but kept Bel's cold hands. "She's not eating well, is she?" She ran a dismayed glance over Bel's neat black suit. "James, you must make sure she's taking care of herself!" She blinked tear-brightened eyes. "I know *I* haven't much influence over Belinda but she'll listen to you, I know she will! You must promise me. Promise me you're looking after her!"

"I am, ma'am." He patted her shoulder. Bel stared helplessly, her pulse thudding ominously in her ears. She wasn't going to pass out, was she?

Vivi drew in a shuddering breath, released it and looked around the packed great room. "Oh, dear. I'm not late, am I?" She offered Bel a tremulous smile but satisfaction was rich in her voice. "I'd hate to cause a scene."

James eyed her hat. "I'm sure."

Bel snapped back to herself. *Oh, hell, no.* This woman was *not* hijacking Bob's funeral. Bel could tolerate a lot but that was beyond enough. *So move, damn it. Do something.*

"You won't cause a scene," Bel assured her. It was amazing how calm she sounded. How cool and rational. She

299

took her mother's elbow and drew her to the still-open door. "Because you're leaving now."

"Oh, but Bel!" Vivi gazed up with huge, hurt eyes, but Bel knew her mother. The hurt was a thin layer slapped over eager appetite. Vivi loved nothing more than a scene. "I know we've had our differences, darling, but you must know I wouldn't allow you to walk through this tragedy, to bear your grief, alone!"

"Vivi." James stepped forward, gently disengaged Bel from her mother's grip. He folded her tiny hand in his and smiled warmly down at her. "Actually, I'm glad you're here. I wonder if you could come into the study for a moment."

Bel's heart took a sudden unpleasant lurch. *Déjà vu.* "James, I don't want—"

"I know." He met her eyes evenly and she sucked in a sharp, focusing breath. Because what she saw there wasn't *I'm sorry* or *Grow up* or even *Come on, Bel*. What she saw there was *Trust me*. Which she did, completely. So she just nodded and stood silently as James offered Vivi his arm.

Triumph was a split-second flash over Vivi's beautiful face, covered almost immediately with sorrow and dignity. Then her mother sailed into the crowd on James' arm like a grief-stricken prom queen.

He gave no signal that Bel could see, didn't speak to anybody he passed. But somehow Bel found herself leading a parade into the study that included Drew and Audrey, Ford and Annie. Vivi sank gracefully onto the settee before the massive desk and Drew snicked the doors shut behind them.

James went to the desk and withdrew a large rectangular envelope. He caught Bel's eye and nodded her toward the settee beside Vivi.

Everything in her resisted but she trusted James so she sat. Audrey and Annie took up posts behind the couch like foot soldiers while Drew and Ford manned the doors. She wondered what the hell was going on.

James sent Vivi a grave smile. "I'm glad you stopped by, Vivi."

"Bel's my daughter," Vivi whispered. She reached out as if to touch Bel's knee. Bel gave that hand a stony glance and it fluttered weakly back to her mother's lap. "I needed to be here for her." Her lashes drooped. "Whether I was welcome or not."

"How commendable."

"Oh, you're sweet." Vivi's dimples winked sadly. "But it's a mother's duty to put her child first, and I—"

"So true." James drew several sheets of paper from the envelope and came around the desk to hand them to Vivi. "I wonder, then, where that conviction was the whole time Bel was growing up."

"Excuse me?" She peered at the papers, confusion knitting her brow. "What are these?"

"Belinda's school records." He leaned back against the edge of the desk and folded his arms. "That's fourth grade you're looking at. Five separate schools in the one year alone. Four of the schools were in the U.S.—New York, Seattle, DC and then, let's see, LA, was it?—and the fifth was in Switzerland."

"I was a single mother." Vivi blinked bravely. "I had to provide—"

"I've seen your tax returns, Ms. Pietrantoni." James pinned Vivi with a cool look. "You have an impressive trust fund. And while I'll admit you *were* a mother—biologically speaking, at least—you were hardly ever single. Each of these moves corresponds exactly with the start or end of a high-profile romance. Of which you've had more than a few." James' smile was distinctly unfriendly. "It appears that you're addicted to love, Vivi."

Drew snorted out a laugh. "*She's so fine, there's no telling where the money went.*" Even Bel turned to blink at him. He grinned. "Robert Palmer. You don't know that one? "Addicted to Love?" Video of the eighties, man. It was..." He cleared his throat. "I'll stop now."

"Three more schools in fifth grade," James went on. "Only two in the sixth. Not bad. Then seventh grade happened."

Bel's stomach went cold and Vivi looked away. "I gather that's supposed to mean something to me?"

"That's the year you decided to drop Bel off with your parents for a few months while you followed your race car driver boyfriend all over Europe."

"She needed to be in school," Vivi said airily. "I should put my life on hold in order to supervise algebra homework?"

"Your father died of a massive stroke two months after Bel moved in, and your mother overdosed on sleeping pills two days after that. It was ruled accidental, of course."

"I know when and how my parents died, Mr. Blake. Thank you for bringing up the memories."

"So you should also remember that it took the executors of your parents' estate six weeks to even determine your whereabouts. It took another three weeks for you to wrap up your European vacation and head home. Nine weeks, Ms. Pietrantoni. Did you ever wonder where Bel was during this time? Who was caring for her?"

Bel stared at James. He knew. All this time, he'd known?

Vivi lifted a languid shoulder. "My parents were extremely well-off, Mr. Blake. I assumed there was a nanny or a maid—"

"She was made a ward of the state," James said, and Bel couldn't suppress the flinch. Even after all these years, she couldn't suppress the flinch. Annie's hand came gently to her shoulder, then Audrey's to the other. "She spent nine weeks in Juvenile Hall—eating, sleeping, learning, and bathing with troubled, unstable and potentially violent girls while you jetted around Europe with your boyfriend."

"I came for her," Vivi said petulantly. "I did come for her."

"Eventually, yes." James took the stack of papers from Vivi's unresisting fingers. "And cooperated fully when she petitioned to become a legally emancipated minor at age sixteen."

"Belinda's always had a strong mind. She knew what she wanted. Who was I to—"

"Her *mother*," James spat, fury finally snapping his control, and Bel blinked. She'd seen him slip his civilized skin a time or two, but never on her behalf. This was...revelatory. And hot. He leaned down into her mother's face, rage pumping off him with almost tangible heat. Bel felt warm for the first time in weeks. "You were her *mother*."

But Vivi didn't shrink. Bel knew she wouldn't. She watched as Vivi latched onto his anger, drinking it in like a woman dying of thirst. She leaned right back into his face, greed and gratification sparkling in her eyes.

"That's right. I was. I *am* her mother, and I always will be."

"James, don't." Bel watched with dull disgust as her mother all but bloomed under the attention. "You're just giving her what she wants." She sat back, weary beyond description. "She's nothing but a junkie looking for a fix."

"A junkie!" Vivi sounded genuinely outraged at that one but Bel didn't even look at her.

"I know," James said grimly. He ignored Vivi, too. "It took me a bit but I figured it out. The endless string of troubled relationships, the constant moving around, the pathological selfishness. Her decision to ambush you at the biggest, most important event of your career in the name of motherly duty, and in a very flattering period costume." His lips twisted. "I didn't figure she could possibly resist anything so juicy as a funeral, so I came prepared."

"To what?"

"To cut her off. She's not your family anymore." He shifted his gaze back to Vivi. "I am." He glanced around the room. "*We* are."

Vivi smiled. "You don't choose your family, Mr. Blake."

"Of course you do." James eased forward until his shadow fell across Vivi's lap. "Your actions choose for you, every single day. That's why you're nothing to Bel anymore. She kicked you to the curb when she was sixteen, and I have nothing but admiration for the wisdom it took to see you for the parasite you are. For the courage to do something about it."

A splash of hectic color glowed at Vivi's cheekbones but her eyes were murderously cold. "I'm getting bored of this conversation, Mr. Blake."

"Yes, it's clear you're bored easily and often. My mother used to say it was a sign of poor intellectual development. Smart people are rarely bored. But as I have no desire to tax your limited attention span, I'll get right down to business." He put the papers back in her hand. "Have a look at those, Vivi."

Vivi frowned down on them.

"That right there is a copy of Bel's academic record. You've also got a transcript of her emancipation hearing. Last in the stack, though? Those are written evaluations of your psyche by, oh, half a dozen or so of the country's most well-respected psychiatrists." He smiled coldly. "As it turns out, you're a narcissistic sociopath, Vivi. Not a well woman. And if you ever again show your face on this property or at a public event Bel or I are attending, you'll see the inside of a mental institution before you can say *But I'm not crazy*."

"Excuse me?"

"I'd recommend moving back overseas, myself. Because you may not believe this, but I'm a likeable guy. I have a *lot* of friends. Famous friends. Rich friends. The kind of friends gossip columnists really like. The kind they can't make a living without, actually. All of whom have agreed to blackball any journalist who gives you so much as a blog mention." He leaned forward, his face cold and hard. "You understand what I'm saying here, Vivi?"

"I understand that coming here was a colossal mistake." Vivi's lips were a quivering line. "One I won't be repeating." She turned to Bel, her face pale and tragic, her eyes blazing with fury. "I only ever wanted to love you, Belinda. How you turned into such a vindictive, ungrateful—"

"Finish that thought and every poor bastard who looks at you twice gets a copy of what's in your hands."

Vivi's voice cut out abruptly.

"I *can* ruin you, Vivi. Happy to do it, in fact. So you'll want to step right carefully there."

She sucked in a sharp breath, tipped her nose into the air and sailed toward the exit. Drew stepped aside and helpfully pulled open the door for her. The crowd parted before her like the Red Sea and then she was gone.

Bel stood up on shaking legs. She tipped her head and eyed James like she'd never seen him before. She let a beat of ringing silence pass. He shifted uncomfortably.

"You hacked into my school records," she said finally.

Drew raised his hand like an eager pupil. "No, that was me."

"It was all of us." James tried a smile. "But it *was* sort of an accident, if it helps. We were combing the internet for old addresses after you took off and sort of...stumbled across some stuff."

"Your court records, too." Drew shook his head. "The great State of Virginia really ought to look into better computer security."

"I see," Bel murmured, and Ford excused himself to take a phone call that she suspected didn't exist. Self-incrimination made him nervous.

James sank back onto the desk behind him. He gripped the edge at his hips and stared at his shoes. "Listen, I'm sorry if I stepped on your toes, or embarrassed you or anything, but I underestimated Vivi once before and she almost destroyed us. And, worse, she *hurt* you." He looked up abruptly and what she saw blazing in his eyes had her sucking in a sharp breath. "And I will *never* let that happen again. Do you hear me? So I'm sorry if I hung out your dirty laundry or whatever but don't ask me to apologize for going to war, because I won't. I'd do it again tomorrow. Five minutes from now. Whenever I need to. I—"

"I wasn't going to." She stepped forward on wobbly legs. "God, James, I wasn't going to. I'm just surprised, that's all. I mean, I never expected—" She twitched a shoulder and groped for words to describe what she'd just experienced.

"Never expected what?" he asked softly.

"To face the enemy with an army at my back," she said finally. "No, not an army. A *family*." She reached a trembling hand to him while wonder blew sweet and wild inside her. "Thank you. James, I—"

He came off the desk with the speed and deadly grace that justified everything the DC Statesmen paid him. Before she had any idea he was even planning a move, his arms were around her, banded so tightly she could hardly breathe. Her throat was too tight for breathing anyway so she didn't bother trying. She just threw her arms around him and held on.

"You're mine now, Bel." He murmured it into her hair, low and fierce. "You're not hers, you're *mine*. I'm your family, I'm your home, I'm your port in the fucking storm or whatever. Your fight is my fight, Bel."

"What we have, we share?" She gave a watery laugh. "Even my crazy mom?"

"Yeah." He cupped her shoulders in both hands and drew back to glare at her. "So get used to it."

She could do that.

"Hey, James?"

"Yeah?"

"I love you."

He didn't answer. He just hauled her up onto her toes and kissed her until her toes curled inside her sensible black pumps and her greedy hands had wrinkled the hell out of the crisp white shirt she'd ironed just that afternoon.

She could, she thought vaguely, get used to this, too. But she hoped she never did.

EPILOGUE

Will was standing on the front porch of the Annex—had been for five minutes, probably—when the door opened of its own accord and Bel's mom stalked out. Well. That probably wasn't good. He ought to get in there. He eyed the door Vivi had left conveniently open.

Go on, you cowardly goat fucker. It was Bob's voice in his head, gravelly and amused. *Get your ass in there.*

Will sighed. Upon his death, Bob had given Will his business, a month to dry out, and now—Jesus—his voice as a conscience. Evidently Bob had been stone-cold serious about that haunting-your-lazy-ass-into-eternity thing.

Nice.

It's not going to be easier in another five minutes, Nancy. Grow a pair, why don't you? Just face her and get it over with.

Will wondered if Bob was talking about Bel or Audrey. Because God knew he hadn't left either relationship in precisely good repair. He was too sober now to go around laying fat wet ones on unwilling women—and thank Christ for that—but sobriety wasn't a Get Out Of Jail Free card. Or so he'd been told, and at length. It had been a long thirty days. As a result, however, he accepted that he had a couple well deserved face-slappings coming his way, and James owed him a solid punch. He also accepted that he would have to take them like a man.

Would they all swing on him at once, he wondered? Line up? Take turns? Here in front of the crowd, or maybe in private?

You're right. This is some hard shit. Let's forget it and go get a facial.

Will almost smiled at that one. He and Bob hadn't been close but he'd appreciated the guy.

307

Or a drink.

Ouch. Below the belt, Bob. Because, Jesus, that was exactly what he wanted.

Are you going to do your job or not?

Yeah. He was going to do his damn job. He stepped through the open front door and pulled it shut behind him. He was disgusted to discover his hands weren't precisely steady on the knob.

Almost immediately, they were on him. Bob's people. Mourners, funeral goers, whatever the hell you called the black-draped crowds that cooed over caskets like morbid birds. He suppressed a shudder—last funeral he'd endured had been his parents'—and found himself shaking sympathetic hands, accepting shoulder pats and exchanging cheek-pecks.

It's not that hard when you're not being a dick.

Thanks, Bob. I'll remember that.

"Hey, listen." He grabbed the nearest shoulder. He had no idea who it belonged to, though the guy seized his hand and shook it like a fucking pump handle. "Any idea where Bel and James are?"

Seconds later, he was standing outside the closed study doors. Rumor had it they were all in here. James, Bel, Drew, Ford and Annie. And Audrey. The whole package, God help him. He wiped clammy palms down the seams of his black suit—it was a funeral, after all, and he wasn't a total asshole—and let himself quietly into the study.

Bel and James were in front of the desk, locked in a steamy embrace just this side of get-a-room territory. The rest of his family stood around gazing at them with fond, damp eyes. He wondered what he'd missed. A showdown with Vivi? A marriage proposal?

Good God, marriage. Wouldn't that be a kick in the pants?

His heart ached, just a little, faint and bittersweet. James—the sunny, funny middle child who skated through life with fucking rainbows on his feet—was getting married. Manning up. *Growing* up.

A sharp pang of envy came next. But why? Because James had grown up and left him behind? Or because James had lucked into a woman who smelled like sugar cookies and sported the deepest, sweetest dimples Will had ever seen? A woman who looked at James and all his shit and saw somebody worth loving?

It was possible that a sigh escaped him. Small and, yes, pathetic. It couldn't have been more than a breath of sound but it was enough. Audrey saw him first. He knew the instant she registered his presence. Her spine went instantly and hostilely stiff. She turned slowly, regally, nostrils flared like she smelled something off and was about to check her shoe.

He braced himself for the slapping he knew he deserved. He thought about trying a conciliatory smile but Bob said *bad idea* so he went blank and non-committal.

"Hey, Audrey."

"Will." A single, frosty syllable was all she gave him but she didn't wind up for the slap. That was something.

"Holy shit, *Will*!" Drew's eyes went wide, and a grin spread across his thin face that was equal parts *welcome home* and *this ought to be good*. Drew did love a scene. He loped forward and threw a skinny arm around Will's shoulders. Gave him a solid squeeze and a back thump. He drew back to eye him suspiciously. "You didn't bust out of rehab, did you?"

"Nah. I graduated."

"Hey, congrats."

"Yeah, thanks."

Drew released him, and Will absently accepted similar greetings from Ford and Annie. Nothing from Audrey but he'd already gotten more than he expected there. No, he had his sights on James and Bel now.

They stood at the desk, still loosely wrapped in each others' arms. Will approached them slowly, warily. Giving them plenty of time for the wind up if they were planning to take their shots. James met his eyes, a smile flickering at the corner of his mouth. Not that it meant anything, Will told himself, sternly squashing a flare of hope. James was always right next to a smile. It was like the pilot light on his native good humor. It didn't mean Will was welcome here. God knew he hadn't earned any such thing.

Bel straightened slowly. James' hand fell away from her back and she stepped forward. She looked cool and pretty and grave, not at all like a woman who'd just kissed his brother into a happy, disheveled stupor.

He forced himself to keep walking until he was close enough to touch her. Not that he did. He just wanted her to be able to slap him without reaching for it. He owed her that, didn't he?

The boy can be taught.

Shut up, Bob.

"Hey, Bel." He didn't smile. Didn't have the stomach to even try. He was exquisitely aware of Audrey, her beauty almost blinding, her eyes cold and watchful on him as he faced Bel's judgment. He groped for words, any words. Magic, pretty words that would put him at rights with this woman his brother had chosen and he'd wronged. Nothing presented itself—he doubted words that powerful existed, actually—so he just said, "I'm so sorry."

She gazed up at him and the silence strung out between them. It stretched, thinned, then narrowed to an achingly fragile thread. It went on and endlessly on, beyond awkward and into irretrievable. His throat tightened with shame—*well-deserved*—but he cleared it away. All he could do was deliver the apology. It hers to accept or—

And then Bel did something so unexpected, so outrageous that Will failed to even comprehend it at first. One second he was standing there in an agony of shame, the next her arms were around him and the vanilla and cinnamon smell of her hair was flowing into his lungs like oxygen and forgiveness. And only then did it register that she was *hugging* him. She'd just thrown open her arms, all warm and strong and welcoming, and Will had fallen into them. And now she was laughing and hanging on and maybe he was, too. Or maybe he wasn't making a single sound, because nobody had hugged him quite like this since his mom, and his throat was a little tight. Hard to say.

"Will! Oh, Will," she said into his collar. She pulled back and squeezed his hands, her smile a thing of beauty and wonder. "Welcome *home*."

Now his heart was tighter than his throat and he could only beam back at her like an idiot. Then James was pounding his back and squeezing him. Then Drew was on him, too, and even Ford and Annie got in on it. It was chaos of the very best kind, and it buoyed him up and over all the rocky places still left in his heart. Even if just for a minute.

"Hey, Bel," he said finally. "Listen. I have something for you."

"You do?" Her eyes were bright and interested.

"Delivering it is my first official act as an agent."

Her brows rose. "As my agent?"

"As Kate's." He drew a sealed envelope from his inside pocket. It was the size of a thank you note, and had a large snow flake embossed on the flap. He handed it over. "For you."

Bel blinked, exchanged a glance with James that said *huh*, and slid her finger under the flap. She withdrew a piece of thick, creamy stationery and unfolded it. She read, then turned troubled eyes up to James. "She wants us at the taping of her Christmas special tomorrow." She shifted that sharp gaze to Will. "Why would she want that?"

Will shrugged. "I honestly don't know. I'm just the messenger boy."

James slung an arm around her shoulders, took the paper and inspected it himself. "Guess we'll find out tomorrow, won't we?"

"Guess we will," Bel said.

But Will wasn't listening. Because sometime during the laughing and the weeping and the hugging, Audrey had slipped away. He'd felt her go—his Audrey radar was evidently still powered up and sensitive as hell—but didn't try to stop her. He'd go after her later. Because what he had to say to Audrey, what lay between them still?

That business would be dealt with in private.

Coward, Bob said.

Damn straight.

311

Susan Sey

About the Author

Some years ago, Golden Heart Award winner Susan Sey gave up the glamorous world of software training to pursue a high-powered career in diaper changing. Two children and millions of diapers later, she decided to branch out and started writing novels during nap time. The kids eventually gave up their naps, so now she writes when she's supposed to be doing the laundry. She currently resides in St. Paul, Minnesota, with her wonderful husband, their charming children and a very tall pile of dirty clothes.

For more about Susan or her books, feel free to visit her website (_www.susansey.com_) where you'll also find links to her Twitter and Facebook pages, and the occasional deleted scene or bonus chapter. Which have usually been deleted for very good reasons but still.

Blake Brothers Trilogy Book 2:
Talent for Trouble

For a sneak peek, read on…

William Blake's fresh start went live bright and early the morning of December third. Not that he'd done anything to deserve a fresh start. Had he needed one? Oh, yeah. Desperately. Deserved one? Not so much. But while people said a lot of things about Will—the majority of them unrepeatable—nobody had ever suggested the man was stupid.

So when Hunt House's door bell rang at precisely eleven-oh-two a.m., Will was right there waiting for it. Had been for the past fifteen minutes, just in case they were early.

He pulled the door open and found his brother and the woman who would surely become his sister-in-law one of these days standing on the front porch. "Hey, James. Bel. You're right on time."

"You sound surprised." Bel grinned at him, her elegant cheekbones flushed with cold, her hair a sleek swing of maple.

"Well, I figured *you* for the punctual sort." He gestured them into the soft gleam of the foyer that millions of viewers would recognize from *Kate Every Day,* the south's answer to *The Martha Stewart Show*. "My brother, though?" He shook his head. "That's some powerful laziness right there."

"Hey, I practically jogged over here." James nudged Bel over the threshold and followed her in, blowing on his hands. He kicked the door shut with one heel. "It's *cold* out there."

Will cocked a brow. "It's December."

"It's *Virginia*."

Will rolled his eyes and reached over to help Bel out of her coat. She blinked in surprise but turned her back and allowed it. "It could be high summer," Will said, his arms now full of navy wool that smelled like frosted sugar cookies. "If not for Bel cracking the whip on your lazy ass, you'd be sitting in the Annex kitchen in your shorts right now, eating last night's pizza for breakfast."

"Wouldn't that be nice?" James shrugged out of his own coat with a wistful sigh. "She didn't even let me comb my hair."

1

"James." Bel ruffled snowflakes from his shaggy blond head with a fond hand. "You never comb your hair."

"True enough." James sent his coat to Will on a no-look pass and gazed soulfully at Bel. "But given an extra fifteen minutes, I *might've*."

She pursed her lips. "I *gave* you an extra fifteen minutes."

"Mmmm. You did, didn't you?" He smiled, slow and hot. He slid an arm around her waist and began to reel her in. "And I gave *you*—"

"The question is," Bel cut in brightly, the color in her cheeks rising, "what are we on time for?"

She jammed an elbow into James' gut, a move his brother allowed with an easy cooperation that suggested he really had started off his morning with—ahem—a bang. Bitterness was an automatic pinch in Will's gut. How long had it been since he'd talked a woman back into his bed after the alarm went off? A long damn time. Longer yet since he'd had a woman in his bed he'd care to see there when the alarm did go off. In his imagination, though? He had a woman *there*. God, did he. Whether he wanted her there or not.

He didn't, in point of fact, want her there. But there she was anyway—that impossible face, that silvery hair, and a set of curves like to break a man's heart. And those eyes? Yep. Present and accounted for. Wide, heavily lashed, and so deeply blue they were almost purple. And filled with cold dislike.

Will's imagination was nothing if not accurate.

Oh, cry me a river. Are you listening to yourself, you self-pitying pussy?

His imagination also excelled at channeling the voice of the late Bob Beck, the man responsible for Will's recent and wholly undeserved fresh start.

Because I am. I'm listening, and it's turning my stomach. And I'm dead, *Will. It's hard to turn a dead guy's stomach.*

Will would take that one on faith.

2

James is a lucky bastard, no question, but that's not why he's got a pretty girl in his bed and you don't.

I know why I don't have a girl in my bed, Bob.

Will wondered vaguely when he'd starting talking back to the voices in his head. Wondered if it was a sign of an imminent mental breakdown or if he was just indulging in talk therapy for the terminally introverted.

Your bed's cold and empty because you're an asshole, Will.

I know, Bob. Thanks for the news flash. Now shut it, will you?

Bob shut it. Will sent up a brief prayer for his sanity. He wasn't the praying sort but figured it couldn't hurt. Then he shoved the Bob situation aside to deal with the Bel-and-James situation in his lap. One mess at a time, right?

"So, Mr. Mysterious." James draped a friendly arm around Will's shoulders and gave him a hearty squeeze. "To what, exactly, have we been summoned?" Then he stopped, eyebrows shooting up over that beaky nose of his. He leaned in, peered suspiciously at Will's jaw. "Hold that question. I have a better one: Are you wearing *makeup*?"

"Makeup?" Bel's eyes went wide and she leaned in, too. Will felt himself flush. "Good lord, he is! Will, you're camera ready."

"I know," he muttered, mortified.

"Is Kate putting you on air?"

"Yes."

Her eyes went wider. "During the *Christmas special*?"

Will gave her a weak smile. James grinned broadly. "I'm totally calling Drew." He dug into his pocket for his cell, presumably to call their other brother and make Will's humiliation complete. "Makeup! Good God."

"Will?" Bel's eyes were dark and uncomfortably shrewd. "What's going on? Are you—"

"I don't have time to explain." He glanced at his watch and winced. "Come on."

Bel frowned at James, who shrugged a *hell, I don't know* and put away his phone with an air of deep regret. Will shoved the coats into a handy closet then headed down the

3

hall at a near-trot. They followed him as he punched through the heavy door into the kitchen. Or what would look like a kitchen on-camera, anyway.

He put Bel and James beside one of the cameras, right where Kate had requested. They stood there in the dimness, lucky slobs, facing a massive counter that stood like an island in a broiling puddle of light. Will stepped up to the counter and faced the camera.

The heat was instant and engulfing. Terror seized him by the throat, shrinking his airway to pin-prick proportions. Millions of people were watching him, he knew. Or would when the tape went live. He could feel them already, those millions upon millions of cold and avid eyes. He felt them mercilessly observing the sharp elbows, the skinny chest, the knees and ankles that could never and had never agreed on a single direction when Will decide to ambulate. They would see his Adam's apple ratcheting uselessly up and down his pencil-neck in a doomed effort to dredge up even an ounce of the sunny charm or easy coordination that came so naturally to James. They would see him fail. And they would enjoy it.

The impulse rose up inside him, savage and fierce, to go to war. To shed blood and make those eyes look elsewhere. If he couldn't be admired, at least he wouldn't be pitied.

Will swallowed with a small click and forced his lips into a genial smile. He nodded to the camera person he couldn't see and waited until the little red light blinked on, indicating that they were rolling tape.

"Hello, everyone," he said to the camera's red eye. "My name is William Blake. Some of you may know of the recent death of Kate Davis' dear friend and long-time agent Bob Beck. Responsibility for Bob's client list has passed to me." Jesus. It was still a shock, that one. "As Kate's acting agent, it's my duty to inform you all of Kate's retirement, effective immediately."

Will couldn't see shit beyond the cameras but he heard Bel's sharp, shocked *oh*. Kate had very recently and in no uncertain terms refused to retire, thereby blowing to hell her promise to hand *Kate Every Day* over to Bel, her

4

acknowledged successor. So the news of Kate's retirement
was surely a surprise, but Will was counting on Bel's deep
attachment to personal dignity to get them all through this
without a scene. Or—God forbid—a second take. He kept
his gaze steady on the camera and hurried on.

"It also falls to me to share with you the letter Kate left
in my possession to be read aloud at the conclusion of her
annual Christmas special." He withdrew a folded sheet of
stationery from the inner pocket of his jacket, a creamy,
snowflake-embossed card identical to the one he'd put in
Bel's hand yesterday inviting her to today's taping.

"To my at-home family," he read. "It grieves me to
leave you, to take this final step away from this wonderful
community of friends to discover what else life might hold
for me. It's a journey I've been afraid to take for many years,
and one that I hope will sustain me and feed me for many
more now that I've found the courage to begin it. But I want
to assure you that I've left you in extremely capable hands."

There was an agitated rustle beyond the pool of light
and Will thought *shit, I should have warned her*. Because
Bel was probably out there thinking he was about to give her
dream job to somebody else. Kate could be cruel like that.

"In Belinda West's hands, to be specific."

The rustling went still and Will hoped that meant she
was listening, not unconscious. "Belinda has earned the right
to take my place," he read on. "She's earned it dozens of
times over through her endless ability to endure and to love,
to give and to forgive. Through her ability to place family
above all else, the family she's chosen, the family of her
heart. Because she won't allow her dreams to be taken from
her, not by fate, not by the family she was born into, and
certainly not by bitter old women who are too afraid to love
and be loved. But I'll be working on that in the south of
France. With love, Kate Davis."

Finally the lights went dim and the cameras went blind.
Will wondered if he was sweating through his suit coat or—
Christ—through his makeup. Then he wondered how Bel
was taking the news that she'd just been granted the job
she'd worked and waited for, the job she'd earned that she

thought Kate Davis had refused her. *Kate Every Day* was hers.

He squinted into the shadows and found Bel. She stood right where he'd left her, her hand limp in James', her eyes unfocused and vague. Will came and stood in front of her.

"She okay?" he asked James.

"Not sure." James jiggled Bel's hand. "Bel? Hon? You in there?"

"I'm fine," she said slowly. "Shocked, though." She lifted her eyes to Will's. "The south of France?"

"I know," Will said. "Didn't see that one coming."

"But...why? She was so set on keeping the show. I can't imagine she had a change of heart this dramatic."

"I don't think she did," Will said. "Not entirely."

"What does that mean?" James asked.

He shrugged. "I can only speculate, but I did a little research last night. As it turns out, the highest rated episodes over the past three years were by far the ones featuring Bel. And the segments featuring Bel's almost-wedding knocked Kate's solo shows out of the park. There may have been some sentiment behind it, but Kate's a pretty shrewd business woman." He lifted a shoulder and shifted his eyes to Bel. "Younger viewers wanted you, Bel, and Kate gives the viewers what they want." He smiled then. "Especially when Kate's retaining a producer credit and the pay check that goes with it."

That was it, Will thought. He could almost hear the internal *click* of the last puzzle piece falling into place in Bel's head. *That* was what she'd been waiting for before she could believe—evidence that Kate was still Kate. Because the Kate they all knew didn't give anything away. Not unless there was a healthy profit margin in it for her down the line.

"Oh, and one more thing," Will said, flipping Kate's note over in his hands. "It says 'P. S. Enjoy the Dower House.'"

The Dower House was the third spoke of what had once been a massive estate surrounding the pond in the back yard. The first spoke was Hunt House, the gracious pink-bricked mansion in which they were now standing, the home of *Kate*

6

Every Day. The second spoke was the Annex, the sprawling white-slatted plantation house the Blake brothers called home. The Dower House was a little cottage separated from Hunt House by a lavish rose garden, originally intended as a honeymoon suite of sorts. During the three years that she'd worked as Kate's on-air baking maven, Bel had lived there.

Will handed the note to her. "Any idea what that's all about?"

Bel stared at the note in her hands, dumbfounded. "She gave me the Dower House?" She lifted baffled eyes to James. "Kate gave me the Dower House."

"Well, no," James said. "I did. Merry Christmas."

"Merry—" She broke off, stunned. Then, "You bought me a *house*?"

"Well, yeah. The Dower House. You love that place." He stuffed his fists into his pockets and looked amazingly awkward for a guy whose athletic ability had made him a millionaire several times over. Will watched, fascinated, as color mounted his brother's cheeks. "And since Kate was leaving—"

Bel's eyes went narrow. "You knew Kate was leaving?"

James shifted his feet. "Will might've mentioned something."

She turned on Will. "*You* knew Kate was leaving?"

"Of course I knew," Will said. "I'm her erstwhile agent, aren't I? But I didn't let it slip." He shot James a poisonous glance. "Your beloved is a sneaky little eavesdropper."

"That's true." James tried an innocent smile. "I am."

Bel pressed a thumb to her forehead. "I don't understand. James, why would you buy me a house? We already have the Annex, and it's huge—" She broke off suddenly and two spots of color flared on those sharp cheekbones. "Oh," she said softly and looked down. "Oh, of course. I see."

Will glanced at James who frowned at the perfectly straight part on Bel's bent head.

"You do?"

"James, of course." She lifted her head and smiled bravely. Will didn't like that smile, and James looked

7

downright alarmed. "We've barely known each other three months. Take out the three weeks I spent playing assistant to Bob, and I completely understand. It's too soon to live together. But you didn't need to buy me a house, for heaven's sake."

"Oh, for the love of—" James sighed, snagged her wrist and yanked her in for a—yikes. Will blinked. For a kiss that didn't exactly leave anything to the imagination.

"Excuse me?" Will cleared his throat. "Still here. Still listening. Still—good lord—watching."

James lifted his head just far enough to speak. He threaded his fingers into her hair, rumpling the shiny spill of it over her shoulders. "You love that house, and I love you, so—" He let a shrug fill in the gap. Bel stared at him, a wary joy easing that horrible, stricken smile.

"So this isn't your way of asking for space?"

"Space?" James rolled his eyes. "Did that kiss feel like a request for space to you?"

Bel shook her head mutely.

"It didn't look like it, either," Will offered. "In case you were wondering."

They ignored him handily.

"For God's sake, Bel." James rubbed a gentle thumb over her cheekbone and Will had to look away from the tenderness in that little gesture. He started to ignore the jagged surge of bitterness that came with it, too, but forced himself to look right at it. To name it properly: jealousy. Pathetic as it was, he was jealous of his brother, of this easy, open sweetness. Of its being received without surprise or suspicion.

Good boy, Bob said.

Shut it, Bob.

"Haven't you heard a word I've said to you since Thanksgiving?" James asked Bel. "*I don't want space*. I hate space. I want you. Every day. Always. In my house, in my bed, in my heart."

"I'm, um, still here," Will said. Was that desperation in his voice? Very likely. "Where I can hear you."

"In fact," James went on as if Will hadn't spoken, "I was going to try to wait for this until Christmas but hell, I already gave you a house. Why hold off on the ring?"

"Oh my God," Will said, alarm snuffing out jealousy in a sudden rush. James was happy, and Will was happy for him. Truly. But there was a limit to what Fate could ask of a guy. Wasn't there? "You're going to do this now?"

Bel said, "Ring?"

James shoved a hand into his pocket, came up with a pretty velvet box and held it out to her. "Ring." He looked a little sick, Will noted faintly. That made him feel better. Marginally. "For you."

She reached for the box and set it on the flat of her hand, unopened. "What kind of ring?" she asked. She looked a little faint herself.

"The kind you put on your finger," James said. "Open it."

"No, I mean, what does it mean?"

"Mean?"

Bel swallowed audibly. "Is it a friendship ring? A promise ring? An I-really-like-you-a lot-so-merry-Christmas ring?"

He snatched the box off her palm and wrenched it open. "It's a goddamn diamond solitaire," he snapped. "The I-love-you-for-the-rest-of-my-life, I-might-barf-if-you-don't-put-it-on-soon kind, okay? The *marry me* kind. Is that clear enough for you?"

Bel launched herself into his arms while he was still scowling. "Crystal," she said, and kissed him with an open-mouthed invitation that had Will spinning hastily away from them.

"Well! Congrats, you two. I'm just going to—" They didn't hear him. He didn't care. He located the exit and punched through it with a sigh of relief.

And mowed down Audrey Bing in the hallway.

He stood there like a complete fool and watched her go down in a glorious swirl of moonlight hair and movie-star curves. She landed on her world-class rump in the hall, and stared up at him, her violet eyes wide and startled. Then they

9

narrowed with dislike. Her beauty was, as usual, a short-armed punch to the solar plexus and Will's mouth went desert-dry.

Unfortunately, it didn't go silent.

"Hey, Audrey." He heard his own voice with a sort of horrified surprise. "Fancy running into you here."

There was a knowing smirk in his voice, he noted with a sinking dismay. As if he were subtly accusing her of lurking in hallways in the hopes that she might accidentally-on-purpose plaster herself up against him.

It was an automatic thing at this point, he knew. Some kind of knee-jerk defense mechanism his desperate nervous system had dreamed up to neutralize that disabling blast of sexual awareness Audrey Bing always wrenched from him. To an extent, it worked. She hated him, deeply and truly. Only a self-destructive ass would make a move—a doomed move—on a woman who'd rather see his head on a spike than his hand on her knee.

Good thing you're not a self-destructive ass...oh, wait.

Shut it, Bob.

He sucked in a whistling breath, aware even now of his pulse thundering, of the way the very air between their bodies seemed super-charged and thick with danger. Or something. He pulled a slow hand down his face and forced the breath out of his lungs.

"Jesus, Audrey, I'm sorry." He held out a hand to the woman still glaring at him from the floor. "Are you all right?"

"I'm fine." She ignored his hand and came to her feet with a fluid grace that made his pulse beat in his ears. Was he blushing? Oh, God, he thought he might be. He swallowed, conscious of his stupid, knobby throat working. She brushed off her jeans and glared at him.

"Listen," he said with strained calm. No time like the present. "Do you have a minute? I'd like to talk—"

She brushed past him and disappeared into the kitchen set, presumably to find Bel or James or whoever she'd come here to find. Certainly not him.

She couldn't avoid him forever, he thought grimly. Just like he couldn't avoid her. *Wouldn't* avoid her. Wouldn't allow himself the luxury. No, he'd damaged Audrey Bing. And he was by God going to fix her. Whether she wanted him to or not.

Made in the USA
San Bernardino, CA
10 June 2014